AUTUMN ALIBI

The Wiccan Wheel Series
by JENNIFER DAVID HESSE

Midsummer Night's Mischief

Bell, Book & Candlemas

Yuletide Homicide

Samhain Secrets

May Day Murder

Autumn Alibi

AUTUMN ALIBI

Jennifer David Hesse

KENSINGTON BOOKS
KENSINGTON PUBLISHING CORP.
www.kensingtonbooks.com

KENSINGTON BOOKS are published by

Kensington Publishing Corp.
119 West 40th Street
New York, NY 10018

All Kensington titles, imprints, and distributed lines are available at special quantity discounts for bulk purchases for sales promotion, premiums, fund-raising, educational, or institutional use.

Special book excerpts or customized printings can also be created to fit specific needs. For details, write or phone the office of the Kensington Sales Manager: Attn.: Sales Department. Kensington Publishing Corp., 119 West 40th Street, New York, NY 10018. Phone: 1-800-221-2647.

Kensington and the K logo Reg. U.S. Pat. & TM Off.

First Printing: October 2019
ISBN-13: 978-1-4967-1775-7
ISBN-10: 1-4967-1775-9

ISBN-13: 978-1-4967-1776-4 (eBook)
ISBN-10: 1-4967-1776-7 (eBook)

10 9 8 7 6 5 4 3 2 1

Printed in the United States of America

For Scott, the yang to my yin

ACKNOWLEDGMENTS

With a heart full of gratitude and love, I thank my wonderful family, my fabulous agent and editor, and the entire publishing team at Kensington. Thanks also to all the readers and fans of the Wiccan Wheel Mysteries. I couldn't have done it without you.

Mabon: A modern Wiccan holiday coinciding with the autumn equinox, Mabon is a time of thanksgiving and a celebration of the earth's bountiful harvest. It is also a time to reflect on the balance of opposing forces, as day and night become equal, until darkness overtakes the light for another season on the Wheel of the Year.

Another year gone, leaving everywhere
its rich spiced residues: vines, leaves,
the uneaten fruits crumbling damply
in the shadows . . .
—Mary Oliver, "Fall Song"

Chapter One

The weathered stone bench made a perfect backyard altar. I knelt on the soft earth and arranged the items I'd gathered: rocks, twigs, leaves, acorns. Part of me felt a little bit childish, as if I were playing with toys. I might as well have made a corn dolly. Come to think of it, I might just do that later. The other part of me knew it was best to approach spirituality with a childlike heart—especially for a Wiccan like me. Open-mindedness was vital in Wicca. How else could one expect to receive messages from the Divine? Besides, when it came to magic, a sense of playfulness was a definite plus.

I cupped one hand over a smooth, angular rock and felt for its vibrations. It was subtle, but it didn't take long before I sensed a definite movement of energy. After a moment, I replaced the stone and picked up the next one, and then the next, noting their similarities and differences. The exercise was grounding. It helped calm the faint nervousness creeping around the edge of my awareness.

Why am I nervous? The lack of an obvious cause only added to my uneasiness.

Of course, I was always slightly anxious when performing rituals outdoors. I didn't want to be caught. Although I was fairly secluded by the fat pine trees and shrubbery in my backyard, not to mention our new cedar fence, the neighbors on both sides were mere yards away. More than once, I had been interrupted by the St. Johns' curious pug. How he managed to breach the fence was a mystery to me—and a source of annoyance to my cat, Josie. She prowled nearby now, like a faithful feline bodyguard.

At the moment, though, all was quiet in my little green alcove. Only the wind rustled the orange marigolds and feathery fronds of the tall ornamental grass behind me. I lifted my chin as the breeze washed over me. There was a hint of change in the mild, early-morning air. A foreshadowing in the slant of the sunlight. Summer was giving way to autumn.

In fact, maybe it was the impending change that was making me feel restless. With the birds flying south and small creatures scrambling for extra food, there was a sense of urgency in the atmosphere. A race against the clock. Yet, somehow, I felt that wasn't all. Something else jangled at my nerves, like the echoing chains of an ancient ghost. Something else was coming, and it wasn't just lengthening nights and colder weather. It was something from my past.

I shook myself and laughed under my breath. With a firm resolve, I focused once more on my altar. I was here for a reason. I'd roused myself out of bed early this Saturday morning to give thanks to the Goddess. And I had quite a lot to be thankful for. I had a loving boyfriend, a nice home, a good job—and a deep appreciation for the divinity in nature.

I picked up the paring knife I'd brought from the kitchen and the honey crisp apple I'd bought at the farmers market. There was so much symbolism in an apple, from its beautiful exterior to the very center of its core. With a steady hand, I sliced it horizontally in two, revealing a perfect five-pointed star in each half. It always gave me a thrill to find the secret pentagram in the heart of an apple. Holding a piece in each hand, I lifted my arms skyward and softly recited a spell I had written and memorized.

> Oh, Great Mother, bearer of sacred fruit,
> You nurture all seeds and watch dreams take root.
> You sanctify the earth; you bless the sky.
> You're the fire within; you're the tears I cry.
> Goddess of Nature, you're the wind, rain, and
>   thunder.
> Your awesome power fills me with wonder.
> Our bounty below reflects what's above.
> A life enriched with magic and love.

I lowered my arms and closed my eyes. For a few moments, I simply breathed, basking in the peace. I felt safe now. Inhaling the aroma of trees and dirt, and listening to the chirping birds, I felt I was enveloped in the arms of the Mother Goddess. All was well.

Then I heard another sound. Footsteps crunched on the ground behind me.

Slowly, I opened my eyes and turned. It was Wes, the loving boyfriend I was just thinking about. Tall, dark-haired, and wickedly cute, he ducked his head beneath a branch and approached with an apologetic grin.

"I hope I'm not interrupting. Want me to go away?"

"Never. I'm just finishing up here." I pushed myself to my feet and held out half of the apple. "Want a bite?"

He raised an eyebrow in mock fear, mixed with amusement. "Really? Are you tempting me with the forbidden fruit?"

In a split second, a million images flashed through my mind. Angels and devils and snakes; Michelangelo; women burning at the stake as punishment for the "fall of mankind." Above it all, my most prominent thought was a jumble of questions: *Could* I tempt Wes? Did I have that kind of power? If I were really offering him the knowledge of good and evil, would he take it? Would he be the Adam to my Eve?

Would he be my partner forever, come hell or high water?

Though I wasn't sure why, that was one question I had long been afraid to ask. Instead I waited. For nearly the entire three years we'd been a couple, including the past twelve months in which we'd shared a home, I waited. I waited for a firmer commitment. Waited for him to pop the question. Waited for a ring.

Wes must have taken my silence as a friendly challenge. With a gleam in his eyes, he bit into the apple. Smiling, I bit into the other half. Perhaps I had my answer.

It was on the tip of my tongue to pursue the topic, when Wes placed something in my empty hand. It was my cell phone.

"This has been buzzing for the past twenty minutes. I finally looked at it and decided I better come get you.

Your pal Crenshaw is trying desperately to get a hold of you."

"Crenshaw? What could he want?"

"According to the text I saw, he urgently needs your help. Sounds pretty dire."

I frowned, as my nerves started tingling again. A sense of foreboding returned, and it didn't have anything to do with the changing season. I sat down on the bench and punched in Crenshaw's number.

Chapter Two

An hour later, I was staring up at one of the grandest old mansions in Edindale. It was a sprawling, stately Georgian, standing proud and aloof at the top of a grassy knoll. The home was beautiful and well-kept. Yet something about it wasn't quite right.

I lingered on the sidewalk and tried to put my finger on it. What was the problem? Why did I suddenly feel like the ground had turned to molasses? As I squinted in the midmorning sun, I studied the home's clean lines, red brick, sturdy columns, and shining, black shutters. The no-frills elegance reminded me of Colonial times. Perhaps that was it, I thought. The house was slightly out of place. Edindale was in Southern Illinois, which, for Northerners, might feel like the American South—after all, we're a mere fifty miles from the border of Kentucky as the crow flies. But this is hardly Dixie. Yet this house would have looked right at home on a nineteenth-century sugar plantation.

On the other hand, maybe it was the last-gasp-of-summer heat wave that put me in mind of more southern climes. Though we were only two weeks from the Autumn Equinox, today was shaping up to be unseasonably warm. As I approached the front porch, the stagnant air felt prickly and heavy. I fanned myself, a motion that had more psychological than practical effect, and glanced back at Wes, who was taking photographs of a giant yellow ash tree in the front yard. He sensed me looking and jogged over.

"Sorry. Are you waiting for me?"

Am I waiting for you? I've been waiting for you my whole life.

I kicked myself mentally and held out my hand, which he grabbed in an easy, strong grip. I gave him a self-conscious smile. "I don't know what it is about this place. It gives me a funny feeling. Do you sense it?"

He raised his dark eyebrows. "Don't tell me. Not ghosts again? We had enough of that last Halloween."

I laughed uneasily. "No doubt. But I don't think that's it. It's not like I'm a ghost whisperer or a psychic medium."

"Yeah, but you're awfully intuitive. Isn't that what Mila's always telling you?"

Before I could respond, the front door swung open revealing a tall, ginger-haired chap in a tailored three-piece suit. His trim beard didn't hide the disapproving smirk above his rigid, square jaw.

"Were you planning on ringing the bell, Ms. Milanni? Or would you rather stare at the building's facade all morning?"

"Well, it *is* a lovely house." I was used to Crenshaw's droll sarcasm and superior attitude. After working with him in the same law firm for seven years, I'd learned to overlook his more annoying habits in favor of his few redeeming qualities—such as unfailing loyalty and occasional kindness. It became easier when I left the firm to start my own law practice earlier this year.

Wes stuck out his hand. "Hey, buddy. How's it going?"

"Smashingly. Won't you come in?" He ushered us inside and locked the door behind us. His heels clicked on the parquet floor, which gleamed with reflected light from the crystal chandelier above and the large, gilt-framed mirror on the foyer wall. "Thank you for coming on such short notice, and on a Saturday no less."

He addressed me and barely looked at Wes. There had always been an odd sort of jealousy between the two of them, which was utterly ridiculous. I had never dated Crenshaw, and he'd never asked me out—not even before I'd met Wes.

"You don't mind that Wes came along, do you?" I asked. "He thought he'd take photos of the grounds outside while we talk."

"As long as the photos won't appear in the *Edindale Gazette,* I suppose it's all right."

"I'm off-duty," said Wes, with a grin.

"Very well. I'll show you to the back door, which leads to the English gardens. You'll find the topiaries quite whimsical, I believe. Keli, you and I can sit in the conservatory, while I explain my proposition."

Wes gave me an arch look behind Crenshaw's back, as we followed him through the art-filled great room, past a sweeping circular staircase, and through a vaulted doorway. I had no idea why Crenshaw wanted so badly to see me today. All he'd told me was that he had been appointed executor of the Turnbull Estate, and that Elaine Turnbull passed away a week ago. This had been her home.

The interior of Turnbull Manor was as graceful and charming as the exterior. Glancing around, I couldn't help but admire the antique furniture, polished and plush, with plenty of curves and ornate finishes. I didn't know neoclassical from rococo, but I could tell it was refined whatever it was. And expensive.

As we passed the open French doors of what I supposed was a parlor or drawing room, I felt the same strange, prickling sensation I'd felt outside. My feet stopped of their own volition, and I looked into the room. The first thing I noticed was the strong scent of fresh-cut flowers—and no wonder. The room was filled with bouquet upon bouquet of heady, blooming flowers, from roses, lilies, and carnations, to exotic varieties I couldn't begin to name. Then my eyes fell upon something else that pulled me forward like a magnet. An enormous portrait hung above a stone fireplace. But it wasn't the size of the painting that caught my attention. It was the bright vividness of the colors and the striking loveliness of the subject.

"Is that Mrs. Turnbull?" I asked.

Wes and Crenshaw followed me into the room and stood on either side of me, gazing up at the portrait. It depicted a petite woman sitting tall on a velvet-cushioned, straight-backed chair. Her heart-shaped face, delicate bone structure, and rose-colored cheeks gave her a youthful appearance, even as the silver highlights in her light brown hair and the fine lines beside her eyes indicated a woman in her late fifties.

"That is she," answered Crenshaw. "Probably twenty or twenty-five years ago. It's quite a good likeness, actually." He crossed his arms and tilted his chin thoughtfully. "Except for the hair, which had become entirely gray, this is largely how she looked when I first met her a few years ago."

"Were you very close?" It suddenly occurred to me

that all the flower arrangements had probably been transported here from Mrs. Turnbull's funeral the previous day.

"We were acquainted through the local theater scene. I can't say we were exceedingly close, but I was fond of her. She was a friend." Outside of his law practice, Crenshaw was proud of his second calling as an amateur actor. I was sure he spoke the truth.

Wes raised his camera, then lowered it. It was reflexive for him, I knew, to want to photograph interesting things, but he never wanted to be disrespectful. "Sorry for your loss, man."

Crenshaw nodded in acknowledgment, then looked up at the portrait again. "Elaine had a fiery spirit. You can see it in her eyes. She was an especially passionate and generous patron of the arts and an avid supporter of the Edindale Community Theater. She will be greatly missed."

"I've seen the Turnbull Foundation mentioned in the papers," I said, "but I thought it was usually in conjunction with the fine arts rather than the performing arts. There's Turnbull Hall at the university and the Turnbull Prize for Visual Artists."

"That was her late husband's foundation," Crenshaw explained. "Harold Turnbull made his fortune in coal in the middle of the last century, before turning to his real passion as an art collector and sometime dealer. He was a renowned collector in his time, amassing an impressive array of works from early twentieth-century American paintings, including Grant Wood—he did *American Gothic*, you know—"

"I know."

"—to sculptures by Gertrude Vanderbilt Whitney, to Lalique glass and jewelry. I daresay Harold enjoyed the thrill of the hunt and subsequent bidding wars nearly as much as he enjoyed possessing the pieces themselves."

Wes, who had begun wandering the room, stopped behind Crenshaw's back and rolled his eyes. It was a natural reaction to Crenshaw's habit of speaking like an English lord. I tried not to laugh as I tuned back into Crenshaw's speech.

"The Turnbulls' son and only child, Jim, shared his father's interest in art. When Harold passed away—this was at least twenty years ago, or so—Elaine inherited the art collection and appointed her son to manage it. Jim moved back into the manor house with his wife and daughter. Sadly, Jim passed away only a few years later. That's also when his daughter disappeared."

"What?" I had begun to wonder why Crenshaw was telling me all this. Now I had an inkling. "Who disappeared?"

"Lana Turnbull. Jim's daughter and Elaine's granddaughter. She's also Elaine's sole heir."

"She disappeared?"

"Well, she ran away, really. She was seventeen years old. That was fifteen years ago. In fact, that's what I wanted to discuss with you. If you'll follow me, let's proceed to the—"

He broke off as a uniformed maid hurried into the drawing room.

"Ah, Celia," said Crenshaw. "You found us."

A tiny, gray-haired woman with sharp, black eyes, Celia marched up to Crenshaw with a tray held tightly in her knobby fingers. On the tray was a sweating glass pitcher of lemonade and two highball glasses half-filled with melting ice.

"You said you would be in the conservatory," she scolded. "And you said there would be two of you!"

Wes moved to relieve Celia of the rattling tray. She deftly swerved from his reach.

"I'll get another glass." Quick as a bird, she whirled and stalked out of the room.

Crenshaw pinched the bridge of his nose as Wes and I exchanged an amused glance.

"Maybe we should sit here," I suggested, pointing to a grouping of armchairs conveniently arranged for conversation. "Then she'll know where to find us."

"Very well," said Crenshaw. He gestured for me to lead the way, so I did.

"So, you were saying that Lana Turnbull ran away when she was seventeen. And she lived here at the time, with her parents and grandmother? And this was right after her father died?" My curiosity was piqued already.

A flicker of concern crossed Wes's face. He pressed his lips together and stood to one side as he waited for the answer.

Crenshaw nodded. "Lana's mother reported her missing. Of course, Suzanne was already speaking with the authorities because of Jim's death."

"How did Jim die?" I asked.

"There was an accidental shooting. He collected antique firearms and apparently shot himself while cleaning one. No one knows if Lana witnessed the accident or if she came upon his body afterward, but people assumed she was traumatized by the event. Either way, she fled and did not return."

"How awful."

Wes spoke up in an oddly quiet tone. "Are you trying to find Lana now? To let her know about her inheritance?"

"Not only that," said Crenshaw, "but also to settle the

estate. Everything is in flux until she is found. Or until every effort has been made to find her."

"So, that's why you called me," I said. Although I wasn't in the business of finding things, I couldn't deny the reputation I'd acquired. Somehow I had managed to locate lots of things over the past few years, from lost heirlooms and hidden tunnels to dead bodies—and the secrets, clues, and evidence that led to the persons responsible for the dead bodies. In other words, the murderers. Maybe it was my dogged persistence or my detail-oriented legal mind. Or maybe, as I suspected, it had something to do with the spells I casted and the divine guidance I received. As a Wiccan, I believed wholeheartedly in magic—a belief that was justified time after time.

I didn't think Crenshaw knew the extent of my spiritual practices, though he did know I traveled in some unconventional circles. He also knew about the crimes I'd helped solve.

"As a matter of fact, yes," he admitted. "Of course, the firm already retained a licensed private investigator. I have the agency's report in my briefcase." He leaned over, reaching toward the floor, then straightened and rolled his eyes. "Which is in the conservatory. I'll be right back."

As soon as Crenshaw left the room, I looked up at Wes. He seemed lost in thought. Then suddenly, he chuckled.

"What is it?"

He shook his head. "I don't know. There's just something so *cinematic* about this whole thing, you know? You're called to this grand old mansion and presented the 'Case of the Missing Heiress.'" He raised his fingers to make quotation marks. "It's like the start of an old black-and-white detective flick, or a mystery novel or something."

I grinned. "That sounds about right. Crenshaw does have a flair for the dramatic."

I stood up and wandered over to a large vase of pink and purple hyacinth. Closing my eyes, I leaned down to inhale the sweet, luscious fragrance. It was a springtime scent, out of place on this early September day—which brought back the dreamlike, off-kilter sensation I'd had earlier.

A shadow fell across the floor in front of me. I looked up and gasped. Instead of Crenshaw, I was faced with a strange man, staring down at me in a dour silence.

Wes darted to my side. "Hey, there," he said, in a casual, friendly way, but with an underlying guardedness I shared.

The stranger nodded his head stiffly and remained quiet. He was a tall, solid-looking man with icy blue eyes and a shock of short, white hair. I guessed him to be in his late sixties or early seventies.

Trying again, Wes stuck out his hand and introduced us. "Wes Callahan. And this is Keli Milanni. We're here with Crenshaw."

With apparent reluctance, the man shook Wes's hand. "Ray Amberly," he said, in a gruff voice.

I waited for further explanation, but none was forthcoming. Luckily Crenshaw returned, putting an end to the awkward staring contest.

"Ah, I see you've met Mr. Amberly," said Crenshaw.

"Sort of," I murmured.

"Mr. Amberly was Elaine's personal nurse and caretaker," Crenshaw continued. "He also lives here at Turnbull Manor."

"I was more than that," cut in the older man. "I was

Elaine's companion. I looked after her for almost a dozen years. We were very close."

"I'm so sorry for your loss, Mr. Amberly," I said.

I thought I detected a slight softening in his rigid countenance. "Might as well call me Ray," he said.

"Now then," said Crenshaw. "I have some business to discuss with Keli. Would you excuse us, Mr. Amberly?"

"Is it about the will?" demanded Ray. "I need to talk to you about that."

Crenshaw's eye twitched. I recognized the impatient look. "We've already discussed it. The will Elaine filed a few years ago is her last will and testament, signed by witnesses, notarized, and never revoked. The probate court already established the will is legal and valid."

"I tell you there's another will. She changed her mind and made a new one."

At that moment, Celia entered the room, once more bearing a tray of lemonade. This time there were three glasses, as well as a plate of cookies. She stopped short when she saw us.

"Now there are four of you!"

Crenshaw's cell phone rang. He snatched it from his pocket and retreated to a corner, plainly relieved for the excuse to escape.

Wes reached for a cookie, but Celia pulled the tray away and whirled around, muttering something about preparing a fourth glass. I would have suggested that she leave the tray, but she was gone before I could open my mouth. Ray, meanwhile, had walked over to Elaine's portrait over the fireplace. As he stared at the painting, his stony face took on a morose air.

My ears pricked up at the sound of Crenshaw's deep voice, which was uttering notes of alarm. I sidled over to him as he wrapped up the call.

"Yes. Yes, I will. Thank you for calling. Good-bye."

He slid his phone into his pants pocket, then grabbed a handkerchief from his jacket and began to mop his forehead.

"Is everything okay?"

"Ah, yes. That is, no. I don't know."

"Who was on the phone?"

"That was Dr. Lamb, Elaine's attending physician. He was out of town the night Elaine died, so he didn't sign the death certificate. He was just reviewing the coroner's report and became troubled by something."

"Oh?"

Crenshaw's already lowered voice dropped to a whisper. "Two things, actually. One, the report stated there was a bluish tinge to Elaine's skin and lips, yet the coroner didn't order a toxicology analysis. Elaine had cancer, so the coroner evidently felt an autopsy was unnecessary. However, there was another disturbing item. The list of Elaine's medications in the report did not include the opioid painkillers Dr. Lamb had prescribed."

"What does that mean? What does he think happened?"

"Dr. Lamb is convinced Elaine overdosed on the painkillers. And since the bottles were missing . . . he suspects foul play."

Chapter Three

Right after Crenshaw's bombshell, Celia returned for the third time bearing her tray of drinks and snacks. The lemonade was watery with melted ice, and too sweet for my taste, but I still drank it in big gulps. The prospect of another unbidden murder investigation had made my mouth go dry. I was never particularly keen on practicing criminal law—preferring instead to focus on family law matters and transactional business. Unfortunately, the Universe often had other ideas.

Crenshaw invited everyone to sit and help ourselves to the refreshments. He gave me a knowing look and touched the side of his nose. I took the hint and remained mum about Dr. Lamb's suspicions. Wes grabbed a cookie and squeezed my shoulder before sitting. Ray took a glass but remained standing. I had the impression he didn't feel like being social but wanted to be part of any discussions concerning Elaine's will.

Crenshaw steepled his fingers as if gathering his thoughts, then turned to the caretaker. "Mr. Amberly—

Ray—let's talk about this purported new will for a moment. Did you ever see it?"

"I saw Elaine working on it. About a month ago, she sat at her desk in the library, marking up the old will and drafting a new one. I didn't see it up close, but I know that's what it was." He took a deep breath and let it out with a sigh before continuing. "She even made a joke about it. She said, 'Ray, do you know what a hand-written will is called?' At first, I thought she was telling a riddle. She had a quirky sense of humor. I said, 'What?' And she said, 'A holographic will'!"

"That's correct," Crenshaw put in. "It comes from the Latin *holographus,* meaning 'written in full, in one's own hand.'"

"Yeah, well, we joked about holograms. She said she would love to make a 3-D image of herself reading the will, like Princess Leia in *Star Wars.*" Ray bowed his head and coughed. "The point is, she knew what she was doing. And I know she finished it, because she mentioned asking two of the landscapers to come inside and witness her signing it. She told me that beneficiaries aren't allowed to be witnesses."

Meaning Ray assumes he's a beneficiary. I made a mental note of the information.

"That's correct," said Crenshaw. "Under Illinois law—"

"Have you questioned the landscapers?" I interrupted. Sometimes Crenshaw's love of his own voice detracted from more pressing matters.

"I tried," said Ray with a frown. "They must have been part of the temporary crew that's only here in the summer. I can't find anyone who remembers signing the will."

"Well, where might she have kept a handwritten will?" asked Crenshaw.

"It's hard to say," said Ray. "Elaine wasn't terribly organized with her paperwork. That's why I pay—paid—the bills. There's the desk in the library and some boxes and baskets of papers in her room. I looked in both places and didn't find it. To be honest, I think she might have hidden it."

"Hidden it?" echoed Wes. "Why would she have done that?"

"She probably didn't want Suzanne to see it," said Ray. "Elaine didn't trust her daughter-in-law. Or maybe Suzanne took it herself, after Elaine passed on. I wouldn't put it past her."

"One moment," said Crenshaw, rubbing his temple. "If I have this right, you're saying that either Elaine hid the will or else Suzanne stole it—and presumably hid or destroyed it. And, even if Elaine didn't hide it, you don't know where she would have kept it . . . but she had a substantial amount of papers in her bedroom and she wasn't very organized. Is that correct?"

"That's what I said."

"I wonder . . . if it's not too painful, would you mind walking us through what happened the night Elaine died? Perhaps it will help to refresh your recollection regarding what you saw in her room. I'm sure things were chaotic. Perhaps you or Celia, or one of the paramedics, might have moved some papers and, in the process, misplaced the will."

Crenshaw surreptitiously touched the side of his nose again, while giving me the briefest of glances. I guessed this was his new form of silent communication. Wes looked curiously from Crenshaw to me. I knew he could tell something was up. Ray didn't seem to notice.

"I suppose I can do that," Ray said. "It's true that things

were chaotic. We'd had a dinner party that night, so our regular routine was already all messed up."

"And she seemed all right at dinner?" Crenshaw asked.

Ray nodded. "She was in good spirits. She had made a sizable gift to the Edindale Art Museum. It was a celebratory dinner. Although . . ." He trailed off, squinting his eyes.

"Yes?" Crenshaw prompted.

"Maybe she was a little quieter than usual. At one point I thought she looked worried. I figured she was thinking about her illness. She'd recently had a relapse and wasn't looking forward to starting up chemo again."

"She was a gracious lady," Crenshaw said. "I'm sure she put on a brave face for her guests."

Ray nodded curtly. "Everyone left between eight-thirty and nine o'clock—some people had another event to go to. By that time, Elaine was pretty tired. She said she was going up to her room. At around nine-thirty, I brought up a glass of warm milk with cinnamon, like she had every night. I knocked on her door, but she didn't answer. I thought this was unusual, since I could see that her light was still on and heard the TV. I knocked again, then went inside. She was lying across the bed at an odd angle, like she'd fallen. I called her name and shook her, but she was unresponsive. I gave her CPR, then called nine-one-one. You can imagine the rest."

I studied Ray while he spoke. Maybe it was my imagination, but, unlike his earlier displays of emotion, he seemed to recite these facts like well-rehearsed lines.

"Did you notice any papers in the bedroom?" asked Crenshaw.

Ray crinkled his eyes. "Yeah. Books, papers, magazines. There were papers on the nightstand, on the vanity, on the floor. I don't remember seeing anything that looked like a will."

"Hmm," said Crenshaw, pursing his lips. I felt sure he wanted to ask if there were any pill bottles in evidence, but it would be an unusual query. As for me, I was trying to imagine what had occurred in the half hour since she'd gone upstairs.

"Was she still wearing her dinner clothes?" I asked.

"No, she had on her dressing gown. I believe she was climbing into bed when she had her attack."

Wes voiced the next question I wanted to ask. "Where was Suzanne during all this?"

"I don't know. Somewhere in the house. When I realized Elaine was unconscious, I yelled for help. Celia arrived first. I told her to go downstairs and let the paramedics in. Suzanne must have heard the front door, because she came upstairs right behind the EMTs. She took one look at Elaine and fainted. One of the EMTs had to attend to her."

He didn't sound very sympathetic, I thought. I guessed I couldn't blame him, under the circumstances.

Everyone fell silent. Crenshaw bowed his head and contemplated his fingers in a posture of deep thought.

I checked my watch. "Crenshaw, I'm afraid I'm going to have to leave soon. I have another appointment today." It so happened that the appointment was with my closest pal, Farrah Anderson, whom I saw several times a week and spoke to or texted every day. But Crenshaw didn't need to know that.

"I can stay," Wes volunteered.

I looked at him in surprise. *What the heck?*

"You can take my car, babe," he continued. "I'm sure Crenshaw can give me a ride home. Right, buddy?"

Crenshaw stared at Wes. Apparently, he was as flummoxed as I felt.

"Well," I murmured, "I don't have to leave just yet."

Ray looked at each of us in turn. "What about the missing will?"

Crenshaw pushed himself slowly to his feet and faced Ray. "If the holographic will is found, I will present it to the probate court for review. I'll keep a close eye out for it as I inventory Elaine's things. In the meantime, let me know if you have any other ideas about where it might be."

Grudgingly, Ray nodded and set his glass on the table. "Will you hold off on administering the old will?"

"For the time being, yes."

After Ray left, Crenshaw sat down again and reached for his briefcase, muttering under his breath. "Administering the will is delayed anyhow, in light of the missing heir."

"So the agency you hired didn't have much luck?" I asked. "How did they even know where to start? Was Lana in touch with her family after she ran away?"

"I don't believe she stayed in touch, but she didn't disappear from the face of the earth," he said. "Evidently, Lana had a credit card, which she continued to use for several months after she left. Her grandmother paid the bills."

"Anyone could have—" Wes began.

Crenshaw cut him off with a withering look. "They knew she was the one using the card, because a number of security cameras confirmed as much. Lana traveled by train to Chicago—by herself. She stayed in a hotel at first, and then a youth hostel."

"If they knew where she was at the outset," I asked, "why didn't anyone go after her?"

"Good question," said Crenshaw. "Elaine didn't talk

about it much—at least, not with me. But I believe this
was a source of great regret in her life. She did mention
once that Suzanne was so distraught after Jim's death,
she had to be medicated and was unable to travel."

"Elaine must have been distraught, too," I said.

"No doubt. At any rate, not long after she left, Lana
turned eighteen. As she was no longer a minor, and
not a missing person, the police closed the case. After
a while, the credit card charges stopped. Elaine liked
to think Lana had found a job and was able to support
herself."

Wes stepped toward one of the tall multipaned windows overlooking an expansive green lawn and gazed
outside. I wondered what he was thinking. As for me, I
still found it hard to believe Lana cut all ties with her
mother and grandmother. My own mother's sister, my
aunt Josephine, had run away when she was seventeen,
but at least she sent postcards and letters to let her
family know she was all right.

"Crenshaw, you said Lana is Elaine's sole heir by the
terms of Elaine's will?"

"That's correct."

"I assume that means Elaine updated her will after
her son died. So, her granddaughter ran away, stayed
away for fifteen years and counting . . . yet Elaine still
left her everything?"

Crenshaw nodded solemnly. I wondered how Elaine's
daughter-in-law, Suzanne, felt about being left out of
the will.

Wes turned around and pointed at the file in Crenshaw's hand. "Any leads in there?"

"Very few." Crenshaw scowled with exasperation.
"Somehow the report manages to be both comprehen-
sive and sparse. I believe the investigator's exact words
were 'We've hit a dead end.' While that may be true, I

must admit it is not at all satisfactory." He stood and assumed a position behind his chair, resting his hands on the back as if it were a podium—which forced Wes and me to look up at him.

"As Elaine's friend," he continued, "more so than as her executor, I feel I owe it to her to do better. I feel *compelled,* as it were, to make an extra effort. Which brings me to the reason I called you here today, Keli. I propose hiring you as a consultant on this matter. Now, rest assured, I don't want you to engage in any formal investigation work, such as would require a professional P.I. license. Rather, I was hoping you could, I don't know, poke around a bit. Talk to people. Do whatever it is you do that results in your stumbling upon the solution to a random mystery now and then. What do you say?"

Stumbling upon the solution? Well, maybe. Yeah, that was sometimes true. I wasn't sure how I could help in this case, but I didn't see any harm in trying.

"Okay," I agreed. "I'll see what I can do."

"Excellent. To begin, I had wanted to introduce you to Lana's mother, Suzanne. However, I remember now that she mentioned having tennis lessons today. I don't believe she has returned yet."

"I can come back another time," I offered. "Maybe it would be better for me to make an appointment with her."

"I suppose," said Crenshaw, handing me the P.I. report. "But while you're here, why don't I give you a tour of the house? I'm in the process of making an inventory of all Elaine's personal property—which is no small feat. Say, as my consultant, perhaps you can assist me in the effort?"

I almost said that sounded like a good job for an

intern, but I bit back the retort. Instead I said, "Perhaps we should discuss my consulting fee first."

"Certainly. I assume you'll charge by the hour?"

"Um, yes. I—" I broke off midsentence, distracted by something outside the window. "Sorry. I think someone was just watching us."

Crenshaw and Wes raced to the window. "There's no one out there," said Crenshaw.

"They could have ducked around the corner," said Wes.

"What did you see?" asked Crenshaw. "Can you describe the person?"

"It was a man. He was wearing a hat, like one of those floppy fisherman's hats, I think. He had a mustache and dark hair sticking out from under the hat. He dropped out of sight as soon as I noticed him."

Wes lifted his camera. "Maybe we should start the tour in the gardens."

"Fine," said Crenshaw. "We can exit through the conservatory, which opens to the patio."

"Can you direct me to a restroom first?" I asked. "I'll catch up with you guys outside."

Standing in the hallway outside the drawing room, Crenshaw pointed in the direction of the great room. "Take a left at the staircase. It will be the second or third door on your right. To find the conservatory, come back this way, pass the dining room, and keep going until you see double French doors. Of course, if you go the other way, you'll end up in the same place. Both wings of the house branch off the great room and lead to the conservatory in the rear."

His directions sounded simple enough, but when I emerged from the powder room I found myself completely turned around. As I followed the curving paneled hallway, I realized I'd made my way to the east wing of the mansion. After a moment, I reached a point where the door to the drawing room should have opened on the left. Instead, a parallel door opened on my right. One peek inside told me it was the library. *This must be where Ray saw Elaine working on a new will.*

I couldn't contain my curiosity. I slipped inside the room and glanced about. Heavy drapes blocked most of the sun's rays, creating a dim, grayish light. Tall bookshelves flanked a stone fireplace much like the one in the drawing room. The portrait above this one was of a smiling, distinguished-looking man, presumably Harold Turnbull.

As I looked around, I imagined Harold and his upper-crust friends relaxing in the club chairs, smoking cigars and sipping brandy. But the image soon faded. For the past twenty years, Elaine had been the head of this household. I could see signs of her personality throughout the room, from the crocheted blanket tossed over the back of the sofa and the rose garden jigsaw puzzle on top of a corner table, to the stack of theater magazines on the wide oak desk. I roamed over to the desk, which stood against the wall between a painting of the European countryside, on the right, and a carved door with a shiny brass knob on the left. *Fancy closet,* I thought. Next to the desk was an elegant wooden filing cabinet, of the sort that probably contained important legal documents. Such as a will?

The cabinet was probably locked. I knew this. I also knew I was going to try it anyway. The instant my fingers curled around the handle, the closet door burst open and a man bounded toward me. He was middle-aged and puffy, with fair, wispy hair and mottled cheeks. His eyes were wide and flashing, like those of a terrified horse.

"What do you think you're doing?" he demanded.

It was a reasonable question, and one I would have readily answered—if not for the fact that my heart had jumped to my throat. The sudden appearance of the strange man wasn't the worst part—it was the large, steel-gray handgun he waved in my direction.

Chapter Four

In times of danger, I automatically turn first to the Goddess. Although I believe in divine polarity, and the importance of both masculine and feminine energies, Mother Earth is my go-to. I can always count on her for comfort, guidance, and protection. Maybe I'm biased, being a woman myself. Or maybe it's because I've been surrounded by strong, influential female figures my whole life. Either way, I feel a close, personal connection to the Goddess in all three of her mythical aspects: vibrant maiden, nurturing mother, and wise crone. That's why my first (and only) tattoo depicts the sign of the Triple Goddess: A row of three moons—waxing crescent, full, and waning crescent. It's inked on my right inner wrist as a constant reminder of Her presence within me.

When the wild-eyed man came at me with a gun, I instinctively grasped my wrist, as if activating the tattoo. At the same time, I mentally launched an energetic shield of protection. I also took a step back and prepared to duck.

Almost instantly, the man dropped his hand and looked sheepish. "Oh. Sorry about this. It's not loaded. I forgot I was holding it."

"You forgot?" I managed to say.

"I—I heard a sound and rushed out here without thinking. Who are you?"

"Keli Milanni. I'm an attorney working with Crenshaw Davenport. And you are?"

He set the gun on the desk and held out his hand. "I'm Perry Warren. I'm an art advisor for the Turnbull Foundation. I used to be a curator at the Edindale Art Museum."

As I shook his hand, I tried to muster up a polite smile. Now that my heartbeat had slowed to a seminormal rate, I was more annoyed than frightened. His moist handshake didn't help. "Nice to meet you," I mumbled, as I discreetly wiped my palm on my trousers.

"I really am sorry," he said, with an embarrassed grimace. "I get jumpy back there around the gun collection. That's an antique, you know." He pointed to the gun, a revolver with a wooden handle. I supposed it did look old, though no less deadly. "It belonged to Jim Turnbull," he continued. "He was my friend and business partner."

"Oh. Right. I heard he collected antique firearms." *And accidentally killed himself with one.* No wonder Perry was nervous.

"Elaine asked me to catalog and appraise all the Turnbull collections. I was about halfway through when she passed away. Crenshaw agreed I should stay on and finish the job."

"I see. So, the gun collection belonged to Elaine?"

"It was bequeathed to her. At the time of Jim's death,

he was estranged from his wife, and his daughter was just a child."

"Wait—Jim was estranged from Suzanne? The woman who lives here now?"

Perry nodded. "Elaine asked Suzanne to move back in after Jim died. She still thought of her daughter-in-law as family. But Jim had left all his assets to his mother."

"Oh. That makes sense." Actually, I didn't know if it made sense or not. I just didn't know what else to say. "Well, Crenshaw is waiting for me, so I should be going. It was nice to meet you."

"Likewise."

I left the library with my head spinning. *What an odd encounter.* As I made my way to the back of the house, I pondered what Perry had told me. He must have been a friend of the Turnbull family for many years, I realized. Maybe he would have some insight into why Lana had run away and where she might be now. I'd have to find time to talk with him again—preferably someplace far away from the antique gun collection.

There was something else he said that came back to me now. It was something about "staying on" after Elaine passed away. Did that mean he was staying here in the house?

I asked Crenshaw as much when I found him and Wes on the tile patio in the courtyard behind the conservatory.

"That's correct," Crenshaw confirmed. "Perry Warren was Jim's fraternity brother. From what Elaine told me, he was a frequent houseguest, both before Jim died and afterward. Most recently, he was helping Elaine manage her art collections."

"Perry mentioned that Jim and Suzanne were separated at the time of Jim's death. Isn't it odd that Elaine invited Suzanne to move back in?"

"Not necessarily," said Crenshaw. "Elaine probably felt that having Suzanne live under her roof was the right thing to do. I think she always hoped Suzanne would do more to find Lana and bring her home."

Wes snapped a picture of me, then moved to my side and draped an arm around my shoulder. "How many people actually live here?" he asked.

"At the moment, only three—Suzanne, Ray, and Perry. Plus the staff."

"The staff?"

"The people who take care of the house and grounds. You met Celia. There are a few others. I've informed everyone they may remain here under the existing arrangements for the time being. Of course, if the estate is sold, everyone will have to leave. I'm hoping Lana will show up to claim her inheritance. She'll have a number of decisions to make."

"Assuming a second will doesn't name different beneficiaries," I pointed out.

Crenshaw grunted. "To be honest, I would be perfectly content to dismiss Ray's claims as wishful thinking. However, I must admit it is entirely possible Elaine made another will. Since the recurrence of her illness, she talked about making certain changes with her affairs. She mentioned downsizing and taking stock. And she did ask Perry to appraise Harold's collections. Whether or not she had time to finalize a second will, I have no idea."

"Speaking of time, I really ought to get going. I'll take a rain check on the house tour." I reached into my purse to find my cell phone. I needed to let Farrah know I was running late. "But wait," I said, remembering.

"What about that phone call from Dr. Lamb? Does he plan to go to the police with his suspicions?"

"I believe so. He wanted to warn me to be careful around here."

"What are you talking about?" asked Wes.

Crenshaw repeated what the doctor had told him about Elaine's missing pain medications and the possibility her death was the result of an overdose.

Wes furrowed his brow. "Hang on. Let me get this straight. You've got a missing heiress, a missing will, and now some missing pills? Instead of hiring Keli, you need to hire a bloodhound. It's like the Bermuda Triangle around here!"

Crenshaw narrowed his eyes, and I snickered. "Don't joke about it," I said, in spite of my grin. "It's not really funny."

"It's funny, all right," Wes insisted. "Funny-strange."

I was about to agree when a movement near a twisting, sculpted evergreen bush caught my eye. I could have sworn I saw a person in a hat. Was it the same man I saw outside the parlor window? I ran over to investigate, but there was no one behind the bush. If anyone had been there, he had disappeared again.

The Bermuda Triangle indeed.

I climbed into the passenger side of Wes's car and placed the Lana Turnbull file across my lap. It was too large to fit into my purse. As Wes settled in behind the wheel, I shot off another text.

"Farrah's waiting for me at the nail salon," I said.

"Can you drop me off? She'll give me a ride home later."

Instead of starting the car, Wes reached for the file. "Don't you want to look at this first?"

I narrowed my eyes in suspicion. "Wes Callahan, is there something you want to tell me? Why are you so interested in this case?"

He gave me a small smile, tinged with something like regret. In that instant, I knew what he was about to say.

"I knew Lana Turnbull. We were classmates in high school."

Of course.

"Why didn't you say something before?"

"I don't know. It was so long ago, and I haven't thought of her in years. I didn't really know her that well . . ." He trailed off.

"What do you remember about her?"

"We were lab partners one year, and we did some group projects together." He wrinkled his forehead as he remembered. "She was a great artist, always drawing or sketching. She used to skip class sometimes, especially senior year. One time I asked her why, and she said she was bored, or something like that. Tired of school and tired of this town. She was itching to get out, move to a big city."

"So, maybe she was planning on running away even before her father died," I guessed.

"Maybe. Eventually she stopped coming to school altogether. I figured she dropped out or else switched to a private school. Everyone knew her family was rich, though you couldn't tell by the way she dressed. She never showed off her money."

I eyed Wes carefully as he squinted through the windshield. It seemed clear he was wrestling with some old memories, but I decided not to press him. I opened the file and skimmed the contents.

"It looks like the P.I. searched all the obvious datasets and came up with a string of negatives," I said, flipping through the top sheets of paper. "Lana has no criminal history. She's never applied for a marriage license. She owns no real estate nor any registered vehicles; she pays no property taxes, has no employment records and no voter information. She doesn't even have any social media presence that they could find."

"In other words, she dropped off the grid," said Wes.

"Almost. It looks like they did find at least two possible leads." I pulled out two sheets of paper that had been marked with red tabs. One was an article in an old Chicago neighborhood newspaper. It was a short piece covering an art and literature contest a few years ago, and there was a group photo of the prize winners. Highlighted in the caption was the name *Lana Turnbull.* "Check it out," I said, handing Wes the paper.

Wes took one look at the picture and nodded definitively. "That's her."

I leaned over. "Which one?"

"There. Front row, second from the end." He pointed to a somber-faced girl with round cheeks and short, spiky hair. "I knew that was her even before reading the caption."

"You're sure?"

"Yeah. I mean, the hair is different and she's obviously a decade older than she was in high school. But that's her."

"Then this places her in Chicago five years ago and tells us she became an artist." I returned my attention to the file and found a note the investigator had made. "The P.I. firm looked up the other nine winners. They reached eight of them by phone—all of whom claimed not to know Lana. Evidently, they had each entered the art contest independently and didn't know one another."

"What about the ninth one?" Wes asked.

"Let's see. The ninth person is a woman named Penny Delacroix. It turns out she has a vast online presence, with YouTube videos and blogs, et cetera. She was easy to find on the Internet, but not easy to find in person. It says here she never returned the P.I.'s calls."

"That's kind of suspicious, isn't it?" said Wes.

"Not necessarily. I can think of a few reasons someone might not return a phone call. But there's more here." I picked up the second tabbed document. It was a blog post Penny Delacroix had published four months ago.

Wes and I read the post together. The bulk of the piece was Penny lamenting the cost of housing in Chicago and her difficulties in finding a suitable roommate. Then we came to the part the P.I. had highlighted.

> I almost convinced my arty friend to move in
> with me, but then she bailed, the wuss. Lana T.
> decided to leave Chi-town altogether.
> Supposedly she missed the farm-fresh air
> back home. If I don't find a roommate soon,
> I may have to follow her . . .

Wes looked up at me with a spark of excitement in his eyes. "So, this Penny person *does* know Lana. I can't believe the investigator didn't try harder to reach her."

I didn't know how hard the investigator had tried, but I did know one thing: I would have to try harder. Considering Wes's interest, how could I not?

Chapter Five

There's nothing quite like a professional mani-pedi to make a gal feel pampered—and, at the same time, as trapped as a parrot in a pet store. With freshly painted fingers and toes, I couldn't get up and leave, couldn't browse on my phone or send text messages. I couldn't even unwrap the protein bar in my purse to appease the rumbling in my stomach. At least I had Farrah to distract me from my hunger. When Wes dropped me off half an hour ago, she was waiting for me in front of the Color Me Happy Nail Salon. Now we sat side by side in soft leather vibrating chairs. We would be heading out for dinner and drinks as soon as our nails were good and dry.

In truth, I felt a little reluctant to go out on an evening when Wes happened to be home. Usually I had girls' nights with Farrah when Wes was working at one of his two jobs that sometimes required evening hours—as a part-time bartender and a full-time photojournalist. But I had agreed to make an exception tonight. Farrah was all in a state. She was having man troubles.

"What should I do?" she asked. "I really like Randall, but I don't know if he's the one. You know?"

Randall was another partner at the law firm where I used to work. Farrah was a lawyer, too, but she had decided long ago to become a legal software salesperson instead of a practicing attorney. It better suited her outgoing personality and gave her more time for extracurricular pursuits. After dating Randall for a few months, she'd put on the brakes because of his long work hours. Recently, he'd called her bluff by agreeing to make more time for her, and it was freaking her out.

"You think he wants to get serious?" I asked.

"You tell me. Last night, I was complaining about how he stays so late at the office, and you know what he said? He said if I wanted to see more of him, we should move in together!"

"And he meant it?" Randall was known for his ironic sense of humor. He was prone to bursts of good-natured sarcasm.

"Yeah! I think he surprised himself, but once he said it, he started to warm to the idea. His house is bigger than my apartment, and he said it could use a womanly touch." She paused and blew on her fingernails. "He might have been teasing about the last part."

"So, what did you say?"

"I changed the subject. I'm not ready for that conversation right now. Especially considering who I ran into at the gym yesterday morning."

"Who'd you run into?"

"Three guesses."

I didn't need three guesses. The situation with Randall immediately called to mind another guy Farrah had pushed away as soon as things turned serious. And he worked at the gym.

"Jake?"

"You got it. I hadn't seen him in ages. It was really awkward. I mean, we were both cool, but he gave me that soulful, puppy-dog look that always left me feeling guilty for no reason."

"Mm," I said, noncommittally. I'd always felt a little bad about how things had ended between Farrah and Jake. He was a nice guy, and she'd broken his heart more than once. But if he wasn't the one, he wasn't the one.

"Oh, and get this," she said. "I might have a stalker. Probably another ex-boyfriend."

"What do you mean?"

"Earlier this week, somebody broke into my mailbox. They must have picked the lock, because the little door was hanging open when I got home, and I know it was closed when I left."

"Was your mail stolen?"

"I don't know if anything was taken. I don't think so. The box was still full of bills and stuff. But some of the envelopes seemed wrinkled. Anyway, then last night, Ed, the super at my building, told me he saw a guy messing around my car. He ran off when Ed yelled at him."

"What was the guy doing?"

"I don't know. Ed couldn't tell. He also couldn't describe the guy except to say he was older than a kid and younger than an old man. Ed isn't very observant."

"That's helpful," I said dryly. "But maybe the dude was just a carhead or something. You know, into Jeep convertibles."

"It's possible," she conceded. "But I also think someone has been following me."

"What? Really?"

"Yeah. Like just a little while ago, I noticed a shiny black coupe behind me—I think it was a Bentley. It had tinted windows and was very mysterious-looking. It was on my tail for a few blocks, turning everywhere I turned."

"What did you do?"

"I parked, and it kept going." She shrugged. "It might have been a coincidence. But you don't believe in coincidences, do you? Or is it that there *are* coincidences, but they always mean something? I can never remember."

I smiled. In spite of her quintessential bubbly-blonde persona, Farrah was a very smart, down-to-earth woman. She was fascinated by my Wiccan practices and respected my beliefs, even if she didn't one-hundred-percent understand them. But I thought I knew what was really going on here, and it didn't have anything to do with uncanny coincidences. Farrah was bored. In the past, she and I had had some fun and frights as an accidental—and very amateur—crime-fighting duo. It definitely brought an element of excitement to our lives. I hadn't had a chance yet to tell her about the multiple mysteries Crenshaw had laid at my feet.

Speaking of feet, the proprietor of Color Me Happy tested our toes and declared us good to go. We slipped on our sandals, paid the woman, and stepped outside into the late-afternoon sun.

"Shall we go on to the Loose now?" Farrah asked. "Or do you want to—"

"Yes," I said, cutting her off. "I didn't have lunch. I'm more than ready for food and drinks. Where's your car?"

"It's in the lot around the corner. I was browsing in the shoe shop while waiting for you earlier."

As we made our way to the small municipal parking lot, I asked Farrah if we should stop off at her place and take a cab to the bar. She thought about it, then shook her head. "I'm not gonna overindulge tonight. I have to get up early tomorrow. I'm meeting Randy for—"

She stopped short, staring at the wheels of her Jeep.

"What's wrong?" I asked. Then I saw it for myself. "Oh, jeez. Who would do such a thing?"

Someone had slashed both of her rear tires, not once but twice, to make a large letter X in each tire.

"A creepy stalker, that's who! Now do you believe me?"

"I never doubted you," I murmured.

At least, not anymore.

By the time the police, a tow truck, and a cab all arrived, and we'd made all the necessary statements, Farrah and I were both ready for a stiff drink. We sat across from each other at a scarred wooden table in the back of our favorite night club, the Loose Rock, and clinked beer mugs.

"Here's to roadside assistance," Farrah proclaimed. "I mean, I could have changed one tire myself, but who carries two spares? Nobody, that's who."

"You would have changed a tire with a fresh manicure?"

"Well, no. Not if I could help it. Hey, do you think

the creep following me saw me go into the nail salon and wanted me to mess up my nails? Talk about adding insult to injury."

"Mm, I don't know. I think you're giving the perp too much credit. Anybody who engages in juvenile property destruction probably isn't that bright."

"Juvenile? I've dated a few boys who fit that description."

I couldn't argue with her there. Instead of replying, I selected another marinated vegetable kabob from the platter in between us and slid the veggies off the skewer and onto my plate. Farrah absently reached over and plucked a piece of zucchini from my plate and popped it into her mouth.

"I wonder who he is." She squinted across the empty dance floor, as if the answer might materialize in thin air. "I haven't rejected any guys lately . . . have I?"

I shrugged. "You shouldn't assume it's a guy. It could be a jealous woman. Maybe you attracted someone's wandering eye."

"Ooh, good point." Rummaging in her purse, she pulled out a lipstick, an eyeliner pencil, and an eyebrow comb, before looking up with a frown. "Do you have a pen?"

"Yeah, I think so. But do you really have enough names to start a list? Tell me more about your run-in with Jake."

"Jake? It couldn't have been him. He'd never do anything to hurt me or my car."

"You're probably right, but that's not what I meant. Why did running into Jake make you question your relationship with Randall?"

"Oh, look who's here!" said Farrah, conveniently avoiding my question. "It's your witchy friends."

I followed her gaze and was pleasantly surprised to see Mila Douglas, the owner of Moonstone Treasures. Mila was a Wiccan High Priestess and a mentor to me, as well as a dear friend. She was with her young assistant, Catrina Miller. They both appeared unusually disheveled.

"I don't think I've ever seen Mila in here," Farrah commented. "I thought she only drank tea."

"Not always," I said, waving at the pair. "Though you're right this isn't her usual hang."

As Farrah and I moved over to make room for the newcomers, I took a closer look. Mila's peasant skirt was twisted, and the scarf wrapped around her brunette shag was askew. Catrina's flower-power T-shirt was rolled up at the sleeves, baring her narrow shoulders. With her G.I. Jane buzzed haircut and men's work boots, she looked like a pixie mechanic. In fact, the oily black smudges on both women made it look like they had just come from an auto repair shop instead of an herbal-scented New Age gift shop.

"What happened to you guys?" I asked.

"Nothing a couple strong females can't handle," said Catrina, flexing her twiglike arms.

"We've been changing tires," explained Mila.

Farrah's mouth dropped open. "Your rear tires? Were they slashed?"

"That's right," said Mila. "Luckily, Catrina's spare fit my car, since I had only one."

"The same thing happened to my car!" said Farrah. "It was in the lot at Main and Willow. Where was yours?"

"In the alley behind the shop, at Main and Magnolia."

"The cops told us Mila's wasn't the only one," put in Catrina. "They think it was some punk bent on destruction. I'm calling him Xorro—spelled with an *X* instead of a *Z*. Get it?"

Mila sighed and used a napkin to pat her face. Farrah still looked dumbfounded. I nudged her and smiled. "There goes your stalker theory. That should be a relief, right?"

"Yeah, I guess." She appeared doubtful.

"That thing with your mail was probably not what it seemed either," I went on. "You probably didn't close the mailbox door tight last time you opened it. It happens."

A waitress came to take Mila's and Catrina's orders and refill our drinks. When she left, I turned to Mila. "Did you close the shop early because of what happened to your car?"

"No, Steve is minding the shop. Catrina and I were heading to the craft fair in Fynn Hollow. Our plans changed when we saw my car. Luckily, the fair is going on tomorrow, too."

"That reminds me. Isn't Applefest coming up soon?"

"Oh, yes," said Mila. "It falls on Mabon weekend this year, and Moonstone will have a booth."

"What's Mabon?" asked Farrah.

Mila, Catrina, and I all spoke at once.

"It's the Witch's Thanksgiving," I began.

"It's a harvest celebration," said Mila.

"It's a time of mystery and death, when darkness overtakes the light," said Catrina.

We all looked at Catrina, and she raised her hands in defense. "What? It is!"

"You're right," Mila conceded. "We often talk about balance and equilibrium at the Autumn Equinox, but it's true that this time ushers in the dark half of the year. It's a prime time for reflection and planning."

"I always feel close to the Goddess in early autumn," I

said. "I think this is the most sensual season. There's such an abundance of sights, scents, tastes—everything."

"Absolutely," said Mila. "We can thank the Goddess Pomona for our abundant gardens and flourishing orchards." Chuckling, she added, "That's what makes Applefest such a perfectly Pagan festival—unbeknownst to the town's event planners!"

Farrah's expression took on a dreamy quality. "I just love Applefest. All the yummy apple treats, and the music, and craft tables. We should go, Keli. We can make it a double date."

"I'd love to," I said, halfway wondering who Farrah intended to bring. "I'll ask Wes to keep that day free."

As we chatted, the bar started to fill up and become louder. An indie rock band took the small stage and began tuning their instruments. I looked over my shoulder to check them out, and when I turned back I spotted a new arrival to the bar. He scanned the room until he zeroed in on me and made a beeline for our table.

Farrah saw him, too, and sat up a little straighter, with an amused look on her face. "Well, if it isn't Crenshaw Davenport the Third!" she said brightly. "What a surprise! Say, what's your middle name? Let me guess. Crenshaw Maximillian Davenport."

"No," he said shortly. "Keli, may I have a word?"

Mila, ever the gracious one, smiled up at Crenshaw. "Why don't you join us?" she asked.

Catrina grabbed a chair from a nearby table and plopped it at the end of our booth. As Crenshaw hesitated, the waitress returned with drinks for Mila and Catrina, then set a glass and napkin at the new place.

"Very well." Crenshaw took a seat and folded his hands primly in his lap. He was still wearing the same suit he'd had on this morning, buttoned up as tightly as ever.

"What's up, Crenshaw?" I took a sip of my beer, enjoying the mellow buzz I was beginning to feel. Something told me I should relish it while I could. Crenshaw appeared more uptight than usual.

"For one thing," he began, "nearly all of the staff at Turnbull Manor have tendered their resignations. With ownership of the manor uncertain, they decided to seek employment elsewhere. Only Celia and one of the gardeners agreed to remain."

"I can't say I blame them," I said. To the others, I explained that Crenshaw was the executor of Elaine Turnbull's estate.

"Oh, I know that mansion," said Farrah. "I attended a party there once. Gorgeous place."

"Yes, well, I'd like to keep it that way," said Crenshaw. "It's way too big for one maid to keep clean, tidy, and properly functioning, not to mention stocked with food and necessities. There are twelve rooms in the main house, plus a number of outbuildings, including two guesthouses."

I wanted to ask why the current residents couldn't clean up after themselves, but Crenshaw was on a roll.

"To top it off," he continued, "right after the staff quit, Celia asked me whether the upcoming gala would still be happening. I asked her what gala, and she informed me that Elaine had agreed to host a fundraising gala for the Edindale Arts Council this coming Friday. Perry Warren—the curator you met—suggested we have the event at the museum instead. However, the council wishes to keep it at the mansion and announce a special tribute to Elaine. Ray Amberly is also pushing to go ahead as planned. He said it's what Elaine would have wanted."

Catrina stared at Crenshaw, then rolled her eyes. "Rich people. Forgive me if I can't muster up sympathy for their so-called problems."

Mila remained silent, but Farrah leaned forward eagerly. "Can you get us tickets?" she asked. "A gala sounds fun! If it's happening this Friday, all the arrangements must already be in place."

"That's true," Crenshaw conceded. "At least, the caterers have already been hired and partially paid for. But that's not the point. I'm trying to conduct an inventory and get the estate settled. I'm not sure it's wise to have a bevy of strangers in the house, especially—" He broke off, as if weighing his next words.

"The caterers usually handle the cleanup," Farrah pointed out. But I didn't think that was what worried Crenshaw. He fixed me with a pleading look.

"Keli, the mansion has a lot of empty bedrooms. I've decided to stay there for a few days, and I'd like you to do the same. Please, I implore you, come and help me finish the inventory and search for the purported missing will."

"Um, did I miss something?" asked Farrah. Mila and Catrina each raised their eyebrows.

"I thought you wanted me to find Lana," I said. "That's why you said you were hiring me. How am I supposed to look for her if I'm confined to the house?"

"You won't be 'confined,'" Crenshaw said. "The house would be your base of operations, as it were. And who knows? While there, you might pick up a clue as to Lana's whereabouts."

I opened my mouth to respond, then promptly closed it. I didn't know what to say. I could easily have said no. I never agreed to commit one hundred percent of my time to this case, and I had plenty of my own work to keep me busy. Besides that, I had definitely picked up a strange vibe at Turnbull Manor.

Still, I couldn't help feeling intrigued. Like a multi-tiered wedding cake, there were so many tempting layers to dig into. Maybe I was crazy, but I couldn't shake the image of Elaine looking down on me from her portrait, practically begging me to make things right.

Oh, who was I kidding? Whatever the reason, I had already been sucked into this unlikely mystery. I was all in—ready or not.

Chapter Six

Since Farrah and I were without wheels, and Mila had four good tires, she offered to take us home. During the whole drive, Farrah pressed me for details about what was going on at Turnbull Manor. I gave her and Mila the condensed version, leaving out the part about Crenshaw's phone call from Dr. Lamb. I didn't want to spread unproven rumors. To be honest, I also didn't want to believe his suspicions were true—especially if I was going to be spending a few days at the mansion.

When we pulled up in front of my cheerful brick town house, Mila turned to me and smiled. "Stop by Moonstone when you can. I received a new shipment of crystal jewelry I think you might like."

"Sounds great. I'll come in soon," I promised.

Farrah tugged on my ponytail. "And call me! I want to know more about this sketchy situation Crenshaw has brought you into. It all sounds very bizarre, if you ask me."

I waved away her concern and assured her it was

fine. But as I climbed the steps to my lit-up front porch, festively decorated with a country-style harvest wreath and barrel planters bursting with flowers of rust-red, butter-yellow, and gold, I began to have second thoughts. Maybe I should have discussed it with Wes before saying yes to Crenshaw.

The house was quiet, except for faint strains of jazz music coming from upstairs. I kicked off my shoes, dropped my purse in a chair, and followed the sound to the bedroom—where I found Wes tossing clothes in a suitcase sitting wide open in the center of the bed.

"And here I thought things were going so well," I said from the doorway.

He looked up and grinned. "Hey, babe. You'll never guess what happened. Al called and said the *Gazette* has an extra ticket for the Chicago Journalism Conference this week. He asked if I wanted it, and of course I said yes. I'm taking the early train tomorrow morning."

"Really?" I was a little confused at his enthusiasm. "Do they have a lot to offer photojournalists?"

"I don't know. There will probably be a couple of panels. But that's not my main reason for going. I can cut out early and track down that friend of Lana's."

"Oh." Now I understood. "You think you'll have more luck than the P.I. firm?"

"Yeah, maybe. I mean, Crenshaw didn't seem very impressed with the job they did. He thought you could do better, so why not me? It's the perfect opportunity."

I glanced at the pile of shirts, pants, and socks on the foot of the bed and noticed a sizable book sticking out from underneath. I pulled it out and looked at the cover. "Your senior yearbook?" I shoved the clothing aside and sat down with the yearbook on my lap. "Why have I never seen this?"

"It was at my folks' house. I stopped by to get it earlier this evening."

I flipped through the pages, pausing when I came to the senior students whose last names began with the letter *C.*

"And there you are, cute little Wesley Callahan." Seventeen-year-old Wes had longish hair, curling at the neck, and a devilish grin on his handsome face. "What a fox you were. I bet you drove all the girls crazy."

Wes snorted. "I don't know about that. I was about as anxious to get out of that place as Lana was."

I turned next to the *T*'s and found Lana Turnbull's senior picture. She had a pretty face, if slightly plump, and fair skin and hair. Her tailored silk blouse and side-swept hair gave her a refined, moneyed appearance. But she didn't look happy. If anything, her expression was defiant as she stared, unsmiling, into the camera . . . with haunted eyes. Or maybe that was my own projection based on what I knew. The photo must have been taken shortly before her father was killed and she ran away.

"I took a picture of her photo with my phone," Wes explained. "That way I can show it to people when I ask if they knew her."

I raised my eyebrows. "You're really serious about this, aren't you?"

"Of course. I want to help, you know?"

I just looked at him, waiting for him to elaborate. He sighed and sat down next to me. "Maybe I'm also trying to make up for past mistakes. The truth is, I feel bad about not being more of a friend to Lana. I keep thinking back to the last time I saw her. It was obvious she was lonely and troubled."

I reached for Wes's hand and gave it a squeeze. "You couldn't have known what she was going through."

"I knew enough to see she could use a friend. Like, this one time, she asked if I would stop by the art room after school to help her with a project. The assignment was to sketch a friend, or something like that. I said I would, but I forgot. I only remembered later when I was out with my buddies. Lame, huh?"

"Did you apologize?"

"Sure. I apologized the next time I saw her, and she said it was no big deal. But I could tell she was hurt. I tried to tell myself it was nothing, like she said. But deep down I knew better."

"Well, if you want to help find her, that's cool with me. Crenshaw keeps expanding my so-called consulting role anyway." I told Wes about Crenshaw's request that I stay at the manor for a few days.

"But that's great!" said Wes. "Now you won't be here alone while I'm out of town."

"I suppose." I stood up and headed for the adjoining bathroom. "I'm going to get ready for bed."

"I'll be done here in a minute," he said, tossing more items into his suitcase.

As I washed my face and brushed my teeth, I realized Wes had a point about me not being alone. Although I lived by myself before he moved in, I'd become somewhat jittery in recent months. It all started when a mad killer decided to terrorize me with bizarre phone calls—and then set a fire on our deck. To make matters worse, a second weirdo bugged my office with a hidden camera and sent me cryptic, vaguely threatening notes. Luckily, the first criminal was no longer a threat, but the second one was still at large.

After changing into pajamas and a well-worn satin robe, I slipped out of the bathroom and headed straight for the spare bedroom, which I'd converted into my personal sanctuary. It was where I sat in meditation, drew tarot cards, and performed a variety of spells. Beneath the window was my altar, fashioned from a long narrow console table with decorations that changed with the season. I lit a pillar candle and looked outside to the backyard, where it was dark and quiet.

Immediately, my mind flitted to Farrah's possible stalker, and I once again recalled my own ordeal last spring. Whenever I thought about the one who wasn't caught, who even now might be lurking about somewhere in the darkness, I always felt fear first, followed by anger. It was so bizarre. What did this person have against me? I figured it must be somebody who felt I'd done them wrong, but I had no idea who it was. From what I could tell, the whole reason for planting the hidden camera seemed to be to sabotage my law practice. Yet I also had the impression the creep was toying with me. In fact, because of the dubious gifts sent to my office, I had nicknamed my enemy the Giftster. Use of the goofy name made the whole situation slightly less scary.

I hadn't received any tricky gifts in a few months—*knock on wood*. But that didn't mean I had lowered my guard. I constantly had the urge to look over my shoulder, and I couldn't sleep at night unless I'd cast an iron-clad protection spell to shield the whole house—which I now set about doing.

Since I had done this so many times, all my supplies were readily at hand. I pulled open a slim drawer in

the altar table and brought out four items correspon-
ding with the four ancient elements: a vial of purified
water, a bundle of sage, a black candle, and a bowl of red
brick dust. As I placed each item in the direction asso-
ciated with the element, I mentally created a circle of
light and intoned a simple chant to "call the quarters":

> *By the Sun of God and Moonlight's daughter,*
> *I now invoke earth, air, fire, and water.*
> *From the north, dust of earth,*
> *From the east, scented smoke,*
> *From the south, a flame so bright,*
> *From the west, water's light.*

I lit both the sage stick and the black candle, and
took three deep, centering breaths. For a moment, I
contemplated the flickering candle flame until I felt the
presence of Spirit within my sacred circle. Then I traced
a pentagram in the center of the altar and placed a ce-
ramic bowl on top. Next, I poured some of the red
brick dust into the bowl. Wafting sage smoke over the
dust, I chanted a spell I knew by heart:

> *Guarded by angels of the Goddess,*
> *I am safe.*
> *Strong as a mighty fortress,*
> *My home is safe.*
> *Shielded by Nature's highest forces,*
> *Those I love are infinitely safe.*
> *Defend, protect, repel*
> *Defend, protect, repel*
> *Evil halt and danger quell*
> *By my power, all is well.*

I blew gently into the bowl, then picked it up and carried it with me as I made my nightly rounds. Room by room, I sprinkled red dust along the threshold of every window and doorway in the house. Somewhere along the way, I became aware I had picked up a shadow.

"You should be used to this by now," I said to Josie, the cat.

She purred in response.

I had to smile. It had been a little less than a year since I'd brought her home, but I couldn't imagine being without her. A sleek black feline with keen yellow eyes and a tendency to stick close to me, Josie was a perfect witch's familiar—though I didn't usually call her by that term. She certainly wasn't my spirit animal. She was much too independent. Besides, by now she belonged to Wes as much as to me. Still, when we found each other last October, our connection was undeniable. And like her namesake, my late aunt Josephine, Josie the cat seemed to look after me, sometimes in uncanny and mysterious ways.

Now, however, she was kind of in the way. While I tried to smudge the back door, she wound herself around my legs and kept purring for attention. I had to be careful not to step on her.

"Watch out, kitty! If I didn't know better, I might think you're trying to keep me from doing this spell. Fat chance."

I had been performing this ritual every night for the past four months. Since there had been no further incidents with the Giftster in that time, I assumed the spell was working. I wasn't about to stop now.

Of course, I wouldn't be doing it tomorrow night, or the night after that. I'd be in a strange house then. I couldn't exactly go around scattering red dust all over Turnbull Manor. Someone would be bound to notice.

But maybe there was something I could do. As I washed my hands and went back upstairs to clean off my altar and extinguish the candles, I thought about the talismans and amulets I could take with me on this little getaway. Maybe I would bring along some lucky red powder after all. I would just wear it close to my body.

It couldn't hurt.

Chapter Seven

I woke up early Sunday morning, not because I wanted to, but because I was uncomfortably hot. Wes had kicked off the blankets in the night, and they all landed on me.

After a quick trip to the bathroom, where I splashed water on my face, I slipped quietly downstairs and stepped outside onto the back deck. The cool morning air was refreshing. I turned my face toward the rising sun and breathed deeply. Sometimes there was nothing more to be done—no magic words to say or elaborate rituals to perform. It was enough simply to be present beneath the open sky. To simply *be*.

Balance.

That's what I needed. All the banishing, repelling, and shielding work I'd been doing lately was starting to take a toll. It was making me feel heavy and constricted, like I was wearing a thick, woolen cape—or like I was being buried under a pile of blankets in a hot bed. I almost laughed as the realization hit me. I was creating too much negative energy. It was time to work some light magic and balance out the darkness—and I ought to do it before we entered the dark half of the year.

In fact, with the approach of the Autumn Equinox, it was the perfect time to think about balance. In two short weeks, night and day would be nearly equal, and the sun would be entering Libra, the sign of balanced scales.

For starters, I could bring a bit of nature inside. I went back in for scissors, then trotted out to the back-yard in my bare feet. Bright yellow sunflowers were just the thing to lighten up my mood.

On my way to the flower patch, I was sidetracked by the tomato plants in my vegetable garden. They were dripping with fat, ripe cherry tomatoes, begging to be picked. I plucked one and popped it in my mouth, the tart juices bursting with flavor. Eating directly from the earth made me feel close to my ancestors, who had lived off the land. It also made me think of the other reason this time of year was so special. Besides offering the gift of balance, the Autumn Equinox coincided with the Wiccan holiday Mabon: a celebration of the earth's bounty and the second of the three harvest festivals, including Lughnasadh and Samhain. A boun-tiful harvest was cause for thanksgiving indeed.

Finally, I moved along and cut a bunch of miniature sunflowers, which I took inside and placed in a tall, metal vase. After arranging the cheerful flowers with sprigs of greenery, I set them in the center of the table and admired the effect. Then I mentally kicked myself. What was I thinking? With both Wes and me leaving the house for a few days, it probably wasn't the best time to bring fresh flowers inside.

"Pretty," said Wes, coming up behind me. "The flowers aren't bad either," he said with a grin.

"Cute." I smiled in return, then noticed his bags. "Are you leaving already?"

"Soon. The crew from the paper is meeting for coffee, and Al has my ticket."

"Oh. I thought we'd at least have breakfast together."

"I have a few minutes." He pulled me in for a hug. "I wish you could come with me."

"Really?" I looked up at him in mock surprise. "Yesterday you seemed determined to track down Lana on your own. Like a regular Sam Spade."

"What's the matter?" Wes asked, matching my teasing tone. "Don't you think I can do it? I have skills, you know. You're not the only one who can ask questions and follow clues."

"Oh, I'm sure you can do it. But it's not as easy as all that—especially when the person you're pursuing doesn't want to be found."

"Is that so?"

"Yes, that's so. I do have a bit of experience in this area, as you might recall."

With a twinkle in his eye, he lifted my hand and held it between his palms like a supplicant. "Oh, most experienced one, please tell me your ways. Share your wisdom so that I might follow in your footsteps and one day be as great a detective as you are."

Suppressing a smile, I jerked my hand away. "You don't need my help. You have skills, remember?"

"True. Never mind, then." He turned away and grabbed a banana from the fruit bowl on the counter. He peeled it and took a bite, then paused and regarded me thoughtfully. "I just had an interesting idea."

"Do tell."

"How about we engage in a friendly competition? Let's see which one of us can solve one of the Turnbull mysteries first. Who can find Lana first? Or the missing will, or whatever else Crenshaw wants you to get to the bottom of. What do you say?"

"I say you're awfully sure of yourself. You know, it's more likely Lana is near Edindale than in Chicago, based on that blog post in the P.I.'s file."

"So, is it a bet?"

"What are the stakes?"

"Hmm. Besides bragging rights . . . how about if the winner gets a pass on kitchen cleanup duty for the rest of the year?"

"The loser does the dishes after every meal?"

"Absolutely. I'm sure you can handle it."

"Ha! You've got yourself a deal."

After Wes left, I had breakfast alone in the quiet kitchen and considered what to do with my Sunday. Part of me was itching to start looking for Lana right away. I had no intention of letting Wes win the bet. But then I checked my email and realized I had a number of things to take care of before I could devote any time to Crenshaw's assignment. I took a quick shower and dressed in a nice pair of jeans, a soft cotton blouse, and a pair of faux suede boots. Then I grabbed my purse and keys and set off for my office downtown.

The drive took all of five minutes. As a college town, county seat, and nature-lover's destination, Edindale had a lot to offer, but it was still on the small side. That suited me just fine. If not for all the errands I had to run today, I might have walked to work.

I pulled into a parking space on the street in front

of the square brick building that housed my office. A 1950s-era former bank, it had once conveyed solid trust and respectability. Now it was a somewhat dusty relic offering cheap office space. But the location, one block off the town square, was ideal, and the antique aura held a certain charm. My footsteps clicked along the tile floor as I made my way down the quiet hallway to the door bearing my name in gold lettering: KELI MILANNI, ESQ.

I paused, feeling a familiar twinge of apprehension. Following the incidents last spring, I had changed the locks here and installed a host of magical talismans and enchantments. Still, I always felt a little wary when I inserted the key and pushed open the door.

"Hold it!"

I almost jumped out of my skin at the sound of the voice behind me. Whirling around, I gaped at the petite woman rushing toward me. It was my fellow building tenant, Annie Chapin. She giggled at my reaction.

"Sorry to startle you. I wanted to give you this package before I leave. I've been trying to catch you for days."

"Oh," I breathed, accepting the brown envelope. "Thanks."

"The delivery guy wouldn't leave it without a signature," she went on. "He didn't want to come back yet again, so he knocked on my door, and I signed for you."

I glanced at the return address on the envelope and recognized the name of a law office in a nearby town. "This must be the signed settlement agreement I've been expecting."

"You should have important mail held at the post office, if you won't be here every day. Either that or hire an assistant."

"Yeah, maybe. I'm sorry for the trouble. I guess I'm still figuring out the ropes as a solo practitioner."

"No worries. I'm not always here either, you know."

I knew. It seemed like all of the occupants of this building were rarely here. Many were small-business owners who worked from home or in other towns and kept a small office here for the occasional appointment. Annie was a physical therapist who spent most of her daytime hours at the hospital. She used her rented office space to meet with private clients in her off-hours. As a result, I often felt like I was the only person in the building—which could be lonely and a little eerie, especially in the evening. That was part of the reason I didn't spend as much time here as I had at my old law firm.

I thanked Annie again and went inside. Everything was in order, just as I had left it a few days ago. There was the tidy little reception area, outfitted like a miniature living room with two plush chairs facing a small coffee table. In the far corner was a discreet kitchenette tucked next to a vintage wooden storage cabinet. And to the left were two doors, one to a locked closet where I kept my clients' files and one to my private office. I entered the office and flipped on the light.

This room was smaller than the first, but tastefully decorated with pictures, books, and shimmering crystals. I tossed the envelope on my desk and turned on the computer. While it booted up, I checked on the plants that hung from the ceiling and lined the cabinet behind my office chair. They weren't doing very well. The only window in the place faced an alley, but it let in an ample amount of sunlight. The problem was some of the plants needed watering more often than I made it here.

I broke off the dead leaves and gave the plants a

drink, then got to work on client matters. For the next two hours, I knocked out some quicker tasks, then set about rearranging things on my schedule to free up time for the "Turnbull Project," as I noted it on my calendar. I did have one court appearance on Wednesday that I'd have to keep, but everything else could wait.

Ever since branching out on my own, I had become more of a general practitioner than I had been before. While the bulk of my caseload still fell under the umbrella of family law, I wasn't picky. If I felt I could handle it, I was willing to take on just about any case that happened to walk in the door.

Of course, no one was actually walking through the door. Clients usually called or emailed. Even if they wanted to walk in, I might not be here to greet them.

My stomach growled, telling me it was time for lunch. I wandered over to the kitchenette. The minifridge contained a bottle of soda water and a container of soy yogurt—expired. I wrinkled my nose and went back to my desk. I'd have to go out for food, but first I needed to work on billing matters and prepare invoices for mailing.

I sighed. Annie was right. I really could use an assistant.

My cell phone rang, and I snatched it up. It was my cousin, Ricki Day. "Hey, cuz!" I said brightly.

"Hey, Keli. Doing anything right now? I have some time to kill while my car is at the auto shop."

"I was about to go grab some lunch. Can I pick you up?"

"That would be great." She told me where she was, and I gathered up my things and headed out. A short while later, we were sitting across from one another at the Cozy Café diner.

I loved the Cozy Café, not only for the convenient

location, friendly staff, and pleasant ambience, but also because of its decent selection of vegetarian options. It was one place in town where I felt comfortable inviting both my meat-eating friends and fellow vegans. My cousin fell into the former camp, so I was a little surprised when she asked the waitress to make her order the same as mine: a black bean burger without cheese, sweet potato fries, and a side salad.

"I've been thinking about my birth mother a lot lately," she explained. "Josephine was the quintessential hippie, you know? Living close to the land, advocating for the environment. I mean, I may be an environmental inspector, but I never really thought about how my own lifestyle impacts the environment." She paused, searching for the right words. "Don't get me wrong—I wouldn't have traded my adoptive parents for the world. I had a wonderful upbringing. But sometimes I imagine how different my life would be if I'd been raised by Josephine."

I nodded and, for some reason, my mind jumped to Lana Turnbull. To understand the girl who ran away, I was going to have to learn about the family she left behind.

Ricki and I continued chatting as we ate our lunch. When the check came, we divided the bill, and I asked her if she wanted me to take her back to the auto shop.

She checked her watch. "Yeah, might as well. My car should be done soon. It doesn't take that long to repair two tires."

I froze with my hand on my purse. "Tires? Don't tell me. Did someone slash your two rear tires?"

"Yes! How did you know?"

"Didn't the cops tell you? Apparently, there's a mad slasher on the loose. I have two other friends who had the same thing happen."

"Dang. I hope they catch him soon." Ricki pushed her chair back and stood up. "That's too bad for your friends, but I'm glad to know I wasn't targeted. At first I thought someone was getting even with me for issuing them a violation notice."

We stepped outside and headed to my car parked along the curb. I immediately checked my tires, which were fine. But something about Ricki's assumption that she had been targeted wasn't sitting well with me.

"Where was your car parked when it happened?" I asked.

"In my driveway, in front of my house."

"And none of your neighbors had their tires cut?"

"Nope. Just my luck, huh?"

I didn't respond. I was starting to have a funny feeling about these tire-slashing incidents. Maybe they weren't so random after all. So far, I had only heard about three victims—and they all happened to be friends of mine.

Chapter Eight

For the rest of the afternoon, I crossed items off my to-do list, finishing up at the drop-off box outside the post office. With my last errand out of the way, I decided to reward myself by paying a visit to one of my favorite people at one of my favorite places: Mila Douglas and Moonstone Treasures.

In the past, I tried to be discreet when patronizing the occult gift store and witchcraft emporium. I had been afraid of being caught buying tarot cards, herbal potions, or pentacle-adorned trinkets, for fear that my more conservative clients and colleagues might judge me as frivolous—or worse. In fact, I did lose a couple of clients last spring, when a reporter implied I might be a witch. But around the same time, I ended up attracting some new clients for the very same reason. *Where one door closes, another opens.*

Besides that, over the last year or so I had dared to show my true nature a little bit more, and the world hadn't ended.

I entered Moonstone Treasures to the tinkling of

bells and the scent of cinnamon and patchouli. Soft
lighting, combined with velvety rugs underfoot and
flowing tapestries on the walls, added to the soothing
atmosphere. Mila was helping a customer at the counter,
so I gave her a wave and turned to admire the newest
display near the entrance.

Mila changed the decorations in her shop windows
every eight weeks to match the turn of the Wiccan
wheel. Showcased in the window today was the traditional Mabon cornucopia, surrounded by other symbols
of autumn abundance, including apples, pomegranates,
and Indian corn. Nearby, a round table held a fat orange
pumpkin encircled with assorted scented candles. I was
sniffing one when Mila came up to join me.

"What are your feelings on pumpkin spice?" she
asked. "Love it or hate it?"

I set the candle down. "This one's not bad. It's
subtle, which I like. Some of them can be too over-
powering."

"I agree. Given its ability to evoke strong emotions,
scent can be a powerful tool in magic. But it's so personal. A scent that's attractive to one person might be
repellant to another." She beckoned me with one
finger. "Crystals, on the other hand, derive their power
from the earth, so their magic is more universal. Come
see the jewelry I was telling you about."

I followed her to the jewelry case in front of the
checkout counter. Mila unlocked the glass door and
brought out a flat, velvet-lined box containing five
rows of pendants. They were various sizes, from the
delicately small to the chunky and bold. Most were
fashioned in silver or gold and inlaid with a stone or
crystal—amethyst, tourmaline, and hematite among
them. In spite of their variety, there was one thing

they all had in common: Each pendant was designed in the shape of an eye. I looked down at an assortment of eyes—the Eye of Horus, the all-seeing eye, the evil eye—and they all stared back at me. Their message was clear: "Watch out."

I looked up at Mila in amazement. "How did you know?"

"How did I know you could use a little extra protection? I couldn't say. Just a feeling, I suppose."

"Of course." I smiled and shook my head, then turned my attention back to the charms. After a moment's consideration, I selected an Eye of Horus with a dark green moldavite gem in the round center. When it came to connecting with a higher power, I drew from an eclectic pantheon, and I had always been fascinated by the myths of ancient Egypt, so solemn and regal and magical. Mila slipped the pendant on a chain and fastened it around my neck, and I felt instantly braver.

"Anything else you're looking for today?"

I smiled at her choice of words. "Actually, yes. I'm looking for a few things, though not here. Honestly, I could use all the help I can get." She waited expectantly, as I considered how much I should say. "I've cast finding spells before, as you know, but this is a tough case. Two cases, really. I need to find a missing person who probably doesn't want to be found and a missing will that may or may not exist."

"Hmm." Mila narrowed her eyes, already coming up with ideas, I was sure.

"Plus, time is short for a few reasons," I went on. "I have my other clients to attend to, and—"

"Say no more. I have just the thing."

I blinked. Of course she did.

"Astral projection."

"Astral projection?"

"Right—the act of traveling through non-ordinary reality without your body. You've done this before in visions and dreams. You can also do it very deliberately for specific purposes."

I nodded. "Yeah, I have done that before. But it's not always clear what I'm seeing. My visions are usually symbolic, and sometimes I see only part of the picture." I looked away. "And sometimes it's scary."

"There are ways to make it less scary," Mila said gently. "But when you're looking for answers, you won't always like what you see. Visions, like all divine messages, almost always require interpretation. Step one is to be clear about what you're looking for."

I smiled ironically as a thought occurred to me. "Is this how psychics help locate missing people? Through astral projection?" I had told Wes I was no psychic, yet here I was about to act like one.

"Mm-hmm." Opening a cabinet behind the counter, Mila rummaged through an assortment of bottles, vials, and jars as she spoke. "First, you need to get yourself into a relaxed, open, trancelike state. Make sure you're in a safe, quiet place where you won't be disturbed. Concentrate on the object of your quest . . . then prepare to take flight."

I couldn't help snickering. "All I need is a broomstick, right?"

She found what she was looking for and held out her hand. "That, and some flying ointment."

My house was quiet when I returned home. Even Josie was curled up in a patch of late-afternoon sun shining on the living room floor. With Wes out of town, I almost wished I could go ahead and leave for Turnbull Manor today instead of tomorrow. I didn't relish the idea of being home alone.

In the kitchen, I noticed a basketful of apples practically begging to be cooked up into something delicious. *That's what I need to do,* I decided. *Some kitchen witchery.* Mabon was about honoring the harvest, and the best way to do that was in the kitchen.

As I washed and sliced the apples, I hummed a tuneless melody. My intent was to raise my spirits and reinforce my stronghold, both in heart and hearth. Yet my mind kept returning, unbidden, to darker thoughts: memories of stalkers, smugglers, murderers, and thieves—all of whom I had encountered in recent years.

As much as I loathed to dwell on the past, the truth was there were several people out there who had reason to feel ill will toward me. One way or another, I'd helped send more than one criminal to prison. And they all knew it.

I dumped the chopped apples into a large pot and covered them with water. Then I measured in the fragrant ingredients, including cinnamon, cloves, and ginger. These potent spices reminded me of all the protection spells I'd casted since meeting so many bad guys.

Thankfully, I'd never had to testify against any of them in court. They had all entered into plea deals. As far as I knew, they were all still safely behind bars. Surely I would have heard if any of them had been released. *Wouldn't I?*

"That's all I need," I muttered. "A felon on the loose—with a grudge against me."

I stirred the apples, then fired up the burner and covered the pot. As I cleaned the kitchen, setting aside the apple cores for the compost bin, I tried to alter my negative train of thought. On the plus side, I had helped a lot of people in my short career as an amateur detective.

I had even helped myself, I realized with a start. After all, it was a mystery that had brought Wes and me together.

As the apples simmered and the kitchen filled with the warm scent of cinnamon spices, I recalled the circumstances of our meeting. It all started with the death of Wes's grandmother and the theft of a valuable Shakespearean heirloom. The treasure belonged to Wes's family by rights, but someone thought otherwise. For a while, I had thought the thief might be a wayward member of the family—maybe even Wes himself! Luckily, it turned out to be a former colleague of mine who had his own dubious claim to the folio. As it happened, he was also involved in an illegal money-lending scheme that targeted gamblers.

Nice guy, I thought ruefully.

I got up to give the apples a stir—something I'd have to do every fifteen minutes or so, until they were soft enough to purée. Every time I did so, I recited the same little incantation:

> *Bless this kitchen, bless this food*
> *Fill my home with a happy mood*
> *With a pinch of luck and a lot of love*
> *Let magic flow from high above.*

In between stirrings, I made labels for the glass jars I would fill. I planned to make gifts of my special

Mabon recipe. *"Apple butter like no other,"* I thought with a giggle. By this time, the spell had worked, and I was in a much better frame of mind. I had succeeded in pushing away negative thoughts of intruders and enemies.

Mostly.

Chapter Nine

My second visit to Turnbull Manor was a far cry from the first. Without Wes, there was none of the Saturday-in-the-park, carefree feeling that had offset the strange vibe I'd picked up from the house. Now the mansion appeared almost foreboding under the slate gray sky. The lack of sun didn't help. Overnight, the September winds had shifted, letting loose a chill dampness in the morning air. As I stood on the doorstep, the collar of my coat turned up, a suitcase in one hand and a cat crate in the other, I couldn't help feeling a bit forlorn myself. *Like a maiden in a Gothic novel,* I thought. *Sent to live with peculiar relatives in a rundown castle . . . on the moor.*

"Good grief, Keli," I said to myself. *Get a grip.*

I rang the bell and waited. There was no response. I dug out my phone to give Crenshaw a buzz and saw that he had sent me a text: Held up at the office. Get settled in and I'll meet you at the manor by ten.

Great.

When no one answered my next two rings, I tried the doorknob. It was unlocked, so I let myself in. With hesitant steps, I walked through the foyer and into the great room. A lit Tiffany lamp on a marble-topped console table was the only sign of life.

I set my suitcase down at the foot of the broad staircase and checked on Josie. She was being exceptionally docile in her traveling crate. It was like she knew she'd better be on her best behavior if she wanted to stay with me on this unusual adventure. Of course, I could have left her home, popping in once a day to freshen her food and water. But I felt better having her with me.

"I'll let you out of there soon," I murmured. "I hope."

I removed my coat and draped it over the bannister. I was glad I'd opted to wear nice clothes—a cream-colored turtleneck sweater and long pleated skirt—the better to fit in with my surroundings. Gazing around the spacious room, I took in the wide variety of artwork adorning the walls and pedestal tables. I hadn't paid much attention when passing through the other day, but now I was in awe. There was one piece in particular, a striking bronze sculpture, that captured my attention. At about twenty inches high, it depicted a male nude bearing a rock on top of his head. A small plaque indicated the artist was Gertrude Vanderbilt Whitney. *Amazing.*

Wandering around the room, I was struck by the apparent quality and authenticity of all the paintings. These were no reproductions. I ventured up to one oil painting, a pastoral scene in vibrant shades of green and gold, and was startled to recognize the printed signature: *Grant Wood.*

I whistled softly. *If this is an original, the occupants of this house should really keep the front door locked.*

A faint creaking sound came from the east hallway. It

could have been a door opening or someone's weight upon a loose floorboard. I peered around the corner and saw nothing but an empty corridor.

"Hello!" I called.

Feeling like an intruder, I moved quietly down the hall to the open door of the library. The room was dark. Another step down the hall, and I yelled out a little louder. "Hello? Anybody home?"

From somewhere within the depths of the house came another sound, dull but abrupt, like a door slamming. "Some welcome," I muttered, turning back to the great room.

As I approached the staircase, I stopped short. A woman was leaning over my suitcase.

"Hello?" I said, more sharply this time.

She stood and whirled so quickly, she almost toppled over in her four-inch heels. Regaining her balance, her pink-tipped fingers fluttered at her chest.

"Oh! You scared me!"

For a moment, we looked at one another questioningly. Though she was old enough to be my mother, there was a vulnerable youthfulness in both her looks and manner. With her bronzed skin, expertly applied makeup, and golden red hair tied up in a baby blue silk scarf, she reminded me of a maturing Hollywood starlet in denial about her true age.

Suddenly, she laughed lightly and held out her hand. "I'm Suzanne Turnbull. You must be the other lawyer. Keli, right?"

I shook her hand and smiled. "Sorry I startled you. The front door was unlocked. And just now I thought I heard someone in the hallway."

"Probably Celia or Ray," she said, waving her hand

dismissively. "I was just heading to the kitchen. Have you had breakfast?"

"Maybe I should put my things away first," I suggested. "I hope it's okay that I brought my cat. She's very friendly and doesn't scratch."

"Oh, the darling! I wondered what was in there." Suzanne leaned over and unlatched the crate, making kissing sounds as she offered her hand to be sniffed. Happy to be free, Josie stepped daintily past the woman and leaned her paws forward in a full body stretch.

"Bring her along," Suzanne said brightly. "Ernesto will take your things upstairs. Celia made up a room for you."

"Ernesto?" I scooped Josie up and followed Suzanne down the curving hallway to the large kitchen, an elegant, airy room with gleaming white cabinets, marble countertops, and a large center table.

"He's the groundskeeper and head gardener," Suzanne explained. "But he does a lot of other things around here, too. Especially since most of the other staff took off." She filled a bowl of water for Josie, then set about making toast, chattering as she went. "I am *so* glad you're here! You're going to be a big help. Crenshaw means well, but men aren't really good at this sort of thing, are they? And Elaine had *so* much stuff! Clothes, jewelry, shoes, books, photo albums . . . I can't fathom sorting through it all. I'm overwhelmed just thinking about it!"

"I can imagine," I murmured. I felt a little breathless just listening to her—and somewhat puzzled. As far as I knew, the burden of going through Elaine's things wouldn't have fallen upon Suzanne. Crenshaw was the executor, and Suzanne wasn't a blood relative. Still, I supposed it was natural for her to feel some responsibility. After all, she had lived with her mother-in-law.

She placed a crock of butter and a jar of marmalade on the table, along with a stack of toast. "I suppose it will all have to be sold, won't it?" she asked, taking a seat across from me. "All of Elaine's possessions—even the house?"

"Crenshaw will have to complete the accounting first," I said. "After all the debts are paid, it will be up to the beneficiary to decide what to do with the remainder. Which, of course, is why we're trying to find your daughter. Were you surprised Elaine left everything to Lana?"

Suzanne dropped her butter knife with a clatter. Recovering, she spoke quickly, eyes focused on the toast. "No, not really. Lana is Elaine's only heir, after all. And Elaine always did dote on her."

"They hadn't been in touch, had they?"

"Not that I know of."

"Has anyone heard from Lana in recent years, that you know of?"

Suzanne shook her head, still not meeting my eyes.

"I'm sorry," I said gently. "I can only imagine how difficult it must have been for you . . . back then and even still."

Abruptly, Suzanne scraped her chair back and sprang to her feet. "Forgive me! I should have offered you a drink. Would you like coffee or tea? Or—better yet, let's have mimosas!"

Without waiting for an answer, she went to the refrigerator and took out a container of orange juice and a bottle of sparkling wine. From a glass-doored cabinet, she grabbed two champagne flutes and set them on the table. As she filled them, she shot me a sly look.

"I don't know about you, but I *do* enjoy the finer things in life. I mean, it's not like I married for money. Jim was just a student when we met, with a dual degree in art history and business. His parents didn't support him. After he graduated, he worked in the corporate world for a couple years, until his mother asked us to move in with her. But then, let me tell you, it didn't take long to get used to the perks of living here!"

"I can imagine," I said, looking around. We clinked glasses and sipped our drinks. It was surprisingly refreshing.

"Are you married?" asked Suzanne.

"Um, no. But my boyfriend and I live together."

"Girl, you better lock him down!" She wagged a finger at me, then laughed. "Of course, it doesn't always work out. Jim and I were separated by the time he died. I had moved out, more or less permanently. I only came back later when Elaine asked me to."

"That was nice of you to come back."

"Yeah, it was kind of surprising, since I wasn't exactly her favorite person in the world. To be honest, we butted heads all the time. So, even though I've lived here for years, I never expected it to be forever. That's why I've always got my eyes open for new husband material. Preferably in the form of a wealthy, older man, if you get my drift."

I only smiled, as she took another swig of her drink. Then she laughed again.

"Look who I'm talking to! Don't listen to me. You're a lawyer. You can bring home your own bacon."

"True."

"Same here. I'm a businesswoman. I was a makeup artist before I met Jim, and now I'm an independent saleslady for Carrie Cosmetics." She raised her glass. "To women's lib!"

I took another sip, then set my glass down and pushed it away. The sweet-tart cocktail was going down a little too easily. "Suzanne, I wondered if I could ask you a few questions about Lana. As you probably know—"

"My, you have gorgeous cheekbones!"

"Excuse me?"

"I can show you some contouring tricks to enhance them. And your eyes! They're hazel, right? So pretty. But with a little shading here, a little highlighting there, I can make them really pop. You should let me give you a makeover!"

I sighed. I wasn't particularly interested in making my eyes pop. On the other hand, if it would give me more time to question Suzanne, it was worth a shot. "Sure. Why not?"

"Wonderful! Your boyfriend will flip by the time I'm through with you. The bombshell look is my specialty."

I had to laugh. "Oh, well. My boyfriend is actually in Chicago for a few days. In fact, he's following up on a possible lead to Lana. He's trying to track down a woman who might have been friends with her."

Suzanne's face clouded over, and she took a gulp from her drink. I was about to apologize again, when she spoke up, a hard edge to her voice. "You know, even if you do find her, it doesn't mean she'll come back. You can't make her come back."

"Er, you're right. She could disclaim her inheritance. Or she could hire an attorney to handle everything for her. But first we have to locate her."

I waited for Suzanne to say something. When she didn't, I pressed on. "You might be able to help. If this lead doesn't pan out, I think I'll post a public notice in a few area newspapers. Would you like to help craft the message?"

She shook her head. "I don't think so."

"Oh." I was beginning to wonder if Suzanne didn't want to find her daughter.

"You don't understand. Lana doesn't want to hear from me."

"Are you sure? After so many years, how—"

"I'm sure! Lana will never come back, because . . . because she hates me!"

Suzanne jumped to her feet, pushing against the table with such force that her glass tipped over. Without a backward glance, she bolted from the room.

Stunned, I looked from the doorway, to the puddle of spilled mimosa, to my cat, who stood stock-still in the corner.

"Yeah," I said softly, grabbing a towel. "That just happened."

Chapter Ten

I sensed a presence behind me even before I heard the familiar throat-clearing. It was like his own personal introduction before every *bon mot* he fancied himself saying.

"When I asked for your help," said Crenshaw, "I didn't intend for you to become *the* help."

"Ha ha," I replied, thrusting a mug into his hands. "Pour yourself the last cup of coffee. I need to check my phone."

After cleaning up the mess Suzanne had left, I'd loaded the dishwasher, rummaged through the pantry, and made another pot of coffee. My phone had buzzed a couple of times, and I was only now ready to see who had called. When I recognized the name of one of my clients on the caller display, I had the sinking feeling I should have answered it sooner. I quickly punched in her number.

"Hello, Allie?" I said, when she picked up. "I'm sorry I missed your call. What can I do for you?"

"I think I might have made a mistake," Allie said

apologetically. "I thought we had a ten o'clock appointment. I waited outside your office for twenty minutes, but I started to feel awkward just standing there, so I left. Did I write down the wrong day?"

I slapped my forehead. "Oh, dear. I think I'm the one who messed up. I'm so sorry. Let's pick a new date, and this one will be on the house. No fee."

After finishing up the call with Allie, I made sure to enter the new appointment in the calendar on my phone—something I neglected to do when I'd made the first one with her two weeks ago. Then I immediately placed another call, this time to the classified ad department at the *Edindale Gazette*. My help-wanted ad would run the next day.

When I turned back to Crenshaw, he was leaning against the counter sipping coffee and watching Josie. She had made herself comfortable on top of the wine cabinet. Twitching her whiskers, she stared right back, as if daring him to defy her. He raised one eyebrow.

"Is this your cat?"

"She's mine and I'm hers. We're kind of a matched set."

"There's a dog on the premises someplace. Belongs to Ray, I believe. You might want to keep her inside."

"Thanks. She looks after herself pretty well, but I do intend to keep her close."

He poured me a cup of coffee and handed it to me, inclining his head toward my cell phone. "Everything all right?"

"Yeah, perfect." I blew on my coffee and took a careful sip. "I met Suzanne. Have you talked to her much?"

"I tried. She wasn't very forthcoming with me. She talked a lot without saying anything and effectively changed the subject every time I asked about her daughter."

"Same here. I mean, I get that it must be upsetting to talk about a child who ran away. But she acted . . . almost guilty. And a little angry. I wonder if she and Lana fought before Lana took off."

Crenshaw shrugged. "I'm sure you'll get to the bottom of it. Would you like a tour of the house now?"

He showed me around the main floor first. We made a large circle, pausing at each doorway, including the dining room, parlor, library, and conservatory. Josie followed us, sometimes veering off to explore on her own, but never straying far. I wondered if she sensed the strange, melancholy atmosphere I'd picked up the first time I laid eyes on the house.

When we returned to the kitchen, Crenshaw led the way to the back staircase. On the second floor, there were two wings, divided by a central gallery at the top of the main staircase. We made a quick pass through the loftlike gallery, with Crenshaw pointing out some of the more valuable paintings. The most interesting one, to me anyway, was a family portrait: Harold Turnbull, seated like a king on his throne; Elaine, his dutiful wife, standing next to him with her hand resting lightly on his shoulder; and their young son, Jim, with freckles and a cowlick, sitting on his father's knee. The pose was formal, but their facial expressions were natural, almost playful, even, as if the family were sharing a private joke with the artist. I smiled softly and felt an unexpected lump in my throat. Was it because this family was now gone? Their lives, their happiness, a thing of the past? Or was it something more personal, a sort of longing for something missing in my own life?

"Are you coming?" asked Crenshaw, breaking into my maudlin daydreams.

"Yes. Carry on."

Each wing on the second floor contained a master suite, a guest bedroom, and a lounge. In the east wing, Crenshaw pointed out Suzanne's room, with its closed door, and the guest room, which used to be Lana's. "They didn't preserve it," Crenshaw informed me. "After Lana's twenty-first birthday, Elaine and Suzanne boxed up her things and converted the room to another guest bedroom. Whatever they kept is now in boxes in the attic."

Elaine's master bedroom was in the west wing. We didn't linger, because Crenshaw was eager to show me the rest of the house. When we came to the guest room in that wing, I was happy to see my luggage had been placed on a cedar chest at the foot of the bed. I dashed in to set up Josie's portable litter box and a bowl of food in the en suite bathroom. She made herself comfortable on top of the bed, so I closed the door to keep her inside.

The back staircase continued upward to a third floor, which consisted of four rooms: three bedrooms—Celia's plus two that had been occupied by staff who had since departed—as well as a large space used for storage. A tall window in the storeroom offered a panoramic view of the grounds in back of the house. Beyond the gardens, I spotted a hedge maze, a tennis court, and a swimming pool, which was evidently drained and covered for the season. Farther away, a sizable grove of trees gave way to rolling farmland, calling to mind the Grant Wood painting displayed in the great room.

"What are all the buildings down there?" I asked.

"I'm not even sure I know all of them. There are two guesthouses on the property, one used by Ray and the other by Perry. There's a pool house, a garden shed, and, somewhere out there, an old springhouse. And there's a garage, of course. It used to be a carriage house and has an apartment upstairs. That's where Ernesto Cruz lives. He's the groundskeeper and head gardener. He had shared it with the chauffeur before the chauffeur quit."

"Where is everybody now?" I wondered. During the whole of the tour, we hadn't run into a single resident of the manor. We hadn't even heard any creaking floorboards.

"I have no idea. I expect they're around here someplace." He peered out the window once more. "Look. There's someone now."

Following his gaze, I spotted the slight figure of a dark-haired man in work clothes. He wore a fisherman's cap.

"That's the man I saw at the window in the drawing room!"

"That's Ernesto. He was probably trimming the shrubbery when you saw him before. It looks like he's doing garden work now, too."

"Are you sure about that?" As we watched, Ernesto glanced over his shoulder in a move that could only be called furtive. Seeing no one around, he left the path and made his way to a shadowy enclave behind a pine tree. Then he just stood there. He would have been hidden, if not for Crenshaw and me spying from the third-floor storeroom. We looked at one another, then looked back down at Ernesto. He kept glancing around and checking his watch.

"Who do you suppose he's waiting for?" I asked.

"I think we're about to find out."

Crenshaw was right. Another figure emerged from the trees along the border of the English garden. It was a petite woman, dressed in a light blue maid's uniform under a long brown cardigan. Celia.

"Seems a rather unusual place to discuss household matters," said Crenshaw.

"I wish I had binoculars." I squinted at the pair, doll-like in the distance. From what I could tell, Celia seemed to be doing most of the talking—and Ernesto was not happy about what she had to say. A moment later, they parted, each leaving the way they had come.

"Interesting," I said.

"And so it begins," said Crenshaw.

For the rest of the morning, Crenshaw worked in the library going through Elaine's paperwork. While Ray made sure the monthly bills were paid, Elaine had filed her own taxes and managed her own investments. Crenshaw was still trying to sort through her various accounts. He left me in Elaine's room to catalog her personal things and search for anything resembling a handwritten will.

Armed with a clipboard and pen, I walked slowly around Elaine Turnbull's spacious bedroom. *King-size bed with ornately carved headboard. Matching mid-century bureau, dressing table, and two nightstands. Faded Persian rug. Flat-screen TV on the wall. Overflowing bookcase in the corner*—Elaine was evidently fond of historical romances. *Crushed-velvet daybed by the window. Walk-in closet filled to*

the brim with racks of dresses, skirts, blouses, and pantsuits;
shelves of shoes; boxes of scarves; and a wall-mounted jewelry
cabinet filled with necklaces, bracelets, rings, and pins.

I dutifully recorded everything I saw, knowing that an appraiser would likely have to come through and do it all over again. Still, it would be useful for Crenshaw to at least have a starting point. Throughout my inventory, I kept an eye out for any scrap of paper that could be the missing will. Though there were plenty of papers on both sides of the bed, none of them were particularly interesting. It wasn't until I had given the closet a thorough once-over that I found something of any real promise. In a far corner, beneath a stack of throw pillows, was a fireproof, steel lockbox.

It was locked, of course. After dragging the heavy box to the center of the closest, I stood up and looked around. *If I were Elaine Turnbull, where would I hide a key?*

I went first to the jewelry case, which, now that I thought about it, probably should have been locked, too. There was no sign of a key there. Next, I looked carefully in every drawer of every piece of furniture in the bedroom. There was nothing hidden among her delicates other than a couple of old lavender sachets.

With a sigh, I gazed around the room one last time. I was sure the lock could be broken if necessary, but I wasn't sure how to do that. And I was eager to open it now.

Suddenly, I had an idea. Feeling slightly self-conscious, I closed the bedroom door. Then I kicked off my shoes and climbed up onto Elaine's bed. I sat on top of the bedspread on the left side—I deduced this was the side she favored, based on the reading glasses left on the nightstand.

Taking a deep breath, I closed my eyes and thought about the woman who had lived—and died—in this room. Elaine Turnbull. Friend of Crenshaw, patron of the theater, a generous lady, who had shared her time, money, and home . . . Also, a wife without a husband, a mother without a son, and a grandmother without a grandchild. For an instant, a rush of sadness filled me like a sob. Unwittingly, I had opened myself to this woman's emotions. But it wasn't all sadness. There was a jumble of feelings—a lifetime of feelings: freedom, elation, fear, worry, joy, pain.

With a gasp, I opened my eyes. What was I doing? I was no medium. I wasn't even an empath. I wasn't prepared to handle information like this. Perhaps this wasn't the best idea.

Scarcely had these doubts crossed my mind when my eyes slid over to a framed picture on the dressing table. It was a faded photo of a little girl. I got up and went over to examine it. It was a candid, outdoor shot; the girl sat cross-legged in the grass, tilting her sun-kissed face to the sky. Her hair was in pigtails, her bangs blown back by the wind. Her gap-toothed smile was happy and carefree, that of a child who didn't yet know the meaning of anxiety or self-consciousness.

This has to be Lana, I thought. *I should look for more family photos.* But first . . . Turning over the frame, I removed the cardboard backing. There, taped to the other side, was a small silver key.

"Thank you, Elaine," I whispered.

Swiftly, with a feeling of authority, as if I'd been granted permission by the owner, I went to the closet, unlocked the steel box, and lifted the lid. Then I frowned. There was nothing inside that resembled a will. The box was filled with small notebooks. Hardbound journals. Diaries.

This could be useful.

I reached inside and pulled out the topmost journal. Gently turning the pages, I skimmed a few entries. Written with blue ink, in neat, flowing cursive handwriting, was a chronicle of Elaine's thoughts and activities.

Happy to see attendance at the theater is up this summer. I must remember to compliment the new director. Think I'll send her a gift basket . . .

Pesky "Uncle Arthur" is acting up today, making it difficult to write. Ray said I might need to go on steroids, but I think I'll try massage first . . .

The dahlias are blooming in the English garden. Ernesto has an eye for beautiful landscape design, on top of his other creative talents. I knew I was right to give him free rein in the backyard . . .

Been thinking a lot about Harry lately. Today would have been our fifty-ninth wedding anniversary . . .

I shut the book, feeling conflicted. Reading someone's personal diaries was a clear invasion of privacy. Sure, I'd found the hidden key, but that didn't really give me a right to read this woman's private thoughts.

On the other hand, there could be vital clues here. If Elaine had really written a new will, she might have mentioned it in her diary. She might even have noted where she put it. And her granddaughter . . . Surely she would have written about Lana and the efforts to find her.

My mind flashed to Dr. Lamb's suspicions about the cause of Elaine's death. It sure would be interesting to know what was on Elaine's mind in the final days of her life.

I flipped to the last entry and read it quickly. There was nothing earth-shattering. The only thing that jumped out was Suzanne's name.

Suzanne keeps pestering me for info about Harold's old friends—even that old silver fox, Winston Betz. And here I always thought Winston was too old for me! I told her she was being too obvious—she's only interested in him for his money. It's unseemly. I asked her what would happen if someone told Winston the truth—or, better yet, told his children and grandchildren. She turned so red, I thought she'd pop a gasket. I had to tell her I was only joking, but I don't think she believed me.

I found the date and saw that the last entry was written in July, just over two months ago. A cursory check of the other journals revealed that they were all older, going back for years. Elaine was a faithful writer. So, where was her most recent diary, covering the past several weeks? I felt certain she must have started a new one.

I closed and locked the box, then pushed it back into the corner of the closet. Pocketing the little silver key, I returned to Elaine's room. It had begun to rain. Pattering droplets thrummed against the window-pane in a rhythmic, soothing refrain. Standing at the foot of Elaine's bed, I looked around the room once more. She would have written in her diary in here someplace, I felt sure. Maybe she sat on the daybed beside the window or at the desklike dressing table. Or, more likely, right there in her bed. Propped on her pillows, with a glass of milk or tea on the night-stand, reading glasses on, perhaps the TV playing in the background . . .

She wouldn't have left it lying about in plain sight—

not when she wrote about the people living in her house and was so careful to lock up her journals. But would she have had it out that night after the dinner party? If she had, and it was with her when she died, that meant someone had taken it. But I didn't think that was the case. She reportedly wasn't feeling well that evening. From what Ray stated, she had come up to her room, turned on the television, and changed out of her dinner clothes. Wherever she kept her diary, I had a feeling it was still there.

The low sound of distant thunder rumbled outside the window. Briefly, I contemplated trying the same little trick I'd done to find the lockbox key. I quickly dismissed the thought. It was bad enough the first time. And the more I thought about Elaine's recent demise in this room, the more nervous I was becoming.

How 'bout good ol' common sense? I walked over to Elaine's bedside and looked once more in the drawer of the nightstand. *Hand lotion, handkerchiefs, ink pens, puzzle books . . . No diary.* Next, I knelt on the floor next to the bed and reached my hand between the mattress and box springs. Feeling nothing, I started to pull back. Then I hesitated and reached in farther. Did my fingertips just bump up against something?

A resounding chime gave me a start.

Ignoring the bell, I once again reached my hand beneath the mattress. This time, I was certain I felt something, but in trying to grasp it, I only pushed it farther away.

The doorbell rang again, three times in a row. "People really don't like to answer the door around here, do they?" I said aloud. With a sigh, I pushed myself to my feet and crossed the room to open the bedroom door. Now the ringing was joined by an urgent pounding. Hurrying down the hall, I was beginning to feel alarmed—even more so when a muffled voice hollered my name.

"Keli! Open the door!"

Chapter Eleven

Farrah stood on the doorstep, dripping water from the tips of her long blond hair to the ends of her flared plaid skirt. When I opened the door, she pounced like a cat to give me a soggy hug. Something crinkled between us. Pulling apart, she handed me a squished paper to-go sack from the Cozy Café. We both spoke at once.

"Oh, my gosh, Keli! What took you so long?"

"What in the world, Farrah! What's going on?"

"I was getting soaked out there! I saw your car out front, but you didn't pick up your phone. And when you didn't answer the door, I started to get worried. This place is kind of eerie, isn't it? And have I mentioned I'm soaking wet?" She spoke in a rush, her voice rising with every syllable.

"You were worried? I'm fine. I was just in the middle of something and didn't hear my phone. But why are you—are there sandwiches in this bag?"

"I brought you lunch! I want to hear all about your case." She looked past me, taking in the size and opulence of the great room, from the gleaming parquet floor to the heavy, crystal chandelier. Her eyes grew big. "Is this where the gala's happening on Friday?"

Just then, Crenshaw strode in from the east wing. He froze when he caught sight of Farrah. Or maybe it was the puddle she'd left on the floor.

Farrah directed her dazzled gaze to him. "The lord of the manor! Crenshaw . . . Alistair?"

"No."

"Augustine?"

"No."

"Humperdinck?"

He whipped out a handkerchief and offered it to Farrah. "No," he said.

She smiled cheekily as she patted her forehead and lips.

"Where were you a few minutes ago?" I asked Crenshaw. "Didn't you hear the doorbell?"

"I was out back talking to Ray. Then I received a call from—" His words were interrupted by the chime of the doorbell. "Ah, here he is now."

Farrah and I watched as Crenshaw opened the door to admit a stocky, middle-aged man in a wrinkled, tan trench coat. He held a leather notebook over his head, and when he ducked inside he stamped his feet on the entry rug. His eyes flicked from the foyer to the great room. "Nice place."

"Detective Rhinehardt!" I had crossed paths several times with Adrian Rhinehardt, chief homicide detective on the Edindale Police Force. Somber by nature and good at his job, he'd always proven himself to be fair-minded and reasonable. He was also both smarter and kinder than he usually let on.

He nodded at me curtly. "Hello, Keli. And Farrah, right?"

Farrah grinned and held out Crenshaw's handkerchief. Shaking his head, the detective pulled out his own hanky.

A gasp from the hall made us all turn our heads. Celia came running over, a stack of white bath towels in her arms. I wondered where she'd been when Farrah was pressing madly on the doorbell. She evidently knew she would find rain-soaked guests congregating in the foyer.

"Doesn't anyone know how to use an umbrella anymore?" She clucked disapprovingly as she handed a towel each to Farrah and Rhinehardt, then used one to wipe up the floor.

"Sorry," said Farrah. She pulled off her boots and leaned down to help dry the floor.

Crenshaw cleared his throat. "Mr. Rhinehardt, why don't you come with me to the library? We can discuss . . . *matters* there." As he ushered the detective ahead of him, Crenshaw gave me a sidelong glance and tapped the side of his nose. I rolled my eyes and grabbed Farrah by the arm.

"Let's go to the kitchen. Think those sandwiches stayed dry?"

"Probably. They were double-wrapped."

By now, I'd learned my way around the kitchen pretty well. I half expected Celia to march in and scold me for messing up her domain, but she didn't follow us. I put on a kettle of water to make hot tea, while Farrah filled me in on the latest happenings in her life.

"Any more suspicious stalkery stuff?" I asked.

"No." She looked almost disappointed. "I guess I was

wrong. After all, I wasn't the only one who had my tires cut."

"True. But your super did see a guy hanging around your car, and then you thought you were being followed not long before it happened. Maybe it wasn't so random that your car was selected."

"Wait, what are you saying? Now you think I *do* have a stalker?"

"I don't know. I just think you should stay alert, that's all."

As we ate our lunch, Farrah peppered me with questions about the Turnbull assignment. I told her everything. I knew she was eager to help, and I was grateful for her friendly, supportive energy. When I told her I thought I might have located Elaine's last diary, she hopped to her feet.

"What are we waiting for? Let's go!"

I waved her back to her seat, as I finished off my sandwich. "In a minute."

A sound at the doorway cut off her response. I brought my fingers to my lips to shush her, but she didn't see me.

"Hello!" she called out. "Is somebody there?"

Half a second ticked by before Suzanne poked her head in. "There you are, Ms. Lawyer Lady! I've been looking all over for you. And you brought a friend—perfect!"

Suzanne was all smiles again, with no hint of her earlier distress. She clacked into the room, dragging a wheeled, pink suitcase behind her. The letters *CC* were embroidered on the side. *Carrie Cosmetics.*

"Suzanne, this is my friend, Farrah Anderson. Farrah, meet Suzanne Turnbull."

"Lovely to meet you," said Farrah. "I'm so sorry for your loss."

For an instant, Suzanne wore a blank look. Then she cast her eyes downward in an expression of appropriate solemnity. "Thank you. My mother-in-law was a feisty ol' gal. It's not the same around here without her."

I stood up to throw away our lunch wrappers and wipe off the table. Farrah checked her phone. "I'm free for the next couple of hours, Kel. So, if there's anything I can do to help you out . . ." She trailed off, waiting for me to take the lead.

"Join us for a makeover!" insisted Suzanne. "You have gorgeous bone structure. I have just the thing to enhance your natural beauty."

"Um." Farrah shot me a questioning look. I gave her a slight smile and barely cocked one eyebrow. It was all I could do not to touch the side of my nose. Crenshaw might have been on to something with his corny wordless hand signals. But Farrah didn't need a sign. She was already on my wavelength.

"Sounds like fun!"

"Wonderful! Let's go to the conservatory," Suzanne suggested. "Even on a cloudy day, the natural light will be nice. And I think it's starting to clear off anyway."

She was wrong about the weather. It was still slate gray outside the wall of windows in the conservatory. But Suzanne had a lighted mirror in her pink suitcase, along with a trove of other makeup supplies. She spread them out on the table and asked us who wanted to go first. Farrah nominated me.

"It's a shame your man is out of town," Suzanne said, as she wiped makeup remover across my face. "We'll have to take your picture when we're through. You can send it to him and show him what he's missing." She giggled like a teenager at a slumber party. Farrah smirked with amusement.

"We'll have to take Farrah's picture, too," I said. "She can send it to her boyfriend, so he'll stop working so many late nights. Of course, he already wants her to move in."

"You girls and your live-in boyfriends," said Suzanne, with a shake of her head. "It must be a generational thing. I'd never move in with a man until he makes it *official.* I want the ring, the name, the works!"

Suzanne was brushing various powders across my face, which made me reluctant to open my mouth. Then she began to describe all the products: primer, foundation, concealer, bronzer, blush. I let her rattle on for a few minutes—I knew it was all part of her sales pitch. When she finally paused to rummage through her vast collection of eye shadows, I directed the conversation away from makeup.

"Suzanne, I hear there's a gala at the manor this Friday evening. Will you be attending?"

"Oh, yes. Everybody who's anybody will be there. I wouldn't miss it. The university orchestra will be performing, and Ruby Plate Catering is providing the food. They always do a fantastic job."

"I understand there was a party here the night Elaine passed away. Was that a gala, too?"

"Not quite. But Ruby Plate catered that one, too. There were four courses, all delectable, from the appetizers to the dessert. You have to try their chocolate lava cake. It's to *die* for."

Maybe it was the expression on my face, or maybe Suzanne realized for herself how insensitive she sounded. "Oh, my goodness! Bad choice of words. Don't get the wrong idea. Elaine didn't die of food poisoning! She'd been ill for a while."

I nodded. "I heard she wasn't feeling well that night and went to bed early. Did you see her at all after dinner?"

"No, I was walking out with some of the guests. When they all left, I went to my room to work on my business. Social media is *so* important for entrepreneurs, you know. I have to do promo work every day."

"Who's selling tickets for the gala?" asked Farrah. "Are there any left?"

"Perry Warren is on the Arts Council. I'm sure he'd still sell you a ticket or two. Ooh, I can do your makeup that night, too! Unfortunately, there won't be a lot of attendees your age—most are in the silver-haired set. But oh! There is one you might want to impress. I know you girls have boyfriends and all, but since you haven't tied the knot, you really should meet Xavier."

"Who's Xavier?" Farrah asked eagerly. She was definitely less committed to her relationship with Randall than I was to mine with Wes. Plus, she generally loved all men.

"Xavier Charleston. He's a young, wealthy art collector from LA. He's new to this area. I can't imagine he'll stay long, but who knows? He's trying to buy pieces from several local collections, and he's been talking shop with Perry. Wait 'til you see him. He's a real suave guy. Kind of reminds you of James Bond, if 'double-oh seven' had a beard."

"I'd love to meet him," said Farrah, her eyes shining. "Men with beards are so sexy."

I gave Farrah a sideways glance, before turning back to Suzanne. "Is he interested in the Turnbull collection?"

"Uh, no, I don't think so."

"Really? I thought it was one of the largest, most valuable, private collections around."

"Well, I wouldn't really know. I never paid much attention to what all Harold acquired. That was Jim's thing."

"Jim?" echoed Farrah.

"My late husband. He managed the collection after his father died. Elaine didn't focus on it much either. Now then, should we give Keli smoky eyes or cat eyes?"

"You decide," I said. Suzanne's evasive answer was only making me more curious. "Was Xavier at the dinner party the other night?"

"Yes, for a while. He didn't stay for dessert. Can you imagine?" She laughed boisterously, but it sounded false.

"So, if he wanted to buy something from the Turnbull collection," I pressed, "would he have spoken to Perry or Elaine?"

"Shut your lips, hon."

"Excuse me?"

She held up a lip liner pencil. "You need to be still while I outline your lips. You wouldn't want crooked lips, would you?"

Farrah snorted. "Yeah, Keli. You don't want to look like a Picasso, all disjointed and off-center."

I tried to smile without moving my lips. "Mm-hmm."

I couldn't talk now, but that didn't mean I was done asking questions. I hadn't failed to notice Suzanne's smile drop away when Farrah mentioned Picasso. Something about the Turnbull art collection was making her nervous—and I intended to find out what.

When Suzanne finally finished with my face, Farrah insisted on doing up my hair to match my new glam look. She had plenty of extra hair ties and bobby pins in her purse, along with a travel-size bottle of hairspray. As soon as she was satisfied, she pulled out her phone and snapped my picture.

"Va-va-voom!" she gushed. "Hashtag: no filter."

Suzanne was upbeat again, too, launching into her sales pitch with an enthusiasm that bordered on feverish. Everything was on sale, it seemed, but only if multiple items were purchased. "The more you buy, the more you save!"

I knew I wasn't going to get out of there without dropping a little cash. Then Farrah, the traitor, announced that she had to leave.

"I'm a saleswoman, too," she told Suzanne. "Only, I don't get to sell anything half as fun as cosmetics. I represent a legal software company, and I have a client meeting this afternoon."

"No worries," chirped Suzanne. "You'll be back. Come by early before the gala on Friday."

"Maybe I will," said Farrah. "Keli, do you need me to bring you some dinner later? Or are you allowed to leave?"

"Of course I'm allowed to leave. This isn't the Hotel California." I laughed lightly, but I heard a nervous tinge in my voice that surprised me.

"Have dinner here," said Suzanne. "Celia loves to cook. You might offend her if you don't join us."

"Oh, I don't want to put anyone out."

"Keli's a vegan," Farrah volunteered.

"That's no problem," Suzanne said, with a flick of her wrist. "Celia is used to dealing with dietary restrictions. Elaine didn't eat red meat, Ray can't stand seafood, and Perry is lactose intolerant. You'll fit right in!"

A knock on the doorframe drew our attention. It was Crenshaw.

"Sorry to interrupt, ladies. Detective Rhinehardt would like to speak with Suzanne for a moment."

"Me?" she said, looking alarmed. "What did I do?"

Rhinehardt ambled in behind Crenshaw, with his hands in his pockets and his face pleasantly neutral.

"Don't worry, ma'am. I'm talking with everyone. Just trying to confirm a few things about Mrs. Turnbull's passing."

Suzanne's alarm transitioned to confusion. I would have loved to stay and listen in on their conversation, but Farrah tossed her purse over her shoulder and linked her arm through mine. She pulled me with her to the doorway, where she linked her other arm through the crook in Crenshaw's elbow.

"What do you think of Keli's new look?" she asked him, as she led us through the dining room and toward the hallway.

Flustered, he looked at Farrah's arm on his before giving me the barest of glances. "Er, very nice."

"You flatterer, you," I said.

Farrah laughed and let go of our arms. "Of course, we all know Keli is gorgeous with or without makeup. But this is a look I can't wait to see again at Friday's gala."

"You're coming to the gala?" Crenshaw asked.

"I hope so," she said. "You'll be there, won't you?"

"Yes. As executor, I feel I ought to keep an eye on things for the estate."

"Ah. Strictly business." She gave him a wink, then squeezed my arm. "I'll call you later, girlfriend." She pulled her boots on in the foyer, then dashed outside.

I turned to Crenshaw and told him about the front door being unlocked when I arrived. "Is there a security system here?"

"There is, but I don't think it's been armed lately. The butler who handled that resigned last week with the other staff."

"Maybe you should hire a private security company," I suggested.

"Yes, I'd thought of that. At least, I planned to do so for Friday night. Perhaps it would be wise to bring on a full-time guard before then." He gazed thoughtfully at the paintings and sculptures in the great room.

"So, what's Detective Rhinehardt up to?" I asked. "Did you ask him to come?"

"No, he called me. Dr. Lamb went to the police with his concerns about Elaine's death. Rhinehardt is only asking questions at this juncture, trying to determine if there's any cause to open an official investigation. Unfortunately, it's too late for an autopsy. Cremation occurred a week ago."

A door slammed somewhere in the house, causing me to jump. Crenshaw checked his watch. "I need to be going soon," he said. "Let's touch base again in the morning."

"What? What do you mean, 'in the morning'? Where are you going?" I heard my voice take on a whiny quality.

"I need to stop by the office. Then I have a rehearsal this evening at the community theater. Our fall play opens a week from tomorrow. You should come. We're performing *Pygmalion*. I play the part of Professor Henry Higgins."

"Of course you do. But why can't you come back here after the rehearsal? I thought you were staying here. You asked *me* to stay here!"

"Yes, well, I'm afraid I'm needed at the office and can't devote all my time here. Anyway, I trust you'll make headway on this project without my presence."

He paused, apparently noticing my apprehension for the first time. "What's the matter? You're not *afraid* to be here, are you?"

"Afraid?" I scoffed. "I just thought I'd have a little help, that's all. I'm not afraid."

What could I possibly be afraid of in a potential murder house?

Chapter Twelve

When Crenshaw left, I found myself alone once again in the quiet manor. I returned to the conservatory, hoping to have a word with Detective Rhinehardt, but both he and Suzanne were gone. I thought about looking for them outside, until the echoing jangle of a telephone drew my attention. I followed the sound to the library. There, in the center of the large desk, like something out of an old movie, was a vintage-looking rotary phone. It continued to ring as if waiting for me to answer. The receiver felt heavy in my hand as I lifted it to my ear.

"Hello?"

There was a slight pause, and then a husky, gravelly voice. "Hello. Is Perry there?"

I glanced around the dark library. "Not at the moment. Would you like to leave a message?"

"How kind of you. This is Xavier Charleston."

The art collector Suzanne described as James Bond with

a beard. I couldn't say why, but there was something about this man that put me on alert.

"I'll tell Perry you called, Mr. Charleston. I'll probably see him at dinner."

"I appreciate it. He isn't answering his mobile phone, and we have some business to discuss." There was another pause before Xavier continued in an even softer voice. "I must know—who is the lovely woman I'm speaking with? Your voice is enchanting."

I almost laughed. Only politeness kept my response even. "This is Keli Milanni. I'm an attorney working with the Turnbull Estate."

"Ah, wonderful. I hope I have the pleasure of meeting you before I leave town."

"Are you leaving soon?"

"Not immediately. But my business here will be concluded in the near future."

Okay, that's vague. I wanted to question him further, but before I could say another word, he abruptly hung up.

"Good-bye to you, too," I said to the dead phone line.

For a moment, I considered searching the library while I had it to myself. Then I remembered Elaine's diary. Turning on my heels, I ran down the hall and up the back staircase to her suite in the west wing.

Outside the bedroom window, the clouds parted in time to let in a shaft of late-afternoon sunlight. I closed the door softly behind me and hurried across the shadow-dappled carpet. With my heartbeat thudding, I lifted the edge of the bedspread, shoved the mattress over, and stretched my arm beneath it.

Bingo.

I pulled out a slim, leather-bound notebook. Eagerly,

I carried it over to the daybed beside the window and settled in to read. What was going through Elaine's mind on the last days of her life?

Right away, I saw that this wasn't going to be a quick read. As I flipped through the pages, skimming the contents, I noticed Elaine's handwriting often deteriorated to a shaky scrawl. And several entries seemed to break off midthought. I thought I knew why. In one entry, she complained about her arthritis again. In a few others, she mentioned being tired and listless.

But that wasn't all she wrote about. Sometimes she reminisced about the past, and other times she dished on the people around her. I would have to start from the beginning and read every page, I decided. I didn't want to miss any references to her will or comments about Lana. First, though, I had to peruse the very last entry.

It was written the day before she died. In a return to her neat, flowing penmanship, Elaine wrote about looking forward to the dinner party the following evening. She apparently felt good about the gift she would be making to the museum. A few lines later, she mentioned being irritated with Ray and Perry for keeping some information from her. She also seemed to be upset with Celia for messing up a grocery run, and with Suzanne for generally being annoying. I smiled as I pictured Elaine as a stereotypical grumpy old woman, shaking her cane and grousing about every little thing. Then I turned the page and my amusement evaporated. Elaine's words rang with foreboding.

Am I being paranoid? Maybe it's the new medication. It makes me drowsy and uneasy. But I swear . . . it seems like everyone around me is hiding something. I don't know who I can trust anymore. I don't feel safe in my own house.

Dinner was served in the formal dining room. Since there were only four of us, we sat in the center chairs at the long table, with Suzanne and me on one side and Ray and Perry on the other. Celia bustled about pouring drinks and bringing dishes to the table: vegetable soup and crusty French bread to start, followed by mushroom rice pilaf with a side of sautéed broccoli and cauliflower. There was roasted chicken for the meat eaters. I was glad to have the food to focus on, because conversation quickly turned awkward. It started when I walked in and Ray, after one look at me, barked out a laugh. It was the first time I'd heard any hint of humor from him—though it wasn't exactly merry.

"I see Suzanne got ahold of your face," he said.

"Don't be rude," Suzanne snapped.

I touched my cheek self-consciously. Perhaps I should have wiped off a layer or two of the heavy makeup.

Perry was the only one with the grace to look embarrassed. "You look very nice," he said to me. "Suzanne's a pro, you know. She went to beauty school and everything."

I nodded. "She definitely knows a lot more about cosmetics than I do."

"Don't pay any attention to Ray," Suzanne said. "He's only jealous I'm able to make a career out of my art. He sits in his little studio making his little paintings, and then he's too timid to let them see the light of day."

"Did you say art?" Ray asked. "Is that what you think you're doing with lipstick and rouge?"

Suzanne gave him a dirty look, and Perry shook his head like the long-suffering parent of squabbling siblings. He shot me a rueful smile and changed the subject. "So, Keli, Crenshaw tells me you're a fine lawyer—specializing in family matters, I believe?"

"Yes. I handle a variety of issues, from marital conflicts to trusts and estates. And Crenshaw is a fine lawyer, too. We've been colleagues for years."

"Well, I don't blame him for bringing on reinforcements in this case. The Turnbull Estate is . . . not small. And Elaine wasn't especially organized with her finances."

"How would you know?" Ray interjected. "Elaine was very organized, in her own way."

Before Perry could respond, Celia scuttled into the room with a plate and glass. She sat down next to Perry and helped herself to a serving of rice and vegetables. For a moment, I was surprised, and then felt chagrined at myself. Why shouldn't she have dinner with the rest of us? She had probably worked for the Turnbulls for so long that she'd become like part of the family. Now I felt bad for not offering to help her with dinner. Even though she earned a salary, it still seemed wrong, somehow, to be served by this tiny woman who must have been pushing eighty.

I leaned toward her. "Celia, everything is absolutely delicious. I'd love to get your recipe for the pilaf, if you don't mind sharing it."

"I've had a lot of practice," she said briskly. In spite of the brush-off, I thought she seemed pleased.

"Where's Ernesto?" asked Suzanne.

"Outside," replied Celia. "He wanted to finish up

some yardwork, now that it's stopped raining. He said he would eat later."

Ray's eyes took on a devious glint. "Guess you'll have to manage without your little pet for one evening."

"He's not my pet!" Suzanne protested. "He's just very handy."

"He's also a nice young man," Perry offered diplomatically.

At that, Suzanne pulled out her cell phone, and Ray stared morosely at his plate. Casting about for a new topic, I turned to Perry.

"Oh, I almost forgot! Someone called for you earlier. Xavier Charleston. He was trying to reach you on your cell to discuss business. I told him I'd let you know."

"Ooh la la!" interjected Suzanne. "You spoke with Xavier? Lucky girl!"

"Thank you," said Perry. "I'll call him back later."

"That reminds me, do you still have tickets for the gala?"

"I do, yes. Just let me know how many you'd like, and they're yours."

"Great, thanks." I took a sip of water and tried to think what else I should ask Perry. "I take it there's a lot of significant artwork here in the house? I wish I knew more about art history. I enjoy art, but I know so little about the famous artists."

"Have you ever been to the Edindale Art Museum?"

"Yes, but it's been a while."

"I'd be happy to give you a tour sometime. I used to work there, you know."

"That would be nice. Thank you."

The rest of dinner passed in a somewhat strained silence, broken only by the clink of silverware on porcelain and the occasional exchange of words between Perry and me. When Celia stood up and began to clear the table, I made a move to help her. She slapped my hand away with startling strength. "Sit down! I'll bring coffee and dessert."

Perry chuckled, and Suzanne rolled her eyes. As soon as the older lady had left the room, Suzanne patted my hand. "You'll get used to her. She thinks she runs this place." Then she lowered her voice and leaned forward in the posture of a gossipmonger. "I used to wonder why Elaine kept her on. Celia is kind of disrespectful for a maid, and not very friendly. She was Harold's housekeeper before he married Elaine, and I don't think the two women ever did see eye to eye. But she's efficient enough and an excellent cook. Good help can be so hard to find."

I didn't know what to say, so I said nothing. Celia brought in dessert, warm apple cobbler with dairy-free coconut ice cream, and we all tucked in without a word. As soon as I finished, I thanked Celia again, said good-night to everyone else, and left the dining room. Ray followed me out and called for me to wait.

"How's the search for the will going?" he asked gruffly.

"Well, I don't think it's in Elaine's bedroom. I've looked in there pretty thoroughly."

"I don't think you're going to find it in anyplace Elaine put it. I think someone else took it."

"In that case, the search may be pointless," I said matter-of-factly. "If someone took it, don't you think they would have destroyed it by now?"

"Nah, that doesn't make sense. Think about it! The only reason to take the will would be to change it. The Turnbull Estate is worth millions. Nobody wants to see Elaine's wayward granddaughter get it all. Whoever took it probably wants to make sure they'll benefit from it."

It was on the tip of my tongue to point out the obvious: that the same could be said for Ray. But I had no interest in arguing with him. Instead, I promised I would keep looking and excused myself to go upstairs.

I opened my door to find Josie curled up on a cushioned bench beneath the window. It was immensely comforting to see her. She lent a warm, homey air to the otherwise plain, sparsely-furnished room. I picked up my clipboard and walked around, listing the room's contents—and searching them—as I went. It didn't take long. There was a large bed, draped with a simple, white duvet; two bedside tables holding brass, spindle lamps; and a six-drawer oak dresser with empty drawers. The chest at the foot of the bed contained extra blankets, and the bench by the window had no storage. I was hopeful the closet might yield something, but it stored only a few winter coats and extra toilet paper. In fact, the only items of interest in the room were an antique-looking oval mirror standing in a corner, a pair of pastoral paintings on the wall, and a small collection of glass perfume bottles on the bureau. These all looked like they could be valuable, but they hid no secrets that I could see.

"I hope you weren't too bored in here," I said to Josie. She flicked her tail in response and turned her head toward the window. "Right. At least you could watch the world outside." I took a look through the window but couldn't see much in the darkness. Discreet ground-level lights lined a curving pathway and cast a narrow glow through the trees. Glancing to the grove at the bottom of the hill, I thought I saw something—a pinprick of light wavering among the shadows, like a lost fairy. Then it disappeared.

I found the lighted path again and noticed that it led to one of the guesthouses. The small cottage was visible only because of a winking yellow light in one of its windows. I wondered if the house was occupied by Ray or Perry and resolved to find out the next day.

As I gazed at the partially-obscured cottage, I thought about Elaine's belief that everyone around her was hiding something. Perhaps it was something about the manor that encouraged secrets, because I was hiding a few things, too. I'd hidden Elaine's diary in the chest at the foot of the bed, along with the key to her lockbox. I was also hiding a protection amulet, next to my new Eye of Horus necklace, on a slender chain inside my sweater. I pulled out the amulet—a cloth medicine bag filled with dried sage leaves, red brick dust, and assorted, tiny crystals—and cupped it over my heart. Closing my eyes, I whispered my oft-repeated mantra: "I am safe, guarded in this hour, sheltered by divine power."

My cell phone rang. Before reaching for it, I already knew who it was. I would have called him soon, if he hadn't called me first.

"Hey, good-looking," I said, keeping my tone light and flirty. No need for Wes to know about my frayed nerves.

"Hiya, doll," he said, sounding like a character in a 1930s talkie. "Is this Miss Keli Milanni, aka Boopsie, the dame in the pinup portrait? I got a picture here that's making all the newsmen drool. You ever think of making a calendar?"

"Maybe I have, and maybe I haven't," I said, doing

my best impression of Mae West. "Know any good photographers?"

"You're talkin' to one, cupcake. Though, I tell ya what, after this trip I might have myself a new career as an investigative journalist. O' course, I'd still take your picture any ol' day."

"What do you mean, you 'might have a new career'?" I asked, dropping the goofy chitchat. "Did you find something?"

"I did. Surprised?"

"Not a bit." He'd been in Chicago barely more than twenty-four hours. Why should I be surprised?

"I found Penny Delacroix," he said, with an obvious note of pride. "You know, the blogger who eluded Crenshaw's P.I. firm? I noticed she reviews a lot of art shows at this studio space in the West Loop. I took a little field trip this afternoon and spoke with the manager. He gave me Penny's number."

"You've spoken with her already?"

"Yes, ma'am. She admitted that her Lana is our Lana. But she refused to give me contact info for our mutual friend."

"I suppose we can't fault her for being a good friend. Did she tell you anything about Lana?"

"Not really. However, she did agree to give her a message."

"That's great! I'll write up a message and email it to you."

"No need. I've already given her the message."

"Oh."

"Yeah, you might want to go ahead and pencil in your kitchen-cleaning duties. You know, to plan ahead and all."

"Ha! You haven't won yet. You have to physically locate the woman. You have to produce a mailing address."

"I'll get it. Don't you worry. So, how's it going there? Find any 'clues in the old mansion'?"

"As a matter of fact, I have. I found Elaine's diaries."

I filled him in on all I'd learned so far. It helped to vocalize my thoughts and observations. Wes agreed Suzanne's behavior was odd—as was everyone else's at Turnbull Manor.

The moment I hung up the phone, I pulled Elaine's diary from the chest and flopped on the bed. If Elaine wrote a single word about her last wishes or the existence of a new will, I was determined to find it.

Ten minutes and several pages later, my optimism waned. Elaine wrote about a lot of mundane things, from the current weather to her favorite television shows. So far, there was nothing about a will.

Yawning, I stretched my arms and decided to take a break. But as I moved to close the diary, a few words jumped out at me. Something about a "valuable painting." Quickly, I read on.

I asked Perry about the Edward Hopper. At first he acted like he didn't know what I was talking about. I had to jog his memory. 'Remember—the one I always told Jim we shouldn't keep?'

It's not that I was nervous to keep such a rare and valuable painting in the house. We've always had a lot of those. Rather, it was the cultural value. When Harold was alive, I left him alone about his collections. But when Jim took over I told him some of our pieces really belonged in a museum, for everyone to admire and learn from. He finally agreed to lend the Hopper to the Edindale Art Museum.

*But then it was never displayed! Jim said it was
being cleaned or restored or reframed. It was always
something.*

*Anyway, I forgot all about it until the other day
when I was talking to Perry about the collection. He
said he'd check with the museum director. But I got
the feeling he didn't like me asking. I wonder if he
knows something he doesn't want to tell me.*

I stared out the window, mulling over this latest information. Josie snapped me out of my reverie by batting at my feet.

"What's up, Miss Kitty? Is it time to wind down?"

I unpacked my toiletries, brushed my teeth, and took a shower. After getting myself ready for bed, it was time to get the room ready. I took another small travel case out of my suitcase and removed the contents—not soap, lotion, and makeup, but consecrated salt water, loose chamomile petals, and sage spray mist. I walked the perimeter of the room, sprinkling and spritzing, as I murmured my protection spell.

> *Defend, protect, repel*
> *Defend, protect, repel*
> *Evil halt and danger quell*
> *By my power, all is well.*

By the time I'd made a complete circuit, I felt a noticeable change in the room's energy. Everything now had a familiar cast—the bed, the mirror, the glass bottles on the bureau. It felt safer. I was no longer a stranger in a strange land. I'd made my psychic impression here and invited in my guardian angels. I could have closed my eyes and imagined I was at home.

Then someone screamed.

Chapter Thirteen

Josie yowled and darted under the bed. After a frozen second of disbelief, I threw open the bedroom door and stepped into the hallway, listening. The scream hadn't come from an adjacent room, but it wasn't far. I headed to the back staircase and started down, trying not to make a sound. A few steps from the bottom, I heard another high-pitched yelp, followed by a string of angry words. And then a man's voice, equally agitated. I followed the voices to the kitchen, where I stopped short in the doorway. By the glow of an outdoor security light shining through the window, I recognized Celia, in a long flannel nightgown. She gripped a cast-iron skillet like a billy club. Her ire was directed at a man who cowered in the corner, one arm shielding his face.

"Put that thing down!" he roared. "You know who I am!"

"Intruder! Sneaking in the house in the middle of the night!"

"I wasn't sneaking! I was trying not to awaken anyone."

I decided I'd better intervene. Holding my robe closed with one hand, I stepped into the kitchen and flipped on the light. "What's going on here?"

The man lowered his arm and straightened to his full height. I'd thought his voice sounded familiar. It was Crenshaw, looking highly affronted.

"That's what I would like to know," he said, as he smoothed the front of his jacket.

Celia lowered her arm and set the pan on the counter. "I heard someone breaking in," she said defensively.

"I wasn't breaking in," he countered, addressing me. "I have a full set of keys for the manor. It may have taken me a moment to locate the correct one for the side door, but I wasn't making a lot of noise. When I let myself in, Celia was lying in wait. In the darkness."

I turned to Celia. "You heard him from your bedroom?"

"I was in here getting a glass of water, when all of a sudden a strange man comes in. What was I supposed to think?"

I didn't know what Celia was supposed to think. I didn't even know what I should think. According to the digital clock above the microwave, it was after midnight. It seemed unlikely to me that Celia would come down three flights of stairs for water, when she could have kept a pitcher in her room or used a sink in one of the upstairs bathrooms. It also seemed strange that she wouldn't have turned on a light.

Instead of answering Celia, I directed my next question to Crenshaw. "What are you doing here, anyway?"

"That's your fault, actually. You made such a fuss

about my not staying here, I decided perhaps I should spend the night after all."

I opened my mouth to protest, but he cut me off with his raised palm. "And," he continued, "I realized it's only fair. I wouldn't want you to think I'd hired you under false pretenses." He picked up the brown leather overnight bag sitting at his feet and gestured toward the back staircase. "Now then, I believe there's a guest room already made up in the east wing. Shall we retire?"

Celia looked from Crenshaw to me as if we were both crazy. At that point, I might have agreed with her.

Back in my room, I found I was too wired to sleep. Crawling into bed, I grabbed Elaine's diary and picked up where I'd left off. It was worth paying attention. Interspersed with day-to-day trivialities were juicy tidbits that wouldn't have been out of place in a tell-all memoir:

*I caught Celia rummaging through my jewelry
again. I think she was looking for items Harold gave
me. I know she was in love with him, even though he
never could see it. From the very beginning, she was
always so cold to me. She thinks I have the life she
was meant to have. I just feel sorry for her. To let
her go now would be cruel.*

I looked up from the diary. Was reliable Celia a spurned lover? Still bitter after all these years? I supposed that would explain why she wasn't on the best of terms with Elaine.

As I read on, I kept an eye out for other familiar

names. When Elaine mentioned her gardener, I took notice. Most interestingly, she wrote:

Ernesto is a sweet, talented boy, but so impulsive and hotheaded—not a good combination! We had a little misunderstanding over his use of my car. He thought I was accusing him of taking advantage of me, but I wasn't. Before we cleared things up, he'd punched a hole in the garage door and tried to turn in his resignation! Some men . . .

Yikes. I had yet to meet Ernesto, but Perry and Suzanne seemed to like him. From what I'd seen, his behavior seemed a little shady—he always seemed to be lurking or disappearing. I wondered if he was avoiding me for some reason.

The room was growing chilly, so I pulled my covers up higher. My eyelids were growing heavy, too, but I didn't want to stop reading. I perked up again when I read what Elaine had to say about her live-in nurse:

Ray asked to borrow money again. His painting hobby sure is expensive! All the paints and canvases and doodads and whatnots. I've been telling him for years that I don't really need a full-time nurse—he's welcome to go back to the agency for more patients. I know he doesn't want to do that. I also told him he's lucky I don't charge him rent. I was only teasing, but he got a worried look, like he never even gave it a thought.

Had Ray overstated the nature of his relationship with Elaine? It was hard to tell, but Elaine didn't sound quite as fond of him as he seemed to be of her.

I was so engrossed, I lost track of the time. When I

finally glanced at the alarm clock, I was surprised to see it was after 2:00 A.M. I set the diary on the nightstand and switched off the light.

The first night in a strange bed is always hardest, and this was no exception. I tossed and turned, drifting in and out of cloudy, muddled dreams. Josie was restless, too. I could feel her walking around on the foot of the bed, hopping off and back on. Once she knocked something off the bureau, and another time she scratched lightly on the door. I grumbled at her to go to sleep and pulled the covers over my head.

I awoke to bright sunlight and a persistent buzzing noise. For a moment, I forgot where I was. Sitting up, I rubbed my eyes and looked for Wes in the bed beside me. Then Josie meowed from the bathroom doorway, and everything came back to me.

"Why did you keep me up?" I asked her. "That wasn't very nice."

I refreshed her food and water, then checked my phone, which was the source of all the buzzing. I had seven voice mail messages, all from different, unfamiliar numbers. Perplexed, I listened to the first one. It was from a woman who had seen my ad for a legal assistant.

"Ah. Of course." I set my phone down, resolving to listen to the rest of the messages later. I was glad there was a lot of interest in the ad, but at the moment it wasn't my highest priority. Recalling everything I'd read in Elaine's diary the night before, I felt an increasing sense of urgency to read the rest. I also wanted to hurry up and get dressed, so I could find Crenshaw and bring him up to speed.

I reached for the diary where I'd left it on the nightstand. It wasn't there. Frowning, I looked on the floor. It wasn't there either. I dropped to my hands and knees, looked under the bed, and then beneath and behind the nightstand. The diary seemed to have vanished.

What in the world?

I stood and looked around the room. Josie watched me curiously from her perch atop the bureau. "Do you know something about this?" I demanded. My cat had been known to hide small objects in the past, although never anything as large or heavy as a diary.

Suddenly, I recalled the strange sounds I'd heard in the night, and my heart jumped to my throat. My eyes slid to the bedroom door. It was unlocked. Had I locked it the night before? I couldn't remember. But even if I had, it would be easy to pick. It was a simple doorknob lock, with a keyhole on the outside.

Instinctively, I reached for the amulet around my neck. Surely someone hadn't come into my room . . . had they? Nothing appeared to be disturbed. And, of course, there was nothing as obvious as a footprint.

I made one more search of the room to no avail. *This is ridiculous.* Who even knew I had the diary with me? I'd told only Farrah and Wes. I supposed someone could have overheard me. Any eavesdropper might know about the diary I found under Elaine's mattress—and the lockbox in her closet.

With a mounting sense of worry, I slipped out of my room and dashed over to Elaine's. I went immediately to her closet, flipped on the light, and pushed aside the pillows in the corner.

The lockbox was gone, too.

Chapter Fourteen

Crenshaw didn't answer my repeated bangs on his bedroom door. With an exasperated sigh, I returned to my room and called his cell phone.

"Finally awake?" he said, by way of hello.

"Where are you? You didn't leave again, did you?"

"I'm in the dining room." He paused, listening to someone else. "Celia wants to know if you'll be joining us for breakfast. She says the grapefruit is drying out and the coffee is getting cold."

"I'll be right down."

I threw on a pair of corduroys and a cotton blouse and ran a brush through my hair. Before heading out the door, I took a last look around the room. With a thief in the house, I'd better not leave any valuables lying around. I snatched up my purse and hurried downstairs.

When I entered the dining room, Crenshaw was the only one at the table. He set aside the newspaper he'd been reading and looked up at me. One eyebrow popped up in surprise.

"I have the hardest time keeping up with modern fashions," he said. "Is the witch-doctor look in vogue now?"

"What?" I looked down at my chest and saw I'd forgotten to tuck in my amulet and necklace. Rolling my eyes, I pushed the medicine pouch under my shirt but left out the Eye of Horus necklace. It was too pretty to hide anyway.

Crenshaw passed me a carafe of coffee and a basket of poppy seed muffins. "Celia advised me that Tuesday is laundry day. She's off gathering towels and such. Perry left for the museum, and Suzanne went shopping."

"What about Ray and Ernesto?"

"They both headed outside. Do you have something to report?"

I nodded and took a bite of sliced grapefruit. It was slightly tart, but still juicy. I chewed slowly as I collected my thoughts. Here it was, day two of my stay at Turnbull Manor, and I seemed to be losing things as fast as I found them. When I finished the grapefruit, I stood up and peered around the corners of both doorways. Satisfied no one was eavesdropping, I returned to my seat and leaned forward.

"Someone was in my room last night."

Now both eyebrows darted up. "You saw someone?"

"No, but it's the only explanation." I told him about finding Elaine's diaries—the most recent one I'd had in my bedroom, as well as the collection of old diaries. "On the plus side, the lockbox seemed to be heavy-duty, and whoever took it doesn't have the key. I made sure it's still where I put it, under the blankets in the cedar chest."

Crenshaw stroked his beard thoughtfully. "Why do you suppose someone would take the diaries?"

"Why?" I echoed. "Because they don't want me to read them, that's why. The thief must know, or suspect, there's something incriminating in them."

"Regarding Elaine's last will and testament?"

"Maybe. Or about her death."

"About that," said Crenshaw, reaching for the coffee-pot. "Detective Rhinehardt doesn't think there's enough evidence to open an investigation."

"Really? He told you that?"

"Yes. I spoke with him this morning. He acknowledged it's entirely possible Elaine overdosed on opioids, as Dr. Lamb suspects. However, there's no proof they weren't self-administered. Although . . ." Crenshaw trailed off, tapping his finger on his lips.

"Although what?" He could be maddeningly slow to get to the point.

"Yesterday the detective showed me the coroner's report. It included an interesting detail the doctor neglected to mention in our phone call."

"What detail?"

"The coroner noted that there was a substance resembling dried milk on the front of Elaine's night-gown. It smelled of cinnamon."

I set down the muffin I'd been about to bite into. For some reason, the mental image of a coroner sniffing a dead body had killed my appetite.

"As you'll recall, Ray told us Elaine used to drink warm milk with cinnamon," Crenshaw said.

"I remember. He said he was bringing her a cup when he found her. Could he have spilled it on her?"

"I don't think so. At least, he told Rhinehardt he didn't. The coroner opined that she had spilled it on

herself when she passed out—meaning she'd already
had her milk by the time Ray came to her room."

"Was there a cup on the floor or bed?"

Crenshaw shrugged. "No one mentioned seeing one
that I know of. In any event, returning to my original
point, if Elaine overdosed on her opioid pills, she
might have taken them herself—either accidentally or
on purpose."

I considered the possibility. Had Elaine been so depressed at the return of her illness that she no longer
wanted to live? Or was she so tired, and in so much
pain, that she didn't realize she'd taken too many
pills? Neither of these scenarios rang true to me. I
shook my head. "If she took the pills, then where's the
pill bottle?"

"It could have rolled under some furniture. It could
have been tossed in a wastebasket and discarded without anyone being the wiser. Its absence doesn't prove
it was used by a murderer."

I knew he was right. Logically, there were any
number of possibilities. The idea that there might be
an innocent explanation should have given me comfort. The problem was, I didn't believe it.

"We've got no murder weapon," Crenshaw continued. "No apparent motive."

"That's where you're wrong," I said. "Elaine made
some very suggestive comments in her diary. From
what she wrote, it sounded like everyone around her
had a possible motive."

"All right. Let's turn, then, to hypothetical number
two. If the pills were not self-administered, someone
must have given them to Elaine, presumably without
her knowledge. Given her habit of drinking warm milk,

and the stain on her dress, let's suppose that someone spiked her milk."

"I was already supposing that."

"Let us further suppose," Crenshaw went on, ignoring my comment, "that she drank the milk in her room. Rhinehardt told me that everyone he questioned agreed that Elaine was empty-handed when she went upstairs after the party. Moreover, Celia and the last of the catering staff confirmed that Elaine passed through the kitchen without stopping. Therefore, someone must have brought the milk to her room."

Nodding, I picked up the thread. "After she drank the milk and passed out, that same person left with both the mug and the pill bottle. Or maybe just the mug. They must have already had the pills, right? They probably mixed the pills into the milk in the kitchen— or someplace else—before bringing the poisoned cup to Elaine."

"Yes, well, there's one problem with this whole scenario."

"What's that?"

"Based on everything we know—the estimated time of death, the dosage of the missing pills, the spilled milk on her nightgown, et cetera—Elaine would likely have ingested the tainted milk between nine o'clock and nine-twenty."

"So?"

"So, everyone living in this house has a solid alibi for that period."

I frowned at this piece of news. "They do?"

"They do. This is what Rhinehardt explained to me a little while ago."

"Well, what about the dinner guests? Or the staff who quit?"

"It was a rather intimate gathering, and all the guests had already left by that time—"

"Even Xavier?" I cut in. "Suzanne mentioned he arrived late to the party that night."

A flicker of doubt crossed Crenshaw's face, but he seemed to brush it off. "I assume so. In any event, as for the staff, all but Celia and Ernesto had left as well. Most had clocked out, figuratively speaking, and gone home when the caterer left—around eight-thirty. The three former staff who still lived at the manor, the butler, a kitchen maid, and chauffeur, had also left. The former two spent the evening at the hospital with a friend, while the chauffeur drove to his brother's house out of town. Rhinehardt assured me their stories checked out."

"Could someone have sneaked back in?"

"Evidently the butler armed the security system before he left. Only the residents of the manor have the code to come in and out of the house. And, as I said, the residents all have verifiable alibis." He used his fingers to tick off each alibi. "Ray was walking his dog in the neighborhood. Perry was on the telephone with someone. Suzanne was online. Celia was with the caterer. Ernesto had gone out with friends."

I scowled into my coffee. Rhinehardt was a good detective, but I wasn't satisfied with his conclusion. I wondered how closely he'd probed everyone's statements.

"I wish I would have taken notes when I was reading Elaine's diary," I said, half to myself. "Or, better yet, photos of certain pages. Then Rhinehardt could see there's a reason to investigate further."

Small creases of worry appeared between Crenshaw's eyebrows. "I agree it is troubling that someone took the diaries. All the more so given that they entered your room while you were sleeping. That was extremely risky."

"It's troubling and it's telling. We should tell Detective Rhinehardt."

"Yes. I do believe it's worth mentioning—do you need to get that?"

"Get what?"

"Isn't that your phone buzzing?"

I looked at my purse in surprise. I'd been so focused on hypotheses of murder, I'd tuned out the ceaseless drone of my cell phone. I took it out now and saw that the incoming call was from yet another unfamiliar number. I decided to answer it.

"Keli Milanni here."

"Hi," said a woman's voice on the other end of the line. "I'm calling about your ad for a legal assistant. I have four years of office experience, and I think I would be a great fit for the job."

"Oh! That's great. Um, let's see. I'll be scheduling interviews in the near future. In the meantime, would you mind calling back and leaving your name and number in a voice mail?"

"I can't do that. Your voice mailbox is full."

"It is? Of course. Sorry. Um, just a sec." I rummaged through my purse for a scrap of paper and a pen and took down the caller's contact information. The moment I hung up, my phone buzzed again. I sighed and tossed it back into my purse.

Crenshaw gave me an amused look and shook his head. "So, what can you tell me about the search for Lana?" he questioned. "Any progress on that front?"

"What? Oh, yes. Wes found a promising lead in Chicago." I took a sip of cold coffee and made a face.

"Knock-knock!" said a friendly voice from the doorway.

I looked up to see Farrah, radiant in a wrap dress and loose chignon.

"Farrah! Come in. Want some cold coffee and a muffin?"

She sat down and grabbed a muffin. "I can't stay. Just thought I'd stop by on my way to the university. I'm giving a guest lecture on legal research. I tried your phone, but your voice mail is full and you don't answer texts anymore."

"How did you get in?" demanded Crenshaw. "I expressly requested everyone to keep the doors locked at all times."

Farrah flashed him a wry grin. "Well, I didn't break in. The maid was shaking out a rug when I walked up. She told me where to find you."

"Ah, I see. Er, I apologize for being so abrupt. It's just that security in this place is woefully lacking."

"I can vouch for that," I added. "I'm thinking about booby-trapping my bedroom door tonight."

Farrah's eyes grew wide. "Why? Did something happen?"

"I'll fill you in outside. Come on. I'm following you downtown." I pushed back from the table.

"You're leaving?" said Crenshaw, sounding like me the day before. "There's still quite a lot of work to do here."

"I want to see Detective Rhinehardt. I also need to stop by my office, clear all my voice mail messages, and schedule some interviews."

My expression must have betrayed how little I was looking forward to the latter tasks. Farrah gave me a sympathetic look. "Do you need help, sweetie? I have time after my class. I can schedule those interviews for you. All I need is your voice mail password."

"I couldn't ask you to do that."

"You don't have to. I just offered."

Crenshaw cleared his throat loudly. "How long will you be gone?"

"Don't worry," I said, as I shouldered my purse and headed for the door. "I'll be back."

Chapter Fifteen

Unfortunately, I was back a lot sooner than I wanted to be. Detective Rhinehardt wasn't in his office, and the desk sergeant didn't know when to expect him. I left a message asking the detective to call me as soon as possible. Next, I swung by Moonstone Treasures to talk to Mila. Much to my disappointment, she wasn't available either. Catrina informed me her boss would be in the divination parlor all morning giving back-to-back tarot readings. While Catrina was always up for a chat, especially about witchy matters, what I really craved was Mila's calm guidance and experienced advice. I wanted to know why my protection charms hadn't worked last night.

I picked up a few items in the shop, including a new bundle of dried sage and a black tourmaline stone. If I was going to stay in that room again another night, I was going to have to double down on my energetic defenses.

When I'd told Farrah someone came into my bedroom while I was sleeping, she'd nearly flipped out.

"Are you kidding me? This is insane! That does it. I'm going to stay there with you tonight—and every night until you're done with this crazy job."

"Wait, what? You want to stay at the manor?" I'd been sure she was going to urge me to leave the place.

"Obviously Crenshaw isn't watching your back like he should be. Wouldn't you feel better having a real friend nearby?"

"Well, yeah, but—"

"But nothing. It's settled. I'll meet you there this evening. What time is dinner?"

I laughed and gave her a hug. It was a relief to know I wouldn't be alone in the guest room. Plus, Farrah could help me search the mansion. In my head, I ticked off the ever-growing list of things I was looking for: a missing will, clues to Lana's whereabouts, the missing pill bottle, the filched diary, and the stolen lockbox. There was probably more. It was hard to keep track.

With Crenshaw's sense of urgency and Wes on pace to win our bet, I decided to return to the manor. I headed back to Edindale's historic district and drove up the broad, tree-lined boulevard leading to the Turnbull property. After parking in front of the mansion, in the same spot as before, I slowly stepped onto the grass and lingered by the car door. I kind of dreaded going back inside.

Tilting my face toward the sky, I breathed in the fresh, rain-washed air. A strong breeze blew in from the east, lifting my hair and ruffling the feathery branches of a mature honey locust tree near the boulevard. It lifted my spirits as well. I marveled at the swirl of tiny yellow leaves fluttering to the ground like gold coins from heaven. Reaching down, I scooped up a small handful, letting the cool, slippery leaves slide through my fingers.

All around me, Mother Earth whispered her irresistible invitation: *Stay outside.*

"All right then," I responded. "Why not?"

I gazed across the sloping front lawn and took another look at the stately Georgian mansion. I guessed the home was probably built in the early 1900s. Although the interior had been modernized to some extent, the grounds appeared to be timeless. There were no visible satellite dishes or telephone wires, no tacky lawn ornaments, children's toys, or Adirondack chairs. Nor were there any high gates, intercom systems, or security cameras. Anyone could walk right up to the house, from any of its sides.

I took a quick scan of the neighborhood. The Turnbull home occupied a corner lot, with a row of mature pine trees blocking the adjacent street to the west. To the east, a short stone wall separated the Turnbull land from its nearest neighbor, another elegant, old mansion. Across the street, expansive, well-tended lawns provided a natural buffer for the nearly-hidden homes set at a distance from the boulevard and from one another.

Between the mansion and the old stone wall a blacktop driveway wound to the rear of the house. I followed it now, all the way to a three-car carriage house garage. At least, I figured it was a garage because of the wide doors. Emerald green ivy climbed the whitewashed walls, while delicate flowers spilled charmingly from two upper-story window boxes. More than anything, it resembled an English country cottage.

This must be where Ernesto lives.

As I admired the carriage house, I thought I de-

tected movement in one of the curtained windows. Or
maybe it was just the flowers dancing in the wind. An
exterior staircase on the side of the building led to a
second-story portico-covered entrance. *I should introduce myself to Ernesto,* I decided. *Then maybe he won't be
so bashful.*

I had just started for the stairs when I heard someone whistling on the other side of the house. It was
such a jaunty, unexpected sound. Walking around the
house, I soon spotted Ernesto in his ever-present fishing cap. Only, this time he carried a fishing pole over
his shoulder and a tackle box in his hand. He was heading down the hill toward the grove of trees.

My first impulse was to follow him. He was hiding
something, I felt sure. But what was I going to do, lurk
in the trees and watch him fish? *Now who's the weirdo?* I
laughed at myself and realized I should just go introduce myself to the fellow as I had originally intended.
However, by this time he was already out of sight, and
I didn't feel like running after him. Better to meet him
at dinner—or any other situation with other people
around.

I proceeded to the gardens instead. The moment I
stepped through the wrought-iron arched rose trellis,
I felt I'd been transported to a fairy land. While the
plantings were tidy and organized, as English gardens
usually are, there were personal touches throughout.
Spouting fish bubbled over a basin fountain. A chubby
Buddha smiled mischievously among decorative
grasses. A glass, mosaic butterfly glittered in the sunlight. As I strolled along the crushed oyster-shell pathway, past sculpted boxwoods and clusters of white,
orange, and pink flowers, I smiled at the whimsical
statues and fountains.

When I emerged, I found myself near the kitchen garden at the back of the house. Now that I had my bearings, I made my way to the guesthouse I'd seen from my bedroom window. As I approached, I noticed a side door was ajar. A golden retriever bounded over to me, tail wagging. After sniffing my hand, the dog turned in a circle and went back inside. Naturally, I followed.

The door led to an enclosed porch that seemed to have been converted to an artist's workshop. Paint-splattered cabinets lined one wall, beneath which were cluttered tables stacked with pictures, props, and paints. In the corner beside a window was Ray, sitting at an easel and squinting in concentration. He gave a start when he caught sight of me.

"The dog let me in," I said, with what I hoped was an engaging smile.

His stony countenance cracked, revealing the first hint of his own smile. "I lose track of time when I'm in here. Sometimes Barney has to run off with my brushes before I remember to feed him."

Barney trotted over to Ray and placed a paw on his knee. "He looks well-cared for to me," I said, noting the dog's shiny coat, bright eyes, and lolling tongue.

Ray scratched Barney behind the ears. "He's spoiled is what he is."

I took another step toward Ray, but not too close. I'd clearly entered his private domain, and I was afraid he'd kick me out at any minute. "So, you're a painter," I said casually. "You must have fit right in with the Turnbull family."

He gave me an odd look. "I never knew Harold Turnbull. He'd passed away years before I met Elaine."

"You knew their son, Jim, though, didn't you?"

"Not well. I met him a few times, if he happened to be around when I stopped in to see Elaine. It was only after he died that she asked me to move in."

"Did you meet Lana, too?"

He nodded. "Yeah. She was a teenager, but she'd still come to see her grandma almost every day after school. They'd talk and work on puzzles together. It was Elaine's favorite part of the day."

"It sounds like they were close."

"You could say that. Had a lot in common, too. Independent, creative, stubborn." A sad smile flickered across his face. "Lana's named after her grandmother, you know. *Lana* is a nickname for Elaine." He looked out the window, almost as if he were peering into the past. "Elaine was called 'Laney' when she was younger. At least that's what she told me."

I had the impression Ray wished he'd met Elaine many years earlier. But I didn't want to go back in time quite that far. I wanted to know more about Elaine's granddaughter. "Given how close they were, it seems surprising that Lana didn't keep in touch with Elaine after she left. Or did she?"

Ray pursed his lips into the frown he so often wore. "It broke Elaine's heart when Lana ran away— and right on top of Jim's death. Whatever Lana's problem was, Elaine would have understood. She would have helped her or forgiven her or whatever Lana needed."

"Forgiven? Did Lana do something that needed forgiving?"

"I have no idea. And now Elaine will never know either."

Ray seemed close to slipping back into his gloomy funk. I cast about for a change in subject. The dog provided one when he came up to sniff my shoes. I patted the top of his head. "Barney sure is friendly. I noticed the yard here isn't fenced in. Aren't you worried he'll run away?"

"Nah. He has the run of the place. He always comes back. He's a loyal pup."

As if he understood, Barney returned to Ray and settled down on top of his feet. Ray chuckled, then took on a thoughtful look. "I'm sure Elaine never stopped loving her granddaughter. I believe she still remembered Lana in her will. But she didn't leave her everything. She'd made up her mind about that a long time ago. That new will has to be found. You have to make sure Elaine's real wishes are honored."

"I'm working on it." I glanced around the studio again. "Did Elaine ever come out here?"

"Not often. I don't like to show my works in progress, and she respected that."

From the look of things, he had a lot of "works in progress." I thought again how tenuous his position was. If Lana came back to claim her inheritance, he could lose it all. I recalled Elaine wrote that she'd teased Ray about charging him rent—and that he didn't find it funny. His entire livelihood and lifestyle depended on Elaine's generosity. That must have been on his mind as Elaine's illness returned and she talked about making a new will.

Now that I thought about it, if Elaine *was* murdered, Ray should be a prime suspect. He was in charge of Elaine's medication. He admitted he brought her nightly cup of milk on the night she died. And he'd found her body. He could argue that it would be crazy to bite the hand that fed him. But if he believed he was slated to receive a generous inheritance, and she was already suffering from a terminal illness, might he have wanted to speed up the process before she could change her mind?

"Ray, what did you think of Detective Rhinehardt's questioning yesterday? Do you think there could be something to Dr. Lamb's concerns?"

"I think it's nonsense. People always want to blame somebody when someone dies suddenly. Families blame doctors. Friends blame the family. People point the finger when they feel guilty themselves. Dr. Lamb felt bad he went on a cruise just when Elaine was taking a turn for the worse. He wants to find someone else to blame. Simple as that."

"Hmm. Maybe. I can't help wondering, though . . . What happened to Elaine's pain medication? The coroner made a list of all the medicines in Elaine's bathroom medicine cabinet. Her new painkillers weren't there."

Something shifted in Ray's expression, and his bearing turned hard again. "I told you Elaine was stubborn. She didn't always follow my instructions. I helped her organize her pills each month, but she took them on her own. And she didn't like those new pills. Didn't like the way they made her feel. She complained about it all the time. She didn't want them in her daily pill organizer. She probably threw them away."

I nodded. It was a plausible explanation. But I was more interested in Ray's reaction to the question than his answer. He seemed excessively defensive to me. He had just given me a speech about how people shift the blame when they feel guilty, and here he was doing the same thing. Did he feel guilty because he was Elaine's nurse and should have kept better track of her meds?

Or did he feel guilty for another reason entirely?

* * *

After leaving Ray's place, I explored more of the gardens, taking a walk through the Zen maze and pausing at an old sundial to try to figure out the time. As attuned to nature as I was, sundials were still a mystery to me. I found it was much easier to look at the sky and notice the position of the sun. Given how high it was, I guessed it was somewhere around noon. Based on the emptiness in my stomach, I guessed it was more likely sometime *past* noon.

Before heading inside, though, I wanted to find Perry's guest cottage. I figured it couldn't be far. Sure enough, I soon caught sight of a well-worn footpath that led to the second guesthouse, a twin of Ray's. Crenshaw said Perry had gone to the museum, and it appeared he was still gone. When I knocked on the door, there was no answer. Trying not to appear too nosy, I strolled around the cottage—looking for what, I had no clue. Through an open curtain, I caught a glimpse of a tidy living room. The only evidence of occupancy was a soda can on an end table and a stack of magazines fanned across a coffee table. From what I could see, they seemed to be art and travel magazines, and maybe an antique car magazine or two. Nothing suspicious there.

At this point, my hunger was overtaking my desire to be outside, so I headed back toward the house. Crenshaw had given me the security codes before I'd left, so I thought I'd try the side door. I had made it to the kitchen garden when I stopped, overcome with a strange, exposed feeling. I felt like I was being watched.

Slowly, I peered over my shoulder. No one was there. I scanned the trees and nearby gardens, tuning in my ears as well as my eyes. I thought about how Crenshaw and I had stood at the third-floor window the day before. Looking up at the house now, I was somewhat startled at the number of windows facing the grounds. They were all dark, opaque with the reflected sun. Anybody could be watching. With a slight shiver, I jogged to the door, out of sight of prying eyes.

Chapter Sixteen

I found Celia baking a cake in the kitchen. I tried to engage her in light conversation, but she would have none of it. She thrust a covered platter into my hands and practically pushed me into the dining room. I sat down at the long, empty table and lifted the lid. On the plate was a peanut butter and jelly sandwich, cut into two triangles, and a serving of potato chips. And they were delicious. I was halfway through the first half of my sandwich, when Celia bustled in bearing a pitcher of lemon water and a tall glass.

"Celia, I really appreciate this," I said. "It's great. But you don't have to keep serving me. I can—"

One look at her hurt expression, and my words died in my throat. "I mean . . . never mind. This is so nice. I feel like I'm on vacation."

She breathed a sigh of relief and went to gather up a glass someone else had left at the end of the table. Before she left, I decided to try one more time to get her to talk.

"Celia, do you know where Elaine kept her important papers? Some things seem to be missing."

She looked at me like I must be dense. "She kept papers in her desk and filing cabinets. I don't know any other place." She swiveled on her feet, but I stopped her again.

"Celia, one more quick question. Did you know Lana very well?"

Now she looked startled—on top of a range of other emotions. I couldn't tell if she was angry, sad, or confused. Maybe all three. When she finally found her voice, it was clipped and no-nonsense. "Yes, I knew her. She moved here with her parents when she was ten years old. I helped raise her."

"Do you have any idea why she left when she was seventeen?"

She hesitated, then said, "I guess I didn't know her that well." And with that, she scurried out of the room.

After lunch, I stowed my purse in my suitcase and checked on Josie. Although she had plenty of food, water, and room to roam and lounge, she was clearly bored. With barely a nod in my direction, she slipped out the door and stalked down the hall, ready to make this castle her own. I decided to follow her example. With a renewed determination, I returned to Elaine's room for one more thorough search. If that pill bottle was in here, I would find it, by gosh.

For the next hour, I searched high and low. I pulled furniture away from walls, lifted the rug, and crawled the floor from corner to corner. I also removed and replaced the contents of every drawer, bin, and closet. Finding nothing, I stood in the center of the room and closed my eyes. With a deep breath, I sought to tap into my intuition. *Is there anything else to find in this room?*

In my mind's eye, the answer surfaced like the reply in a Magic 8 Ball.

No.

I opened my eyes and sighed. *I should have done that in the first place.*

Gathering up my clipboard, I moved on to the west wing sitting room. As I began taking inventory, methodically documenting all personal property as I'd done in Elaine's room, my thoughts veered from things to people. I was originally hired to find a missing person. I hadn't heard from Wes today, so I assumed Lana was still at large. I wondered if she'd really moved back to the Edindale area as her friend's blog had suggested. If so, how near was she? Could she have come to her grandmother's funeral? Or perhaps she visited the cemetery all alone, after everyone else had left, and placed a single white rose on her grandmother's grave.

At that moment, I glimpsed the shadowy outline of a person in front of me. I gasped, fairly jumping out of my skin—until I realized it was my own reflection in the mirror above the fireplace mantel. *Good grief. That's what I get for entertaining such fanciful thoughts.* I laughed softly as I picked up and studied the decorative glass globe that had captured my attention.

Still . . . what had become of Lana? More to the point, at least as far as the estate was concerned: What were Elaine's true wishes? Did she really intend to leave everything to the girl who ran away? If only I still had her diaries. Or the new will.

One thing I knew for sure; I wasn't going to find answers in the sitting room. It was time to employ a more subtle tactic. It was time to go flying.

Before leaving the sitting room, I rifled through the drawers of a vintage sewing cabinet until I came up with a roll of tape. Returning to my room, I made a sign that said NAPPING—PLEASE DO NOT DISTURB and taped it to the door. Of course, I wouldn't really be napping—though it might look that way to anyone who happened to see me. I needed to stay awake for what I had planned.

First, though, I had to prepare the space. My room had been violated last night. I needed to cleanse it and strengthen my wards. I took out my purchases from Moonstone Treasures and lit the sage bundle. Humming softly, I smudged the entire room. I was beyond worrying about anyone catching a whiff of smoke. If I had to, I'd make up an excuse about burning incense for relaxation. But I didn't expect to be disturbed.

Next, I smudged the black stone to clear any energies it might have picked up in the store. Finished with the sage bundle, I placed it in the bathroom sink to let it burn out. (Safety first!) Using my left, or receiving, hand, I then held the black stone close to my heart and whispered words of intention:

> *I dedicate this crystal for its highest purpose,*
> *To repel all negative energies*
> *And bring me the greatest protection.*
> *As I will, so mote it be.*

With its power now activated, I placed the stone on one of the bedside tables. For my final bit of preparation, I took out the "flying ointment" Mila had given me. As soon as I unscrewed the tube, I inhaled the sweet, heady aroma of jasmine, sandalwood, ylang-ylang, and lemon. Mila's special blend was sure to take me on a trip. The scent was intoxicating.

I squeezed a dab of the mixture onto my finger and proceeded to anoint myself. I decided to trace a sigil—in this case a pentacle—with the ointment as I applied it to my forehead, sternum, wrists, and navel. For good measure, I also touched some to the back of my neck and the bottoms of my feet. Finally, I crawled onto the bed and lay on top of the covers.

For the next few minutes, I concentrated on my breathing. It didn't take me long to enter a meditative state. It was something I did on a regular basis. Astral projection, however, was somewhat new for me. I understood the concept but wasn't quite sure what to expect. All I knew was that I needed to keep my physical body still but awake and remain in a trancelike state. If I was lucky, my perceiving consciousness—my soul—would separate from my physical self and I would have an out-of-body experience. Exactly where that experience would take me, I wasn't sure. The astral world was a vast realm. Not only did it form an invisible layer upon the material plane, but it also extended into space as far as the imagination could go.

Gradually, I became aware of a slight pulsating sensation in my limbs. Then I felt myself floating upward, toward the ceiling. In the back of my mind, I wondered if I had fallen asleep and was now dreaming. But then I turned and looked back at myself lying peacefully on the bed. Unconcerned, I rode the current that had pulled me upward and continued rising. I went through the ceiling and through the roof as easily as if they were made of mist. When I was above the house, I looked out across the open skies and perceived majestic mountains in the distance. I had a strong urge to fly toward them, but I resisted. I had a job to do.

Elaine. What did Elaine want?

Willing myself not to fly away, I dropped back down into the house and found myself in the parlor, hovering before Elaine's portrait. It was exactly as it had appeared the day before. In fact, everything was the same—the chairs, the tables, the flower arrangements. This wasn't a facsimile of the parlor. This *was* the parlor.

I moved toward a vase of lilies and noticed a petal had dropped to the floor. It was velvety white with brown along the edges. I reached to pick it up, thinking I would bring it back with me as a souvenir of my travels. But before I could grasp it, I heard a rustling sound, as of the swish of silk skirts. I looked back at the portrait and saw Elaine stand up from her tufted chair. She stepped out of the picture frame and stood before me.

I felt no fear, really, nor any awe. Only curiosity.

"Hello," I said politely. "How are you?"

She smiled graciously, as if welcoming me to her home. "Very well, thank you. And you?"

"I—I'm fine. But I need your help."

She smiled and inclined her head, waiting for me to elaborate.

"I'm looking for something. Answers. I need answers. Can you help me find them?"

She nodded and lifted her arm, pointing with her elegant gloved hand. I turned, following her direction, and saw that she indicated the south-facing window. Outside was a walnut tree, its golden leaves flapping like banners. A green-hulled nut dropped from the tree and thudded to the ground.

"Is the answer out there?" I asked.

Suddenly, there was a scuffling, scratching sound at the window. I drew closer and saw a squirrel come into view. It crouched on the windowsill, attempting to carry one walnut between its front paws and one in its mouth—and struggling to keep hold of both. I smiled at the squirrel's antics. I was sure there was a message there. Nature always had something to say to those who paid attention. No doubt it was a lesson about maintaining balance, juggling priorities, and not taking on too much at once. But that wasn't the kind of message I was looking for right now.

I turned back to Elaine. "There's so much I want to ask you. For starters, where—"

A faint tapping sound cut me off. Elaine looked toward the closed door and smiled, as if she knew who was on the other side and was fond of the person. I sensed time was running out.

"What happened the night you died?" I asked, a note of desperation in my voice.

Her eyes shifted to the window again. Before I could say another word, the tapping grew louder, more insistent. All at once, I felt a rush of wind, then an abrupt jolt. My body gave a jerk and my eyes popped open.

I was back in the guest room, lying on top of the covers. I sat up, feeling disoriented. There was a knock on the door followed by Crenshaw's penetrating voice.

"Keli! Are you in there? Open up at once!"

I swung my legs to the floor and stumbled to the door. When I opened it, I was faced with two vexed stares, that of Crenshaw and of Josie, who nestled somewhat awkwardly in Crenshaw's arms.

"Your cat was scratching on your door," he said, by way of explanation. "I feared something was amiss."

"Everything's fine. I was just taking a nap." I pointed at the sign on the door.

Josie jumped down and sniffed my feet. Crenshaw's nose twitched as well. "Is that a new perfume?"

"Um, yeah. Do you like it?"

He tilted his head, considering. "It's a bit strong—but not bad. Natural and earthy."

"Just like me," I quipped. "So, what's going on? Did Josie get herself into trouble?"

"Josie? Oh, the cat. No. I stopped by to tell you I'm

leaving for a little while. I'm going to the art museum to talk to their head of security. I'm hoping they can spare a guard, or at least recommend someone, to watch over things here."

"Good idea. Can I come along? I have a few questions for the museum folks myself."

"I suppose so—if you're ready now."

"Just one sec."

I dashed into the bathroom, pulled my hair into a low, loose ponytail, and applied a touch of brick-red lipstick. It was a far cry from Suzanne's multi-part makeover, but it suited me just fine. Simple, natural, and understated—all the better for a detective who would rather remain unnoticed.

We took the back stairs to the main floor and started down the west hallway through the mansion. I halted at the parlor door.

"What's the matter?" asked Crenshaw.

"Nothing. I just want to check something."

I crossed the room and stood before Elaine's portrait, in the same place I'd stood in my astral projection. Looking around, I confirmed that every detail was exactly the same, from the arrangement of the furniture and placement of the flowers to the walnut tree outside the window. I walked over to the vase of lilies on a pedestal table and looked down. There, on the floor, was a brown-rimmed white petal. I picked it up and dropped it into my purse.

"Okay," I said. "I'm ready now."

Crenshaw opened his mouth to say something, then seemed to reconsider. He was learning not to question my ways. *Smart man.*

Chapter Seventeen

The Edindale Art Museum was affiliated with South-Central Illinois University, a mid-sized public research university with half a dozen colleges, including the School of Law. Coming to law school here was one of the main reasons I'd left my home state of Nebraska eleven years earlier. It didn't take long for me to fall in love with the town and decide to stay.

Walking through the leafy campus, watching the play of light and shadows across the landscape, I felt the old familiar thrill that always comes at this time of year. When I was in school, September brought the promise of new friends and a fresh slate. Now it was the start of the fall season itself that engendered feelings of anticipation and excitement. Either way, change was in the air.

If Crenshaw felt any of it, he didn't say. He'd seemed preoccupied on the drive over. I wondered if he was worried about all the complications that had cropped up since I came on board. *Maybe I should say something, let him know he doesn't have to pay me the full amount we agreed on.* I'd figure something out.

"Your friend Farrah has been dropping by a lot."

"What?" Where had that come from?

"At the manor."

"Yeah, I suppose. That reminds me—she wants to sleep over tonight. She can share my room."

He gave me a sharp glance. "A sleepover? Will she be a distraction?"

"Not for me. She'll be a help, actually. Another pair of eyes to search the mansion." I patted his arm reassuringly. "Don't worry. She's not going to charge you."

If he had a comeback, he let it go. We'd arrived at our destination. The art museum was housed in a 1970s-era brick-and-glass building with a windowed front entrance at the top of a short flight of steps. Crenshaw paid the suggested donation, while I studied a Rodin-like sculpture in the vestibule. Then we took the stairs to the second floor and found our way to the director's office. Crenshaw had called ahead, so she was expecting us.

"Good afternoon, Ms. Rawlins," said Crenshaw, with a little bow at the waist.

"So formal," she said with a smile. "Please—call me Mavis." She invited us to sit in the upholstered captain's chairs across from her desk. Her office was chock-full of artistic touches, as befitted the director of an art museum. I noticed her taste seemed to run more toward the traditional than the post-modern, with several nineteenth-century prints and a collection of reproduction Fabergé eggs. Her attire was slightly old-fashioned as well. With her polyester skirt suit, pearl necklace, and short, flat-ironed black hair, she reminded me of a schoolteacher I'd once had.

"Rudy, my security chief, will join us shortly," she said. "Attendance is a little higher than normal this evening because of the reception downstairs."

"Thank you for taking the time to see us," said Crenshaw. "I didn't realize there was an event here tonight."

"We have a weekly concert series featuring the university jazz band. Sometimes it coincides with various college events—tonight it's a reception for a visiting professor from Italy. You should stop by. Perry Warren is down there. I saw him earlier."

"Perry used to be the curator here, right?" I asked.

"One of them. For many years, he curated the European art exhibit. We have four permanent exhibits: African, Asian, European, and American Folk Art." She smiled again. "As I always say, I'd like to cover the world, but we'd need a bigger building."

"I prefer smaller museums," said Crenshaw. "I always run out of time when I visit the Louvre."

I decided to jump right in with the questions I wanted to ask. "Does the museum own all the artwork here? Or do you ever display items that are on loan?"

"We own the permanent exhibits, but we always have two or three temporary exhibits. They're often on loan from other museums."

"Do you ever display works from private collections?"

To my surprise, she seemed to bristle at the question. "All the major museums do," she said. "The EAM is no exception."

Crenshaw cleared his throat. "Keli hit on a touchy subject without realizing it." To me, he said, "I'll explain later."

"Um, okay." Crenshaw never could resist a chance to show me up. He probably wasn't even aware of how obnoxious he was. I decided to ignore it and carry on. "What I really want to know is whether the museum has ever borrowed anything from the Turnbull collection. In particular, I came across something that indicated they may have lent the museum a painting by Edward Hopper."

"Hopper?" She laughed as if the idea was preposterous. "Oh, my. I wish!"

"This would have been almost twenty years ago, I think. Maybe a little less."

"Oh, well, I haven't been here that long. We have records, of course, but it might take a while to locate the right one—especially without an exact date. You see, I'm short-staffed at the moment, and my archivist is on an extended medical leave."

Crenshaw gave me an inquisitive look. "This reference you mentioned. Was it in the journal whose whereabouts are currently unknown?"

"You got it."

"And you think this painting is important for some reason?"

"I do. I think."

Mavis followed our exchange like a tennis fan. "You know, Perry would be the one to ask. He's been a friend of the Turnbulls for ages. And he started working as a full-time advisor for the foundation, oh, probably eighteen to twenty years ago."

"Yes. I should ask him." I didn't say that Elaine already had, to no avail.

"Speaking of the Turnbull collection," said Mavis, "I'm sure you know the art world is chomping at the bit, just waiting for the auction gates to open, so to speak. Perry tells me the heiress likely won't be coming forward."

"I'm not so sure about that," said Crenshaw. "Ms. Milanni here has a stellar reputation for bringing people in, as it were. We may meet the heiress yet."

At that, I took a quick peek at my phone. Still no

word from Wes. I was beginning to think his beginner's luck had run out.

"Of course," Crenshaw continued, "Miss Turnbull may very well wish to liquidate the estate—in which case everything will wind up on the auction block anyway."

"Well, I hope it does. I would rather the art be sold at auction than through a private deal. It seems fairer that way." Mavis smiled ruefully. "I'm biased, of course. It might be more beneficial to the estate if Perry can negotiate a private deal."

"Mavis," I said, "did you know Elaine Turnbull?"

"Oh, yes. We crossed paths many times. She was a lovely lady. I'll be at the gala on Friday. Such a fitting tribute." She glanced at the doorway. "Ah, here's Rudy."

Mavis introduced us to Rudy Canyon, the museum's head of security. He was a tall, middle-aged man with a ruddy complexion and a soft-spoken manner. Mavis stood up and walked around her desk. "Rudy, you can use my office to talk to Crenshaw. I need to put in an appearance at the reception. Keli, if Crenshaw doesn't mind, you should come along with me. There are cocktails and hors d'oeuvres. It's quite nice."

"I'd love to."

I left Crenshaw to discuss security matters with Rudy and walked with Mavis down to the courtyard. Strains of jazz mixed with muted conversation as guests mingled on the brick and grass terrace. Strings of lights hung from slender trees, giving the place a romantic ambiance.

"I hope I didn't sound derisive of private collectors," Mavis said, as she handed me a glass of wine from a passing waiter. "Many of them are our greatest patrons. We couldn't survive without them."

"It's a whole new world to me," I admitted. "I didn't realize there's such an important cadre of collectors right here in Edindale."

"Oh, wealthy people everywhere like to own rare, beautiful things. But yes, we are lucky to have such generous families here—like the Turnbulls, the Harrisons, and the Betzes."

"What do you know about Suzanne Turnbull, if you don't mind my asking?"

"Not much. I see her at community functions now and then. I know Perry was close to her husband, Jim. When Jim took over management of the family collections following his father's death, he brought Perry on full-time. That's when Perry left his job here. I believe he and Jim partnered up to expand the collection."

"So, Suzanne isn't involved with the foundation? And she's not a patron herself?"

"Oh, no. I'm not sure she has the means herself. Not to tell tales, but it's my understanding that Jim and Suzanne were never independently wealthy. Harold Turnbull didn't believe in trust funds. That's why Suzanne moved back in with Elaine after Jim passed away."

Mavis beckoned a waiter to refresh my glass of wine, then excused herself to make the rounds. I stood on the edge of the crowd, not far from the jazz band. As I listened to the music and sipped my wine, I thought about Suzanne's odd reaction whenever I'd brought up the family's art collection. Maybe she was resentful because her father-in-law spent so much money on his artwork instead of providing a nest egg for his son. Or perhaps she really had no interest in it at all.

I gazed around the courtyard, wondering if I'd see any familiar faces. I didn't recognize anyone, but my eyes did fall upon a striking figure near the bar. At first, he was surrounded by a group of people, but as soon as they dispersed, I got a good look at him: slim build; tailored, expensive-looking suit; smooth, almost glossy black hair; full lips set in a mildly cocky smirk. And the most eye-catching feature—a thick and trendy Garibaldi beard. He also wore mirrored sunglasses, which gave him a sheen of celebrity. If this was who I thought it was, it was obvious why Suzanne was smitten. Farrah would be, too.

As I studied the man, I gradually became aware that he hadn't turned away in several seconds. Because of the sunglasses, I couldn't see his eyes. Was it possible he was staring at me the whole time I was staring at him?

As if reading my mind, his smile broadened and he lifted his martini glass. I glanced quickly to the left and right, but there was no mistake. He was looking right at me. A slow blush warmed my face. When Perry walked by, I jumped at the excuse to turn away.

"Perry! Hi!"

"Hello, Keli. How nice to see you. Did you come here for that tour I promised you?"

"I'll have to take a rain check on that. I'm just enjoying the music while I wait for Crenshaw."

"I see. Well, better enjoy the nice weather, too, while we can. It will be cold before we know it."

"Yeah. Say, Perry, who is that man over by the bar?"

He turned to look. "Do you mean the older gentleman in the bow tie? That's Winston Betz."

"No, I'm talking about the young guy with the beard." I tried to spot him again, but he was gone. "I guess he left."

"Ah, you must mean Xavier. He does stand out in a

crowd." For some reason, I thought Perry sounded slightly annoyed by this.

"Oh, right. The guy who called for you," I said. "He's a new collector in town, isn't he? Is he interested in the Turnbull collection?"

"As a matter of fact, yes. I've been talking to him about just that."

So, Suzanne was wrong. The question was, had she lied? Or was she really just oblivious to matters pertaining to the art collection her late husband had managed? Either way, I ought to find out more about Xavier Charleston. After all, he was one of the last guests to leave Elaine's home the night she died.

At last, Crenshaw came over. He nodded at Perry. To me, he said, "Shall we go?"

I showed him my wineglass. "Don't you want to have a drink? Listen to some music?"

He checked his watch. "I think I should get back to the manor and tell Celia to expect another guest for dinner. That is, assuming Farrah will be joining us for our evening meal?"

I cocked my head, ready to tease him for being so uptight. Then I shrugged. "That's probably a good idea."

We said good-bye to Perry, who said he'd be leaving shortly, and left the museum. The light was fading fast as we made our way across campus. Students and staff all seemed to be in a hurry, anxious to get inside before the sun disappeared entirely. The temperature was already starting to drop.

When we reached the visitor parking lot, Crenshaw strode up to his car, then froze, keys held aloft. "Do I have a flat?" he asked.

I ran to the rear of the car and saw exactly what I expected—two slashed tires.

I don't know why it should have affected me so badly, but for some reason I started to shake uncontrollably. And I didn't stop until Farrah arrived in answer to my call and shuffled me off to her apartment.

Chapter Eighteen

"I almost wish I didn't have to go back there." I clutched a mug of hot, black tea with both hands, as if it were a life preserver. "That place gives me the heebie-jeebies."

"So, don't go back," said Farrah, ever the loyal friend. "Stay here tonight."

"I can't. I left Josie there!"

"We'll go get her then, and your stuff, too."

I sipped my tea and sank further into Farrah's sofa. It was a tempting idea. I didn't feel safe at the manor, and no one there was giving me a straight story.

On the other hand, no one's tires had been slashed at the manor. And all the unsolved mysteries there were driving me crazy. I felt sure I could uncover the answers if only I kept looking.

My cell phone rang, and I snatched it up, hoping it would be Wes. Instead, it was Detective Rhinehardt, finally getting back to me. There was so much I wanted to tell him, the words burst out of me like water from a fire hose.

"Whoa, hold on a minute," said Rhinehardt, when

he could get a word in edgewise. "Did you say someone's following you around, vandalizing your car, and watching you sleep?"

"Not my car—my friends' cars. Someone is toying with me. *And* something's going on at the manor. Weird sounds, lights, secrets. I don't know if it's related to the tire-slashing stalker, but there's definitely something up at that place. And I really think Mrs. Turnbull was murdered!"

"Where are you right now, Keli?"

"I'm at Farrah's place."

"Don't leave. I'll be right there."

True to his word, Rhinehardt arrived in less than ten minutes. That was one of the advantages of living in a small town—traffic rarely held people up. He declined Farrah's offer of coffee, tea, or beer and got right to the point.

"Start from the beginning, nice and slow, and tell me everything."

I told him everything—minus any witchy workings, of course. As soon as I finished, he made a call to the station to let them know about the thread connecting all the tire-slashing incidents—namely, me. Then he leaned forward and looked me directly in the eye.

"You're a level-headed gal, Keli. I know you have good instincts—I've seen it time and again. Do you really think Elaine Turnbull was murdered?"

I didn't miss a beat. "Yes. One hundred percent. I found one of her diaries—which, unfortunately, is now missing. But she mentioned feeling unsafe. I don't think she trusted the people around her."

He leaned back and bit his lip, a rare display of emotion for the stoic officer. "We're going to have an uphill battle proving it. We've got no murder weapon, no obvious motive, no body—anymore—and a houseful of people with alibis."

"A houseful of people who are lying," interjected Farrah.

"Crenshaw told me a little about the alibis," I said. "Do you mind going over them with me?"

Rhinehardt looked from me to Farrah and then down at his notebook. "Well," he finally said, "there's not technically an open investigation. So, I suppose there's no harm. To be honest, I'd like a reason to dig further. Maybe you can help."

"That's what we're here for," said Farrah.

I almost giggled at that, more from sheer nerves than anything else. Rhinehardt only raised his eyebrows a smidge. He rifled through his notebook until he found the page he was looking for.

"On the evening of Saturday, September first, beginning at six-thirty or so, twelve people gathered for dinner at Turnbull Manor. Eight were outside guests and four were residents of the manor: Elaine Turnbull, Suzanne Turnbull, Perry Warren, and Ray Amberly."

"Ray is the nurse, right?" interrupted Farrah.

"More like a companion," said Rhinehardt.

"Who were the outside guests?" I asked.

"Let's see. Winston Betz was there. And there were three couples: a Mr. and Mrs. Lancaster—they're trustees of the museum; Mavis Rawlins, the museum director, and her husband, William; and Bruce Stevens and Mary Chaser, an unmarried couple."

"I know Bruce," I commented. "Or Wes does, anyway. He owns a gallery that promotes local photographers."

"That's right. In fact, all three couples, as well as another of the guests, Xavier Charleston, went to an opening at the gallery right after dinner."

"Twelve people for dinner," I murmured. "That would have been a tight fit around the table."

"Actually, make that thirteen," said Rhinehardt, checking his notebook. "I forgot that Elaine had invited her groundskeeper to join them for some reason. Ernesto Cruz. I think she was trying to help him out by introducing him to some of the other guests. However, he left early to meet a couple friends at a local bar. The friends vouched for him."

"Of course, they did," said Farrah. "That's what friends do. What about the bartender or any other patrons? Can anyone else provide an alibi besides the friends?" She hopped up and began pacing her living room.

The detective wrinkled his brow. "I haven't got that far."

"There was a catering company there too, wasn't there?" I asked, as I reached for my purse. I'd belatedly realized I ought to be taking notes. I found a pen and paper and jotted down the guests' names.

"There were three individuals from Ruby Plate Catering," Rhinehardt affirmed. "The owner, who is also the chef, plus two servers. They cleaned up and left by eight-forty-five. The housekeeper, Celia Meeks, helped out in the kitchen. She then left with the caterer to deliver the leftovers to a food pantry on the other side of town. She didn't return until nine-thirty."

"Aw, that's nice," said Farrah.

"At some time around eight-thirty or so, Elaine said good-bye to her last guest and informed the household she was going to her room. She passed through the kitchen on her way to the back staircase. She did not stop for a nightcap, water, or any other refreshments."

At this point, I stopped writing and focused on

listening. These were the last moments of a woman's life he was talking about.

"Over the next half hour or so," he continued, "Ray took his dog for a walk around the neighborhood, Suzanne went to her room to post on social networking sites, and Perry went to his cottage and made a telephone call."

"Who did he call?" asked Farrah.

"Xavier Charleston. He had left for the gallery opening, as I mentioned. Several attendees confirmed he was in the lobby on his phone during the time in question. And Mr. Charleston himself offered to produce his phone records. But, again, I hadn't gotten that far."

"They could be in cahoots," Farrah pointed out. "Perry could have set his phone down while the call was still connected. Phone records don't necessarily prove he was really talking."

"Plus Xavier is a suspect, too," I added. "If two suspects each provide an alibi for the other, shouldn't that cancel out both alibis?"

Rhinehardt raised his eyebrows, though I couldn't tell if he was impressed or bemused.

"Okay, what happened next?" I asked.

"Next," the detective continued, "a little after nine o'clock, Ray returned from his walk and put his dog in his cottage. He went to the kitchen in the manor and prepared a mug of warm milk with cinnamon for Mrs. Turnbull. He took it upstairs, found her unresponsive, and called nine-one-one."

My mind whirred, poking a million holes in Rhinehardt's account of things. "About Ray's walk—do you have a list of the neighbors who saw him?"

Rhinehardt gave me a patiently questioning look, as if to say, "What do you take me for?" Of course, he had a list.

"I mean, may I see the list?" I amended.

"I suppose you could go door to door as easily as I did," he muttered, as he flipped to a page and handed me his notebook. I grabbed my phone and took a photo of the page.

"How about the names of Ernesto's buddies at the bar?" asked Farrah. "And the name of the caterer?"

Rhinehardt's radio squawked, and he stood up. "I need to get going, ladies. I'll text you the names, if you promise me one thing."

"What's that?" I asked.

"Keep me informed of anything and everything you uncover. And be careful."

The detective's visit, combined with Farrah's enthusiasm, had reignited my curiosity. I was ready to go back to the manor. Farrah quickly packed an overnight bag, and we bustled outside to her Jeep convertible. I made a habit, now, of checking the tires of every vehicle I was about to board. Luckily, the vandal hadn't struck the same car twice—yet.

On the drive across town, I used my phone to look up Suzanne Turnbull. As an official spokeswoman for Carrie Cosmetics, she was all over social media. I browsed a few of her profile pages, then clicked over to Facebook. It took me a couple minutes to scroll all the way back to her posts on the night of September 1. Sure enough, starting at 8:45 she had uploaded a new post every two minutes—complete with pictures, emojis, and hashtags. I read the names of some of the products she was promoting.

"Evidently she sells more than makeup," I said. "Listen to this. She's got 'glowing serum,' 'anti-aging firming cream' . . . 'Bee venom lip plumper.' Ouch."

"Sounds a little intense even for me," said Farrah.

I snickered lightly as I hopped over to another Web site and found similar results. I read a few snippets out loud, together with the date-stamped times. "Eight forty-eight: 'Check out this BOGO deal . . .' Nine o'clock: 'New product! Gold-plated eye bronzer.'"

"Eye bronzer? Who ever heard of eye bronzer?"

"Nine o-four: 'Get your sexy on with . . .'" I trailed off as a thought occurred to me. Farrah must have been thinking the same thing.

"You know," I began.

"Isn't it possible to—"

"Schedule your posts?"

"Yes!" said Farrah. "Of course, it is. At least, I know you can on business accounts."

"I bet there's an app for that, too. These time stamps prove nothing!"

"Call Detective Rhinehardt."

"Not yet. I have a feeling I'll have a lot more to tell him before too long."

Farrah stopped at a gas station to fill up her car and stock up on snack food. We didn't know if there would be anything to eat when we arrived at the manor. Crenshaw had called Celia to let her know we would be absent from dinner. He was dealing with his car when Farrah whisked me off to her apartment. I had told him we'd see him later.

While Farrah was inside the store, I took the opportunity to shoot a text to Wes.

"Where's my check-in?" I demanded. "I miss my sexy newsman."

He replied at once. "Miss you, too, babe. Sadly, my investigation has stalled."

His investigation. It still made me smile to picture him

gadding about Chicago like some kind of modern-day
Dick Tracy.

"Too bad," I replied. "So, I'm still in the game?"

"Ha! Never fear. I'm still working on Penny. I may
get more out of her yet."

I wasn't sure I liked the sound of that. Now I was picturing him interrogating Veronica Lake . . . On the
other hand, Penny was the only concrete tie we had
to Lana's current whereabouts. If Wes could get her to
talk, more power to him.

Right?

I asked Farrah as much when she returned to the
car. She pondered it for a moment, then nodded. "Absolutely. You've got nothing to worry about. Wes is so
gaga over you, he'd never stray. You and he have a sto-
rybook romance. I'd even call it epic." She turned the
car onto River Road, and we were soon in Edindale's
historic district. Old-fashioned street lamps lined the
boulevard, creating a cozy, almost romantic atmosphere. "Sometimes I envy you," Farrah added wistfully.

"Envy me? You've had your own 'epic' relationships.
And how many proposals have you had now? You could
easily settle down if you wanted to."

"Yeah. I suppose." She concentrated on driving and
didn't say any more. I might have pursued the topic,
but we soon arrived at the mansion. Farrah parked her
Jeep behind my car and cut the engine. I grabbed the
snack bag, and she reached for her overnight satchel
in the back seat.

The neighborhood was dark and quiet. As we walked
up the sidewalk, I raised my hand, motioning for
Farrah to stop. "Let's go in the back," I said softly.

"Lead the way."

We walked down the driveway toward the rear of the
house. I wasn't quite sure why I wanted to go back

there. Something about the night air and abundance of greenery seemed to beckon me. Invisible crickets croaked rhythmically, echoing in the underbrush. As we passed by the garage, I noticed a light shone in Ernesto's apartment. But the moment I looked, it blinked off.

When we reached the topiaries at the entrance to the English garden, Farrah slowed her steps and looked around. "Talk about atmosphere," she said, in a hushed tone. "Where is this fog coming from?"

Sure enough, a fog had begun to roll in from the bottom of the hill where the trees grew thicker. I remembered seeing Ernesto walk off with a fishing pole. "There's a pond or lake down there somewhere. And Crenshaw mentioned a springhouse, so maybe there's a spring, too."

Suddenly, a dog barked and I jumped. For an instant, a howl sliced through the peace like in *The Hound of the Baskervilles*. Then Barney came trotting down the path.

"Hey, little guy," said Farrah. "Are you lost?"

"He's not lost," I said. "He lives here. This is Ray's dog."

Farrah checked the time on her phone. "It's almost nine o'clock. Shouldn't he be on his nightly walk right now?"

"I'm not sure how routine it is. But Ray did say Barney has the run of the place, so I guess he gets his exercise."

I patted the top of Barney's head, but he didn't want to sit still. He pranced happily from me to Farrah, tail wagging.

A flash of light caught my attention by the Zen maze several yards away. I peered into the gloom. The light disappeared and all was still—until something moved in the shadows. Watching intently, I gasped when I saw a person glide behind the rose arbor.

"Did you see that?" I hissed.

"See what?" Farrah was busy scratching Barney's belly.

"There's someone over there in the trees."

"It's probably Ray, looking for his dog."

"No. It was a woman."

We heard footsteps coming from the house and turned to see Crenshaw walking toward us. The crisp smell of his aftershave preceded him. I figured he must have showered after changing his tires.

"Do the two of you plan on coming inside anytime soon?" he asked, impatient as ever. "Celia wants to know if she should warm up dinner."

"In a minute," I said, edging toward the shadows.

"Keli, where are you going?" asked Farrah. "Let's go in now."

"I'll be right back."

Before they could stop me, I jogged over to the arbor and slipped inside. I looked around, straining to see in the darkness. The path lights barely illuminated the ground in front of my feet. I crept along slowly so I wouldn't trip.

On one hand, I realized it wasn't unusual to come across a person out here. Several people lived on the Turnbull property. But there was something about the woman I saw that was not at all usual.

A soft metallic creak reached my ears. *The garden gate.* Picking my way around flowers and statues, I reached the wrought-iron gate in time to see it barely swinging on its hinges. Outside the formal garden, the manicured lawn gave way to bushy trees. The ground lights stopped here.

I took another step into the darkness and paused. Where had she gone? She must know the property well, I thought. I hadn't heard any sounds of tripping, falling, or bumping into trees—like I was in danger of doing.

After about a minute of blind groping, I had to stop. If I went much farther, I was liable to fall into the pond. Disappointed, I started to turn back. I also didn't want to get lost. As it was, I could no longer see any lights from the house or gardens.

I was trying to locate the gate again when the clouds parted, finally allowing a beam of moonlight to penetrate the fog. At that moment, I perceived the rustle of a low-hanging tree branch. I made myself still as a statue and waited, my heart thumping loudly in my ears. Before long, a shadow emerged from the trees and took the form of a woman. For a split second, she crossed into the moonlight before disappearing into the grove at the bottom of the hill.

I couldn't have followed if I'd wanted to—I was paralyzed from shock. Of course, I might have been mistaken. I *must* have been mistaken.

Because if I wasn't, then the woman I just saw was none other than Elaine Turnbull.

Chapter Nineteen

By the time I returned to the gardens behind the house, I had begun to doubt my own eyes. The atmosphere here was the perfect setting for a ghost story. Plus, after my interrupted astral experience this afternoon, I was only too eager to see Elaine again. If anything, my subconscious probably conjured an imaginary ghost. It was probably only Suzanne creeping about in the yard—for Goddess knew what purpose.

As I rounded the corner at the topiary garden, I caught sight of Farrah and Crenshaw, side by side on a stone bench. Farrah was swinging her legs and Crenshaw was talking with his hands. I heard the murmur of their voices but couldn't make out their words. They were probably talking about me.

With my eyes on my friends, I failed to see the man rush toward me from the opposite direction. We nearly bumped into each other.

"Oh!" I exclaimed, taking a step back.

"*¡Dios mio!*" Apparently, he hadn't seen me either. He pressed his hand to his chest and sprang aside. I reached out with both hands to keep him from running away.

"Ernesto? What's your hurry?"

"*Sí.* Yes. Sorry." His eyes darted around. I wasn't sure if he was expecting someone or looking for an escape route.

"I've been wanting to talk to you," I said. "My name is Keli Milanni. I'm staying at the mansion for a few days." I offered my hand for a handshake, leaving him no choice but to take it.

"Ernesto Cruz. Nice to meet you."

He was an attractive man, maybe in his late thirties or early forties—a few years older than me at any rate. He was also just a little taller than me. In spite of his baggy work clothes, I could tell all his outdoor labor kept him in good shape.

By this time, Crenshaw and Farrah noticed us and sauntered over. "Is everything all right?" said Crenshaw. "Oh, hello, Ernesto."

"Hello." Ernesto nodded, and looked down. Was he really that shy, I wondered, or was he hiding something?

"Ernesto," I said, "I thought I saw a woman out there, under the trees. Did you see anyone?"

"Woman?" He acted confused.

Farrah laughed lightly and touched my arm. "You should have your eyes checked, Keli. As you can see, this is no woman." She held out her hand to Ernesto. "I'm Farrah Anderson. You must be the landscape designer I've heard so much about. I can't wait to see the gardens in the daylight."

"Let's all go in for a bite to eat, shall we?" said Crenshaw. "Ernesto, Celia mentioned you weren't at dinner either. You'd better come along or risk offending the cook." He ushered the gardener ahead of him, leaving no room for argument.

Celia's eyes lit up when she saw the bunch of us file into the kitchen. "One, two, three, four . . . Everyone to the dining room! I'll bring in the food."

Ernesto said something to Celia in Spanish. From his tone, I gathered he was protesting. He probably didn't want to sit down for dinner with three lawyers he barely knew. Who could blame him?

They were still arguing when Suzanne came in by way of the back staircase. "What's going on in here?" she asked. "Is there any food left?" *So, she missed dinner, too*, I noted.

Celia turned on Suzanne. "Mr. Betz called."

"Winston? What did you tell him?"

"I told him you weren't here. I didn't know where you were. How would I know?"

Suzanne let out an exasperated sigh. "These old coots who don't believe in cell phones," she said to the room. "They have a home computer they sit at all day, but cell phones are 'too modern.' I better go call him back."

After Suzanne left, Celia handed Ernesto a covered plate, and shooed the rest of us into the dining room. Ernesto left out the side door, presumably to eat alone in his apartment.

Farrah, Crenshaw, and I settled in at one end of the long table. Crenshaw picked up a bottle of wine from the sideboard and filled three glasses.

"Is it presumptuous of me to assume you both will join me for a wee nip?"

"No," said Farrah. "But it was presumptuous of Celia and Ernesto to assume we don't speak Spanish."

Crenshaw raised an eyebrow, and I stared at Farrah. "They'd be right, wouldn't they?" I asked.

"No way! I had, like, six years of Spanish in school. Plus, I used to date a guy from Puerto Rico. I may not be fluent, but I can get by."

"You're full of surprises, aren't you?" said Crenshaw, sounding impressed.

"Well, what did they say?" I asked.

"It's funny. At first—"

She broke off as Celia teetered in with a giant tray loaded with food—including three bowls of hearty bean soup, a basket of crusty bread, and a dish of home-made red cabbage slaw. Crenshaw jumped up to help her, and for once she didn't argue.

"Oh, wow, this looks heavenly," gushed Farrah.

I agreed. "It smells wonderful. Celia, please let us clean up after ourselves tonight. I insist."

"Very well," she said after a short pause. She looked rather relieved.

We tucked into the food before she left, duly exclaiming over how delicious everything was. A few minutes later, I pointed my soup spoon at Farrah. "Well?"

"Well? Oh, yeah. So, at first I thought Celia was going to be motherly, you know? She was telling Ernesto he needed to eat. But then it got a little weird. She said something like 'Don't forget what I know.' And, 'I'm not a fool.' He said, 'You have it all wrong. You don't know what you're talking about.' And then she said, 'I saw you with my own eyes. I saw you with the lady.'"

"The lady? What lady?" I asked.

"I don't know," Farrah said. "But then Celia said, 'You owe me. *Quiero mi dinero.* I want my money.'"

"Interesting," said Crenshaw. "What do you make of it, Keli?"

For a moment, I was stunned Crenshaw was asking for my opinion. *He must really think I'm some kind of detective,* I thought. *I guess I'd better get to detecting.* I took a sip of wine before answering. "I'd say Celia is black-mailing Ernesto. Remember when we saw them down in the gardens, having their surreptitious little rendezvous? She was probably shaking him down then."

"What's the big deal about being seen with a lady?" asked Farrah.

We were all silent, as we considered the possibilities. "Perhaps," Crenshaw finally said, "the 'lady' in question was the lady of the house. Meaning Elaine."

Farrah put down her wineglass. "You mean, Celia saw him with her before she died?"

"Or immediately afterward," I suggested. "In Elaine's diary, she mentioned that Ernesto was a bit hot-headed. And there was an incident not long ago. Evidently, Ernesto was upset because he thought Elaine had accused him of taking advantage of her."

"Meaning?"

"I don't know. I wish I had the earlier diaries. I wonder why Elaine took such a special interest in her gardener anyway? Rhinehardt said she'd even invited him to her dinner party on the night she died."

"Elaine liked to help people," Crenshaw said. "It wouldn't have been terribly unusual for her to introduce her staff to other wealthy homeowners. She might have been thinking about his future employment options."

"Do you think he resented her for it?" asked Farrah. "Was he embarrassed?" She picked up her wineglass again and shook her head. "I don't know. I just can't picture that sweet-faced gardener killing his kind-hearted employer. It doesn't make sense."

"Maybe not," I conceded. "Unless there's more to the story that we don't know."

"I find it difficult to picture *anyone* murdering Elaine,"

said Crenshaw, his face sober. "Yet, as much as I hate to admit it, I'm starting to believe someone did."

Later that night, I answered a knock on the bedroom door to find Crenshaw standing in the hallway. "I thought you might need an extra pillow."

"Thanks," I said, taking it from him.

"Are you sure you'll be all right in here? Do you want to trade rooms?"

"We'll be fine. Besides, I'm all settled in here with Josie and everything." Not to mention the fact that this room had already been smudged, blessed, shielded, and consecrated, three times over. I wasn't about to do it all again in a new room.

"Well, good night, then."

"'Night!" called Farrah, from the adjoining bathroom, where she was washing her face.

She and I took turns freshening up, then decided to turn in. There was plenty of room in the king-sized bed. Farrah plumped her extra pillow and began to pull on a satin eye mask. Then she paused.

"Oh, gosh, should I not wear this? I can take it off real quick if something happens. See?" She proceeded to demonstrate, whipping the mask off and on several times in quick succession, until her hair looked like a static plasma ball.

"I'm not worried," I said, with a grin. "Just get some sleep, okay?"

I turned off the light and lay on my back. In the darkness, I took a few deep, calming breaths. I had it in mind that I might try astral projection again. Maybe I could learn more about what was going on from Elaine herself.

But scarcely had I closed my eyes, when a shrill rock

anthem blared into my awareness. I sat up with a start. It was morning.

"Sorry, sorry, sorry," mumbled Farrah, blindly hitting her cell phone on the nightstand until the music stopped.

I rolled out of bed. "It's okay. I need to get ready anyway. I have a court appearance this morning."

"That's right. And then you have the interviews."

"What interviews?"

She pulled off her sleeping mask and blinked against the sunlight. "Didn't I tell you? I scheduled five interviews for you today at your office, starting at eleven o'clock."

"Oh, right. The interviews." This was going to be a busy day. First, I needed to run home and change into a business suit. Then I needed to go over my file for the hearing and get to the courthouse. And then there were the interviews.

On top of all that, I was acutely aware that this was my third day at the manor—and time was money. Crenshaw was counting on me. Perhaps, on the astral plane, Elaine was counting on me, too.

At this point, I almost hoped Wes would win our bet and find Lana already. Because I sure wasn't having much luck.

Chapter Twenty

I hurried down the courthouse steps and jogged across the square. The hearing went fine, but the judge was a bit chatty afterward. He wanted to tell everyone about the New England fall foliage tour he and his wife would be taking in a few weeks. Someone mentioned that the foliage here in Southern Illinois was just as beautiful, especially in Shawnee. I had to agree. I loved hiking in the national forest. I always felt close to the Goddess and at one with the living earth under the majestic canopy of trees.

Unfortunately, I hadn't had time to hit my favorite trails lately—and I definitely didn't have time to talk about it now. My first interview was scheduled to begin in five minutes.

I rushed down the sidewalk, barely noticing the fall decorations gracing storefronts and light poles, or the brown, orange, and yellow banners advertising the upcoming harvest festival. By the time I burst through the doors of the old bank building, I was out of breath and starting to perspire. The line of applicants outside my office door did little to calm my nerves. Had Farrah scheduled all the interviews for the same time? Plus, I thought she'd said there were only five appointments today. There had to be at least three times that many people crowding in the hallway.

"Hello," I said, as I fumbled with my door key. "Sorry to keep you waiting. Um, just one more minute." Once inside, I flipped on the light, set down my briefcase, and grabbed a yellow legal pad.

"Okay," I said to the first person in line, a middle-aged woman wearing a smart suit and a rather severe high bun. "Come on in." I led her to my inner office and invited her to have a seat at the single guest chair opposite my desk. As soon as I sat down, I asked for her name and a copy of her resume.

"My name is Cheryl Finch," she said briskly. "Currently, I'm an office manager at an international accounting firm based in Carbondale, where I lead a staff of twelve clerks and secretaries. I've been employed there for the past ten years. Before that, I managed a mid-sized law office for several years, overseeing billing, budget, personnel, and more. I value hard work, efficiency, directness, and, above all, *punctuality*."

She gave me a pointed look at the end of her spiel. Was she implying I was late for the interview? I glanced at the clock. It was only five minutes past the hour now. I swallowed and looked down at her resume. It was three pages long, including references.

"Um, Ms. Finch, if you don't mind my asking, why are you interested in this position?"

"Why? I should have thought it obvious. The pay rate eclipses what I'm currently earning. After working here for two years, I'll be able to retire early." She gazed around my small office with barely disguised distaste. "I've always heard nice things about Edindale. But . . . this isn't the job site, is it? I would like to see my actual working environment before accepting the position."

I stared at the woman, at a loss for words. She was either missing a marble or two, or she'd been sorely misinformed. I hadn't included any pay rate in my ad. Even if I had, there was no way it would come near to what she must be making now. I thanked her for coming and walked her to the door.

The second person in line was a preppy-looking young man with short blond hair and a smug grin. He shook my hand with a grip so firm I flinched.

"Have a seat," I said, glancing at his resume, "Mr. Bigsly."

"Call me Ace." He sat down and unbuttoned his blazer. "First off, I want to confirm that this is a nine-to-five job, right? Monday to Friday? 'Cause I have a very active social life and a heavy sports schedule at the club. So, overtime is not an option for me."

Oh-kay. I tried not to let my surprise show. He was young, after all. "I don't anticipate overtime being necessary, Ace, but we can talk about your schedule later. Let's talk about your experience first."

"Yeah, sure. I have *lots* of experience."

"Have you worked in an office before?"

"Oh, you mean that kind of experience."

I glanced at his resume again. "I see here you majored in political science. What are your career goals?"

"Yeah, well, I thought about going to law school, but I figured there are easier ways to make money. Then I saw your ad in the paper this morning and knew I was right."

"This morning? You mean yesterday."

"No, this morning. You didn't give much notice, but that was kind of smart. Otherwise a lot more people would have showed up. This way you get only the ones who are really on the ball."

I was so confused. Maybe *I* was the one short a marble or two. "Do you happen to have a copy of the ad with you?"

"Yeah, sure." He pulled a newspaper clipping from his jacket pocket and handed it to me. I almost fell out of my chair when I read it.

Office Assistant for Rising Attorney
Open Call Interviews
Wednesday, 10–3
Law Offices of Keli Milanni
132 Hawthorne Street, Suite 102
Starting salary: $70,000. No experience necessary.

The only part of this ad that matched the one I had placed were the words *office assistant*.

"This must be some kind of joke," I muttered.

"Excuse me?"

"I'm sorry, Ace, but there's been a mistake. This isn't the salary I'm offering. And I actually *am* looking for someone with relevant experience."

When Ace left, I looked down the hallway in dismay. The line now snaked around the corner and out the front door. I had to raise my voice to be heard over the din of chattering voices.

"Hello, everyone! Did anyone here receive a phone call with a scheduled interview time?"

"I did!" yelled a voice at the far end of the hall.

"Come on up, please!"

As I waited for the applicant to make her way through the crowd, I heard grumblings all around me.

"I was here first!"

"I've been waiting for more than an hour!"

"Unfair!"

When the woman reached me, I steered her inside and closed the door. "Sorry about all that," I said. "There was some kind of mix-up with my newspaper ad."

"Oh, that's okay. I have time. Yes, ma'am." She bobbed her head, making her silver curls bounce. She had a pleasant, if slightly manic-looking, smile. Regrettably, she also smelled strongly of cigarette smoke.

I sat back in my chair to put a little distance between us. "I'm Keli. And you are?"

"Berty Finkle. Yes, ma'am. Like I said, I have time, because I'm not currently working. There was a little incident at my last job, but it really wasn't my fault. Anyway, there were two other ladies here with appointments, but they took one look at the line and turned around and left. They said they didn't have time for this. But I have time."

"I see. Well, I'm glad you have the time."

"Yes, ma'am."

I conducted the rest of the interview as quickly as possible. Berty Finkle might have had plenty of time, but I didn't. And I was starting to fear a revolt from the masses in the hallway. As Ms. Finkle pushed her way toward the exit, I bit my lip and tried to decide what to do.

A booming voice from the end of the hall cut through the noise. "Make way! Coming through."

The crowd parted, and a large man came clomping

up to my door. He was an imposing figure, with shoulder-length, curly hair as black as his buckled combat boots. The horn-shaped silver earrings spiking through both of his earlobes gave him an extra fierce look, as did the clench of his beefy, skull-ringed fingers. But the most incongruous part of his appearance was the gray business suit and pin-striped, white Oxford shirt.

"Hiya, Miss Keli," he said, when he caught sight of me. "Everything all right here?"

"Arlen! What a surprise." Arlen Prince, aka the necromancer, was a former client of mine. I hadn't seen him in months. "There's been some kind of crazy misunderstanding, and all these people think I'm hiring for a position that doesn't exist."

"You mean you're not lookin' to hire an assistant?"

"Don't tell me you're here because of the ad, too?"

He furrowed his heavy eyebrows. "Well, yes, I called you after I saw your ad on Monday. A gal named Farrah gave me a call-back."

"Oh! You have an appointment then?"

"I was supposed to be here at eleven-thirty. Thought I'd be early, but there's no place to park out there. Now I see why."

No kidding. "You're right on time. I'd be happy to interview you. Um, do you mind making an announcement for me? I need to tell these people the interviews are now closed—with my apologies for the inconvenience."

I slipped back into my office and let Arlen disperse the crowd. Evidently no one was inclined to argue with him. He came inside a moment later.

"How have you been, Arlen?" I asked, after we sat down across from one another at my desk.

"Not bad, not bad." He gave his collar a little tug

and popped a button. Shrugging, he pulled a rattling bone necklace outside his shirt, letting it drape across his wide chest. *Talk about the witch-doctor look,* I thought, remembering what Crenshaw had said when he saw my amulet. But on Arlen it made sense. As a necromancer, he worked with animal bones to contact the spirit world and work magic. Like me, he was a Pagan. He just communed with nature in a slightly different way.

"I've been thinking of going back to office work— with a little nudge from my partner. The taxidermy business is slow. Not as many hunters want trophies as they used to." He crinkled his eyes good-naturedly. "I suppose that makes you happy."

I smiled. It was true, it did make me happy. But I didn't want to be rude about it. "To each his own," I said. "But what did you mean, 'back to office work'?"

"Believe it or not, I worked the front desk at a dentist office a while back. Made the appointments, handled the billing. I have a degree in bookkeeping. In fact, I even worked for a lawyer for about a year after college, until he up and retired."

"I had no idea," I murmured.

He handed me a bundle of papers. "That's my resume, college transcripts, writing sample, and references."

"Wow." I almost whistled, as I reviewed his resume. On paper, he was surprisingly impressive. But I still had a hard time picturing him as a receptionist. He seemed uncomfortable in his suit. When I'd first met him, he was wearing black motorcycle pants and a black tank top under a long, black trench coat. And *lots* of chunky jewelry. As much as I hated to think it, I wondered if he would scare away potential clients.

"I can type seventy words a minute, if that sort of thing is important," he said.

I set down his papers and gave him a thoughtful look. "Are you sure you'd be happy working in an office? I always thought of you as an outdoor type."

"Of course I'm an outdoor type—just like you are. But I can work anywhere." He leaned forward, with a twinkle in his eye. "I may not look it, but I'm actually pretty flexible."

I laughed out loud at his joke. And suddenly I felt ashamed for judging his appearance.

At that moment, the beep of a car alarm sounded from the alley outside my office. It cut off abruptly, as if it had been activated by mistake. Arlen nodded at the open window behind my desk.

"Somebody must be lost," he remarked. "The same fancy, black car has gone by at least three times since we've been sitting here."

I hopped up, opened the window wider, and looked outside. At the end of the alley, a black car stood idling. From what I could tell, it seemed to be a sporty-looking luxury car with tinted windows. *A Bentley, maybe?* That was how Farrah had described the car she thought was following her the other day.

"I wonder what they're up to," I muttered.

Arlen came around and stood next to me to have a look. "Huh. Want me to go ask?"

I glanced up at him, towering at my side like a pro wrestler. Or a bodyguard.

The mysterious car took off suddenly, spraying gravel in its wake. As I closed the window, it dawned on me that having an intimidating figure at the front desk might not be such a bad thing after all. In fact, it could be exactly what I needed.

Chapter Twenty-One

After Arlen left, I peeked down the hall to make sure there were no lingering job applicants. I was glad Annie and the other first-floor tenants weren't around today. The fiasco in the hallway was bad enough as it was. I would have felt even worse if it had disrupted my neighbors.

Relishing the quiet, I sat back down at my desk to make a few phone calls. The first was to the classified ad department at the *Edindale Gazette*. When I asked who had placed the ad for the open interviews at my office, there was some confused stammering on the other end of the line.

"What do you mean, Ms. Milanni?"

"I mean, who bought this ad? And when?"

"Why, you did. Just yesterday."

"No, I didn't. I called on Monday about the ad that ran yesterday. But there was another ad today. That's the one I'm asking about."

"But I have it right here in my database that you bought the second ad. I even took—no, wait. Now I remember. It was a gentleman who called. But he said he was calling on your behalf!"

"Did he give you his name?"

"No . . . I only got your name."

I went around and around with the newspaper clerk and didn't learn a thing. The unknown "gentleman" had used a prepaid debit card to pay for the ad. I hung up in frustration and called Wes. Hearing his voice made me feel instantly better.

"Hey, babe," he said when he answered. "I was just thinking about you!"

"Now who's the psychic?" I teased.

"Nah, I just miss you. I feel like I've been gone for ages."

"I miss you, too. Things here have been . . ." I trailed off, not wanting to worry him.

"Things have been what? What's going on?"

"Things are weird. You're not going to believe what happened this morning." I told him about the flood of misinformed job applicants.

"Man, that's crazy! I'm gonna talk to Al. Somebody messed up big time."

"I don't want to get anybody in trouble," I said. "Anyway, on the bright side, I think I found an office assistant who will work out nicely. He's actually a former client."

"He? Your new assistant is a man?"

"Yeah. So?"

"I don't know. It just seems unusual, that's all."

"Not really. Men can be administrative assistants, too." I smiled in spite of myself. I could have told Wes that Arlen wasn't interested in women in any romantic kind of way. But it didn't seem especially important at the moment.

"So, tell me," I said. "How is it going with your search? Any word from Lana yet?"

"No," he said, sounding a bit defeated. "And I think Penny is getting tired of all my messages."

"How many have you sent?"

"A few. I really thought Lana would respond to me."

"Are you sure Penny is passing along the messages?"

"Yeah, she is. She's been helpful. In fact, she finally dropped a useful hint. She let it slip that Lana might have gone to stay with an old friend for a while. She wouldn't tell me the friend's name, but she said she thought it was someone Lana went to school with."

"High school?"

"I assume so. I don't remember Lana hanging out with anyone in particular, but then again we weren't close. And I wasn't all that observant. As soon as I get back to Edindale, I'm gonna look up some old class-mates and see if anyone else can come up with a name."

"Sounds like a good plan," I said. "And I can ask Suzanne. If Lana had any good friends, you'd think her mother would know."

"Ah, so the race is still on?"

"Of course!"

I only hoped Suzanne wouldn't flip out this time.

By the time I returned to the manor, it was well past noon. Farrah was on her way out the front door as I walked up.

"Where ya goin'?" I asked. "Want to go grab a bite to eat?"

"I have to meet a client, but I'm glad you got here before I left. There's something I have to tell you."

She grabbed my arm and lowered her voice. "I talked to some of the neighbors this morning."

"Oh? What did you learn?"

"*Nobody* saw Ray the night of Elaine's death. They only saw his dog, Barney. They assumed Ray wasn't far behind, since he always lets Barney off the leash. But they admitted they never actually saw him."

"Another bogus alibi," I said.

"Exactly. So, I went to ask Ray about it. He was super-defensive."

"Wait—you didn't accuse him of lying, did you?"

"Not in so many words. I told him I was trying to clear up some confusion about the sequence of events that night."

"What did he say?"

"He got real angry. Said we're wasting our time, and Dr. Lamb doesn't know what he's talking about. He said we should be trying to figure out where Elaine hid her new will."

"So, he thinks she hid it? I wonder why he's so sure of that."

"You can try asking him," said Farrah. "I'm pretty sure he's done talking to me. Speaking of which—I also tried talking to Ernesto. I waved at him across the lawn and started toward him. Instead of waiting, he just tipped his hat at me and jumped on a riding lawn mower. You would have thought I was trying to sell him some Carrie Cosmetics."

I shook my head. "Well, Suzanne seems to know Ernesto fairly well. I'll try to get some more information out of her. I want to talk to her more about her daughter anyway."

"Good luck. I'll be back later, but first I'm gonna stop by that bar Rhinehardt mentioned. I want to see if

anyone remembers seeing Ernesto. It would be nice to
be able to cross at least one name off the suspect list,
you know?"

"I'm with you there, sister. That reminds me: I'd still
like to track down that art collector, Xavier Charleston,
and ask him a few questions, too."

"Leave it to me. I'm on it."

"Are you sure? How will you even know where to
find him?"

"Easy. I'll start at the most expensive hotel in town."

With a smile and a wave, Farrah took off down the
sidewalk toward her car. A small flock of geese honked
overhead, drawing my attention skyward. In that
moment, I felt a whisper of gratitude fill my heart. Part
of it felt like my ever-present gratitude for Mother
Nature, but another part seemed to come from without—like a ghostly prayer from the departed family
who had once inhabited this place.

Rubbing my arms, I turned back toward the house.
The main focus of my appreciation right now was
toward Farrah. I was grateful not only for her help, but
also for her enthusiasm. Otherwise I might start to get
discouraged by the daunting task we'd taken upon
ourselves. Sometimes it seemed like we had more suspects than a game of Clue—and none with convincing
stories.

I was still thinking about all the flimsy alibis as I went
to my room to change out of my suit and play with
Josie for a few minutes. In the interest of eliminating
suspects, I decided to double-check Celia's alibi. I
looked up Ruby Plate Catering and dialed the company's phone number. A man picked up.

"Ruby Plate, offering fine food and impeccable service, fit for the royals."

"Hi," I said. "May I speak with . . . Ruby?"

"Uh, Ruby isn't a person. Do you mean Sylvia?"

"Yeah, sorry. Sylvia is the owner, right?"

"Yes, ma'am. Owner, chef, and mom—to me. I'm her son, Trevor."

"That's nice," I said. "You must be proud of your mom. I've heard great things about her food."

"Oh, yeah. It's the best."

"Is she around now?"

"No, she's on a job. Can I take a message?"

"Hmm, no, I guess not. I wanted to ask her about a particular job—and give her my compliments. It was a private dinner at Turnbull Manor about a week and a half ago."

"Oh, sure. I worked that one."

"You did?"

"Yeah, I help out sometimes. I can pour water, bus tables. Stuff like that."

"That's cool. Did you go along to take the leftovers to the food pantry as well?"

"Yeah, we always do that on our way home. Mom would rather die than throw away any of her food."

I was liking Sylvia more and more. "That's awesome. Say, do you happen to remember what time it was when you dropped Celia off back at the mansion?"

"Huh?"

"Celia Meeks. She lives and works at the manor. Didn't she go along with you to deliver the food?"

"Nah. It was just me and mom in the van. Gloria, the other server, drove herself and went on home."

"Are you sure? Do you remember seeing Celia in the kitchen that night? Do you know who I mean?"

"Yeah, sure. Mom and Cee Cee go way back. They were neighbors when my mom was a kid."

"They were friends?"

"Sure, family friends. Cee Cee—Celia—is closer to my grandma's age."

Interesting.

"Thanks, Trevor. You've been helpful. Maybe I'll see you at the gala on Friday."

So much for crossing off Celia's name from the list. The fact that she lied made her more suspect than ever. But what should I do about it? Confront her? Ask her to explain herself? At a minimum, I would tell Detective Rhinehardt. Alibis were falling apart around here like cheap furniture.

I went downstairs to the kitchen to scrounge up some lunch. Celia was nowhere to be seen, and I was kind of glad. I was feeling increasingly nervous about being in a house with a probable murderer. And if Celia was the one who poisoned Elaine's milk, I definitely didn't want her preparing my food.

I found the makings of a lettuce salad in the refrigerator and set about putting it together. As I peeled a carrot, chopped a bell pepper, and washed a handful of cherry tomatoes, I thought more about the headstrong maid. Did she really have a motive for murder? Elaine wrote in her diary that Celia had been in love with Harold. I wondered why Celia stayed on after he married Elaine. Maybe she needed the job and didn't have a choice. Or maybe she still wanted to be close to Harold. Maybe she even hoped he would one day leave Elaine.

I sprinkled some sunflower seeds on my salad and drizzled on some vinegar and oil. I ate at the kitchen table, still feeling a little funny about making myself at home here. Out of all the residents, this place felt most like Celia's home. She had been here the longest, and she seemed to take charge of things, at least when it came to food and cleaning. Then I had a darker thought: *Maybe that's how she wanted it.* She wanted to be the lady of the house. Did she finally decide she was done answering to the "other woman"? Did she decide to do away with her? I shivered at the thought.

Elaine had also mentioned she caught Celia going through her jewelry. Was that more evidence of Celia's wanting to take Elaine's place? Or was she just a thief? *If only I still had the diaries. Who knows what else I might have learned?*

There was one thing in Celia's favor, I realized. She was a small, elderly woman. I wasn't sure if she could have managed carting off the heavy lockbox, especially up or down the stairs.

On the other hand, I had noticed more than once that she seemed to be stronger than she looked.

The side door opened with a rattle, and Ray came in carrying two bulging grocery bags. He gave me a startled look when he caught sight of me, then nodded his head and set the bags on the counter.

"Hello," I said, feeling like Goldilocks face-to-face with Papa Bear. I might have to reconsider my idea that Celia was the head of this household. Ray had lived here for many years, too. As he unpacked the groceries, I took my lunch dishes to the sink and washed them out.

"Celia sure is a good cook," I said, by way of small talk. I was curious about the living arrangement at the manor. It was such an odd dynamic, when I thought about it. The residents here weren't quite family, yet they shared meals and a living space. It called to mind the early twentieth-century boardinghouses I knew only from old movies and books.

Ray must have sensed my curiosity. "The guest cottages have small kitchens. It's easier to have most meals here in the house."

Of course, it is, I thought, *when someone else is doing the cooking and cleaning.*

"In fact, Elaine used to insist on it," he continued. "She joked sometimes about 'the boys out back,' meaning Perry and me, and the staff who lived above the garage. She liked to have people around her and was always inviting people to dinner. It kept Celia busy, too, which made her happy."

"Sounds lovely," I said.

"Yeah, well, it's all going to change if the real will doesn't turn up."

It's already changed, I wanted to say. It changed when Elaine died. How could Ray even imagine things might go on as they always had? Did he think Elaine was going to bequeath the manor to him, complete with the staff and the money to keep it running? Or was it his plan to make it *look* as if she had? Could he have made a fake will and then somehow lost it?

"Ray, tell me again what you think happened to the will?"

He turned his back to me and reached into a grocery bag again. "I don't know," he finally said. "All I know is Elaine was acting odd the last couple days before she died. I think it was the medication. She was paranoid and suspicious. I think she hid the will, so Suzanne wouldn't see it and beg for a bigger inheritance."

Or any inheritance, I thought. Under the existing will, Suzanne didn't receive a thing.

As I watched, Ray hefted a plastic jug of milk and tried to set it on the counter. He missed. The carton dropped to the tile floor and split open, splashing milk in all directions.

Ray cursed, and I sprang back. Wanting to help, I looked around for a towel, but Ray pushed me aside.

"Get out of here," he growled. "I'll take care of it."

He didn't have to ask me twice.

Chapter Twenty-Two

I went to the library to find Crenshaw—and stopped short at the doorway. There were books everywhere—piled on the tables, desks, and chairs, stacked waist-high on the floor. At first, I thought the place must have been ransacked. Then I saw Crenshaw on the far end of the room, methodically removing books, fanning through them, and adding them to a tall stack beside him. His sleeves were rolled up to his elbows, and he seemed to be absorbed in his task. I walked right up next to him and folded my arms.

"Are you crazy?" I asked.

He gave a start and looked up. "Keli! Hello. I'm glad you're back. I could use a hand in here."

"A hand? It looks more like you could use a platoon of librarians. And some boxes."

"I'm not packing the books. These all need to go back on the shelves."

I looked around in consternation. "Are you searching for the will inside the books? Why didn't you just replace each book after looking through it?"

"I'm not looking *only* inside the books. I'm also

looking behind them. It occurred to me that the space behind a row of books would make an ideal hiding place for a folded piece of paper."

"Still . . ."

"Yes, yes, I know," he said, a touch defensively. "This is not the most efficient course of action. I admit I became a bit zealous in my search and didn't want to lose track of where I'd already looked."

I picked up the nearest book and read the title: *The Castle of Otranto, A Gothic Story,* by Horace Walpole. I set it back onto the stack. "Do you have someone lined up to come in here and do an appraisal? I have a friend in the old-book business."

"I would be most obliged if you would call your friend. That would be helpful. If we don't find another will by the end of this week, I'm going to have to proceed with the only one we have."

For the rest of the afternoon, I helped Crenshaw remove and glance through the remaining books, and then replace them all back onto the shelves. It was slowgoing, especially since I kept finding myself wanting to read the book flaps. The Turnbulls had an eclectic taste in literature. They seemed to own everything from art history and poetry to pulp fiction.

At one point, I found myself standing near the portrait of Harold Turnbull. "You were quite a diverse collector, weren't you?" I said to the painting.

"I beg your pardon?" said Crenshaw, walking up behind me.

"Old man Turnbull." I pointed to the portrait. "He didn't seem to favor any particular period or style in his collections. His books are as varied as his paintings."

"Ah. I'm sure some of these were Elaine's or Jim's, but it's true that they represent a broad range of tastes."

"That reminds me. At the museum yesterday, you said something about me raising a touchy subject when I asked if the EAM ever displays private collections. What was that all about?"

"It's a question of ethics." Crenshaw sat down at a library table and took on a professorial mien. "When a museum chooses to display certain works, it indicates those works have artistic merit. In turn, this serves to increase the value of the works. Therefore, showcasing a private collection can be seen as benefitting the collector. If a museum or curator is accepting money from the collector, one might wonder if they're being bought, so to speak. Perry did the right thing by leaving his museum job."

I supposed that made sense. I didn't know how much curators made, but the Turnbulls must have paid more. Still, it wasn't like this was New York City or LA. "It's hard to imagine private art consulting would be a lucrative field here in Edindale, especially if you work for only one collector."

"You'd be surprised."

I didn't doubt it. I'd been surprised so many times in the past few days, it was becoming my new normal.

I glanced over at the door to the gun room and remembered how Perry had surprised me in a big way on my first visit to the manor. As I recalled, I had been about to open the antique filing cabinet. I wandered over to it now.

"What's in here?" I asked, pulling open the top drawer.

"Nothing anymore," said Crenshaw, turning in his chair. "It was filled with old receipts and provenance documents for the artwork Harold bought and sold over the years. I took it all to the office to be scanned. And no—there was no sign of a will among the papers."

"I figured as much," I said. "But wouldn't Perry have needed those documents to assist with his appraisal?"

"He's already been through them and entered the information on his own spreadsheets." Crenshaw joined me at the cabinet and opened the bottom drawer, as if to confirm it was empty. "Perry mentioned that Jim had begun to create an electronic database of his father's collection. He died before he had a chance to finish it, and now the software is outdated."

I stared at the nearby hand-carved oak door and engaged in an internal debate. On one hand, I knew every room of the mansion should be searched. On the other hand, I wasn't exactly eager to see the place where Jim had accidentally shot himself to death. Crenshaw made the decision for me by unlocking the door and pulling it open.

"I neglected to show you the gun room on our tour the other day," he said. "It's one of the few rooms that is kept locked at all times." He went in and flicked on the overhead light.

I followed him inside and blinked. More than an armory, the room resembled a den—or an upscale man cave. To be sure, there were plenty of guns. They were prominently displayed in glass-doored cabinets and on hooks above a stone fireplace. But the dark paneled walls were also adorned with mounted antlers and animal skulls, as well as scenes of fox hunts painted in oil. To the left was a large executive desk. To the right was a brown leather couch, which faced the fireplace—and a shaggy bearskin rug on the floor near the hearth. A few well-preserved birds perched here and there,

while a moose head stared balefully from the far wall.
I shuddered involuntarily.

"Harold liked to hunt," Crenshaw said dryly.

I was reminded of Arlen's comment that his trophy
mounting business had slowed down. Surely there was
still a demand in some places, but it was definitely an
old-fashioned look.

As I took in the room, my skin began to prickle. I
took a tentative step toward the desk. "Is this where Jim
was when . . ." I didn't have to finish the question.
Crenshaw knew what I meant.

"I believe so."

Almost against my will, my mind jumped to that
tragic day fifteen years ago. I pictured Jim sitting at the
desk, cleaning an antique gun. Though, come to think
of it, didn't people usually clean guns after they had
fired them?

"Was Jim a hunter, too?" I asked.

"I'm not sure. However, it's my understanding he
would frequent the shooting range at Stag Creek Hunting Club."

I looked up sharply. Crenshaw was examining a
stuffed pheasant in the corner of the room—and stu-
diously avoiding my eyes. A couple of winters ago, he
and I had shared a harrowing ordeal at that gun range.
He didn't seem inclined to relive the memory. Neither
was I.

I returned my attention to the desk. There wasn't
much on it: a reading lamp, an ashtray, and a glass pa-
perweight. The drawers contained folded maps, binoculars, pencils and paper, and little else.

"So, Jim made a fatal error in judgment," I said. "It's
hard to believe such preventable accidents still occur,
but I know they do."

"With devastating consequences." Crenshaw circled the desk, eyeing the chair and everything around it, as if he, too, was envisioning how it might have happened. He looked at the floor for a moment, then examined the cabinet behind the desk. "I would venture to say this floor was once covered by an Oriental rug, likely matching the runner in the library. And the door on this cabinet is not the original. Rather than replace the glass, Elaine must have had the whole door replaced."

"Well done, Sherlock." My voice was light, but I wasn't really feeling playful. The circumstances were way too horrible—especially if Jim's daughter had happened upon the scene.

I went to the cabinet Crenshaw had indicated and opened the door. Four old rifles hung vertically in a row. I assumed they weren't loaded, but I wasn't about to touch them. I was more interested in the nick in the wood of the cabinet's interior. I ran my finger across the rough spot.

Turning, I caught sight of a cow skull on the wall above. "If only the bones could talk," I murmured.

"I beg your pardon?"

I faced him and had another thought. "Do you think we could get a copy of the police report? From the night Jim died, I mean."

He narrowed his eyebrows. "I can ask Detective Rhinehardt. What are you thinking?"

"I don't know. I just want to learn all I can about the night Lana disappeared."

He nodded and agreed to make the call. I took another slow walk around the room. The eerie vibes I'd felt on my first visit to the manor were magnified in here. As soon as I was satisfied that there were no apparent hiding places for Elaine's will, I headed to the exit. I was more than ready to get the heck out of Dodge.

Farrah returned to the manor shortly before dinner. We had a few minutes to catch up in our room before Crenshaw would be summoning us to the dining room. She filled me in on her efforts to gather info "in the field."

As for Ernesto, she didn't have much to report. The staff at the bar didn't remember seeing him the night of Elaine's death. Neither did any of the regulars. So, she wasn't able to substantiate his alibi. Her investigation of Xavier, however, proved to be a little more entertaining, if nothing else.

"I'm impressed you found him so quickly," I said.

"It was nothing," she said, waving her hand lightly. "When I mentioned his name at the Harrison Hotel, the concierge pointed me toward the bar upstairs. Happy hour was just getting started. It was easy to spot Xavier with his full beard and preppy California-style suit. He was at a table by himself, having a drink and a bite to eat."

"And you just, what, walked up to him and said you'd like to ask him some questions?"

"Yeah, basically. I told him I wanted to get into art collecting and wondered if he could give me some tips. Of course, I coated it all with a lot of flattery and flirtation."

"Of course."

"Unfortunately, I didn't learn much. He admitted he had hoped to purchase some pieces from the Turnbull collection, but now he thinks that will have to wait. He said he might come back after the estate is settled."

"Did he say anything about knowing Elaine?"

"He said he was glad he had a chance to meet her before she died. It sounded like he'd never met her before."

Farrah brushed her hair and touched up her makeup, while I checked my buzzing phone. It was Crenshaw, letting us know dinner was ready.

"By the way," said Farrah. "I think Xavier has been to Edindale before."

"Oh? Why do you say that?"

"Because of a couple things he said. Like, at one point, a bachelorette party came into the bar. He said something like it was 'louder than Ladies' Night on the *River Queen.*'"

"The *River Queen?* As in, the gambling boat here in Edindale? That went out of business three years ago."

"How could I forget?" said Farrah. "It went belly-up shortly after you tipped off the feds to a loan shark operation connected to the casino. Probably not a co-incidence."

I flinched at the memory. "Well, the casino's closure might also have had something to do with the death of the owner a few months later—at the Harrison Hotel, no less. But that's beside the point. Did you ask Xavier about it?"

"Nuh-uh. He distracted me with his sparkling eyes and pouty lips."

"Farrah—"

"Just kidding. I actually didn't think anything of it until later. But he did say something else that struck me as kind of funny. He mentioned all the community festivals we have here. We were talking about local artists, and he said he's not interested in amateur crafty stuff."

"What a jerky thing to say."

"Yeah. He said he buys museum-quality artwork, not the stuff they sell at all the street fairs and park festivals they have every other month in small towns like Edindale."

"Again, what a jerk. But that doesn't mean he's been to Edindale. He probably saw the signs for Applefest, and it reminded him of other small-town festivals."

"Could be. Anyway, we should keep an eye on him. Maybe we can get more info from him at the gala."

"Yeah, him and everybody else."

Crenshaw buzzed my phone again, so we headed down to dinner.

Everyone was already seated when Farrah and I took our places at the table. That is, everyone but Ernesto. He was absent once more, even though Celia had set a place for him. She uncovered a casserole dish, served herself, then passed it around the table, family-style. When the dish came to me, I hesitated for half a second before spooning out a generous portion. The creamy potato and veggie concoction, topped with crispy, browned onions, was too delectable to pass up. Besides, even if Celia had laced Elaine's milk (which I sincerely hoped she hadn't), what were the odds she would poison six other people, half of whom she barely knew? *Knock on wood.*

Fortunately, everyone behaved like civilized adults during dinner. Conversation centered on the upcoming gala. Ray and Celia conferred about last-minute details regarding house cleaning and the caterer's instructions, while Suzanne chattered excitedly about the guest list and what she would be wearing. Perry listened politely to Suzanne. When he could get a word in, he told Crenshaw, Farrah, and me about a scholarship the Arts Council would be announcing in Elaine's honor.

As soon as she had cleared her plate, Suzanne announced that she would be skipping dessert and left the table. Ray and Perry excused themselves a short while later. I was glad to see they at least took their plates to the kitchen. Then Celia stood up and said she would be back to clean up. "I'm going to prepare a plate and take it out to Ernesto. He's so busy, it's no wonder he doesn't have time to come to dinner."

Farrah shot me a significant glance. I shook my head in response.

"More wine?" asked Crenshaw, raising a bottle. Farrah and I each held out our glasses.

"Where did this come from anyway?" I asked, noting the high-end label.

"Perry brought it up from the wine cellar."

"So, it belongs to the estate?"

Crenshaw nodded and patted his breast pocket. "Not to worry. I made a note of it in my logbook. I'm keeping track of everything."

"I'm not worried."

"As long as people still live and work here," he said, "I believe they may continue to be supported by assets of the estate. To a point. Of course, the sooner it's settled, the better."

Farrah sipped her wine and licked her lips. "You know, a wine cellar would make a good hiding place. Have you searched it yet?"

Crenshaw cocked his head, as if intrigued by the idea. "I have not."

"Let's check it out now!" She pushed back from the

table and nudged me with her elbow. "Come on, Keli!"

The entrance to the basement was through a nondescript door at the back of the mansion. Crenshaw led the way, with Farrah close behind him. I followed somewhat reluctantly. I had a thing about enclosed, underground spaces. I'd found myself in life-threatening situations belowground—more than once.

Stepping off at the bottom of the narrow, wooden stairs, I was relieved to see the area was well-lit, if a little cramped. The low-ceilinged basement was unfinished, but the appliances to the right appeared to have been upgraded in recent years. Straight ahead was an arched wooden door. Crenshaw opened it to reveal a lavishly rustic-looking wine cellar. Along all four brick walls, elegant racks held an impressive variety of wines. In the center of the room a round tabletop perched quaintly atop an old wine barrel.

Farrah whistled as she ran her fingers along some of the bottles. "There must be thousands of dollars' worth of vino down here."

"No doubt," said Crenshaw. "Perhaps this would make a good task for you—helping me to document the stock in here. Perhaps tomorrow?"

"Perhaps," she agreed.

I stopped paying attention to the two of them when I glanced through the arched doorway and noticed another door. *Another escape route?* It was along the opposite wall of the basement. I left the wine cellar and went to investigate.

The door was made of gray wood and appeared solid and heavy. It was barred by a thick board. I was trying to get my bearings and figure out which direction

I was facing, when I heard a dull thud. It came from the other side of the door.

"You guys!" I called. "Come here!"

"What is it?" said Farrah, from the threshold of the wine cellar.

I pointed at the old door with a trembling finger. "I think someone is in there!"

Chapter Twenty-Three

If not for my surging adrenaline, I might have laughed at the picture we made. After Crenshaw heaved open the old door, the three of us crouched in various states of readiness: Crenshaw armed with a penlight, Farrah wielding a wine bottle, and me clutching the board I'd removed from across the door. But it was all for nothing. There was no one behind the door. The only danger I faced was the risk of getting a splinter from the board.

Crenshaw, the Boy Scout, shined his light onto the dirt floor and crumbling walls of the cavelike room. Decrepit shelves hung precariously along one side.

"This must have been a root cellar once upon a time," I said, finally finding my voice.

"Once upon a *long* time ago," said Farrah. She sneezed and backed away.

I wished we had a bigger flashlight. I wasn't confident in the tiny beam from Crenshaw's penlight. I was sure it wasn't covering every inch of the room. Even so, I had to admit the space appeared to be empty, save for a few dusty cobwebs and unknown creepy-crawlies.

"You probably heard someone walking upstairs," he said. "Things often sound strange in basements of this vintage."

"I know that," I snapped. I was feeling petulant. Crenshaw's adult-talking-to-a-child tone of voice didn't help. I knew the difference between a sound above me and a sound in front of me.

At least, I thought I did.

While I got ready for bed a while later, Farrah and Crenshaw stayed up late chatting in the second-floor sitting room. I was happy with how well they seemed to be getting along. In the past, Farrah would have considered Crenshaw a bore, while he would have thought her frivolous. I thought it was very mature of them to find common ground—though what they found to discuss, I couldn't imagine.

After putting on my pajamas, I took out Mila's flying ointment from my suitcase. I sniffed the tube appreciatively, then dabbed a bit on all my pulse points. Leaving a night-light on in the bathroom for Farrah, I went ahead and crawled into bed. Lying on my back, I took three deep breaths and recited my protection mantra to myself. Then I focused on raising the vibrations in my body in another attempt at astral projection.

To my disappointment, it didn't seem to be working. Once I thought I felt myself pulling upward, away from my body, only to drop immediately back down. I tried a few more times, but I couldn't seem to make it happen. *Maybe I'm trying too hard. I'm too tense.*

I resorted to a well-practiced relaxation exercise instead. Predictably, I fell asleep. At least, I must have, because I awoke with a start sometime later.

Farrah was beside me, fast asleep. What had woken me? A noise outside?

Quietly, I got out of bed and looked out the window. It was a clear night—the waxing moon would be full in just a few days. Everything appeared to be still on the grounds below.

Then I heard another noise, unmistakable this time. It sounded like a door closing, and it came from the direction of the garage. Straining my neck, I could just barely make out the edge of the garage—and then something else. Two figures emerged from the back of the building. Side by side, they headed down the hill, staying in the shadows.

I itched to go after them. Who were they, and what were they up to? Was it Ernesto and a buddy going night fishing? Somehow I didn't think so.

In the darkness of the bedroom, I fumbled for my shoes. And where were my jacket and phone? I would have to use my phone as a flashlight.

Just then Josie purred at my feet, and Farrah stirred in the bed. I sighed and set down my shoes.

Oh, well. This probably wasn't the wisest idea I'd ever had. I decided to do the smart thing and save my sleuthing for the morning. I got back into bed and stared at the moonlit tree branches outside the window until, eventually, I fell back to sleep.

First thing on Thursday morning, after showering and dressing, I marched outside and climbed the steps on the side of the garage. As I rapped on Ernesto's apartment door, I tried to decide which question I'd ask first—and which approach I should take to coax him to talk. Should I be friendly, flirty, or firm? Good cop or bad cop? Confident or casual?

There was no answer.

More insistent this time, I knocked again. I thought I heard a noise inside, but no one came to the door.

Darn it. Was I going to have to leave him a note? I couldn't force him to talk to me. But maybe Rhinehardt could. I'd have to add this to my ever-growing list of things to discuss with the detective.

For the bulk of the morning, Farrah and I searched and inventoried all the unoccupied bedrooms in the mansion. We were on the third floor, in the former living quarters of two maids, when Farrah flopped onto one of the beds. "Not much to see in here, is there?"

"You don't have to stay." I appreciated her company and her help, but I couldn't blame her for being bored. This was thankless work.

"No, no. I want to stay. But you know . . ." She trailed off with a thoughtful gleam in her eye. It was a gleam I knew well. It usually spelled trouble.

"What?" I asked suspiciously.

"Think about what we're looking for: a will that either Elaine hid or someone else stole. If someone stole it, then it's going to be in that person's room. The diaries were definitely stolen. So why are we looking in empty bedrooms? We should be searching the occupied rooms."

"We can't do that, Farrah." Sometimes I had to be the voice of reason for my impulsive friend. It was hard when I secretly agreed with her.

"Why not? Are we detectives or what? Detectives snoop!"

"We're not detectives! Not really." I walked to the window and looked down at the grounds far below. Someone was crossing through the gardens, but I couldn't tell who. "People have a right to their privacy,"

I continued, trying to convince myself as much as Farrah.

"We're not cops," she retorted. "We don't need a warrant. We're working for the executor of this estate, and he's responsible for all the assets on this property. Everyone who still lives here must realize that."

"Well, there's still one problem." I turned to face her.

"What's that?"

"How do we snoop without getting caught?"

Farrah's face broke into a grin. "We just have to wait for the right opportunity. Celia runs errands sometimes, doesn't she?"

Before I could respond, my cell phone rang. I held up one finger, indicating Farrah should hold her thought, and took the call. It was a client, Tia Richards, in the midst of a minor meltdown. Her ex-husband had picked their daughter up from school without letting her know. The daughter was fine—they had only gone to get ice cream. But the ex had done this before, and Tia was fed up. She wanted me to draw up a petition to have his custody rights revoked. I had a feeling she would change her mind once she'd calmed down, but I agreed to meet her at my office.

"I have to go," I said, when I'd hung up. I explained the situation to Farrah, and she waved me away.

"Go on. Take care of your client. I'll go find Crenshaw and see if he wants to start on the wine cellar now."

"Better you than me," I said, heading for the door. "Keep your eyes and ears open down there!"

She gave me a salute, and I took off.

* * *

An hour and a half later, I emerged from my office with a much calmer Tia Richards. I had let her vent her frustrations, and then we came up with a plan. It involved me writing a friendly letter to her ex-husband's attorney, requesting her to remind her client about the terms of the current custody arrangement—and the importance of following it. Tia agreed to keep her temper in check for the sake of her daughter.

As we said good-bye in the hallway, Annie stepped out of her office. *Her* attitude was somewhere near the opposite of friendly.

"Keli," she said shortly.

"Hi, Annie. How's it going?"

She waited until Tia had left the building before answering. "It's been quiet today. Unlike yesterday."

"Oh, no!" I didn't have to ask what she meant. "You were here yesterday? I didn't think you were in."

"I couldn't *get* in. I couldn't even get in the front door. I had to cancel all my appointments."

"I'm so sorry! There was a . . . mistake. Or something. It will never happen again." *I hope.*

Her expression was doubtful. "I have another package for you." She grabbed something from inside her office and thrust it at me. "This came on Tuesday."

"Thank you, Annie." I poured sincerity into my words and inwardly vowed to bring her flowers. "I'll be hiring an assistant soon, so—"

She grunted and turned away before I could finish. Her door snapped shut like a bite.

Time to call Arlen.

After sleeping on it the night before, I was now certain. I would never find anyone as qualified, good-natured, or interesting as Arlen Prince. As a bonus, I could be myself around him, witchy ways and all.

When I called to offer him the job, he asked me how soon he could start.

"The sooner the better, as far as I'm concerned," I said. "But let's go with Monday." I hoped I'd be able to get away from Turnbull Manor for at least a little while on Monday. Maybe I'd even find some answers by then and be able to wrap up my involvement in the whole thing.

Somehow I doubted it.

I told myself I should get back to the mansion, but first I drafted the letter I promised Tia. Once that was done, I sent it by email, responded to a few other messages, and then finally shut down my computer. I was heading for the door when I noticed the package Annie had given me. I'd forgotten all about it.

It was a small cardboard box, about six inches square, with computer-printed postal labels. The return address was a P.O. Box here in Edindale. There was no name. As I examined the package, shaking it gently and even sniffing it, I felt a growing sense of unease. Nothing was obviously amiss, but something still felt off.

I took the box to my desk, used scissors to slit the tape, and opened one end. Whatever was inside was wrapped in tissue paper. Touching my Triple Goddess wrist tattoo, I said a quick protection spell—and pulled out the contents. When I unwrapped the paper, I was slightly confused at first. But not for long. Inside the package was a toy car. Its rear tires had both been cut to shreds.

Chapter Twenty-Four

There was no doubt in my mind now that the tire slasher was the same person who had tormented me last spring. The Giftster. Once I got over my initial shock, I immediately checked the toy car for any bugs or hidden cameras. But I resisted the urge to destroy it. I'd learned my lesson the last time around. After discovering a concealed spy cam in a fairy figurine, I'd smashed them both to bits—along with any clues. This time I would preserve the thing as evidence. I tossed the toy back in its box and stuck it in a filing cabinet in the closet.

For a moment I paced my office. The message of the toy car was clear. The stalker wanted me to know that all the recent tire slashings were for my benefit. He—or she—wanted me to know how much they knew about me. And my friends. They targeted my cousin at her home and Mila at her shop. Farrah's car was vandalized in a public parking lot, after she thought someone had followed her from her apartment building. Crenshaw's car was hit at the university when he and I were at the museum. I shuddered as the realization set in. This person knew a lot, was practically omniscient, and seemed to relish scaring me.

Then I thought about the phony job posting. That had to be the work of the same person. After finding the spy cam last spring, I'd realized it was being used to sabotage my law practice. Was that what this was all about? The fake job posting had certainly caused a disruption to my work and life.

It was all really juvenile, when I thought about it. Now I was more irritated than scared.

By the time I sat behind the wheel of my own car, on the street by my office, my fear had somewhat dissipated. I was especially relieved to see that all four of my tires were completely fine. The vandal could have cut them like the others and hadn't. *Why?*

Probably to keep me on edge.

Before driving off, I picked up my cell phone and called Detective Rhinehardt. He wasn't available, so I left a message. Next, I started to call Wes, then reconsidered. He would only worry, and there was nothing he could do in Chicago. In fact, there was nothing much *I* could do here in Edindale. I decided to go back to the mansion.

On the way, I kept looking in my rearview mirror. This latest incident wasn't going to help my peace of mind. At least the happenings at Turnbull Manor weren't about me. Puzzling through whatever was going on there was actually a good distraction from my own worries.

I let myself in the front door and heard voices in the grand hall. Farrah and Crenshaw were at the base of the staircase, on their way up. They came over when they saw me come in.

"Hey, Kel!" chirped Farrah. "You just missed lunch, but there's still soup simmering on the stove. How was work?"

"Fine." I would fill her in later. I didn't feel like giving the prankster-terrorist any more of my energy right now. "What's going on here?"

"We finished our inventory of the wine cellar," said Crenshaw. "Now we're going to tackle the east wing second-floor sitting room. It's stuffed with antiques, including a cabinet of memorabilia from Harold's mining company."

"Have you seen Suzanne?" I asked. "I really need to talk to her."

"She was late to lunch," said Crenshaw. "She might still be in the dining room."

I told Farrah and Crenshaw I would catch up to them later. As it happened, Suzanne was just getting up from the table when I entered the dining room. I intercepted her before she could leave. "Hi there. Can I chat with you for a minute?"

She looked at her wrist, as if her tennis bracelet were a watch. "Sorry, hon. I have someplace I need to be."

"Please? It's important and won't take long."

She looked at me expectantly, her eyes telling me I should just get to the point.

"We have another promising lead on where Lana might be," I said. "She might be staying with an old friend. Can you remember any of her friends from school? Was there anyone she was especially close with?"

Suzanne slumped her shoulders. "Don't you think the police asked me the same thing when she ran away? I've already been down that road. She had playmates when she was a child. By the time she started high school, she had stopped talking to me. She never brought anyone home, and she never talked about anyone special. At least not to me."

"Oh. Well, did she happen to leave behind any scrapbooks or diaries? Anything like that?"

She shook her head. "Nothing of any use. Like I said, I've already been down this road."

A scrape at the door drew our attention. Suzanne narrowed her eyes. Without warning, she yanked the door open—causing Celia to stumble into the room.

"Aha!" said Suzanne. "I knew it! You're always spying on people, aren't you? Trying to spice up your dull little life? Is that it?" She brushed past the maid and stalked out of the room. I stared after her in dismay. *Was that really called for?*

"Wow," I said to Celia. "She's over the top, isn't she? I think she's under a lot of stress right now. I'm sure she didn't mean what she said."

I didn't know why I was making excuses for Suzanne. Anyway, Celia didn't seem the least bit embarrassed. She looked after Suzanne with a mean glint in her eye. "The only thing that gives her stress," she spat, "is the thought of cleaning her own toilets."

Yikes. Evidently there was no love lost between Suzanne and Celia.

She started to leave, but I stopped her. "Maybe you can help me," I said. "I don't think Suzanne was very close with her daughter. You might know more about Lana than she does."

"I don't know anything."

I didn't believe her. She had her ear to the ground— and the door. I was sure she knew things.

She moved for the exit again, but I was quicker. I blocked her way, like a goalie on a soccer field. "Celia, *I* know something you might be interested in."

That got her attention. "What do you know?"

"I know you lied about your whereabouts the night Elaine died."

She hadn't seen that coming. Fear flashed across her face, and for a moment I was afraid she might faint. I continued more gently. "If you tell me what I want to know, I . . . I won't tell the cops you didn't really leave the house that night."

If I lie to a liar, is it still wrong? Yeah. But I was pretty sure Crenshaw had been keeping Rhinehardt updated on all we'd learned, so I wouldn't have to break any promises to Celia. Technically speaking.

"What do you want to know?" she asked warily.

"I want to know about Lana as a teenager. What was she like? What did she do for fun? And who did she hang out with?"

The old woman squinted, as if trying to remember. "She was a quiet girl. She liked to draw and swim. She worked on puzzles with Elaine sometimes. She played golf with her father sometimes."

"She was close to Jim?"

"Oh, yes. He doted on her. I wouldn't say she was spoiled exactly, even though she was an only child. But he would do anything for her—even if Suzanne didn't approve." There was that look of distaste again. Celia really didn't think much of Suzanne.

"Lana wasn't a popular girl. She was the shy type." Celia wrinkled her forehead as she thought. "But she was on the school swim team for a year or two. She had a friend on the team who came over to swim a few times."

"Oh?" Now we were getting somewhere. "What was the girl's name?"

"Let's see . . . Jenny something. She was a skinny little thing. Jenny . . . Burg. That's it."

"Jenny Burg. Great. Anyone else?"

"I don't think so. Lana would go off and spend time by herself a lot. She'd go sit down by the pond and draw. Especially when her parents were fighting."

"Suzanne and Jim fought?"

"Something fierce. Suzanne even moved out of the mansion, which goes to show how angry she was. Of course, she still came back a lot to get things. And eat the food, drink the wine, and leave her dirty clothes." Celia sneered.

"How long had Jim and Suzanne been separated before he had his accident?"

"A few months. They fought that very morning, you know."

"On the day he died? What did they fight about?"

Celia shrugged. "I didn't hear them myself. Elaine did. I remember she came downstairs with a headache, complaining about the noise. She asked me to fix her tea and call Ray to come see her."

"So, Ray was here on the day Jim died, too?"

"He was here a lot." She shifted on her feet. "Can I go now?"

"I have just one more question. Why did you tell Detective Rhinehardt you left with the caterer the other night?"

For a second, I could have sworn she gave me a calculating look. Then she seemed to shrink in on herself, looking like nothing more than a tired, elderly woman. "I get mixed up sometimes. I meant to go with them. I've gone before. I guess I went to lie down instead."

I let her go after that. It wasn't until later that I remembered the caterer had corroborated her story. Why would she do that unless Celia had asked her friend to cover for her? Celia was definitely still hiding something.

The rest of the day passed uneventfully. In the evening, Celia said she wasn't feeling well, so everyone would have to fend for themselves for dinner. I felt slightly guilty. I hoped I hadn't badgered her to the point of sickness. More likely, though, she probably just wanted to avoid further questions.

Suzanne announced she was going out to dinner with a friend, and Perry mentioned he was leaving for an Arts Council meeting. Ray and Ernesto each grabbed some food to take to their own places—Ernesto moving so fast, he was in and out before I could even form a complete sentence.

Farrah, Crenshaw, and I ended up ordering pizza. Crenshaw was skeptical about trying pizza without cheese, but it was so loaded with veggies and spices that he forgot to complain. We sat at the kitchen table, drinking flavored seltzer water and discussing our next steps.

"The asset inventory is almost complete," said Crenshaw. "All that remains to search is the attic storeroom. I also need to review Perry's inventory of the Turnbull art collection."

"What about all the guesthouses?" asked Farrah. "And the occupied bedrooms in the mansion?"

"I covered that on my first day here," he said. "I walked through each resident's quarters with the respective resident, and we made a list together. That way they could point out what belonged to the manor and what was their own personal property."

"How do you know everyone told you the truth?" I asked. I didn't fully trust anyone who lived here.

"It was fairly obvious. No one claimed to own any of the antique furniture."

"So much for our excuse to search their rooms," said Farrah, obviously disappointed.

Crenshaw shook his head. "I'm not convinced you would have found anything anyhow. Perhaps it's true that Elaine indicated to Ray that she was making another will, but she could have easily changed her mind. Regardless, I intend to proceed under the existing will on Monday." He gave me a questioning look. "Do you think Lana is going to come forward?"

"I think we're close to locating her. Whether or not she comes forward is an open question."

For the next few minutes, we ate in silence. The one thing we hadn't discussed was the mystery of Elaine's death. It seemed like an impossible quandary. Any evidence there might have been had most likely been destroyed. Short of receiving a confession, I didn't see how we could ever prove she had been murdered. The thought was depressing.

Farrah wiped her mouth and regarded Crenshaw thoughtfully. He and I waited for her to say what was on her mind. I hoped she had come up with another avenue for us to pursue.

She scrunched up her pretty forehead and pointed her finger at my colleague. "Crenshaw . . . *William* Davenport. Is that it?"

He pursed his lips into an amused smirk. "No."

"Alistair? No, wait—I already guessed that one, didn't I? Is your middle name . . . Mortimer?"

"No."

I took my plate to the sink and washed it off. "I'm gonna go call Wes," I said, taking out my cell phone.

"Tell him 'hi' for me!" said Farrah.

Instead of going upstairs, I ambled up and down the halls as I made the call. He picked up right away.

"Hey, babe. One more day! By this time tomorrow, we'll be together again."

"I can't wait! Will you make it in time for the gala?"

"It'll be close, especially if the train runs late, but I'll do my best. I'll have to go home and change, of course."

"You should come, even if you're late. And bring an overnight bag. I'll tell Farrah she'll have to get another room tomorrow night."

"Aren't you ready to come home yet?"

In my meandering, I had ended up near the library. I slipped inside and turned on the overhead light. "Not yet," I said. "There are too many unanswered questions here—not only about Lana and Elaine, but also about the people who live here." I told him about all the false and questionable alibis, as well as the strange behavior of some of the residents. While we talked, I strolled along the bookshelves, casually running my free hand over some of the spines.

"Wait a minute," said Wes. "Are you saying *everyone* is guilty? Like some sort of conspiracy?"

I paused, considering the possibility. "Wouldn't that be a fine plot twist? Only, this isn't an Agatha Christie novel. And besides, some of the people here don't even seem to like each other."

"I'm not sure that matters."

"True. Anyway, on another note, have you reached out to any of your former classmates yet?"

"I've made a couple calls. I'll do more tomorrow and this weekend."

"I have a name for you to try. Do you remember a girl named Jenny Burg?"

"Jenny? Yeah, sure. She was a nice kid. Smart, as I recall. Why? What about her?"

I told him what Celia had shared, about Jenny and Lana being on the swim team together. "She might be the friend Lana is staying with."

"Huh. I'm surprised you told me this," said Wes. "You could have looked her up yourself and won our bet." He sounded slightly suspicious, as if it might be a trick.

"Honestly, I don't care about that anymore. I hope you do find Lana, Wes. I feel like time is running—"

Thump.

I froze, my eyes shooting to the closed door of the gun room. The sound had come from within.

"What is it?" Wes asked. "What's the matter?"

I tried the doorknob. It was locked. I put my ear to the door. I thought I heard another sound, a light scuffling, so faint it might have been my imagination. But I hadn't imagined the first noise.

"Keli?" said Wes.

"It's nothing," I whispered. "But I gotta go. I'll call you later."

I hung up and ran down the hall, all the way back to the kitchen. Farrah was wiping down the table and Crenshaw was tying off a trash bag. They looked startled to see me. I told them what I'd heard and urged Crenshaw to come and unlock the gun room.

A minute later, we all three entered the small, den-like room and looked around. Nothing appeared to be out of place. There were no antlers on the floor or guns on the bottoms of any cabinets. There was nothing to explain the thud I'd heard.

Farrah circled the room with a curious air, then bent down to run her fingers over the bearskin rug. "Shagadelic," she joked.

Crenshaw was more serious, as he eyed me with concern. Whether he was worried about the strange noise or concerned for my mental health, I wasn't sure. "Perhaps you heard Celia walking around upstairs," he said. "In old houses—"

"Stop," I said, holding up a palm. "I know what you're going to say, and you're right. It could have been anything: creaking walls, old plumbing, somebody dropping something upstairs."

He visibly relaxed. "Very well. No harm done."

"Right. Just a little paranoia, that's all."

And who could blame me?

Chapter Twenty-Five

I was afraid I would have trouble sleeping, but somehow I managed. Maybe I was just exhausted from being on edge for so long. Either way, sleep came as a relief. I awoke with the sun on Friday morning, feeling remarkably refreshed. I slipped out of bed without waking Farrah and hurried to get dressed so I could go outside.

The world was quiet and peaceful under the clear autumn sky. I strolled around the grounds, enjoying the fresh air. I hoped the weather would remain this pleasant for the gala. Crenshaw had mentioned the festivities might spill outside, which made perfect sense with gardens this lovely.

I wandered over to the western edge of the property where fat pine cones littered the ground. Out of habit, I started collecting them until my arms were so full, I wound up dropping them all. I laughed at myself. Was this a sign that I was trying to take on too much at once? *Just like the squirrel from my astral visit with Elaine in the parlor.*

Picking up the spilled pine cones, I arranged them

like an offering at the base of a tall pine tree. Then I pocketed a small, cute one and headed over to the side of the mansion where the walnut trees grew outside the parlor window. Elaine had pointed to the window twice in my vision. Was there something out here I was meant to see?

The recently mown lawn sloped gently away from the house. There was nothing much to see on the ground besides a few sticks and walnuts and the first of the fallen leaves. I picked up a green walnut and rubbed the bumpy hull with my thumb and fingers. There were no clues out here—except for nature's subtle reminders to pay attention to the beauty all around. A song sparrow whistled overhead, and I smiled.

Not yet ready to go inside, I headed toward the gardens, then veered off track toward Ray's cottage. The last I saw him in the mansion, he'd said something about helping Celia with the dusting this morning. I wondered if that was where he was now. His windows were dark, and Ray didn't strike me as the type of person who slept late. I walked up to the front door and knocked. There was no answer, either human or canine. After a moment, I went to the side door, which led to Ray's studio. Thinking he might be taking advantage of the early-morning light, I tapped on the door. Again, there was no answer.

I could hear Farrah's voice inside my head. *We need to snoop! We need to search the occupied rooms!*

What would I find in Ray's place? Did he know more than he was telling us about Elaine's will? And was he or wasn't he walking his dog when she drank her final gulp of cinnamon milk?

"Keli?"

I whirled, placing my hand on my heart—the same hand that had been about to reach for Ray's doorknob.

"Detective Rhinehardt! What are you doing here?"

"I was looking for you. Crenshaw said you might be out here."

"He was right. Here I am." I laughed sheepishly and walked away from the door.

"How's your search going?" he asked.

"Not great," I said bluntly.

"Any other incidents here you need to tell me about?"

"Not really." *Unless you count things that go bump in the night. Or bump in the daytime, as the case may be.* "However, we've identified holes in everyone's alibi for the time Elaine was likely killed."

"Crenshaw told me about that. But I still don't have evidence a crime was committed." He held up his hand to keep me from speaking. "I need something concrete. Conjecture isn't enough."

I kicked at a patch of fallen leaves.

"Let's walk," said Rhinehardt, heading back to the path. We moved farther away from the mansion, following a trail I hadn't yet explored. Before long, we came to a thatched roof cabana next to the covered swimming pool. We were on the back side of the cabana, so I couldn't see inside. From what I could tell, it had probably been charming in its day. It was now a bit shabby and forlorn from lack of use. We continued on down the hill toward the grove of trees.

"Did Crenshaw tell you I'd like a copy of an old police report?" I asked. "I'm still trying to figure out why Lana ran away when she was seventeen."

"Yeah, he told me. And I looked into it. But the report won't tell you much."

I glanced over at him. "You've seen it?"

He nodded. "It basically says that two officers responded to an emergency call at Turnbull Manor at four P.M. on November thirtieth. A family friend made the call."

"Perry Warren?"

"Yes. The shooting was ruled an accident and the report was closed out."

"That's it? Wasn't there an investigation?"

For a moment Rhinehardt didn't answer. I wondered if he felt conflicted about sharing so much with a layperson. But since the accident occurred so long ago, I didn't think it should matter.

He squinted against the morning sunlight. "Fact is, I thought the report was unusually brief myself. So, I paid a visit to the reporting officer. He's retired now, but I knew his name from some of the old-timers."

"What did he say? Did he remember the call?"

"Yes, he remembered. Seems he never thought the shooting was accidental."

"What?" I stopped in my tracks, forcing the detective to halt, too. By this time, we were quite a distance from the house. Out of the corner of my eye, I noticed an overgrown concrete structure and heard the trickle of water. I figured it must be the old springhouse Crenshaw had mentioned, but I wasn't interested in that now. "If he didn't think it was an accident, then why didn't he open an investigation?"

Rhinehardt sighed, clearly not happy about the situation. "The officers thought they were doing what was best. They wanted to spare the family any more heartache."

"You mean—?"

"They believed Jim had committed suicide."

"Oh. Well, the family had a right to know that."

"I agree. But there was no note, no definitive proof. The retired officer said it *could* have been an accident. Faced with a grieving widow, a grieving mother—also widowed—and a grieving daughter, they decided to go with the gentler explanation."

The air was cooler among the trees, but that's not why I shivered. My imagination had jumped to the past. Had Lana witnessed her father taking his own life? If so, it was no wonder she didn't want to come back to Turnbull Manor. And if she had heard her parents fight that very morning, maybe she blamed her mother for what had happened.

"It's so sad," I said softly.

"Yeah," Rhinehardt agreed. "There's no question about that."

Rhinehardt declined my offer of coffee and said he'd check in with me later. After breakfast, Farrah and I each went to our own homes for a little while to catch up on some work and pick out our dresses for the gala. I scrounged up some lunch while I was at my house. Before leaving, I decided to seek some spiritual guidance. I went up to my altar room, took out my favorite deck of tarot cards, and made myself comfortable in the center of the spare bed. As I shuffled the cards, I thought about all the questions roiling in my mind like smoke in a cauldron.

Did someone really murder Elaine Turnbull? If so, then why? For her money? Who stood to benefit from her death? Under the only will in evidence, Lana was the only one to benefit. Yet she had left her home, her family, and her privileged life fifteen years ago and never returned. *Again, why?*

Then there was the question of the mystery in my own life. Who in the world was messing with me—and what was the point? More importantly, what would the creep do next?

Suddenly, I felt a wave of vulnerability as I became aware of my solitude in the quiet house. I didn't even have Josie to keep me company. She had been content to prowl around the Turnbull mansion, so I let her stay behind.

Sunlight slanted through the window, illuminating dust mites in the air. I stared at the specks for a few breaths and consciously willed myself to calm down. When I returned to my shuffling, I asked myself what I most wanted to know.

Am I on the right track?

I drew the top card and turned it over. *The Lovers.* I stared at the card, perplexed. What did The Lovers have to do with anything? This was a card about relationships and connections. It also represented choice.

Did I have a choice to make?

When I returned to the mansion, there were unfamiliar people scurrying about, moving furniture, dusting, polishing, and mopping. Crenshaw had informed me he had hired extra help to ensure tonight would run smoothly. I found him setting up a velvet rope on gold stands in front of the paintings in the great room.

"How's it going?" I asked.

He turned and dusted off his hands. "Ah, Keli. I'd like you to meet—where did he go?"

A wiry, weathered-looking man came bounding around the corner. He wore a navy-blue security guard uniform and a broad grin.

Crenshaw beckoned the man to come forward. "Gus, this is my partner, Keli Milanni."

Still grinning, Gus shook my hand and bounced on his feet. He made me think of a tightly-wound spring.

"Keli," said Crenshaw, "Gus is on loan to us from the Edindale Art Museum—as are these ropes."

I smiled in return, slightly touched that Crenshaw had referred to me as his partner. I knew he hadn't been pleased when I left the law firm. I was also amused at Gus's apparent glee.

"I work part-time at the museum," Gus said. "I started my career as a roadie, traveling with bands around the country. Then I moved into security. I work security at concerts and festivals every summer."

"Cool."

"Yeah, it's a trip. No pun intended." He laughed, making me think his pun was totally intended. "This is my first gig at a private home. And, man, is this place palatial! Have you seen the guest bathroom? There's more marble in there than in my mother's kitchen."

"Yeah," I said agreeably. "I've been staying here all week."

"Lucky you!"

"I've been showing Gus around," said Crenshaw, looking slightly uneasy. "We'll try to confine the party to the first floor, with the exception of the gallery at the top of the stairs. Guests will enter through the front door, mingle in the great room and parlor, and points in between. We'll have a bar set up in the conservatory with the doors open to the patio. That's where the band will play and the scholarship will be announced."

"Should I check bags at the front door?" asked Gus.

"Check them for what?"

"You know. Drugs, alcohol, weapons."

Crenshaw touched his forehead as if it pained him. "This isn't a rock festival. Think of this as a museum. Your job is to keep people from touching the artwork."

"Gotcha," said Gus. "No problem."

"I'm going to take my dress upstairs," I said. "Is there anything I can do to help after that?"

"As a matter of fact, there is one thing. There are some chairs in the tool shed that need to be brought to the patio. Ernesto was going to do it, but he had to leave to pick up an outdoor canopy tent. And I need to finish placing these ropes and showing Gus around."

"No problem. I'll do it."

After a quick trip upstairs, I headed out back. The shed was a modern, metal structure near the garage. As I passed the steps leading up to Ernesto's apartment, I glanced up. Would I ever have a chance to talk to the guy? Maybe Farrah and I could corner him tonight.

I was nearly to the shed when I heard voices. It sounded like two men arguing. I slowed my steps and perked up my ears. As I drew closer, I dropped behind a hydrangea bush and listened. I recognized Perry's voice. He spoke rapidly and sounded nervous.

"Calm down, Ray! There's no need to get all worked up."

"Don't tell me to calm down!" Ray sounded angry and, from the shrill edge to his voice, "worked up."

"Really, listen to yourself," pleaded Perry.

"You listen to *me*. You—you—"

"Ray! Come on, now. All this stress isn't healthy. I'm worried about you. *Elaine* was worried about you."

"Don't you dare—" Ray tried to cut in, but Perry kept talking.

"Do you hear how paranoid you sound? All this nonsense about a missing will. You've got those poor lawyers tearing apart the house looking for a figment of your imagination. You need to face reality!"

"I know what you're doing," said Ray, his voice suddenly an octave lower. "I'm on to you."

"Okay, Ray. Whatever you say." It sounded like Perry was walking away. Would Ray go after him?

"You won't get away with this!" Ray hollered. A second later, he stormed past my hiding place. I peeked out from behind the bush and saw he was carrying two patio chairs.

"Looks like things are under control here," I muttered to myself. Avoiding the patio, I made my way around to the front of the house. I had no desire to run into Ray when he was in such a foul mood. From what I'd witnessed, his anger seemed positively . . . murderous.

Chapter Twenty-Six

I found Farrah in our room getting ready for the gala. She turned off the hair dryer and shook it at me.

"It's about time, girlfriend! I was starting to think you got lost."

"I got sidetracked." I told her about the exchange I'd overheard between Ray and Perry. "I don't know what started it, but Perry must have said something to ignite Ray's fury."

"Ray's a touchy one, isn't he?" Farrah remarked.

"Touchy as a time bomb." I looked at myself in the mirror and picked a small leaf out of my hair. "They were talking about Elaine's will—a subject that always seems to upset Ray. It sounded like Perry doesn't think Elaine ever made a second will."

"I tend to agree," said Farrah.

"You do?"

"Yeah. Ray is the only one who supposedly knows anything about it, and we haven't found any evidence to support his claim."

"You might be right." I thought again about seeing

Elaine in the parlor during my astral projection. Although she didn't say or do much, I'd felt sure she was communicating with me. I was going to have to figure out another way to contact her. Only she knew the truth.

Farrah moved aside so I could have more space at the mirror. "By the way," she said, "I passed Suzanne in the hallway a little while ago. She said she's sorry, but she doesn't have time to do our makeup after all."

I rolled my eyes. "Yeah, right. She just doesn't want to answer any more of my questions." It was just as well. I wasn't comfortable with Suzanne's heavy-handed approach to makeup anyway. After doing my own face and hair, I slipped on a long, jersey-knit gown in burgundy, with a front slit for easier walking. Farrah put on a royal blue cocktail dress, which accentuated the vivid blue of her eyes.

I sat down on the edge of the bed to pull on my strappy heels. Remembering something, I glanced over at Farrah, who was putting on a pair of earrings. "Hey, I meant to ask you—did you invite Randall to the gala?"

"Uh, no. He and I are splitsville."

"What? When did this happen?"

"A couple of days ago. I realized I didn't want to be exclusive with him and told him as much. It didn't go over very well."

"I can imagine." I stood up and moved to the mirror, making sure my updo was still up.

"At least I was honest. I'm always honest with guys."

"You *are* honest," I said. "It's one of your best qualities. You're true to yourself and unapologetic about it."

"Why should I apologize?"

"You shouldn't." I turned to face her. "That's my point. You're actually very inspiring to me."

"Aw. Thanks, Kel." She stood before me and brought

her finger to her chin. "If I'm being absolutely honest then, I must say . . . you look absolutely stunning."

I grinned. "So do you, sister."

"Now let's go solve a mystery."

Guests were slowly beginning to trickle in. It was early yet, so I decided to step outside for a few minutes of alone time near the trees. Farrah and I had decided to divide and conquer, working the crowd separately for a while. Our mission was to gather as much information as possible about all the suspects and their relationships with Elaine. Without any physical evidence, we would have to rely heavily on psychology and intuition—and see how far that would take us.

Because of my heels, I stayed on the stone path and didn't venture too far from the house. Twilight rippled across the sky, and a soft breeze rustled the leaves, sending forth an intoxicating, musky-earth scent. I breathed deeply and felt empowered. As I made my way back toward the mansion, I heard strains of music as the band tuned their instruments.

As lovely as the atmosphere was, I still couldn't help feeling a little twitchy. It might have been anticipation—I was eager to see Wes after being apart for five days. But that wasn't all. I couldn't shake the feeling that something was going to happen tonight. Something big. I touched my wrist tattoo and straightened my back. *Goddess, give me strength.*

I reentered the mansion through the kitchen door and caught a whiff of delicious-smelling hot hors d'oeuvres: puffed pastry, garlic, olive oil, and herbs. Even the spicy meatballs smelled mouthwateringly savory. Staff from Ruby Plate Catering buzzed from the kitchen to the dining room, where serving trays were laid out on the table for waiters to pick up and carry around.

Seeing the caterers hard at work made me think of Elaine's last dinner party. Maybe that was the cause for some of my jumpiness. In some ways, tonight was not unlike the night she died. Granted, the scale was much grander, but the caterer was the same, some of the guests were the same, even the art theme was the same.

I caught sight of a young man wearing a white bib apron over black pants and a crisp white shirt. I walked up to him and took a shot in the dark. "Trevor?"

"Yes?"

"I'm Keli. We spoke the other day about the dinner party here a couple weeks ago—and your mom's acquaintance with Celia Meeks."

He paled and looked quickly over his shoulder. "Oh, man, I shoulda never said anything. Can you just forget we talked?"

Yeah, right. I had to suppress a smile at the boy's naivete. "You didn't do anything wrong, Trevor. You only told the truth, right?"

"Yeah, but Mom said I might've got Cee Cee in trouble."

"Is your mom around? I'd like to talk to her."

Now sweat beads popped out on his forehead. "She's real busy."

"I don't want to get anybody in trouble, Trevor. I'm just trying to confirm what everybody was doing during the time Mrs. Turnbull passed away."

That was the wrong thing to say. Trevor staggered backward, almost knocking a tray off the table. I had to catch the tray and grab his arm to steady him. The moment I made contact, I tried an energetic technique I'd seen Mila use. I visualized peace and calmness flowing from me to Trevor like a soft, reassuring blue light. It lasted only a second, but he exhaled visibly. I released his arm.

"Okay, l—listen," he whispered. "I don't want my mom to get into trouble either."

"Why would she be in trouble?" I kept my voice and eyes gentle.

"She was only trying to help. Cee Cee is a nice lady, but she's getting old. She should probably retire. Anyway, she told my mom that after we left that night, she went to her room instead of finishing up her work. She asked Mom to back her up and say she came with us to the food pantry."

"Is that all?"

"Yes, I swear! My mom said she wasn't under oath when the cops questioned her. But if they ask again, she'll tell the truth."

I nodded soberly. "She really should have told the truth in the first place. But I'm glad you're both being truthful now."

I reached for a spinach tartlet and raised it like a toast. Then I left Trevor to his work. I didn't think there was anything more to learn from him or his mother. Either Celia had told Sylvia the truth, in which case she hadn't killed Elaine. Or else she lied to her friend, in which case she was still a suspect. Given her propensity to tell falsehoods, I was inclined to believe the latter.

By now, the house was filling up. Some of the guests mingled in the great room and upstairs gallery, but most seemed to migrate to the conservatory and patio. I said hello to Mavis, the museum director, who introduced me to her husband. They were chatting with Perry and another member of the Arts Council. As we made small talk, I noticed Ray standing by himself in a corner near a potted palm tree. He appeared to be brooding.

At the first lull in the conversation, I excused myself and headed toward Ray. But before I could reach him, he turned suddenly, as if something had caught his eye. Following his gaze, I spotted Ernesto. Apparently, the groundskeeper saw Ray at the same time—he turned tail and slipped out the open French doors. Ray went after him. *What are they up to?*

I followed Ray, who trailed Ernesto through the crowd on the patio, then out toward the gardens. At one point, Ray paused and looked over his shoulder. I ducked behind a sculpted tree shaped like a rabbit. When he continued onward, so did I. I shadowed him in this fashion along the outer edge of the English garden. Before long, I realized he was moving in a zigzag pattern. Then he abruptly altered course and headed toward the rear of the carriage house garage. I wondered if Ernesto was toying with Ray. Or maybe he'd noticed him and changed his planned destination.

Ray slowed down, shortening the distance between us. The whole time, I was being extra careful not to make a peep. I watched every step to make sure I wouldn't crunch on a twig underfoot. I thought I was being the consummate private eye—until my cell phone rang.

Ray whipped around so fast I had no time to hide. All I could do was act as normal as possible. Ignoring Ray, I pulled my phone out of my clutch and answered cheerily. "Hello!"

"Hey, babe." It was Wes. "I have good news and bad news."

I walked back toward the house, already forgetting about Ray and Ernesto. "What's up? Where are you?"

"I'm here in Edindale. My train was on time, but my car is out of commission. Somebody—"

"Slashed your tires?"

"Yeah. Just like Farrah's. Can you believe it?"

I could definitely believe it. So much had been going on, I hadn't told him about all the other incidents—or my theory about who was behind it.

"My car was in the railroad station lot all week," he continued. "So, there's no telling when it happened. Probably overnight earlier in the week, I'd guess."

"Me, too." Did the vandal follow him to the station from our house? Or did the creep already know about Wes's trip—and know what Wes's car looked like? I didn't like either possibility, nor did I want to ponder either one right now. "You'll still come to the manor, won't you?"

"Absolutely. It'll just be a while yet."

Wes and I said our good-byes as I crossed the patio and entered the conservatory. Farrah was in there, chatting up the bartender. We each gave the other a questioning look. No doubt she wondered where I'd been, while I wondered if she was investigating or flirting. Before we had a chance to catch up, the band stopped playing and Mavis Rawlins took the microphone. We made our way outside to listen.

"Ladies and gentlemen," Mavis began. "Thank you all for coming tonight. As you know, this is a bittersweet occasion, as we honor the life and legacy of our own Elaine Turnbull."

As Mavis spoke, I scanned the crowd for familiar faces. I recognized several people, including Gus, the security guard. He stood on the perimeter of the patio with his arms crossed, like a bouncer ready to block fangirls from storming the stage. I inwardly rolled my eyes and kept looking around. A few guests seemed to be missing—but not Ray. He must have abandoned his pursuit of Ernesto. Solemn and doleful, he stood close to the front, even helping to usher guests on and off the dais. Several people took a turn at the microphone to offer words of praise and admiration for Elaine. Of course, Crenshaw was one of them. I had never known him to pass up an opportunity for the spotlight. Surprisingly, his remarks were short and sweet.

At the conclusion of the tribute, the band played another number, and then began to pack up. Guests moved indoors, but there was no indication the party was winding down. People continued to talk, drink, and move from room to room. Bluesy jazz standards now played through a sound system in the conservatory.

Farrah ordered two martinis at the bar and handed one to me. She raised her glass. "To Elaine, a woman of fine taste and many admirers. I wish I'd known her."

"I'll second that." I took a sip from my glass, then touched Farrah's elbow. "Hey, look who just came in. Xavier Charleston."

Xavier glided from guest to guest, greeting people like he was some kind of celebrity. In fact, he looked the part. With his expensive tuxedo and glossy black hair, he exuded confidence. Even his beard appeared stylish, rather than shaggy.

"He doesn't stay in one place for long, does he?" said Farrah, her eyes following him around the room. A moment later, he headed for the French doors leading outside.

"I want to talk to him," I said, "and see if I can confirm Perry's alibi."

"I'll do it," said Farrah, raising her hand like a good little volunteer.

Before I could respond, Crenshaw walked up to us. "Ladies, I'm about to bring out Harold's Lalique glass collection to show the Arts Council. Some of the finer pieces are in a curio cabinet in the formal sitting room off the great room. Would you like to come along?"

Farrah withdrew her hand. "On second thought, Kel, you should be the one to question Mr. C this time." She took Crenshaw's arm and allowed him to lead her away.

I stepped outside and looked around. The patio was empty now, as everyone had gone inside. As I walked toward the English garden, I perceived a faint, sweet aroma drifting through the air. It disappeared as suddenly as it had begun. Peering through the dimly lit gardens, I spotted Xavier leaning against a fountain ledge in the shadow of a giant mermaid statue. He was vaping on a flavored e-cigarette.

"Hello," I said, walking toward him. "Nice night."

"It's a marvelous night," he said, his voice soft and gravelly.

"A bit chilly, though," I added, shivering as a sudden breeze lifted the hem of my dress.

He took a drag on his e-cigarette, releasing a cloud of vapor that momentarily obscured his whole head. Even when it cleared, I couldn't see his face well in the darkness. Still, I had the distinct impression he was scrutinizing me—like he would a monarch under a magnifying glass.

"You look familiar," he drawled. "Have we met?"

"I don't think so. I'm Keli Milanni." I would have offered my hand, but he made no move in my direction. In fact, he appeared quite content to remain where he was.

"Keli Milanni," he repeated, slowly, as if tasting the letters of my name.

"And you're Xavier Charleston, right? Art collector and friend of Perry Warren?"

"It would seem you know more about me than I do about you," he said, with a hint of amusement in his voice. "Are you single?"

For a moment, I was thrown off guard by the forward question. "Uh, no," I stammered. "I'm in a relationship."

"Too bad."

I swallowed and tried to remember what I wanted to ask him. "So, what brings you to Edindale?"

"I'm here on business."

"Art business?"

"Yes. Art business. I'm a buyer for a gallery in LA. I'm on a Midwest tour this month, meeting with a few private collectors in the area." He took another draw on his e-cigarette, releasing the vapor from his mouth like a well-mannered dragon. "Do you think the Turnbull Estate will be settled anytime soon?"

"Good question."

The patter of paws drew my attention, and Barney came into view. I held out my hand to pet him, but he bypassed me and went straight for the bushes. With one short bark, he sniffed and snuffled until he succeeded in drawing out his prey.

"Go away, dog!" she cried. "Not now!"

I narrowed my eyes when I recognized her. *Celia.* Again with the spying. As soon as she noticed I was staring at her, she straightened to her full five feet and stalked off without a word. I shook my head.

"She's something else," I began—until I realized I was

alone by the fountain. Xavier was gone. "*He's* something else, too," I muttered to myself.

So much for my interrogation. Why was everyone avoiding me? If I didn't know better, I might start weaving conspiracies myself.

Chapter Twenty-Seven

I went back inside to catch up with Farrah and Crenshaw. I made it to the great room, and was passing by the staircase, when strong, bony fingers wrapped around my arm. I winced and almost cried out, until I saw it was Winston Betz. He squinted up at me behind thick glasses, looking for all the world like a geriatric owl. He let go of my arm as soon as he had my attention.

"Young lady," he rasped. "Have you seen Miss Suzanne?"

"Not lately. Sorry."

"She went upstairs ages ago. I'm going after her." He put one knobby hand on the bannister and raised his cane to the first step.

"I'll go find her," I said quickly. "Why don't you wait right here. I'll be back in a jiffy."

This mansion is definitely not elder-friendly, I thought, as I hurried up the steps. How awful it would be if poor old Winston tumbled down the stairs.

Suzanne's bedroom was in the east wing, next to the

guest room Crenshaw was using. I knocked on her door and waited. Then I knocked again.

"Suzanne? Are you in there? It's Keli."

She opened the door, looking slightly rumpled. I wondered if she had been taking a nap. "Keli! What can I do for you?"

"Winston is looking for you. I'm just saving him a trip up the stairs."

"Oh! Good. You're such a doll. I had to get away and take some aspirin. My head was killing me. Let me just . . ." She trailed off as she reached behind her for a beaded handbag. Standing in the hallway, she pulled out a compact mirror and a tube of lipstick, then touched up her lips while pulling the door shut behind her. She headed down the hall, patting her hair. "I can't leave him waiting. He's so impatient."

I started to follow her, then glanced back at her door. It didn't shut all the way. *Hmm.*

I took a few more steps in the direction Suzanne had hurried off. As soon as she turned toward the gallery, I tiptoed back to her room. The opportunity to do a little snooping was too perfect to pass up. Quiet as a whisper, I let myself in and shut the door behind me.

She hadn't bothered to turn off her light. Apparently, she didn't bother to do much tidying either. The room was a cluttered mess. Boxes of Carrie Cosmetics vied for floor space with discarded clothes. The tops of both nightstands and the dresser were a jumble of hair accessories, jewelry, and knickknacks. The bed was unmade.

Where to begin?

Halfheartedly, I pulled open a dresser drawer and stared at a pile of filmy lingerie. I closed the drawer. I was rapidly losing my nerve. This didn't feel right. Who was I kidding? It *wasn't* right.

Gazing around the room once more, I noticed two closed doors—presumably the bathroom and closet. I opened the closet, then quickly closed it, lest I release an avalanche of clothes and shoes. With my back to the closet door, my eyes fell upon an open rolltop desk in the opposite corner. I moved closer. The writing surface was covered with customer invoices and receipts for Suzanne's makeup sales. The top shelf served as a display table for framed photographs of Suzanne herself: in her tennis outfit, dolled up in an evening gown, and even a glamourous headshot.

Without touching anything, I peered into the desk's cubbyholes. Nothing struck me as particularly interesting, until I noticed a slightly crinkled portfolio lying on an inner shelf. Carefully, I pulled it out, opened the cover, and turned a few pages. It was an artist's portfolio, filled with pencil drawings. They seemed quite good to me, in my non-expert opinion. I glanced at the signature: *Lana T.* No wonder the portfolio had an aged look to it. It must have been more than fifteen years old.

As I gently turned the pages, I noted the wide variety of subjects, from botanical still lifes and figure drawings to abstract cubist designs. It was touching to me that Lana's mother was keeping this reminder of her daughter in her room.

A sound from the bathroom jolted me back to the present. I froze, as I stared at the bathroom door. *Not again.* This was the third time I'd heard a noise on the other side of a closed door. Was I going crazy?

Gingerly, I replaced the portfolio on the shelf where I'd found it. If Suzanne's bathroom was like the others

I'd seen in this house, I knew there would be a small anteroom, with a dressing table and shelves, which led to the actual facilities. From what I'd seen of Suzanne's housekeeping habits, this space was probably over-flowing with clutter, too.

Another noise broke the silence. This time it sounded like a shoe dropping. I started across the room, making a beeline for the exit. I was even with the bathroom, when the door swung open.

I found myself face to face with Ernesto Cruz. He appeared as stunned as I felt. Though, by the look of things, he might have been even more surprised than me. His hair was damp, his shirt was open, and his belt was loose. He looked as if he'd just gotten out of the shower.

Why would Ernesto be taking a shower in Suzanne's room?

Ohhh. There was only one plausible explanation. Suzanne and Ernesto were having an affair. No wonder she didn't want anyone to come upstairs.

After a fleeting standoff, Ernesto made the first move, bolting from the room. I didn't go after him. I was just glad I didn't have to explain myself. At least for now.

I left the room and closed the door behind me. Ernesto had probably taken the back stairs. I made my way to the front stairs and down to the great room, as casual as could be. Several guests still mingled around the paintings, but the party seemed to be winding down. Suzanne and Winston were nowhere in sight.

I was on my way to the sitting room to find Farrah, when I sensed a strong male presence at my shoulder. Turning, I took in a snazzy, charcoal suit, a skinny tie, and alluring dark stubble across the lower half of a heartbreakingly handsome face.

"Wes!"

We embraced, and just like that I felt a million times better.

"You look *amazing*," he said, holding me at arm's length. "Why was I gone for so long? I must have been out of my mind."

Grinning, I slipped my hand in his. I was about to lead him upstairs, when Celia sidled over. She looked from Wes to me with a strange glint in her eye. "Who's this? I thought the other gentleman was your beau. The one you were whispering with, all alone in the garden."

I stared at her, dumbfounded. What was her problem anyway? She eyed Wes, waiting for his reaction. He raised his eyebrows, then frowned.

"Where is that scoundrel, Crenshaw?" he asked, in mock frustration. "I need to challenge him to a duel—not pistols at dawn, but cameras. I'm sure I can outshoot him."

I tossed my head like a tease. "Actually, Crenshaw isn't the man Celia saw. It was someone else."

"Oh, ho! You've been busy, have you?" He draped his arm over my shoulders, and we sauntered off together, leaving Celia befuddled at this turn of events. Apparently, she wasn't accustomed to a couple who actually trusted each other.

We went upstairs, so Wes could drop off his bag in the guest room. It was tempting to shut the door behind us and call it a night. But Farrah still had her things spread out all over the room. Plus, I was dying to swap stories with her and analyze what we'd learned tonight.

"Are you hungry?" I asked as Wes and I left the guest room. "We can take the back stairs down to the kitchen and see what's left of the party food."

"Sounds good to me."

When we reached the kitchen, the caterers were cleaning up. I intercepted Trevor, who was carrying a bag to a van parked in the driveway. He handed Wes a box of cheesy bacon crostini, which Wes noshed on as we moved on to the conservatory. The bartender was packing up there, too, but he gave Wes a beer and me a bottle of sparkling water. A few guests lingered at a table under the hanging ferns, but Farrah and Crenshaw were nowhere to be seen.

"They must be up front," I said. We took the west hallway and passed the parlor, which was dark. As we rounded the corner into the great room, I heard voices saying good-night, and then the click of the front door. The formal sitting room was also empty, so we headed to the east hallway. Maybe our friends were in the library.

Wes had finished his snack and once again rested his arm lightly on my shoulders. As we crossed the great room, I halted suddenly, causing him to swing forward.

"Whoa, babe. You all right?"

I didn't reply. I was staring at the wall, at a blank space between two paintings. There had been something in that space the last time I'd looked; I was sure of it.

"What's the matter?" asked Wes.

"Something's missing," I said. Pulling Wes with me, I approached the velvet rope Crenshaw had borrowed from the museum. I pointed at the wall. "There should be a painting in this spot. A Grant Wood."

Wes looked down. "Is that it?" He indicated the floor, where a painting leaned against the wall, facedown.

"What's that doing there?" I asked. Something was definitely off.

"Maybe the hanger broke." Wes leaned down and picked up the picture by the top of the frame.

"Be careful," I said. "That's a valuable—"

I broke off as he turned the object over. "Frame?" he asked, as if finishing my sentence. For that's all it was. An empty frame. The canvas was gone.

Chapter Twenty-Eight

My first inclination was to yell for help and raise an alarm. But there was no alarm to pull, and hollering in the middle of the mansion seemed a little ridiculous. So, I pulled out my phone and called Crenshaw.

"Where are you?" I demanded when he picked up.

"Hello to you, too," he said dryly. "I'm in the library with Farrah, Perry, and Gus. We're discussing security matters. I'm working on a plan for Gus to remain on duty here for the next few weeks."

"You might want to reconsider that plan." *At least, the part that involves Gus.*

"Why do you say that?"

"Could you come to the great room, please? We have a problem."

A few minutes later, he saw what I meant. "Good Lord! What happened here?"

"Oh, my gosh!" said Farrah, coming up behind him.

"You've been robbed, buddy," said Wes, clapping Crenshaw on the shoulder.

Perry pushed past Crenshaw to get a closer look. "Oh, no," he groaned. "Not the Grant Wood. That was a two-hundred-thousand-dollar painting. One of the best in the collection."

Gus scratched his head, looking confused. Crenshaw took out his phone to call the police. The moment he hung up, we all stared at one another for a second of silence. Then, of one accord, we jumped into action. Crenshaw and Gus started yelling at each other: Crenshaw alternately accusing the guard of negligence and grilling him for information, and Gus making excuses and deflecting blame.

"Come on," I said to Farrah, Wes, and Perry. "Let's see who's still here and direct everyone to gather in the great room."

They nodded, and we all dashed off like players in a scavenger hunt. Perry took the front of the house, Farrah ran upstairs, and Wes jogged down the west wing. I hurried along the east wing, looking in each room along the way.

When I reached the kitchen, I heard more yelling. It was coming from right outside the kitchen door. I pulled it open and found Suzanne and Ernesto standing under the porch light, facing each other like boxers in a ring. Their fists weren't raised, but their voices were. It sounded like Ernesto was denying some sort of wrongdoing, and Suzanne wasn't buying it.

"Gimme a break!" she shouted, her voice shrill with emotion. "I know you're hiding—" She broke off abruptly when she saw me.

"What is he hiding?" I asked.

"Never mind," said Suzanne, looking away. Ernesto looked like he was about to flee again.

"Could you two please come with me?" I watched them closely to gauge their reactions. "A painting has been stolen, and the police are on their way."

Suzanne gasped theatrically, and Ernesto clenched

his jaw. They came along without argument, Suzanne sputtering questions I couldn't answer. We reached the great room just as Farrah was coming downstairs with Celia. Wes had rounded up Ray, the bartender, and two very tipsy council members. Perry reported that there were no other cars parked outside, so we knew we had found everyone.

For a moment, everyone fell into a shocked silence as they stared at the empty frame. Then the police arrived, and we all began speaking at once.

"Who would do such a thing?"

"How could this happen?"

"I never saw this coming."

"Who was in charge of security, anyway?"

Crenshaw flushed at the last question, which had come from Ray. I could tell my buddy felt responsible, and I felt bad for him. I stepped forward to give my statement first, as much to deflect attention from him as to get the investigation started. After introducing myself to the two patrol officers, I explained how I'd discovered the theft. The cops then spoke to each person in turn, while Crenshaw and Perry worked on putting together a list of all the gala attendees, from the guests and the staff, to the caterers and the entertainment.

I was pacing up and down the great room when Detective Rhinehardt arrived. I took him aside and filled him in. He seemed more curious than concerned.

"Somebody walked off with a painting worth two hundred grand?" he asked. "Right out the front door?"

"I don't know if they used the front door. There are three doors to the outside, and people were using all three this evening." I tilted my head as I looked around the spacious room. "Actually, we don't even know if it was taken out. It could have been hidden somewhere in the mansion."

I snapped my fingers. "We need to search the house! And all the guesthouses! The thief could have stashed the painting anywhere."

He rubbed his chin thoughtfully. "The residents here are like tenants, even if they don't pay rent. Without a warrant, I can't search their personal space unless I have probable cause to believe they committed a crime. I'm not seeing PC here."

"You don't need PC if they consent. I'll ask."

I rejoined the group and clapped my hands for attention. "Hey, everybody! I have a special request."

Driven by a sense of urgency, I laid out my proposal. There was no time to waste. If the painting was hidden on the premises, I doubted it would remain so for long.

The occupants of Turnbull Manor looked at one another with a mixture of discomfort and distrust. I was sure they understood that to object would only make them look suspicious.

Ray was the first to speak up. "I don't see the point. The painting is probably long gone. And nobody could've entered my cottage anyway. The doors are locked and Barney would've raised a ruckus." Scowling, he shook his head like a martyr. "But I've got nothing to hide. Let's get this over with."

Suzanne laughed nervously. "I have nothing to hide either, of course. But my room is a bit of a mess." I shifted uncomfortably at that and carefully avoided meeting Ernesto's eyes. Evidently, he hadn't told Suzanne I was in her room.

Crenshaw stepped forward. "As executor of this estate, I hereby grant permission for the authorities to search all common areas in the mansion, as well as my own room. Will everyone else voluntarily grant consent?"

"By all means," said Perry. "The painting could be suffering damage as we speak. Let's do all we can to try to find it."

Ernesto nodded slowly, but Celia seemed the most reluctant when she said a grudging "okay." Or maybe she was just tired.

At that point, the non-residents were allowed to leave, with the bartender offering to give a ride to the straggling guests. Gus wished us luck, clearly happy the mansion was no longer his problem. Then the two patrol officers began a search of the main floor, while the rest of us trooped, en masse, from one guest accommodation to another.

We started at Ray's place. Detective Rhinehardt asked everyone but Ray and me to wait outside. I was allowed in because I could identify the painting—and, maybe, I liked to think, because Rhinehardt liked and trusted me, and knew I'd be keeping an eye out for clues to the other unsolved mysteries. Crenshaw was asked to ensure that no one left the group. Rhinehardt wasn't going to take any chances that somebody might slip off to hide things they'd left in their rooms.

True to form, Barney barked furiously the instant we entered the cottage. Ray held him back while Rhinehardt looked in closets and under beds. We assumed the canvas had been rolled, but it would still be approximately twenty-four inches long. This limited the range of possible hiding places—which meant I had no excuse to go rifling through small drawers, pockets, or cubbyholes. *Darn it.*

From what we could see, there was nothing obviously incriminating among Ray's things. The same was true for Perry's. He had even fewer possessions, since he hadn't been there as long. In fact, while we were perusing his tidy living room, he mentioned he had begun packing things up. "As soon as my work here is done," he said, "I plan to move to an urban area, some-place where the art market is bigger."

Next we went to Ernesto's apartment. *Finally, I'll get a peek into this guy's private life.* Ernesto unlocked the door and went in first—and somehow managed to knock a metal box fan off of an end table. It fell to the floor with a crash.

"*Lo siento.* Sorry, sorry." Scrambling to pick up the fan, he bumped into a broom, which hit the floor with another clatter. Rhinehardt and I exchanged a glance. Why was Ernesto so nervous?

As we moved from room to room, Ernesto rushed ahead to open closets and cupboards for us. I couldn't tell if he was just trying to be helpful, or if he was pur-posefully steering our attention. In case it was the latter, I made a point of walking through every room twice. But there wasn't much to see. If anything, the place was surprisingly neat, especially for a young guy who lived by himself.

Back at the house, we started on the top floor and searched all the bedrooms, including Celia's. When we were in the maid's room, I couldn't help noticing how her eyes kept darting to the top drawer of an antique dresser. She did it so many times, I felt she was practi-cally begging me to have a peek. While Rhinehardt pulled back the curtain on the room's only window, I made a pretense of looking behind the dresser—and subtly pulled open the top drawer.

"Stop!" Celia cried angrily. "You're not supposed to look in small places. Those are my personal things."

"I'm sorry," I mumbled, as I closed the drawer. I'd only gotten a brief glimpse of the drawer's contents, but it was enough to see what Celia was hiding. Not a painting or a diary, but a pile of jewelry. And I'd bet any amount of money the jewelry had belonged to Elaine. I decided I'd tell Crenshaw and let him decide what to do.

"I think we're finished here," said Rhinehardt. "Let's move along." He gave me a significant look as he ushered me ahead of him. I took the hint and kept my mouth shut. We'd discuss our findings and theories later.

In Suzanne's room, she did all the talking. She apologized for the clutter, complained about Celia's neglect of her cleaning duties, and bragged about how full her social calendar was. Rhinehardt and I largely ignored her as we conducted our search. When Rhinehardt reached to open the closet door, I winced involuntarily and stepped back. Sure enough, a jumble of shoes and tennis rackets came tumbling out. Undaunted, the detective pulled out a flashlight and shined it in every corner of the closet. There were no stolen paintings—or lockboxes.

After a perfunctory walk through Crenshaw's room, we ended our search in the room Farrah and I had shared. Rhinehardt took a look at the doorknob, no doubt remembering the break-in I'd told him about. "Easy enough to pick," he noted. Josie jumped onto the windowsill to watch as we made a quick search of the room.

We reconvened with the other police officers in the gallery at the top of the stairs. They reported that their sweep of both the basement and the first floor had turned up nothing.

"I told you this would be a waste of time," groused Ray.

"Can I go to bed now?" asked Celia.

"You're all free to go," said Rhinehardt. "Thank you for your cooperation."

Farrah squeezed my arm. "Keli, I'm gonna get my stuff and go on home tonight. I'll check in with you tomorrow." She was talking to me, but her eyes were on Crenshaw. Creases of worry seemed to be permanently etched between his eyebrows.

After everyone left, Wes and I helped Crenshaw turn off lights throughout the mansion and make sure all the doors and windows were locked. When we finally settled into our room, Wes's face took on a worried expression that almost matched Crenshaw's.

"What's going on here anyway?" he asked. "Why do things keep disappearing?"

I scratched Josie under her chin as I shook my head. "I'm not sure yet. But I'm going to figure it out."

Chapter Twenty-Nine

I slept in late on Saturday morning. When I awoke, snuggled up next to Wes, I could almost forget where we were. The bedroom was quiet and warm from the filtered sunlight shining through the window. I could hear Josie nosing through the backpack Wes had left on the floor. *My little family, together again.* I sighed with contentment.

Then the memories came trickling in. The tension the night before had been so thick I could've cut it with my athame. Everyone was on edge after the painting was stolen, and no one was happy about having their rooms searched. It was one thing after another in this house. What would happen next?

Reluctantly, I crawled out of bed and took a shower. By the time I got out, Wes was up and texting someone on his phone. "I need to go into the newspaper office for a little while today," he said. "I have to turn in the photos I took in Chicago and pick up my next assignment. Do you want to stay here again tonight?"

I rummaged through my suitcase and found my last clean sweater and a pair of jeans I'd already worn at least once before. "Yeah, I think so. One more night, at least."

After Wes left, I made my way to the kitchen, where I found Crenshaw making cream of wheat. "This place feels deserted," I said, as I poured myself a cup of coffee.

"Celia is visiting friends today," he said. "I believe Suzanne is still in her room. I don't know where everyone else is."

We sat across from each other at the kitchen table, quiet with our own thoughts. Then Crenshaw set his cup down with a thud. "I hate to do it, but I think I had better ask everyone to leave. I'm going to have to shutter the mansion."

I looked up in dismay. "You mean let all the suspects go?"

"Suspects? Perhaps. But keeping them here hasn't brought us any closer to resolving anything. My responsibility is the estate. I had thought it would be best to keep the place open and functioning, rather than closed up to grow dusty and decayed."

"That makes sense."

"I thought so," he continued. "Everyone who lives here is on the payroll, so to speak, helping with the upkeep of the mansion in one way or another. That is, everyone but Suzanne. It will be difficult to ask her to leave, considering this is her home. I don't know if she has anyplace else to go."

We fell silent once more. The future of the mansion and its occupants seemed to hang in the air like a giant question mark. I sipped my coffee thoughtfully, as my mind whirred. I didn't like unanswered questions.

"What are you thinking?" asked Crenshaw. I hadn't realized he'd been watching me.

I gave him a slight smile. "I was thinking about the

naturalist John Muir. He once said, 'When one tugs at a single thing in nature, he finds it attached to the rest of the world.'"

Crenshaw raised one eyebrow. Usually he was the one to spout a quotation or two.

"In other words," I went on, "all things are connected. Native Americans, and others, call it the 'web of life.' I think what we have here is one great big web. Tangled, for sure, but not impossible to follow."

"Meaning?"

"Meaning everything that has happened here is connected. The missing diaries, the false alibis, the stolen painting—even Lana's disappearance." *Not to mention, the strange sounds I keep hearing and the weird vibes I keep picking up. And Elaine's death.*

Crenshaw seemed to ponder this for a moment, then shook his head. "It's beyond me. All I know is that this matter has taken up far too much of my time. I've tried to do my best to honor Elaine's wishes and properly manage the estate, but things are getting out of hand." He pushed his coffee cup away. "And now I need to file an insurance claim for nearly a quarter million dollars."

I clucked sympathetically, but my mind was still occupied with my tangled-web analogy. I wanted to find some paper and a pen and draw a great big diagram.

Crenshaw pushed back from the table and reached for my empty bowl. "I'm going into the office this morning, and then I have a dress rehearsal this afternoon. You might as well go home."

"Do you mind if I stay?"

He looked at me with mild surprise. "By yourself?"

"I'm a big girl."

"Very well. Call me if you need me."

Besides, I thought, as I locked the kitchen door behind Crenshaw. *I'm never really alone.*

The library gave me the heebie-jeebies, and the parlor, with its dying flowers beneath the once-twinkling eyes of Elaine in her portrait, gave me the blues. So, I wound up spending a good part of the morning in the conservatory. The green plants, so full of life and magic, gave me inspiration. I brought Josie in with me and shut the door, so she wouldn't go wandering. She would be my muse as I tried to puzzle through what in the world was going on at Turnbull Manor.

Celia was good about keeping the plants watered, but there were still brown leaves to pick off, and a couple of planters that were beginning to dry out. I tended to the plants as my mind drifted like the clouds outside the windows. Before long, I recalled the tarot card I'd pulled the day before: The Lovers. I still wanted to get Mila's take on the card's meaning. My first thought, of course, was of Wes. Maybe the card was more about my personal life than the mysteries I was trying to solve—the ultimate mystery being the future of our relationship. Would we continue in this casual, limbo state forever? Or would we finally tie the knot? Or, in Suzanne's words, "make it official."

Thinking of relationships brought me back to the connections among the residents of Turnbull Manor. Everyone seemed to have a secret. The question was, how many secrets were out there? Were some of the residents keeping the same secret? Were some of them working together? The relations among the five of them seemed to be more and more strained as time went on.

Celia knew something about Ernesto—something

for which she had demanded hush money. Suzanne apparently liked Ernesto and seemed to be having an affair with him. Was that their secret? But then they argued last night, and she accused him of hiding something. Ray had also tried to follow Ernesto early in the evening during the gala.

At various times, Suzanne had also lashed out at both Celia and Ray. Maybe she was cranky because of her precarious financial position. But she was also evasive about the past, especially about the period when her husband died and her daughter ran away.

Celia had her own secrets. She stole jewelry from her late employer, whom she evidently didn't much like. And she lied about leaving the house the night Elaine died. She also had a habit of spying on people, me included. I remembered how she'd been caught eavesdropping on Xavier and me in the garden, and then tried to make Wes jealous by tattling on me. Was Celia obsessed with lovers and the idea of splitting them apart?

Then there were Ray and Perry. Perry seemed to get along with everyone, whereas Ray didn't seem to like anyone. But the heated argument between the two of them suggested there was more going on that I didn't know about.

"What am I missing?" I asked aloud. Josie flicked her tail as she stalked by.

My ears picked up the sound of chimes. Opening the conservatory door, I realized it was the front doorbell. I still seemed to be alone in the house, so I went to answer it. To my delight, Mila was standing on the front porch. Her gray cat, Drishti, stood at her side.

"What a surprise!" I said. "I was just thinking about you!"

"No wonder you popped into my mind," she said

with a smile. "We were on our way back from a visit to the vet when I had a sudden notion to stop in and see you. Something told me I'd find you here."

"Is everything okay?" I inclined my head toward Drishti, who was now eagerly eyeing Josie. The two kitties approached each other with noses twitching.

"Everything's fine. She was due for her vaccinations, so she'll be a little sore—but no less curious."

"Let's go to the kitchen. Would you like some tea?"

We caught up with one another over herbal tea and crackers with hummus. As we chatted, Suzanne breezed in. She went straight for the refrigerator and pulled out the makings of a Bloody Mary. I introduced her to Mila.

"Hello," she said, raising a bottle of vodka. "Hair of the dog, you know? Would either of you like one?"

We declined, and she shrugged, returning her attention to her cocktail ingredients. Once it was made, she stuck in a stalk of celery and took a gulp. "Have you seen Ernesto?" she asked me. "He's not answering his phone."

"I haven't seen anyone," I said. "Other than Crenshaw, who went out for a while."

"I'm going out, too," she declared. "I need to see a man about a car." With that, she fluttered her fingers at us and left the room, taking her drink with her.

I told Mila a bit about Suzanne and the other residents of Turnbull Manor, and then asked for her opinion about The Lovers card. "I was thinking about Elaine Turnbull, among other things, when I drew the card," I said. "Elaine loved her husband, Harold, but he died when she was still in her fifties. I don't know if she loved her nurse, Ray, but I think he loved her. Her maid, Celia, also loved Harold—and, therefore, thought of Elaine as her rival."

Mila listened politely, as I continued naming people

she didn't know. "Of course, Elaine also loved her son, Jim, and her granddaughter, Lana. Jim's best friend was Perry, who was crushed when Jim died. Suzanne was upset when Jim died, too, even though they were separated and on the verge of divorce. I don't know what their troubles were about, but they fought on the day he died. Now Suzanne seems to be lovers with Ernesto, although she often talks about dating wealthy, older men."

I took a breath, and Mila smiled as she sipped her tea.

"What I can't figure out," I said, "is who The Lovers are supposed to be. Do you have any ideas?"

"Yes, I do," she said, her eyes twinkling. "And I think you do, too, deep down."

Frowning, I conjured up the card in my mind's eye. *A man and a woman, standing naked, side by side. They're in a place that looks like the Garden of Eden. Above them is an angel-like figure, blessing their union.*

"Is it me?" I asked. "And Wes?"

"Tarot readings are always personal," said Mila. "They can provide answers to a host of questions. The Lovers card, while symbolic in many ways, is one of the most straightforward cards in the Major Arcana. What do you think it means?"

My stomach did a little flip-flop. The body always knows. "Now that I think about it, my primary question was whether or not I was on the right track. And I *have* been thinking a lot lately about my relationship with Wes."

Mila smiled serenely, as if the matter were settled.

"But what about all the unanswered questions here? Every time I think I'm getting close to figuring something out, another piece slips away. Or is stolen."

Mila tapped her multiringed fingers together, pondering my problem. After a moment, she nodded her head decisively, as if agreeing with a voice only she heard. "Keli, are you familiar with the Witch's Pyramid, also known as the Four Powers of the Sphinx?"

"Of course. They're the four powers you need to make magic, right?" I ticked them off on my fingers. "To know, to will, to dare, and to keep silent."

"That's right. The Witch's Pyramid is an ancient philosophy widely followed by those serious about learning and practicing the magical arts. It contains foundational steps for casting spells, as well as attributes the magician must develop within. It's a tool, really. What does each step mean for you?"

"Gosh, I haven't thought about it in a while. I was all over the Witch's Pyramid back when I first learned about Wicca and real magic. Let's see . . . 'To know' means to acquire as much knowledge as you can. 'Know thyself,' first and foremost, but also keep learning about the world and your craft."

Mila nodded encouragingly, so I continued. "'To will' is about setting your intention. I think it's also about perseverance and personal sovereignty. It's about making your own decisions and directing your own life—which, by the way, is one of the things I love best about our religion."

"Indeed," agreed Mila. "And 'to dare'?"

"That's about courage, naturally. It's about taking action, daring to face your fears and bring forth the latent power within."

"And now for the tricky one. What does it mean 'to be silent'?"

I nodded, knowing exactly what she meant by it being tricky. "I used to think this maxim was advising me to hide my witchcraft, keep all my spell work a secret. But now I think it's more about receiving. There's a time to talk and a time to listen. A time for action and a time for rest. If magic is the practice of co-creation with the Divine, then 'to be silent' is when you sit back after you've done your part, and you let the Divine take over."

"Good," said Mila. "And what a perfectly appropriate, and balanced, approach to take as we near the Autumn Equinox."

"How do you interpret these four principles?" I asked.

She waved her hand as if her beliefs didn't matter. "My interpretation is very similar to yours. The four principles correspond with the four elements: air, fire, water, and earth. These are all necessary for working magic and advancing in our spiritual journeys. However, the reason I'm thinking of this now is because it might help with your current quandary."

"How so?"

"To find that which you seek you need knowledge, focus, courage, and discernment. In other words, you need to make sure you have all the necessary information about the issue. You need to be clear about your desire in this matter, focused and determined. You must not let fear be a roadblock. And you must be careful about who you speak to and what you say, holding back as needed. Does that make sense?"

"Yes, I think so. As for gathering knowledge, that's what I started out doing. I wanted to learn everything I could about Elaine and Lana. My goal was to help Crenshaw settle the estate and find Lana. I guess I let myself get distracted by all the other strange things going on around here." As I thought back over the past week, I realized I'd also lost my nerve more than once. And maybe I'd done too much talking and not enough listening.

"You can get back on track," said Mila. "Just come back to your center of power. And remember the over-arching element: Spirit. You're not in this alone."

"I was just thinking the same thing earlier!" I said.

Mila stood up and called Drishti to her side. "Keep me posted," she said. "I predict you'll have this all sorted before Mabon."

"Really?" Mila's predictions were not to be taken lightly. I knew this from experience.

"Oh, yes. And tonight's the harvest moon, you know. Why don't you ask Luna to shine her light on the dark-est shadows? She just might reveal the truth you're seeking."

My pulse quickened at Mila's words, as a shiver of anticipation coursed through my veins. "Maybe I'll do that," I said, touching my Triple Goddess tattoo. "That's an excellent idea."

Chapter Thirty

Wes came back in the late afternoon bearing sandwiches and beer. We ate in our room to ensure we'd be alone. Crenshaw was still at his play rehearsal, and Farrah had called to say she needed to catch up on things at home. As for the other occupants of Turnbull Manor, I didn't much feel like seeing them at the moment. I was taking Mila's advice to heart and following the words of the Sphinx: to know, to will, to dare, and to keep silent.

Of course, I wasn't keeping silent with Wes. We discussed the case and shared everything we had each learned over the past few days.

"None of my former classmates has heard from Lana," he said, with some frustration. "That idea was a dead end."

"What about the girl from the swim team, Jenny Burg?"

"I finally got a hold of her this morning. She lost touch with Lana after high school."

"Bummer. Are you sure that artist, Penny whatever, was in communication with Lana?"

"Yeah. I know they were really roommates in Chicago, because she showed me some pictures. And you can just tell when a person is telling you the truth, you know?"

I took a swig from my beer bottle and looked out the window. The moon would be rising soon. "Sometimes you can tell the truth from a lie. But not always. Some people lie so easily it sounds like the truth—especially when it's a matter of self-preservation for them."

"Well, Penny had no reason to lie. Her self-preservation wasn't on the line."

"I wasn't thinking of Penny. I was thinking of Celia and Ray and the others who live here." I stood up and wandered around the room, picking up my crystal and replacing it on the nightstand. Here I was letting myself get distracted again. I cracked open the window, letting in a whoosh of cool air.

"To know," I murmured.

"What'd you say?" Wes crumpled his sandwich wrapper and tossed it in the waste bin.

"There's more I want to know about Lana and what was going on here before she left. I never did see the things she left behind."

"Where are they? In her old room?"

I shook my head. "Her stuff was packed up. It's all in the attic now."

"Well, let's go." Wes reached for his jacket and pulled it on.

"It's more of a finished third floor," I said. "It's not cold up there."

"I've got stuff in my jacket," said Wes, patting his pockets. "Phone, notebook and pen, ziplocks for evidence."

"Evidence?" I stared at him, as a grin broke out over

my face. "All you need now is a deerstalker hat. Or maybe a fedora."

"Nah, it would mess up my hair," he said, pushing me toward the door. Not to be outdone, I grabbed my own phone and jacket on the way out.

With the growing darkness outside, the house was becoming gloomy. We flipped on hall lights as we made our way to the back staircase and up to the third floor. If Celia or Suzanne had come back, they hadn't made a sound. I could imagine how eerie this place would become if Crenshaw decided to go through with his plan of closing it up. I wondered if he'd cover the furniture with sheets.

The storeroom was in a state of semi-organized chaos. Labeled boxes were stacked three and four-high along the walls, while old furniture and dusty sports equipment was piled haphazardly here and there. The overhead light didn't provide much illumination, so Wes pulled out his phone and tapped a button. He then directed a bright, white beam toward the boxes on the far wall. "Flashlight app," he explained.

"Smart," I said, wishing I'd thought to do the same with my phone.

"Look," he said. "There's one with Lana's name on it."

The box he indicated was on the floor in front of another row of boxes. The cardboard flaps on top were hanging open. "Someone must have opened this recently," I said.

"Crenshaw?"

"I don't think so. The day before yesterday, he mentioned he hadn't done an inventory in here yet. And he wouldn't have had time yesterday."

Wes shone his light in the box, and I looked inside. It appeared to contain an assortment of other boxes:

shoeboxes, jewelry boxes, and a miniature treasure chest. I lifted some of the lids and poked around. "Looks like keepsakes," I said. There were button pins and swim team ribbons, costume jewelry and movie ticket stubs. Another container held colored pencils and crayons.

Wes moved on to look for other boxes with Lana's name. "Here's one with clothes," he said.

But I wasn't finished with the keepsakes. I'd found a plastic container that held assorted papers: grade school report cards, a few birthday cards, and even a few snapshots. One photograph caught my eye because it was torn. Holding it up to the light, I recognized Suzanne, maybe twenty years ago. It appeared her image had been cut out of a posed family Christmas photo. Did Lana cut herself and her father out of the picture and leave the rest behind? Or did Suzanne cut herself out of the photo?

I set the picture aside and continued my inspection of the papers. I had nearly reached the bottom of the pile when I recognized part of a hand-drawn family tree. I unfolded the paper and spotted Lana's name in a rectangle at the bottom of the sheet. Her name was also in the top right corner, indicating the family tree was made for a school assignment. It went back only a few generations, and only on Harold's side. I found Harold and Elaine, with a line to their only son, Jim. And from there, a line to Lana. And then I saw something surprising—the name in the space for Lana's mother was not Suzanne. It was someone named Angela. I squinted at the dates beneath her name and discovered that she had died the same year Lana was born. Suzanne's name was in a box to the side, under the label "stepmother."

"How about that?" I murmured. No one had ever mentioned Suzanne being Lana's stepmother. In fact, she would have been the only mother Lana ever knew. But I couldn't help wondering if this was at least part of the reason they didn't seem to be especially close. "Wes, did you know Suzanne wasn't Lana's birth mother?"

"Huh?" He was examining something on the floor. "Oh. No, I didn't know that. Check this out."

I replaced the papers in the container and stuck it back in the box, then joined Wes. "What is it?"

He held something between his thumb and forefinger. "It's a clump of mud and leaves. And it's still wet."

"Did we track it in?" I checked the bottom of my shoes, but they were dry.

"Uh-uh. You know how we thought someone had been looking in the boxes recently? I think it must have been *very* recently. Like shortly before we came up here." He pointed his light on the floor a few feet away. "Look, there's more."

I reached down to touch a bit of the mud and confirmed it was damp. "I wonder who was up here."

"Maybe Ernesto," suggested Wes. "He spends a lot of time outside."

"Yeah. But it could have been anyone else who's been outside, under the trees."

Wes walked to the exit of the storeroom, training his light on the floor. "There's a trail of it!" he said excitedly. "It goes all the way to the stairs. I guess we didn't notice earlier, because the light is dim in here."

"Hmm." Frowning, I went to Celia's door and knocked. Maybe she'd come back after all. There was no answer, and when I tried the knob it was locked.

Wes had already started down the stairs, so I shut off

the light and followed. I found him on the second-floor landing, crouched on the floor.

"There are two separate spots of tracked material here," he said, pointing. "But I don't think there were two people. I think the person left a trail going upstairs and another coming back down."

"Huh. Nice detecting."

Wes grinned up at me. "I feel like one of the Hardy Boys. Nancy Drew's got nothing on me."

I smiled at Wes's enthusiasm. Just then I caught sight of a ray of moonlight shining through a window at the end of the hall. The harvest moon.

"I need to stop in our room for a minute. Are you gonna keep following the mud?"

"Of course I am! I want to know who was looking at Lana's things. Don't you?"

"Uh, yeah. You go ahead. I'll catch up."

Back in our bedroom, I rummaged through my suitcase until I found a small glass jar. It contained what was left of the chamomile petals I'd sprinkled around the room on my first night in the mansion. I dumped the rest of them in the inside pocket of my suitcase and slipped the jar in my pocket. I didn't want to pass up the opportunity to make charged moon water tonight.

I trotted down the back staircase and headed for the kitchen. I was almost there, when Wes called out.

"That you, babe?"

I poked my head around the corner and found Wes at the doorway to the basement.

"What are you doing here?" I asked. "Didn't the trail of dirt come from outside?"

He shook his head. "Our mud-tracking friend came and went this way." He had his hand on the knob of the basement door.

I looked back toward the kitchen. I wanted to fill my jar with filtered water and set it outside in the moonlight. All I had to do was say a few words of blessing and intention and let it sit overnight. By tomorrow morning, I would have a powerful addition to any ritual or spell I wanted to cast this month.

Just then, Wes wrinkled his nose. "Do you smell smoke?"

I lifted my chin and sniffed. "Yeah. I think it's coming from outside." I went to the side door in the kitchen and looked all around. Over on the patio, someone was standing over a steel firepit. It might have been Ernesto, but I couldn't tell for sure, as my view was partially obscured by a potted cedar topiary. Wisps of smoke drifted in the breeze.

"Somebody has a fire on the patio," I said, returning to where Wes waited. "It seems to be under control."

"Okay, let's see what's down here then."

"There's just a wine cellar. They probably went for a bottle of wine. I was going to—"

I stopped myself midsentence. *To will.* The element of fire corresponded with the second rule of the Sphinx. I needed to remember my purpose here and not allow myself to be distracted. Wes was right. If someone else was going through Lana's things, we should find out who.

"Lead the way," I said.

At the bottom of the basement stairs, I turned left toward the wine cellar. Wes turned right.

"Where are you going?" I asked.

He pointed at the floor. "The tracks go there, to that old door."

My heart dropped to my stomach. It was the door to the old root cellar.

"Are you okay?" asked Wes. "You look a little pale."

"I heard noises behind that door the other day. I don't know why, but I'm kind of freaking out right now."

He handed me his phone. "It's okay. I know you don't like to be underground. Just take a deep breath and stand back. I'll take a look." He removed the plank from the front of the door and pulled it open. Once again, I found myself gazing into a dark, empty root cellar.

Wes took his phone from me and stepped inside the small room. His phone-light was a lot brighter than Crenshaw's penlight. It lit up every dingy crack and crevice of the old cellar, including the dirt floor. Wes ran his finger along the dirt. "It's dry," he said. "The person we're following didn't pick up the mud and leaves in here."

"You know what?" I said, trying to think rationally. "This doesn't make sense. They might have walked by this room, but I don't think they went inside. They certainly didn't leave through here."

The moment I said it, Wes shone his light on the far wall—revealing another wooden door. "Looks like they might have left through here, after all," he said.

Goose bumps prickled along my arms. "We didn't see that the other day," I said softly. "I guess somebody could have been in here after all. But wait! What about the board over the door to the basement? I don't see how anybody could have entered the house through this cellar. Or left this way, for that matter. They couldn't have replaced the board behind them."

"They could have if someone was helping them."

Before I could argue, Wes was opening the inside door. There was a brick-walled tunnel on the other side.

"Not a tunnel," I whispered. "Why does it have to

be a tunnel?" I felt a wave of dizziness as my mind flashed back to my nightmare experience in the tunnels under Edindale.

"You don't have to come in," said Wes, already crossing the threshold.

"I don't want you going in there by yourself! I don't think either of us should go. Let's go upstairs and see if Crenshaw is back yet."

"Crenshaw?" said Wes, pausing to look back at me. "You'd feel safer with Crenshaw than with me?"

"No, it's not that. I'm just stalling. Let's call Detective Rhinehardt."

Wes hesitated, clearly torn between a burning desire to continue the pursuit and an equally strong desire to respect my wishes. In the silence, I became aware of a trickling sound. Wes heard it, too. He turned and shone his light a little distance ahead.

"What's that?" I finally whispered.

He took a step forward. "It seems to be a rain barrel or a well or something. There's water dripping from the ceiling."

Water, the third element. To dare.

I pressed both palms into my chest, one over the other, and mentally drew in the power of the Goddess. Then I touched Wes's arm. "Hang on a minute." I hurried through the root cellar and picked up the board he had leaned against the wall. I used it to prop open the door to the tunnel.

"Okay," I said. "Let's just go a little ways and see where we end up."

"Are you sure?"

"Yes. I'm not afraid."

Holding hands, we moved slowly down the tunnel. My heart beat so fast I had to concentrate on my breathing to slow it down. I was so focused on trying to remain calm, it took me by surprise when Wes stopped suddenly. He shone his light on a set of concrete steps leading up from the tunnel. Then he shone it ahead of us. The tunnel continued onward.

"Let's check this out," he said, climbing the steps. At the top was a sloping, wooden double door, like that on a storm cellar. He pushed it open, letting in a welcome rush of night air and moonlight. I ran up the stairs after him and stuck out my head. I took a deep breath and said a silent prayer of gratitude.

Looking around, it didn't take me long to get my bearings. We were behind the garage, just steps from the stairs leading up to Ernesto's apartment. There was no one around that I could see.

"Shall we continue?" Wes asked softly.

I looked down into the darkness behind him. I could have said no, but at this point my curiosity was overtaking my fear. And at least I knew there were two means of escape, if I needed to turn back. "Okay," I agreed.

This time we made our way more quickly down the passage. It twisted and turned, and went on a lot longer than I expected. I was becoming increasingly nervous again, when finally we saw a light in the distance. Wes shut off his phone, plunging us into blackness.

"You okay?" he whispered.

"Just peachy," I replied.

He chuckled softly. "Just keep your eyes on that light. We'll be out of here before you know it."

Creeping along, we at last drew near the light. It came from another slanting double door at the top of a flight of stone steps. One of the doors had been left open. With Wes in the lead, we quietly climbed upward and stepped outside.

We were under the trees by the springhouse, near where Rhinehardt and I had walked a few days earlier. From the smell of wet earth and leaves, I guessed we must be near the spring. The person we were tracking had surely come from this way.

I opened my mouth to suggest we turn back and promptly shut it. A rustling sound came from nearby. It sounded like footsteps.

Of one mind, Wes and I stole away from the tunnel doors and slipped into the shadows. I cupped my hands over my mouth as the footsteps became louder. A moment later, a person came into view. He walked right past us without looking our way, but I recognized him in the moonlight. It was Ernesto.

Once he was a few yards ahead of us, we came out of our hiding place and followed. He must have known the path well, because he wasn't using a flashlight. A minute later, I heard the buzzing of insects and caught sight of reflected moonlight shimmering on water. We had come to the pond.

Wes and I paused, watching, as Ernesto made his way toward a fallen tree. With a start, I noticed something I hadn't seen before: Another person was sitting on the log. It appeared to be a woman, and she faced the water. As Ernesto crept up behind her, I felt Wes stiffen at my side. I had an urge to cry out in warning, but something stopped me. Maybe it was the smell of the earth, and the solid ground beneath my feet.

To be silent.

I nudged Wes to hunker down with me behind a tree.

As we watched, Ernesto put his hand on the woman's shoulder. She gasped, and turned to look up at him.

I almost gasped, too. The instant the moonlight hit her face, I thought I was seeing a ghost. She was the spitting image of Elaine.

Before I knew what was happening, Wes stood up and stepped out of the shadows.

"Lana?"

Chapter Thirty-One

The setting was almost absurdly romantic. Stars glittered overhead, while the swollen moon cast a hazy glow on the shimmering pond. Sweetgrass and cattails swayed rhythmically at the water's edge, and a nearby weeping willow reached graceful arms toward the ground. The young woman by the rocks spun around at the sound of her name. Her eyes were wide with fear, her round cheeks flushed in the moonlight.

If anyone was a Gothic heroine in this story, it wasn't me. It was Lana.

Ernesto stepped protectively in front of her, but she maneuvered around him. Her fear gave way to confusion, and finally recognition.

"Wes Callahan?"

"What are you doing here?" asked Wes, walking toward her.

She lifted her shoulders in a motion of helplessness. "Playing hide-and-seek?" she answered, with a trace of irony in her voice. "What are *you* doing here?"

"I'm with Keli, my girlfriend." He touched my arm, and I joined him at his side. In spite of more pressing concerns, I couldn't help noting how inadequate the term *girlfriend* sounded. I waved hello to Lana.

"Didn't you get my messages?" Wes asked. "Penny Delacroix told me she passed them on to you."

Lana appeared to be embarrassed. "My phone service has been cut off. I haven't gotten any phone messages or texts for a while. Last time I checked my email at the public library, I had one message from Penny. She did say an old friend was trying to find me, but I thought it must be a scam or a mistake. I don't have any old friends."

"I thought of you as a friend," said Wes.

"Penny told Wes you were staying with an old friend," I added.

"Oh, well that's true." She pointed at Ernesto. "I'm staying with him."

"All this time you've been staying in Ernesto's apartment?" I asked. That sure explained a few things—including Ernesto's secretiveness. But I still had a lot of questions.

"I've only been here a few days," she added.

"But why are you hiding at all?" asked Wes. "Why haven't you come forward?"

She sighed. "It's complicated."

"Lana, we'd like to help you," I said. "Can we go back to the house and talk?"

"Not the house," she said. "We can talk at Ernesto's place—if it's okay with him."

"It's okay," he said, speaking up for the first time. "But we better take the tunnel. I saw Ray by the firepit on the patio a little while ago."

Ernesto took Lana's hand and led her to the entrance of the tunnel. I realized she must have been the woman I saw running in the gardens the other night. Ernesto must have been with her right before he bumped into me. I imagined they'd be able to shed some light on a few other mysteries around here as well.

Wes reached for my hand. "Ready?"

"Just a sec." The moon reflecting on the water had grabbed my attention again. I took the small jar from my jacket pocket and dipped it in the pond. Natural water was best for magical workings anyway. And there was definitely magic in the air tonight.

We sat at a small round table in Ernesto's tiny kitchen. He put on a pot of decaf coffee and set out a plate of butter cookies. It was such a cozy, friendly scene, I had to keep reminding myself there were still some serious crimes that had yet to be solved. Lana seemed skittish, so I decided to start with the simple questions first.

"Where were you last night when I came through with Detective Rhinehardt?" I asked her. Then I turned to Ernesto. "Were you warning her to hide when you made all that noise knocking over the fan?"

"Yeah, just in case she was in here. I didn't know if she was or not."

"I wasn't," said Lana. "I overheard Ernesto and Suzanne arguing outside, and then you came out. I heard you tell them the police were on their way because a painting was stolen. Just to be safe, I took the stairs to the garage and hid in the tunnel."

Now that Ernesto seemed willing to talk, I was going to take advantage of the opportunity. "What were you and Suzanne arguing about anyway? She accused you of hiding something . . . or someone. Was she talking about Lana?"

He nodded and picked up his coffee mug with both

hands. He brought it to his face, as if he hoped he could disappear behind it.

"It's okay," said Lana. "I keep telling you I'm not mad at you."

Wes and I waited for Ernesto to speak. I imagined it must be a little awkward for Lana and Ernesto, considering he was having an affair with her mother. Or stepmother.

Ernesto set his mug on the table. "Suzanne and I have been seeing each other on and off for a couple years. It's casual, but she gets jealous anyway. She accused me of seeing another woman—which I'm not. Lana and I are just friends. But she thought I was bringing a woman up here sometimes. I guess she saw some signs or something. She doesn't know it's Lana."

"What does Celia know?" I asked. "I know she's been trying to get money from you."

He rolled his eyes. "Celia always suspects people of cheating and messing around. She actually had the nerve to hide in the garage and spy on me . . . and she saw me with Suzanne."

"What's the big deal?" asked Wes.

"We don't want anybody to know about us," said Ernesto. "It would ruin everything—Suzanne's chance to marry a respectable, high-society man, and my chance to work for any of them."

Their lives sounded like a soap opera, but I wasn't there to judge. I was still trying to sort through who knew what about whom. I remembered the evening Farrah translated what Celia had said to Ernesto in Spanish—something about seeing him with a lady. "Does Celia know Lana is here?"

Ernesto shook his head. "I think she saw Lana and me together from a distance one day, but she didn't know it was Lana."

I took a sip of coffee, as I tried to make sense of what exactly was going on here. "So, does Suzanne even know the two of you are friends? When did you meet anyway?"

"My uncle was the groundskeeper here for many years," said Ernesto. "One summer, I helped him out with odd jobs."

"It was the summer everything fell apart," said Lana, as if stating a fact. "Suzanne had moved out, and Dad was having some kind of nervous breakdown. Ernesto was the one high point of that time. I would sit down by the pond and draw, and he'd take breaks to fish. Before long, we came to be friends."

I smiled at this, but I couldn't help feeling like we were dancing around the edges. It was time to cut to the chase. "Lana, are you aware your grandmother left you her entire estate? This place and everything in it are rightfully yours."

Her face darkened, and she shifted her gaze. "I don't believe it," she said quietly.

"Wait—you think she made another will?"

"Probably. As far as she knew, I was an ungrateful granddaughter who abandoned her for the rest of her life." Her lower lip trembled.

As far as she knew. Lana's choice of words made it sound like she didn't really abandon her grandmother—at least, not intentionally.

"Why did you leave?" asked Wes. "I mean, I knew you were sick of school and small-town life. But was it more than that?"

"I left because this place felt toxic." Her voice took on a steely edge. "My parents fought all the time. Like I said, Suzanne had left and Dad was going through a depression or something. He was always testy and moody. Until one day, he . . . escaped the only way he knew how."

Wes and I exchanged a glance. Then Wes asked the question I was afraid to voice. "Did you see it happen, Lana?"

She shook her head. "No. I had just come home from school." She gave Wes a sad smile. "Actually, I shouldn't have been there at all, but I decided to ditch my last class. I came in the front door and was on my way to the stairs. That's when I heard a gunshot."

Ernesto reached over and squeezed Lana's hand. He seemed like such a kind, supportive friend.

"I'm so sorry," said Wes. "You don't have to go on if it's too painful."

I wanted to kick him under the table. I felt sympathy for Lana, too, but it was important to hear her story. Fortunately, she didn't mind talking.

"It's okay. I've relived this in my mind so many times, it's almost like watching a rerun on TV." She took a deep breath before continuing. "When I heard the gunshot, I froze. I knew something bad must have happened, and I was literally paralyzed for a few seconds. Then I heard another noise down the hall, which spurred me to move. I ran to the gun room, but I didn't get past the library. Perry had heard the shot too, and he got there first. The look on his face told me everything. I cried, 'Dad!' Perry had to hold me back. He said there was nothing we could do, and he was so sorry, but he wouldn't let me in."

I bit my lip, trying not to let my emotions get the best of me. *This poor girl.*

"I heard people coming then. Grandma's nurse, Ray, was at the house, and he yelled something like, 'What was that?' I made one more push for the gun room, but Perry blocked my way and handed me a piece of paper. It was a note, in my Dad's handwriting."

So there was a note. Evidently, the responding police officers were right in their belief that the shooting wasn't accidental.

"That's when I fled," she went on. I turned around and ran out, with the note still in my hand. There were people coming down the hall from the back of the house, so I ran to the front door. My only thought was that I had to get away from there. Otherwise, I was afraid I might end up doing the same thing my father had done."

When she stopped talking, the room was so quiet I could hear the wind rattling the trees outside. Wes looked like he wanted to say something but couldn't find the right words. There really weren't any right words in a situation like this. I was about to utter something about being sorry, when a jarring ringtone broke the silence.

Ernesto dug his phone out of his pocket and read a text message. "It's Suzanne," he said. "She wants me to come to the house. And if I don't, she'll come out here."

"Forgive me," I said to Lana, "but why don't you want to see your—Suzanne? She told me she believes you're upset with her, but she hasn't said why. Also, she never mentioned she's your stepmother."

Lana rubbed her eyes, which ended up making her appear weary and sad. "I used to call her 'Mom,' back when I was a little kid. Then I turned into an angsty teen and began using her first name. Things only got worse when she fought with Dad and then took off." She jutted out her chin slightly, raising the specter of herself as a defiant child. "Dad was clearly going through something, but she was too selfish to help him. She walked out on both of us."

I had handled enough divorce cases to know there was always more to the story than the kids knew. Lana probably had little idea of what was really going on in her parents' relationship. Of course, neither did I.

Wes leaned forward. "What are you afraid of, Lana?"

She shook her head helplessly. "That's just it. I don't know what—or, rather, who—I should be afraid of." She laughed without humor, as if she realized how crazy she sounded. "Someone at the manor was working against my grandmother. I know this now. I tried to contact her over the years. I sent her letters and left messages on her answering machine. She never responded. At first, this hurt my feelings . . . even as a part of me knew this wasn't like her. So, I kept trying. The last time was a birthday card I sent her about a month ago. It was returned to me in the mail—with a warning message. I was so freaked out, I decided to move. Whoever sent the warning had my address."

"What kind of warning?" said Wes.

"Show them," said Ernesto.

Lana stood up and left the room. She came back a minute later with a backpack, leaving me to wonder where her things were hidden. I hadn't noticed a backpack, or anything resembling a woman's possessions, when I walked through the place with Detective Rhinehardt.

She pulled a card from her backpack and handed it to Wes. He read the front and inside, then flipped the card over and sucked in a breath. He handed the card to me. On the back, in cramped black handwriting, was a message as crude as it was sinister: "Stay away from Turnbull Manor—or die."

Chapter Thirty-Two

I had hoped I was done with tunnels. Yet, much to my regret, I found myself once again ten feet under the earth, surrounded by musty smells and unbroken darkness. At least this time I wasn't alone. Not only was Wes by my side, but we were with someone exceptionally familiar with the terrain beneath the Turnbull gardens.

While we were in Ernesto's kitchen, examining the disturbing message Lana had received, we had heard the creak of the exterior staircase. Lana immediately scooped up her backpack and headed for the inside stairs to the garage below. Wes and I followed. With the surefootedness of someone who had done this many times before, she climbed out a window in the rear of the garage, hefted open the storm cellar hatch, and descended quickly into the tunnel. She turned right, in the direction of the pond, until Wes stopped her.

"Hey, hold up. We left the door open in the wine cellar. We can get in the house that way." He pointed his phone light toward the ground, lighting up our feet and leaving our faces dimly shadowed.

She took a step backward. "You don't understand. I can't go to the house. Someone there wants to harm me."

"Who do you think it is?" I asked.

"I don't know." She rubbed her forehead, as if it hurt from racking her brain. "If I had to guess, I'd say Ray. He was close to my grandmother and could have prevented her from getting my calls and letters. But it could be anyone who lives here. Even Suzanne."

Even Ernesto, I thought. As nice as he seemed, I couldn't let him off the hook yet.

"Yet you still came back," said Wes. "Why?"

I really wished we could continue this conversation aboveground, but I kept my mouth shut. I wanted to hear Lana's answer.

She sighed. "After I left Chicago, I came back to Southern Illinois and got a job as a waitress in Craneville. I was worried about the message, but at the same time, I wanted to see my grandmother. Unfortunately, I waited too long. It wasn't long afterward that I heard she passed away, which was a real blow. I decided to move again, this time far away."

"What about your inheritance?" asked Wes.

"I don't deserve an inheritance from my grandmother," she said with a mixture of sadness and self-loathing. "But there is one thing I do want. A ring. It belonged to my grandma, and she gave it to me when I turned sixteen. It's a unique antique ring. The enameled setting is a painted butterfly merged with a woman's face."

"And you can't find it, right?" It had dawned on me that it must have been Lana going through her boxes in the attic.

"That's right. I wore it a lot, but I didn't have it on

the day I ran out of here. I don't remember exactly where I left it. I might have taken if off near the swimming pool, or it might have been in my room. I've been looking everywhere. I really want to find it before my grandma's things are sold."

This was crazy. We needed to bring her to the house and let Crenshaw talk to her. There was no need for her to continue sneaking around the property—and fearing for her life.

"We can help you look for it," offered Wes. *Yeah,* I thought. *Or we can just ask Suzanne or Celia if they know what happened to it.*

"That would be great," said Lana. "I don't think I can stay here much longer. It's too risky, and I've imposed on Ernesto too long already."

"You don't have to stay here another minute," said Wes. "Come home with Keli and me. You can crash with us for a while."

Of course, I had to tell Crenshaw. I had to tell Farrah, too—she and I told each other practically everything. But other than the two of them, plus Ernesto, no one else knew about our secret house-guest.

It didn't take much convincing for Lana to agree to come with us. She was tired of running and eager to get away from the manor. As we later learned, part of the reason she'd been bunking in the old chauffeur's bedroom was that she didn't have anyplace else to go. She had run out of money trying to make a fresh start in Craneville.

At first, I hadn't been thrilled when Wes invited her to stay at our house, especially since he hadn't consulted with me first. But I quickly swallowed my irritation,

conceding that it really was the best course of action. I
made sure the coast was clear, while Wes shuffled her
off to his car. Then I quickly packed up our things,
gathered up Josie, and followed in my own car. Since it
was nearly midnight at this point, I had stuck a note to
Crenshaw's door, letting him know I went home and
promising to explain everything the next day.

When I arrived at the town house, Wes and Lana
were in the living room making light conversation—
though I could tell Lana was struggling to keep her
eyes open. I hurried up to my altar room and put away
a few things, transforming it back into a guest bedroom.

It was wonderful to be home. Waking up in my own
bed on Sunday morning, I could almost forget about
all the strange happenings at Turnbull Manor. Almost.
All the unanswered questions still gnawed at my brain—
not to mention the small matter of the heiress in our
spare room.

We spent most of the day in a quiet, relaxed mode.
Wes and I agreed we should let Lana decompress for a
bit. Hopefully, she would come to some reasonable
conclusions on her own. While we worked around the
house and yard, she made drawings in her sketchbook.
She drew quickly, churning out page after page, which
she always tore out and gave to Wes or me. It was like she
wanted to give us something for helping her, and this
was the only thing she had. She mainly sketched flowers
and plants in the backyard, or Josie in various states of
repose. She even sketched me as I stood over a mixing
bowl in the kitchen.

"I like your tattoo," she said shyly, as she handed me
the drawing.

"Thank you. It represents the Triple Goddess." I
pinned the drawing to the corkboard in a corner of the

kitchen, wondering if she'd ask me to explain what I meant by the Triple Goddess. But when I turned back, she had already started on her next sketch.

"You're very talented, Lana. If you end up staying in the area, you'll find lots of support for local artists, both here in Edindale and down the road in Fynn Hollow. Wes and I can introduce you to some good contacts."

She concentrated on her sketch, her hand flying deftly across the page. "You're very kind," she said, without looking up. "But I don't think it's safe for me to stay."

We'll see about that. I had spent nearly a week trying to uncover the secrets of Turnbull Manor. I wasn't about to give up now.

Farrah and Crenshaw joined us for dinner. I made pumpkin soup and marinated tofu. Wes put together a big salad for all, plus roasted chicken for himself and our guests. As we gathered around the table, we took stock of the situation and tried to come up with a game plan. I had already brought my friends up to speed about what we'd learned from Lana.

"Here's how I see it," said Farrah, raising her fork for attention. "Lana is slated to inherit everything, right? That's public knowledge. And somebody *really* doesn't want her to show her face at the manor—so much so that they sent her a creepy threat. Therefore, it stands to reason that the person who sent the threat doesn't want her to inherit everything."

We all nodded. So far so good.

"Well," she continued, "who keeps claiming there's another will that doesn't leave her everything? Ray, that's who. My vote for the guilty party is Ray Amberly."

"Fair enough," said Crenshaw. "However, I should point out that everyone else at the manor had reason to believe they would be remembered in Elaine's will. Her daughter-in-law lived with her and is technically the closest family she has, even if they're not related by blood. Celia has been with the family for more than thirty years. Perry is a close family friend. And Elaine evidently had a soft spot for Ernesto, which makes more sense now that we know his uncle worked for the family."

"It's not Ernesto who wants to keep me away," said Lana firmly. "He's been trying to get me to come home for years, even after Grandma died. However, I agree that all the people who lived with her are more deserving of a bequest than I am."

"Come on, Lana," said Wes. "Don't talk like that."

"It has nothing to do with how deserving anyone is," Crenshaw pointed out. "All we have to rely on is the existing will. If there is, or ever was, a subsequent version, we have no idea where it is."

I had been quietly savoring my soup while the others talked about the will and all its implications. I agreed with Farrah that Ray was the most obvious suspect. But that conclusion still didn't sit right with me. There were too many pieces of the puzzle that didn't fit, including the stolen painting. I said as much to the group and was immediately met with all the counter-arguments, which, of course, I'd already thought of. The theft of the painting could be wholly unrelated to all the other crimes. But I still wasn't convinced.

By the end of the evening, we had at least come up with a plan for the next day, if not beyond that. Wes would take Lana downtown to see Detective Rhinehardt and show him the threatening note. Crenshaw would summon the residents of Turnbull Manor and inform them that they were going to have to move out. Farrah would go along with Crenshaw. She said she would offer to help anyone who might need assistance finding other housing.

As for me, I needed to make an appearance at my ever-neglected office. It would be Arlen's first day, and I needed to show him the ropes. I was looking forward to having an assistant. At least this was one area of my life I was finally getting under control.

When I arrived at the old bank building the next morning, Arlen was already waiting on the sidewalk out front. In one hand, he held a to-go tray containing two coffees, and in the other a paper sack from the vegan bakery.

"Morning, boss! After being late for my interview, I wanted to show you I really can arrive to work on time."

"I wasn't worried." I smiled, noting that his long hair had been recently trimmed and his broad face was cleanly shaven. He wore a black, button-up shirt and nice black denims with black cowboy boots, which put me in mind of Johnny Cash. *The Man in Black, indeed.* Arlen's only jewelry today was a studded-leather wrist cuff, a couple of skull rings, and a heavy-looking medallion on a chain around his neck.

"I guess the first thing I need to do is make a set of keys for you," I said, as we entered the building. "I would have done it already, but I've had a most unusual past several days."

"Leave it to me," he said. "If you lend me your keys, I can make a copy this evening and open the office tomorrow morning before you arrive."

"Wonderful." I felt lighter already, knowing Arlen

would lift much of the burden that had been piling up ever since I'd started flying solo.

Once we were inside, I invited him to have a seat across from my desk, as I cleared off a space for the coffee and muffins.

"I wasn't sure what kind you like," he said, "so I got one of each. I also took a chance with the java. Do you drink the stuff?"

"I do," I said, gratefully accepting a cup. "This is so sweet of you. I feel like I should have brought something in to celebrate your first day. How about if I treat you to lunch today?"

"Sounds good to me. I gotta say, I'm tickled to be working for you." His wide grin said as much.

"Me too, Arlen." I smiled in return. "Now, let's see. I have some employment forms and contact info for you to fill out. Then I'll show you my filing system and get you set up with shared access to my emails and online calendar. I also want to give you a little training on client confidentiality—though you probably know all about that, since you've worked for an attorney before."

"Absolutely. Attorney-client privilege. Very important."

My desk phone rang then, and Arlen reached for it. "May I?" he asked. I nodded my assent, and he picked up the phone.

"Law Offices of Keli Milanni. How can I help you?"

He listened a moment, then rolled his eyes. "Let me stop you right there. We're not interested in a timeshare in the Florida Everglades, so you can remove this number from your list. Please and thank you."

He hung up, muttering, "Vultures. Don't they know this is a place of business?" Then he met my eyes. "Oh, wait. You weren't interested—"

"Not even a little bit. You did great." I handed him

some forms and a pen, and he used the edge of my desk to begin filling them out.

"I'm sorry I don't have a desk for you yet," I said. "Or a computer or a phone. I had planned on visiting an office supply store over the weekend, but I've had a most unusual past few days."

He put down the pen. "That's the second time you've mentioned your 'most unusual' week. Do you want to talk about it?"

"Hmm. Maybe I should. It's all I can think about lately." I leaned back in my chair and absently pinched off a brown leaf from the plant nearest my desk. "I don't know how I get myself involved in so many peculiar cases."

"Because you like to help people," he offered. "That's why."

"There is that. I've been trying to help people this past week, too." I briefly explained my original assignment at Turnbull Manor, and all the ways it had gone off the rails. "Just when I thought I was starting to make some headway, something else would go missing. It's been frustrating."

"Have you tried asking your spirit guides?"

"My spirit guides? I tried contacting the spirit of Elaine Turnbull through astral projection, which sort of worked one time. Unfortunately, I didn't receive any clear answers."

He raised his eyebrows. "You made contact with a recently deceased woman, whose life had been suddenly and maliciously cut short? That's quite amazing. But I'm not talking about ghost whispering, per se. I'm talking about guidance and divination through necromancy."

"I'm more into Goddess worship, myself. I usually

access the spirit world by invoking the ancient goddesses and gods through spells and rituals."

"That's cool. But you ought to try bone magick sometime. You know, I specialize in communicating with animal spirit guides through the parts they leave behind: bones, teeth, feathers, and the like. I find that animal spirits are generally purer than human spirits, energetically speaking. They're easier to work with."

I had to suppress a smile. It was definitely going to be interesting having Arlen around the office.

"If you want answers," he continued, "I might be able to help. The Turnbull property is pretty big and has lots of trees, doesn't it? I bet you could find animal remains without much difficulty."

"There are animal remains in the house," I retorted. "If you count stuffed animals and mounted antlers."

He cocked his head. "Real stuffed animals or replicas?"

"I'm pretty sure they're real. Harold Turnbull was big into hunting and had his gun room decorated like a hunting lodge."

"Ah, I see. I bet the vibrations in that space are something else."

"They are," I said, recalling how odd I'd felt in the gun room. "And it's not only because of the dead animals. That room holds sadness and tragedy. It's where Jim Turnbull shot himself fifteen years ago."

As I said the words, a prickle of doubt crept up my spine. I couldn't say exactly why, but something about Jim's death continued to bother me.

"Something wrong?" asked Arlen, proving how perceptive he could be.

"I don't know. The thing is, I don't know *why* Jim killed himself. His daughter said he was depressed, and he had been fighting with his wife, but . . ." I trailed off, shaking my head. "I guess such things always seem senseless."

"There *is* one way to find out for sure," said Arlen.

I let my gaze wander to a framed sunset photo on the wall. "I suppose I could try astral projection again, focusing on Jim instead of Elaine."

"I have a better idea." Arlen leaned forward. "Why don't we ask the bones?"

"Ask the bones?" I met his eyes, intrigued by the idea. "You really think animal magick can shed light on what's happening at Turnbull Manor?"

He nodded his head solemnly. "I do. Absolutely. Why not let me show you how? We can do it together. Tonight."

Chapter Thirty-Three

By the end of the day, Arlen had won me over. We had discussed it more over lunch, until I was convinced he knew what he was doing and that there was nothing to lose. Once our plan was hatched, only one problem remained: what to say to Crenshaw.

My colleague undoubtedly knew I adhered to a non-traditional spiritual belief system—what many would call "New Age" ideas. He was an observant man. But we had never discussed my Wiccan practices in any kind of detail. I had no idea how to explain the ritual I wanted to perform without him thinking I'd gone off the deep end.

Fortunately, the stars were aligned in our favor. Crenshaw would be away at his final dress rehearsal for much of the evening. When I told him I'd like to spend some time in the Turnbull library "for research purposes," he wished me luck and said to take as much time as I desired. He didn't even bat an eye when I asked him for the key to the gun room.

Arlen and I arrived to the manor at dusk. If any of the residents observed us come in, they didn't let us know.

I imagined they were all in their rooms packing—or brooding over the fact that they were being forced to leave their home. To be on the safe side, I taped a DO NOT DISTURB sign on the library door. And when we entered the gun room, I shut and locked the door behind us.

Arlen had brought a black case, resembling an oversized medical bag, which he set on the desk. As a man accustomed, and immune, to curious stares, he was already wearing his ritual robes and bone jewelry when I picked him up at his home on the edge of town. I wasn't quite as audacious—I'd brought my ritual robe in my tote bag. I slipped it on over my clothes while Arlen looked around.

First, he walked slowly around the edges of the room, touching objects as he went. When he got to the stuffed pheasant, he patted the top of its head and chuckled. "There was once a living soul in this beautiful creature, but no longer. Now it's filled with synthetic material. This won't be a vessel for any visiting spirits tonight."

With a passing glance at the bearskin rug, he circled around to the desk and looked up at the cow skull on the wall. The bleached bone of its narrow head and the curved brown horns evoked thoughts of ranch life and southwestern art. Arlen reached up and carefully removed it from its hook.

"This will do nicely," he said, handing me the skull. "Hold this for a minute, will you?"

I stood back, cradling the bottom of the skull in both hands, while Arlen cleared off the desk and started removing items from his carrying case. After draping a black cloth over the surface of the desk, he placed a candle in each corner. Then he surprised me by pulling

out a number of other animal bones. I hadn't realized
he would be bringing his own.

I watched as Arlen arranged his sacred objects in an
intricate pattern resembling a mandala. Among the
items I recognized were loose fangs, spiral-shaped
seashells, and the spine of a snake. There was also a
small mammal's skull, decorated with esoteric symbols
painted in black and red.

"The fox is a messenger animal," Arlen explained,
touching the painted skull. "Its spirit offers a channel
between the living and the dead."

Arlen relieved me of the cow skull and placed it in
the center of the arrangement. Then he brought out a
shiny red apple and a bundle of green grass tied with
twine, which he placed at the base of the skull. "It's
important to always bring an offering as a gesture of
good will," he advised.

Finally, he pulled out two long, rattling bone necklaces. He placed one over his own head and held out
the other to me. I didn't take it.

We had already discussed my reservations earlier in
the day. Arlen knew I was an ethical vegan, who
avoided consuming or using anything made from an
animal. This extended beyond my diet to my clothing
and household furnishings. There were no leather
belts, shoes, or seat coverings to be found in any of my
personal possessions.

On the other hand, a major part of my Wiccan religion was to honor nature's cycles of life, death, and
new life. If a creature had lived out its life and died in
the wild, then there was really no harm in taking the
parts left behind—that is, assuming one did so in ac-
cordance with relevant local laws. Arlen assured me
that he only worked with bones he had legally collected
himself. He was an ethical necromancer.

Now he gave me a gentle look, as he continued to hold out his spare bone necklace. "You don't have to wear it," he said. "But I promise you no animals were harmed in the gathering of these bones. And you might like the effect. This is what I call my shamanic necklace. It's made from beaver bones and bits of turtle shell, two creatures that in life traveled between land and water. In death, they help us travel between the earthly realm and the spirit world."

I accepted the necklace and placed it over my head. After all, it was something my ancestors might have done. Of course, as long as alternate forms of sustenance were readily available, I would still never eat meat. But I decided I was okay with using animal bones in a respectful way—especially with Arlen as a guide.

While Arlen tucked away his black bag, I smudged the room with sage smoke for protection and peace. At last, we lit the candles, including a few we had placed on the fireplace mantel and two side tables. When I turned off the lights, the room was instantly transformed into a spooky, shadowy den—a perfect space for holding a séance. I tried not to think about the unseeing eyes of the stuffed animals as I walked up to the covered desk.

We clasped hands over the bones and took a few deep breaths. Then Arlen spoke in a low, rumbling voice.

"Spirits of land, sea, and sky, creatures who have gone before, enter our midst if you so desire. I am Arlen the Necromancer, pure of soul and brave of heart. This is Keli the Witch, also pure of soul and brave of heart. We come in peace with open minds and a desire for communication. Willing spirits enter this vessel we have prepared. Accept these offerings."

For several minutes, nothing happened. We stood quietly, with Arlen repeating his invitation every few seconds. At some point, I closed my eyes, allowing myself to enter a meditative state. The scent of sage smoke and candle wax mingled with a musky oil I realized Arlen must be wearing, and I felt a little lightheaded. After a time, a rattling sound penetrated my awareness. I opened my eyes, half expecting to see the smaller bones dancing on the table. Instead, I saw Arlen bobbing his head as if nodding "yes" over and over again. Then he started whispering.

"The spirit has returned to its host," he murmured. "The old steer comes willingly, trusting that these humans are the good kind. The kind that provide nourishment and not pain. This spirit has seen much and will answer our questions."

I wasn't sure if that was my cue to speak, but I found myself unable to utter a word. This was unfamiliar territory. Luckily, Arlen knew what to ask.

"What happened in this room when blood was shed? What secrets lurked in the heart of the man, Jim Turnbull? What secrets can you reveal?"

He stopped bobbing his head and tilted his chin upward, as if he were listening. His eyes were squeezed shut.

Ask about Elaine, too, I wanted to say. *Who is the thief? Who is the killer? Are they one and the same?*

A moment later, Arlen let go of my hands and bowed his head. "Thank you," he said. "Thank you for sharing this space with us. Thank you for sharing your knowledge." He released a shaky breath, then lifted his head and opened his eyes.

"Is that it? Is the spirit gone?"

"Gone for now," he said. "As soon as the answer was given, the spirit moved on. It saw no reason to linger."

"The answer was given? What answer?"

Sweat beads glistened on Arlen's forehead in the flickering candlelight. "The man who died in this room, Jim Turnbull, wasn't alone when he was shot."

"He wasn't?"

"No. And he didn't pull the trigger. He was murdered."

The gun room was no less creepy after we turned on the lights and put away the bones. But I wasn't ready to leave. I was still trying to understand the message Arlen had been given. The "murder" part was clear enough, but we still didn't know who did it or why.

"What about your question about the secrets Jim was harboring? Was there an answer to that question?" I was pacing back and forth between the fireplace and the large fox-and-hound painting next to the door. I had no desire to curl up on the leather sofa in front of the bearskin rug.

Arlen gave me a patient look. "Most of the time, the answers don't come in actual words and sentences. It's more like images and impressions. The feeling I got was that Jim was very troubled, but not troubled enough to take his own life. There was definitely a second person with malevolent intentions."

"Can you describe the person? Male, female?"

"No, sorry. It was like I was seeing the person's dark soul, not their body."

I shuddered. With that kind of energy, no wonder the room felt so eerie.

Arlen was standing on his toes, trying to replace the

cow skull on the wall. I was facing the hunting scene on the wall, when he lost his balance and reached for the edge of a gun cabinet to steady himself. In the same instant, the painting shifted, as if moving toward me. For a second, I thought I might be hallucinating. Then I realized what had happened.

"Arlen! Check it out! You must have pressed a button or something."

"I did what now?"

He joined me in front of the painting, which I now saw obscured a narrow door. I grasped the edge and pulled the door open. Inside was a small room, no larger than a closet. I grabbed my cell phone, with its newly installed flashlight app, and shined it inside.

"What is this?" asked Arlen. "Some kind of safe room?"

"Or maybe a sort of safe," I posited. "This looks like the sort of secret hiding place a wealthy person would use to hide away special treasures. Too bad it's empty now." My light revealed cedar walls and ceiling, with deep shelves made of the same wood—and not a single coin, bauble, or gem.

"You could hide valuables in here," Arlen agreed. "You could also hide a person. There's plenty of room."

"Are you suggesting the killer hid in here?"

He shrugged. "We've no way of knowing. I'm just saying it's possible."

Suddenly, I recalled the noises I'd heard coming from the gun room a few days ago. Was someone hiding in this space the whole time?

Then I noticed something else. My light picked up a small, flat piece of wood jutting slightly from the wall. It was at eye level. I pushed the wood aside to reveal a single peephole. I looked through it and observed a clear view of the library. *Weird*.

"You see what I mean?" I said to Arlen. "With every secret I uncover in this house, another mystery crops up."

"It's a house of mysteries, all right."

"But I'm getting closer," I said. "I'll figure this thing out yet."

Chapter Thirty-Four

Considering how late it was when we finally left Turnbull Manor, I told Arlen he should feel free to sleep in the next morning. But he still beat me to the office—and had dusted the furniture and watered the plants to boot. He returned my keys when I arrived and told me he'd already made two client appointments for me for later in the week.

"Your calendar showed you were free during the hours I scheduled the appointments. I hope that's okay."

"Yes, for sure. I need you to be able to rely on my calendar. I'll try to make sure it's always up-to-date."

We spent a busy morning with little mention of our adventures in necromancy. But the Turnbull mysteries were never far from my mind—especially since Lana was still moping around my house. Wes had to go into work today, too, so the heiress was on her own. At least Josie had someone to keep her company.

By midafternoon, I was ready to call it a day. Arlen was in the process of creating a new accounting spreadsheet and didn't want to stop. He said he'd lock up the office in a little while.

I left for home, mentally congratulating myself for hiring Arlen as my assistant. He was proving to be a valuable asset in more ways than one.

As I was parking my car in front of my house, my cell phone rang. It was Farrah.

"Hey, girl," I said. "I've been meaning to call you today."

"Do you have news? Wait, don't tell me yet. I thought I'd come over to your house a little early, so we'll have time to catch up."

"Early for what?"

"'For what?' How could you forget?"

I racked my brain. It was a Tuesday, three days before the Autumn Equinox. Farrah's birthday was a few weeks ago. What could I possibly have forgotten?

"Crenshaw's play! Tonight is opening night."

"Oh, yeah! Of course. He's been talking about it for days."

"Yeah. So, I thought I'd wear my short chocolate-brown sweater dress with ankle boots. What do you think?"

"Sounds great. I'll find something complementary."

In truth, I was feeling distracted and not exactly in the mood to go see a play. But I wanted to support Crenshaw. By the time Farrah arrived a little while later, I'd changed into a soft beige sweater, brown leggings, and a gold necklace. Lana and I were in the kitchen putting together a lentil salad with mixed greens. Farrah opened a bottle of white wine and sliced a baguette, and we sat down to a cozy little meal in the kitchen.

"Wes called a bit ago," I said. "He was asked to fill in at the Loose tonight. The regular bartender called in sick. Lana, why don't you come to the play with Farrah and me?"

"Yes, do!" said Farrah. "The more the merrier."

"Thanks, but I don't much feel like going out. I'll stay in and watch TV if it's okay with you."

"Sure," I said. "Whatever you want to do is fine."

Farrah kept up the conversation after that, with light commentary on the latest political scandals and celebrity gossip. She seemed to sense I didn't want to talk about the Turnbull case in Lana's presence. I definitely didn't want Lana to hear about Arlen's message from the animal spirits.

Still, there was one thing I was dying to ask her. As soon as we'd finished eating, I decided to broach the subject.

"Lana, do you mind if I ask you something about the day you left home?"

She shrugged as she said, "I guess not."

"It's about the . . . note your father left. Do you remember what it said?" If Arlen's animal messenger was right, and Jim had been murdered, then the note must be a fake.

"Do you want to see it? I still have it."

I nodded, and tried to avoid looking at Farrah. I could tell from the catch in her breath that she was as moved as I was. This poor woman had been holding on to her father's suicide note her entire adult life.

Lana went to get her backpack, which was on the floor in the living room. She removed an envelope, pulled out a small square of paper, and handed it to me.

"Would you excuse me?" she said. "I'm just going to run up to the bathroom."

I was glad she left the room. She probably didn't

want to read the note again herself, or even be with us while we read it.

Farrah and I silently read the scribbled handwriting together.

I can't go on. It's all too much. I hope my family can forgive me.

We looked at each other then, with matching frowns.

"Pretty generic, huh?" I said.

"It's a textbook suicide note," she said.

"Exactly. It's nothing but clichés."

"What are you thinking?" she asked.

"I think it's a fake—which confirms, in my mind, something I learned last night." Without providing the details, I told Farrah about Arlen's revelation.

Her eyes wide, Farrah practically bounced with all the questions she wanted to ask. But the one she asked was the one I couldn't answer.

"Why would anybody want to murder Jim Turnbull?"

On our way to the Edindale Playhouse, I had half a mind to ask Farrah to make a detour to Turnbull Manor. I was feeling an urgency to get to the bottom of this string of mysteries before anything else could happen. Checking my cell phone, I realized we didn't have time. But that didn't mean I couldn't make a quick phone call.

"Do you happen to have Suzanne's phone number?" I asked. "She gave me her card, but I don't know what I did with it."

"Yeah, it's in my phone." Farrah reached for her purse in the back seat and tossed it in my lap. "It's in there."

I found the number and dialed. Suzanne answered

with a cheery, saleswoman "hello." But as soon as I identified myself, her cheeriness dropped away. "Keli? What can I do for you?"

"Sorry to bug you, Suzanne, but I have a very important question."

"All your questions are important, aren't they?" she said dryly.

"It's about your husband's death. The police may be reopening their investigation into how he died." At least, I hoped they would, as soon as I figured out a way to convince Detective Rhinehardt to do so—ideally without mentioning cow skulls and spirit animals.

"What?" she said sharply, her voice raising several decibels.

"I know this is a sensitive subject," I continued, "but I have reason to believe foul play may have been involved."

"What?" she repeated. This time I had to move the phone away from my ear.

"Now, listen, please. I need to know what you were fighting about the day he died."

"What are you talking about?" she yelled. "Jim's death was ruled an accident! Why can't you let him rest in peace? I'm not going to relive the past. It's too painful. I'm sorry." And with that, she hung up.

"That went well," I said, as Farrah pulled into the municipal parking lot.

"I could tell," she said. "Good job."

"Yeah."

Farrah had bought us front-row tickets, in the very center of the theater. We were so close I felt like we were on the stage, receiving phonetics lessons from Crenshaw right alongside Eliza Doolittle. The story was cute and engaging, and I was able to set aside my worries for at least a little while.

During intermission, Farrah and I walked to the lobby to stretch our legs. While in line to grab a few refreshments, we looked around to see if we recognized any of the other theatergoers.

Farrah nudged my arm. "Hey isn't that what's-her-name? The reporter Crenshaw used to date? He's not seeing her again, is he?"

I followed her gaze. "Sheana Starwalt? Yeah, that's her. And, I don't think they're dating, as far as I know. Then again, it's not like he tells me everything about his personal life."

Farrah narrowed her eyes, and I grinned. I was about to tease her about having a crush on Crenshaw, when someone else caught my eye. On the other side of the lobby, a man stood alone, speaking into a cell phone. His back was partially turned away, but I recognized his dark hair and full beard. It was Xavier Charleston.

"Fancy seeing him here," I muttered.

"Who?" asked Farrah.

I pointed him out, then handed Farrah some cash. "Order me a drink, will you? I'm gonna go hover, so I can nab him as soon as he's off the phone. Our conversation was cut short the other night, and I still have a few questions."

As I made my way through the milling crowd, Xavier suddenly turned his head and looked straight at me. He winked, then headed swiftly for the exit. For a moment, I was taken aback. It was such an unexpected reaction. But I soon gathered my wits and followed him outside.

Stepping onto the sidewalk in front of the theater, I looked left and right. Where had he gone? A moment later, I spotted him walking around to the driver's side of an expensive-looking black car parked along the curb. If I wasn't mistaken, it was a Bentley.

An older man walking by paused next to me and whistled softly. "It's not often you see cars like that around Edindale."

"No," I agreed. "It's not."

Chapter Thirty-Five

I tossed and turned Tuesday night, wrestling with the implications of everything I'd learned. By the next morning, I was in no shape to go to work. I phoned Arlen to let him know.

"No problem," he said. "You don't have any appointments today. I'll open up the office and hold down the fort."

"You're a saint, Arlen. Has anyone ever told you that?"

"Hmm," he said, seeming to consider it. "Hero, maybe. I'm not sure about 'saint.'"

Smiling, I told him good-bye and crawled back into bed. An hour or so later, Wes came in with a cup of coffee and a slice of avocado toast.

"Wake up, sleepyhead. We need to talk."

In my sleep-addled haze, my heart stuttered in my chest. Was this *the* talk? The one about our future? Then I rubbed my eyes and shook off the fog.

"Why aren't you at work?" I mumbled.

"I went in early to pick up my assignment. I'll be

photographing the fall decorations downtown later today."

"Fun. So, what do we need to talk about?"

"Lana. What can we do to help her? We gotta figure this thing out. She can't stay here forever."

At least we were in agreement on that point. I got up to throw water on my face and brush my teeth. By the time I came back, Wes was sitting up in bed flipping through a small notebook. I sat down next to him and munched on my toast.

"Are those your gumshoe notes?" I asked.

He snickered. "Sort of. They're mostly about my hunt for Lana. You were supposed to find the will and whatever else was missing."

"I looked, believe me! But there seem to be a lot of secret hiding places at the manor." I'd already told Wes about the hidden closet in the gun room. Now I wondered if the mansion held yet more secrets waiting to be discovered.

"Maybe we should see Rhinehardt again," said Wes. "He kept the threatening letter Lana received and said he'd follow up on it. But he wasn't clear about what he would do next."

"Did he say anything about the missing painting?"

"Yeah. He said the cops spent all weekend interviewing people who were at the gala, and nobody saw anything. Since the bartender was in the conservatory all evening, and the caterers were in the kitchen, it's likely the thief walked out the front door."

"That would have been a bold move," I said.

Wes squinted, thinking back to Friday night. "You're right. There were a lot of cars parked on the street out front. And it's a fairly long walk from the street to the front door. In some ways, it would have made more sense for the thief to slip out the kitchen door to a vehicle in the driveway."

"A few people did park in the circular driveway in back," I mused. "Some of the older guests came in that way."

"Maybe the caterers were too busy to pay attention to people coming in and out," said Wes.

"They were quite busy," I said. "But I'd like to hear for myself what they have to say. Can you hand me my phone?"

Last time I'd spoken with young Trevor, he was a bundle of nerves—mainly afraid his mom would be in trouble for lying to the police about Celia. I imagined being questioned by the cops was a nerve-racking experience for him.

"Ruby Plate Catering," said the woman who answered the phone.

"Hello. Is Trevor in?"

A minute later, Trevor was on the line. His voice cracked when I told him who I was and what I wanted to know.

"I already told the police everything!" he said. "I didn't see Celia walking around with a painting or anything else."

"They asked you specifically about Celia?"

"What? No. I—I just assumed she was a suspect because of, you know, the lies. I mean, not the lies. The misunderstanding."

I glanced at Wes and rolled my eyes. "Trevor, relax. I'm not calling about Celia. I just want to know if you saw *anyone* exit through the kitchen with *anything* in their hands. Anything bigger than a glass or plate."

He was silent for a moment, hopefully thinking. I waited.

"We were really busy," he finally said. "But I think

most of the guests stayed out of the kitchen. There was an old man who came in that way early in the evening. And some of the people who live there walked through— I think their names were Ray and Crenshaw, or something. I don't think they were carrying anything."

"What about later on? Like, during the speeches maybe?"

"Oh, yeah. There was a guy who went to put his coat in his car, but he came right back."

My skin prickled at this bit of news. "An overcoat?"

"Yeah, I guess. One of those long, heavy coats."

"Who was the guy, Trevor? What did he look like?"

"He was one of the rich dudes. He had a long black beard."

I thanked Trevor and hung up. Wes was watching me expectantly. "Well?"

"It was Xavier," I said. "I don't know why, especially if he's as wealthy as everyone says. But I'm almost positive it was Xavier."

I dressed quickly, then followed Wes downtown to the police station. We took separate cars, since we didn't know how long we would be. As it happened, we had to wait a while to see Detective Rhinehardt. When he finally showed us to his small office, he seemed grumpier than usual. He was even less happy to learn I'd elicited information from a witness his officers had already questioned.

"Never mind that," I said, not wanting to draw any more attention to Trevor, my trusty informant. "What do you know about Xavier Charleston?"

Rhinehardt grabbed a file folder and flipped through some papers. Finding the one he wanted, he read us the highlights. "Mr. Charleston was interviewed at the

Harrison Hotel on Saturday. He's an art dealer from LA. He's been in Edindale for a month. I spoke to him myself regarding the night Elaine Turnbull passed away, and he had a solid alibi. As for Friday night, he told my investigator he thought the painting was still on the wall when he left the party around ten P.M." He paused, frowning. "Huh."

"What's the matter?" I asked, leaning forward.

"It says here there was a problem when the investigator went to run Charleston's driver's license after interviewing him at the hotel. He made a note saying he might have copied down the number wrong."

Rhinehardt snatched up his phone and hit a button. "Get me the Harrison Hotel, please."

Wes and I watched as Rhinehardt made his inquiries. By the time he hung up, his face was flushed a fiery shade of red.

"He checked out?" I asked.

"Late last night," said Rhinehardt. "And he paid his entire bill in cash."

We could tell Rhinehardt was in no mood for help from amateurs, so Wes and I wisely said good-bye—right after I mentioned seeing Xavier at the Edindale Playhouse the evening before. Over lunch at the Cozy Café, Wes and I both used our phones to look up anything we could find on the art dealer from LA. We came up with nada.

"Either he's a super private person, or there is no Xavier Charleston," said Wes.

"I'll bet you he's a con artist," I said. "A smooth swindler. I bet even his beard was fake!"

"I don't know," said Wes. "It looked real to me."

"Yeah, well, I always had a funny feeling about that guy."

Wes gave me a half grin, as if to say, "Sure you did."

I took a sip of iced tea, as I tried to recall all the times I'd come across or heard someone mention Xavier's name.

"He had a lot of people fooled," said Wes. "And all to steal a painting from the Turnbulls. I wonder if he robbed anyone else."

"Or purchased something with a bad check," I said. "He was supposedly buying artwork from other private collectors around here."

"Oh, well," said Wes, sitting back in his chair. "That's one mystery solved, but it doesn't help us with Lana's problem. There's still someone out there who apparently doesn't want her to claim her inheritance. Somebody who murdered Elaine—and probably murdered Jim, too, right?"

"Yeah," I said absently, as I played with the ice in my glass. "But I'm not so sure the mysteries aren't connected. I keep thinking *everything* is connected."

"You mean, like, in a cosmic way?"

I smiled. "That, too."

Wes checked his watch. "I gotta go meet the head of the Chamber of Commerce and take some photos. Let's pick up this discussion later. Are you going into work today?"

"Not just yet. I want to stop by the museum first."

Mavis Rawlins was dumbstruck when I broke the news about Xavier. We were sitting in her office at the Edindale Art Museum, much as we had been the first time I'd met her. Only now, her serene composure rapidly cracked like the marble bust on the shelf behind her.

"It appears he skipped town," I said.

"But he pledged thousands of dollars in donations to the museum! What do you mean he 'skipped town'?"

"Well, he checked out of his hotel anyway," I said. "Do you have a way of getting in touch with him?"

She reached for a Rolodex then picked up her phone. A moment later, she shook her head in disbelief. "His number has been disconnected!"

"Mavis, had you ever heard of Xavier before he came to Edindale? How did you first meet him?"

"Why, I believe we were introduced by Perry Warren. I had the impression Mr. Charleston was well-known in his field, at least on the West Coast."

I stood up to leave. "The police are trying to track him down even as we speak. If you think of anything that might be helpful, be sure to give Detective Rhinehardt a call."

In the meantime, I had a few questions to ask Perry.

I swung by Farrah's apartment on my way to Turnbull Manor. "Are you free for a bit of sleuthing?" I asked.

"Heck, yeah! I'm supposed to be making some sales calls this afternoon, but they can wait." She shouldered her purse and locked her door behind us. "This time I want to be with you when you stumble upon some secret passageway or hidden door or whatever it is you always seem to find."

We were quiet on the drive to the mansion. Farrah probably sensed we were nearing the end of our adventure—and, therefore, wandering into dangerous territory. But my mind was occupied with the sticky strands of a complicated web. Or was it so complicated? Maybe the answer to all the open questions was the same. Someone murdered Elaine, took her amended will, swiped her diaries, and stole the painting—or arranged its theft—all for the same reason. Oh, and killed Jim for the same reason several years before. The killer tried to make Jim's death look like a suicide, but then Lana ran off with the suicide note. When Lana first shared her story, I'd assumed Perry never mentioned the note for the same reason the responding police officers didn't share their theory—to spare Elaine the additional pain of believing her son took his own life. Now I was having other ideas . . .

As I parked my car in front of the mansion, Farrah turned to look at me with a nervous light in her eye. "We're not going to confront Ray, are we?"

"We're not going to confront anyone," I said. "We're just asking questions."

Before leaving the car, I shot off a quick text to Wes to let him know where I was. Since I didn't see Crenshaw's car at the manor, I sent him a text as well.

"About the will," I said, as we walked to the back of the house. "We've been under the assumption that whoever took it didn't like how Elaine had decided to distribute her estate. Ray thought the crook was going to alter the document to benefit him or herself."

"Or destroy it," said Farrah. "Maybe the thief preferred that everything go to Lana. That could apply to her friend, Ernesto, or her stepmother, Suzanne. Or to Lana herself. When did she come back again?"

I shook my head. "I don't think the motive had anything to do with any individual beneficiary. I think it had to do with the assets Elaine was distributing."

"What do you mean?"

"I think her will made specific bequests of specific

paintings. The art collection is the key to this whole thing. I'm almost certain someone hired Xavier to take the painting, because they didn't want it to be part of the collection when Crenshaw put everything up for sale."

"Which he was about to do!" said Farrah. "If you hadn't found Lana, he was going to have to liquidate the whole estate."

"I'd love to be able to find Xavier," I said. "And I'm very interested in how Perry came to meet him."

Chapter Thirty-Six

Perry didn't answer when we knocked on his door. We walked around the outside of his guesthouse, glancing over our shoulders and trying to peek in the windows. At his back door, I knocked again.

"Do you think he took off with Xavier?" Farrah whispered.

"That wouldn't be very smart," I said. "After all, his identity is real. He'd have a harder time disappearing."

On a whim, I tried the doorknob. It was unlocked. Farrah and I looked at each other, and she nodded. "Detectives snoop," she said. "Plus, we have permission to be here. Perry let you in with Rhinehardt the other night."

It was plausible. Besides, the closer we got to the answer, the more imperative it was to act fast.

We crept inside and did a quick sweep of every room. Most of Perry's things were packed up in suitcases and boxes—as they should be, considering Crenshaw's eviction notice. We were back in the kitchen, about to leave through the back door, when I opened the refrigerator.

"What are you looking for?" asked Farrah. "The painting?"

"Anything. A pill bottle, a diary . . . A gallon of milk."

"Milk?" Farrah looked around me to see for herself. "Yep, milk. Real suspicious."

"It is when the only guy who lives here is lactose intolerant. Suzanne mentioned it the first day I was here."

"Maybe he takes a pill for that," said Farrah.

"Or maybe he has the milk because he used it to pour Elaine's last mug."

"Let's get out of here," said Farrah. She turned quickly and tripped on a fringed area rug. She gasped, stumbling to her knees.

"Are you okay?" I reached down to give her a hand. As I pulled her to her feet, the rug shifted. "Hey, look at that."

Farrah turned, and I pulled the rug back. There, in the center of the wood-planked floor, was the clear outline of a trapdoor. Farrah jumped back like it was a poisonous snake.

"Take it easy," I said, trying not to laugh. "It's just a trapdoor."

"If there are stairs under there, leading to a dank, creepy cellar, we are *not* going down them."

"Of course not. We're not fools. I just want to see what it is." I grabbed the handle and gave it a yank. The door came right up.

Farrah crouched down to peer inside. "No stairs."

I used my phone to shine a light inside. The space beneath the floor was about three feet deep and four feet wide and appeared to be used for storage. It contained some dusty picture frames, all empty, and a lockbox. On top of the lockbox was Elaine's last diary. I grabbed the diary and thrust it into my jacket pocket. "Help me with this box," I said.

Together we hefted the lockbox out of the hole in the floor and hurried to the door. My heart thudded wildly, as I expected Perry to burst in on us at any second.

"Shouldn't we cover up the trapdoor again?" asked Farrah, her voice shaking.

"Yes." We set the box on the floor and rushed back to close the trapdoor and replace the rug. "Okay, come on!" I said.

We made it outside and halted uncertainly outside Perry's back door. The route to the mansion seemed longer than I remembered, and much more wide-open. We could be seen from several directions.

"Maybe we should hide this in the trees," Farrah suggested.

"Yeah. Good idea."

Moving in an awkward side-step, we managed to carry the lockbox several yards behind Perry's cottage and park it behind a large bush. "Stay here," I said, handing Farrah the diary from my pocket. "I'll go get the key to the lockbox. It's still in the room where we were staying."

"Are you sure?"

"Yes, there's no time to waste. Go ahead and call Detective Rhinehardt. I'll be right back."

Farrah sat on top of the lockbox and opened the diary, as I dashed off to the house. I let myself inside and hurried up the back stairs. I was almost to the bedroom when I heard raised voices coming from the front of the house. It sounded like a man and a woman were arguing. Bypassing the bedroom, I ran to the gallery at the top of the grand staircase. Over the bannister, I spied Perry standing in the great room. He had his hands up as if in surrender.

Moments later Lana came into view. What was she doing here? Perry sounded like he was trying to calm her down—much as he'd sounded when Ray was yelling at him on the day of the gala.

"Just listen to yourself," he said calmly. "You sound crazy." He was backing away from her, toward the west hallway.

"I am not crazy! All these years I believed my father killed himself. And he didn't!"

"I know it's difficult to accept, but it's the truth. And you can't possibly know otherwise."

I didn't like the sound of this. I hurried down the stairs, plastering a forced smile on my face. After all, Perry didn't know what I'd found in his house. "Hi guys! What's up? Perry, did you know Lana's back? Good news, right?"

Lana rounded on me. "I *know* the truth. This note is a fake!" She shook a crumpled piece of paper in her balled fist, and I mentally groaned. She must have overheard Farrah and me discussing the note.

"I don't know what's gotten into her," said Perry.

"She's clearly troubled," I murmured, hoping to keep Perry in the dark. "Why don't we all go sit down in the parlor and talk about it? You both lost someone special to you. It's such a difficult thing."

I tried to send Lana a message with my eyes, but she was focused on Perry. And he was focused on her, as if the note were a deadly weapon. All I wanted to do was stall. Surely, Detective Rhinehardt must be on his way by now.

Thinking fast, I shouted down the hallway. "Celia! Could you please bring tea for three to the west parlor?" I had no idea where Celia was, or if she could hear me, but I hoped to draw as much attention to myself as possible. Knowing her, she was probably watching us from someplace.

"Come on, you two," I said, giving Lana a small push. Reluctantly, Perry led the way to the parlor. But once inside, neither of them sat down.

Lana walked up to Elaine's portrait, then suddenly whirled on Perry. "All these years! I thought my father took his own life, because . . . because . . ." Tears filled her eyes, as she trembled with rage. "I thought he blamed me for the death of my real mom! She died giving birth to me. He would never admit it, but after Suzanne left he wouldn't even look me in the eyes. He probably blamed me for her leaving, too."

"Lana," I said, reaching out to her. "That's not it at all. Your dad was worried about something else entirely. It had nothing at all to do with you."

Perry threw me a sharp look, and I gasped involuntarily. What had I just let slip?

Lana wiped her eyes and smoothed out the wrinkled paper. "If this note is forged, then that can mean only one thing. Somebody murdered my father." She took a step toward Perry. "You murdered him!"

Before I could react, Perry reached into his jacket and pulled out a gun. I didn't know if it was an antique or a recent model, but I was sure it was loaded.

Lana shrank back, as I instinctively stepped in front of her. "Perry, put that away. What are you doing?" I tried to keep my voice steady. But I should have known the time for reasoning had passed.

"Go," he said, waving the gun. "Both of you, go to the library."

My stomach clenched, as I realized what he had in mind. From the library, he'd force us into the gun room.

Once there, it wouldn't be hard to arrange another "accident." I needed to distract him from his plan.

"Elaine was on to you, wasn't she?" I said. "Is that what she wrote in her diaries? She started asking you about certain paintings that had gone missing, and you didn't have good answers." His eye twitched, and I knew I'd hit on the truth. "She was downsizing," I continued. "She'd told Crenshaw as much. Maybe she wanted to start selling off some of the collection, and she asked you for your appraisal certificates. Is that it?"

He inched closer, forcing us to back toward the door. I could have told him the game was up. We'd found the diaries and the cops were on the way. (I hoped.) But I didn't like the desperate look in his eyes. He might decide he had nothing to lose and kill us right there, then try to make a run for it.

Where *was* Detective Rhinehardt?

"Dad was in on the scheme, too, wasn't he?" said Lana in a small voice. "I remember now how you and he were so secretive sometimes. I wasn't allowed in the library when you talked business. You must have been selling off Grandfather's collection, one by one. And here I always thought our wealth came from investment income."

"I'll bet Jim wanted out," I speculated. "He must have felt guilty cheating his own mother, and he wanted to put an end to it. That's why you killed him."

Perry refused to say a word, but his rapid blinking said a lot. I felt Lana tense up behind me.

"Let me guess," I said, trying to bait him just a little. "You replaced some of the paintings with forgeries, so it wouldn't be so obvious the collection was dwindling. The Grant Wood must have been a forgery. That's why you had to arrange a robbery. The minute the painting was placed on the auction block, the forgery would be discovered—and so would your false appraisals."

He shook his head. "Go," he rasped, waving his gun again. "Now!"

"What I want to know," I said, trying to ignore the gun, "is, who is Xavier Charleston? Is he one of your buyers? Is he your link to the black market?" I was just fishing now, but my guesses seemed to hit the mark so far.

Perry lifted the gun higher and aimed it at my chest. "If you won't go, I'll shoot you right here."

What's the difference? I thought. Why did criminals always expect their victims to make it easy for them? By this time our backs were up against the doorway, and I had run out of things to say. I was about ready to try bargaining with Perry, when I noticed the far wall begin to move. What I thought had been a decorative panel was actually a door leading to another secret room.

Perry jerked his head around. In that instant, I raised my foot and kicked his hand as hard as I could. He dropped the gun to the floor, and I made a grab for it. At the same time, Lana tackled him full on, knocking him backward.

A whole team of people, or so it seemed, came rushing through the hidden door. Wes and Detective Rhinehardt burst through first, followed shortly by Crenshaw and Ray.

Then Celia swung open the parlor door and scurried in, bearing a tray with three cups of tea. She skidded to a halt and began counting the number of people in the room.

"Now there are seven of you!" She set down the tray, threw up her hands, and walked out.

* * *

While Rhinehardt cuffed Perry, I told Crenshaw where to find Farrah. He left to go bring her in from her hiding place in the trees. Ray took one look at Lana and dissolved into tears. I'd always suspected he was a big softie, in spite of his gruff exterior.

Wes gave me a big hug, then pulled back and scowled. I knew he was cross with me, and I couldn't blame him. But, really, this was not how I'd envisioned this day turning out.

The parlor door opened again, and Suzanne and Ernesto walked in. "What's going on?" asked Suzanne. "Perry?"

Rhinehardt had just read Perry his rights and was now waiting for backup. Perry stared at the floor without a word.

"I *knew* he was up to something," said Ray.

That's when Suzanne noticed Lana. She screamed and ran toward her. "My baby! Oh, my gosh! You came home!"

Lana looked up uncertainly, then broke into a smile and allowed herself to be hugged. I hoped they'd work things out between them, whatever their issues were. I had a feeling I knew now why Suzanne and Jim had been fighting. Perhaps Suzanne suspected what Jim was up to and didn't approve. That would explain her nervous behavior whenever I tried to talk to her about the art collection. It could also be why she left him in the first place.

At that moment, Crenshaw and Farrah came up behind me. "Well done, Milanni," said Crenshaw. "I don't know how, but you did it again."

"Not by myself," I said, nodding at Farrah and reaching for Wes's hand.

Ray wiped his face with a handkerchief and stepped forward. He cleared his throat and tried to sound gruff again. "Too bad you never found the new will. I guess Perry must've destroyed it after all."

"Actually," said Farrah, stepping forward, "I don't think he did. I found this in the lining of the diary."

She held up a small tarnished key. With a triumphant grin, she handed it to me. "There was a note on the back inside cover that said 'parlor window.' Any idea what that means?"

A strange sensation passed over me, like a whisper-soft breeze from nowhere. I glanced at the large window—the same one Elaine had pointed to in my astral vision.

I made a beeline for the window and looked outside. Then my gaze dropped to the interior windowsill. Kneeling down, I looked beneath it and saw a small keyhole. I inserted the key Farrah had found and turned. There was a click, and the sill fell forward, revealing a hidden compartment. Inside was a folded bundle of papers. Opening it, I wasn't a bit surprised to read an inscription at the top: *The Last Will and Testament of Elaine (Jane) Turnbull.* I flipped to the last page and saw that it was signed by Elaine and two witnesses.

I walked over to Crenshaw, whose mouth was hanging open.

"Here you go," I said.

Chapter Thirty-Seven

Thursday evening, the day after Perry's arrest, found me at the Loose, enjoying happy hour with Farrah. We clinked appletinis and toasted the end of the Turnbull saga. I was definitely in a celebratory mood. Crenshaw had successfully filed Elaine's subsequent will in probate court. I had been correct in my guess that Elaine wished to donate specific pieces of artwork that were now long gone from the estate. It would take a while for an honest appraiser to go through the collection and figure out how much was left, but a preliminary review indicated that there were still quite a lot of genuine works—including the Whitney sculpture.

Happily, Elaine had also left generous bequests to all of her friends and loved ones, including Lana, Suzanne, Ray, Ernesto, and Celia. The mansion itself was still Lana's to take or leave, and she decided to take it. In fact, she had already moved in, determined to make a go with her interesting little makeshift family.

On his way back from court, Crenshaw had stopped

at my office to cut me a check for all the hours I had put in on the case. When Arlen saw the amount, he nearly dropped his muffin. "Holy cow!" he exclaimed. Then he grinned cheekily. "No pun intended."

Wes, of course, was thrilled for his friend—and even happier to have our house back. He was behind the bar now, making silly faces at me every time I shot him a glance. I was smiling his way, when the bar door opened, and Mila and Catrina came strolling in. I waved them over.

"I feel outnumbered!" Farrah joked, as she made room for the newcomers. "I'm surrounded by witches!"

"*Join us . . .*" Catrina intoned in a crackly voice. Then she snickered.

"Nah, I'll just live vicariously through Keli," Farrah replied.

Mila wanted to hear how everything had turned out at Turnbull Manor, so Farrah and I took turns filling her in. Catrina was spellbound.

"Wow," she said. "That Perry guy was one bad dude. I take it he's the one who faked the suicide note and sent a death threat to Lana?"

"Yeah," I said. "I heard from Rhinehardt today, and he told me Perry decided to confess. He shot Jim and poisoned Elaine with her own opioid pain medicine."

"That's dreadful," murmured Mila. "Where were the other members of the household when he took Elaine the poisoned cup of milk?"

"That was the crazy thing," said Farrah. "Everyone lied about where they were!"

"Yes," I said, "and in some cases for silly reasons. Suzanne and Ernesto were in his apartment—"

"Having a little tryst," said Farrah. "And Celia was trying to catch them! That lady has some issues."

I nodded. "Ray's secret was even more unfortunate. He was hiding away in his art studio as the guests were leaving. That's why he was late in bringing Elaine her nightly cup. When someone mentioned he was walking his dog, he decided to jump on the excuse—false though it was."

A waitress stopped by to take orders from Mila and Catrina. As soon as she left, Mila shook her head sadly. "It's too bad the young woman, Lana, was estranged from her family for all those years."

"That was Perry's fault, too," I said. "After Jim's death was ruled an accident, he knew the suicide note would only draw suspicion—especially since it was so badly forged. That's why he didn't want Lana to come back. Plus, she was the only one who knew he was already on the scene when the gunshot went off."

"By the way," said Farrah, turning to me, "did Lana ever find her missing ring?"

I smiled. "Suzanne had it the whole time. She really does love Lana."

Farrah removed the apple slice garnish from the edge of her martini glass and took a bite. "I suppose the missing artwork may never be recovered," she said. "It's hard to believe Perry thought he could get away with such a large-scale fraud for so long. But he almost did."

"To think," said Catrina, "you were under the same roof with a two-time killer. Good thing you know how to set up protective energy shields."

"Here, here," said Farrah, raising her glass again.

At that moment, the waitress came back and set a bottle of lager on the table in front of me. I read the label: Dos Equis XX.

"I didn't order this," I said, trying to hand it back to her. "It must be for someone else."

"Are you Keli?"

"Yes."

"It's for you. Courtesy of the hottie with the black beard."

I whipped around, scanning the room. "Where is he?" I asked the waitress.

"Oh, he left right after he paid. Too bad."

Farrah and I stared at each other in disbelief. "Xavier?" she said. "What is this, his calling card?" She pointed to the X's on the label.

"Like Xorro, with an X," said Catrina.

"What?" I looked at her, trying to figure out where I'd heard that before.

"You know. Zorro always left a Z. This guy leaves an X."

"Like the X's in everyone's tires," I said, suddenly remembering.

"Wait," said Farrah. "You don't think Xavier is the tire slasher, do you? He doesn't seem like the type who would stoop to something so juvenile."

Juvenile. Just like the pranks of my mysterious Giftster. Xavier drove a Bentley, and Farrah had seen a Bentley following her shortly before her tires were slashed. I'd also seen one in the alley behind my office right after the fiasco with all the unwanted job applicants.

Plus, there were all those times I'd caught Xavier looking at me, and the obscure things he'd said to me in the gardens.

Had I met my stalker in the flesh?

"On the bright side," said Farrah, "he'll never have the nerve to show his face around here again."

"Right," I said. At least not a face I would recognize.

* * *

Day one of Applefest felt like a celebration of all the best fall had to offer. Situated on the county fairgrounds at the edge of town, it provided a perfect showcase for all the area farms. As I wound my way through the grounds, I passed stands bearing all the season's bounty: from corn, squash, arugula, and okra to peaches, tomatoes, and grapes. And apples, of course, in a multitude of varieties. Besides the cornucopia of fruits and vegetables, there were also fresh-cut flowers, dried cornstalks, and other goodies for autumn decorating. The sound of children laughing, and the scent of popcorn and cider doughnuts, only added to the festive atmosphere.

When I finally reached Mila's booth, set up against a backdrop of golden-brown cornfields, I was grinning from ear to ear. It looked like she'd recreated the window display at Moonstone Treasures—complete with her cat, Drishti, who made a perfect witchy mascot. She greeted me with a warm smile and a glass of deep purple grape juice.

"You're such a dear to help me out! Catrina's hay fever kicked in so badly, I sent her straight home for herbal tea and bed rest. But I could really use a second pair of hands today. Just look at all these people!"

"I'm happy to help," I said, as I took in the milling crowds. It was true that the turnout today was larger than usual. This was partly due to the glorious weather. But I suspected it was also attributable to a couple of other events coinciding with the harvest festival, including a kids' beauty pageant and a luxury auto auction.

As I watched the passersby, an unexpected profile came into view. In fact, it was so surprising it made my stomach lurch. There was no mistaking the expensive haircut, movie-star sunglasses, and full, black beard.

Evidently, I hadn't seen the last of Xavier Charleston after all.

"What is he doing here?" I muttered. "Mila, do you need me at the moment? Or can I—"

"Go," she said, taking the glass of grape juice from my hand.

"I'll be right back."

I hurried off in the direction Xavier had headed. For a moment, I lost him in the crowd. But then I spotted him again—standing in line at a caramel corn stand, of all places.

Ducking behind a chrysanthemum-filled wooden cart, I studied the man who called himself Xavier.

Who is he really?

As I watched, he stepped up to the counter and lifted his sunglasses to the top of his head. He flashed a grin at the girl behind the counter. And when she handed him a bag of caramel corn, he tilted his chin and gave her a wink.

In that moment, I recognized the man behind the beard. It had to be him. There was only one cocky young man I knew with a habit of winking and a penchant for caramel corn—and a deep grudge against me.

But no. He was in jail. My former colleague, Jeremy Bradson, was arrested for stealing Shakespeare's First Folio—among other crimes. It couldn't be him.

As Xavier took off again, I followed a few paces behind. With my mind reeling, I took out my cell phone and called Detective Rhinehardt. When he answered, I asked him straight up: "Is Jeremy Bradson still in prison?"

He hesitated for barely a second before saying, "No."

I froze in my tracks, incredulous at the story Rhinehardt shared. Shortly after his arrest, Jeremy had turned state's evidence, agreeing to give up information on all his co-conspirators in the loan shark operation. That was the real reason the *River Queen* gambling boat had been shut down three years ago. Part of the deal allowed Jeremy to go free under cover of a witness protection program. But last Rhinehardt had heard, Jeremy had disappeared from the program.

"I know where he is," I said.

"What? Where?"

Gazing around the crowd of festival-goers, I realized I'd lost him. He was gone.

"Never mind," I said. "I'll talk to you later."

With a sigh, I made my way back to Mila's stand. In my heart, I knew I had seen the last of Xavier Charleston—this time, for good. He had undoubtedly sold his Bentley at the auto auction and would soon shave his beard and change his name. With all the cash he had, he could go anywhere now.

Maybe I wouldn't hear from the "Giftster" anymore either. Maybe he had tormented me enough. At least for now.

Chapter Thirty-Eight

On Mabon morning, I awoke early and went outside to gather fallen leaves. There weren't as many on the ground as there would be in a few weeks, but there were still plenty to choose from. I started in the backyard and ended up wandering over to Fieldstone Park. It was like a meditation-in-motion. A dazzling leaf of gold, red, orange, or yellow would catch my eye. I would lean down to pick it up, admire its beauty, and place it in my basket. In this way, it also became a gratitude ritual. With every unique and gorgeous leaf, in infinite variations and patterns, I would say a prayer of thanks to Mother Nature. As I filled my basket, I reflected on the other ways my life was filled with abundance.

I had a wonderful, loving partner. Awesome friends and a caring family. The sweetest, smartest cat (if I did say so myself). A job I found fulfilling—with an amazing new assistant! I was also grateful for my beautiful little town, quirks and all. And the sun, moon, and stars; the flowers and the trees; the birds and bees.

By the time I returned home, my heart was as overflowing as my basket. I brought the leaves inside, scattered a few across my altar, and placed the rest in a large glass bowl. It would be the centerpiece of our dining room table.

Wes and I had to add a few more leaves to the table—the kind that make it bigger—in order to accommodate all our dinner guests that night. Mabon was the Wiccan Thanksgiving, and I'd decided to go all out. At first, it was going to be an intimate gathering, with just Mila and her husband, Farrah and a date, my cousin Ricki, and Arlen. Then Arlen asked if his partner could come along, and I said, "Of course." Mila mentioned that Catrina was feeling better and didn't have plans, so I called her at once to extend an invitation.

Farrah texted to let me know she didn't have a date, but she hoped Crenshaw would be there. At that, I realized I should have invited him in the first place. He was surprised when I called but delighted to accept.

All told, there were ten of us around the dinner table. We passed the cider and wine and feasted on roasted harvest vegetables, seven-bean soup, spinach pomegranate salad, and corn bread—with assorted apple and pumpkin treats for dessert. It was a laughing, genial bunch—and such an interesting mix of professions, styles, and personalities. The Autumn Equinox was a time to welcome balance, and I had a perfect example of balance sitting right across from me. *Talk about yin and yang.* Farrah and Crenshaw looked at one another with sparkles in their eyes. At one point, I overheard her say, "Crenshaw . . . *Macbeth* Davenport."

"No," he said.

"What *is* your middle name? Are you ever going to tell me?"

"No," he said. "I guess you'll just have to keep guessing."

After everyone left, Wes and I sat on the floor in the living room, watching Josie play with her favorite cat toys. We'd dimmed the lights and lit some candles. I was so content and pleased with how the day had gone.

"What do you want to do tomorrow?" asked Wes. "For once we both have a free Saturday."

"I haven't been to the woods in a while," I said. "Want to go for a hike out at Briar Creek?"

"Sure. As long as I'm with you, I'm happy to do anything."

I smiled and leaned my head on his shoulder. *Am I the luckiest girl in the world, or what?*

Suddenly, a notion took hold of me, making me sit upright. There was one thing that really, truly would make me the happiest I'd ever been. I wanted to marry Wes. I wanted to "make it official," as Suzanne had said.

I should just ask him myself.

I turned to face him and took a deep breath. "Wes—" I began.

But he said my name at the same time. "Keli?"

"Yes?"

"Will you marry me?"

If you enjoyed *Autumn Alibi*,
be sure not to miss all of
Jennifer David Hesse's
Wiccan Wheel Mystery series,
including

Yuletide Homicide

It's Christmas in Edindale, Illinois, and family law attorney Keli Milanni is preparing to celebrate the Wiccan holiday Yuletide, a celebration of rebirth. But this Yuletide someone else is focused on dying . . .

After years of practicing in secret, Keli has come out as a Wiccan to her boyfriend, and she feels like this Yuletide she's the one who's being reborn. But the Solstice is the longest night of the year, and Keli is about to stumble on a mystery so dangerous, she'll be lucky to make it to morning.

Paired with her unbearably stuffy colleague Crenshaw Davenport III, Keli goes undercover at a real estate company owned by mayoral candidate Edgar Harrison. An old friend of Keli's boss, Harrison is being blackmailed, and it's up to her to find the culprit. But the morning after the company holiday party, Harrison is found dead underneath the hotel Christmas tree. The police rule the death an accident, but Keli knows better—and she'll risk her own rebirth to nab a missing killer.

Keep reading for a special excerpt.

A Kensington mass-market and eBook on sale now!

"Blackmail? Really? Someone is blackmailing Edgar?"

Now there was something you didn't hear every day. Before I could stop myself, an image flashed to mind: Edindale's most prominent silver-haired citizen engaged in a steamy, salacious affair. Scandalous! But with whom? I shifted in my leather seat and smoothed my pencil skirt, as I waited for my boss to continue.

Beverly cast a sharp glance at the door to her dark-paneled inner office. It was still closed.

"Let's not use that word from here on out," she said. She pressed her lips together, a visible demonstration that *mum*, not *blackmail*, was the word.

"Right. Sorry," I said quickly, though I still wasn't clear as to why Beverly was telling me this—well, me and my colleague, Crenshaw Davenport III.

Crenshaw cleared his throat from the chair next to me. His long legs were crossed in an elegantly relaxed pose, but I could tell he was just as intrigued as I was. He thrust his bearded chin forward slightly more than usual.

"It's understandable that Mr. Harrison desires discretion in this matter," he said, "especially given his recent announcement." Crenshaw turned toward me and looked down his nose. "Monday was the filing deadline for anyone interested in running for mayor next fall. Edgar Harrison announced his candidacy, along with half a dozen other Edindale residents."

"I know," I said evenly, biting back the snarky comment on the tip of my tongue. Crenshaw took every opportunity he could to school me in front of Beverly. It was one of his more annoying habits—one of many. We had both been with the firm for about six and a half years, and lately Beverly kept hinting that someone might be making partner soon. This only served to ramp up the competitive wedge between us.

Beverly removed her red-framed glasses and rubbed the bridge of her nose before responding. It had been a long week at the law firm, as everyone tried to finish up as much work as possible before the holidays. Of course, Beverly still looked impeccable in her designer pantsuit and expensive makeup, even if her eyes bore telltale hints of exhaustion.

"As I said, he was contacted by an unknown person who claims to have some information that Edgar would not like to be made public. This person has demanded a large sum of money in exchange for his or her silence. Edgar has until Tuesday to produce the cash." Beverly paused and looked from Crenshaw to me with a deadpan gaze. "Obviously, the information is not true. Edgar assured me that the person manufactured their so-called evidence. However, they must have done a convincing enough job that it could still damage Edgar's reputation should it be released."

I glanced at Crenshaw and saw him raise one eyebrow. He must have been wondering the same thing as me: *Why worry about what a blackmailer might reveal if the information is not true?*

Beverly held up her palm. "I know what you're thinking. Don't. I've known Edgar a long time. He has no reason to be involved in anything illegal. His businesses are all doing extremely well."

That was no surprise. Edgar seemed to have a knack for investing in only the most lucrative projects. He owned Edindale's only riverboat casino, its fanciest hotel, and its trendiest residential developments—among other holdings. But did that necessarily mean everything was on the up and up? Evidently, the blackmailer had information that might indicate otherwise. So much for my steamy affair theory.

"Here's the deal," said Beverly, twisting the silver rings on her left hand. She appeared to be choosing her words carefully. "Edgar is convinced that someone hacked into his computer. This person accessed some confidential financial records about some of Edgar's investments . . . and found a way to twist the truth about the records in a manner that might portray Edgar in a less than favorable light. While Edgar has done nothing illegal, the intricacies of business law are not always easy to explain to the layperson."

Out of the corner of my eye, I saw Crenshaw nod his head and steeple his fingers under his lips. *Oh, sure. As if he already knows what Beverly means, even though she's being extremely vague.* I cleared my throat. "Is that why Edgar came to you instead of the police? Because even the police might have a hard time understanding the legalities?"

Beverly frowned. "Not exactly. It's more that the information might make Edgar look bad, in spite of the fact that his dealings were technically legal. In any event, Edgar fully intends to go to the police as soon as he has evidence. He already has a couple of suspects in mind . . . which brings me to why I asked the two of you into my office this afternoon."

"How can I help?" asked Crenshaw.

"How can we help?" I asked, at the same time. I narrowed my eyes and glared at Crenshaw, before turning back to Beverly.

"As Edgar's attorney and close friend, I agreed to help him figure out who is doing this." Beverly stood and paced to her window where she paused and looked outside. Snow was falling in slow, lazy swirls. She walked back to us and remained standing. "Of course, I immediately thought of you, Keli, because of your detecting skills. You seem to have a knack for recovering stolen objects and ferreting out criminals. As for you, Crenshaw, in addition to being one of my most trusted lawyers, I believe your acting skills may be useful in this case." Crenshaw nodded his whole upper body in a seated bow, as if thanking her for a well-deserved compliment. I fought the urge to roll my eyes.

I looked up at Beverly. "How can we possibly figure out who is blackmail—I mean, who is threatening Edgar?"

"The logical place to start is at Edgar's main office. Harrison Properties has a new IT support specialist, a young, tech-savvy guy named Zeke Marshal. Edgar thinks that if anyone could hack into his secured, password-protected files, this fellow would be the one. The only problem is, Edgar can't imagine why he would do it. The young man was just hired. He has a bright future ahead of him, in a career that will compensate him well. It doesn't make sense."

I nodded, beginning to feel more and more curious myself.

"I've arranged for the two of you to set up shop in Edgar's office for a few days. The ostensible purpose will be to conduct a thorough legal audit of his corporation's files. In fact, Edgar will be paying you to do just that. His staff will be told this is a proactive measure to ensure the company is in compliance with all relevant business laws. At the same time, you will keep your eyes and ears open, and see what you can learn about Zeke. You'll start right away. The sooner we can end this headache for Edgar, the better."

After leaving Beverly's office I headed to my own, much smaller office to gather my coat and purse. Crenshaw and I had agreed to meet downstairs in the lobby in ten minutes and then walk over to Harrison Properties to get started on our strange assignment. Shaking my head, I pushed open my office door and stopped short when I saw what was sitting on my desk: a large gold-colored box, topped with a golden ribbon.

"A delivery guy brought it while you were with Beverly," said a voice behind me. I turned to see Julie, our twenty-something front desk receptionist, peering over her trendy glasses toward the gold box. "There's a card, too."

I smiled at Julie's eagerness, then walked over to my desk to check out the package. Right away, I noticed the word *Godiva* embossed on the lid of the box.

"Did someone say chocolate?" I looked up to see Pammy Sullivan standing in my doorway next to Julie.

Pammy was a fellow associate with heavily sprayed hair and a stylish, if somewhat gaudy, wardrobe. Today she wore a salmon-pink skirt suit, which matched her lipstick and fingernails. The buttons of her blazer strained ever so slightly across her plump figure.

"Come on in," I said, laughing. Pammy must have known about the delivery and was just waiting for me to return to my office.

"Ooh, Godiva," said Pammy, squeezing between the two guest chairs facing my desk to get a look at the gift box. "The nearest Godiva shop is in St. Louis. Someone must have ordered this online, unless they brought it in from out of town. Is it from a client?"

Shrugging, I slipped the small plain card out of the white envelope and furrowed my brow. "I don't think so," I said, in answer to Pammy's question. The card simply said *Missed you*. It was unsigned.

"Aw," said Julie, looking over my shoulder. "It must be from that hunky boyfriend of yours. Hasn't he been out of town?"

"Yeah, for a week. Wes helped his brother move to Seattle. He's supposed to get back later today. I'll see him tonight."

"Well, maybe he came back early," said Pammy, her eyes still on the gold box.

"Maybe," I agreed. I lifted the lid and tore off the protective plastic covering to reveal an assortment of fancy chocolate candies. It was a somewhat odd gift, coming from Wes. He knew I wouldn't eat milk chocolate because I'm vegan. On the other hand, he would also know I'd share the candy.

I replaced the lid and handed the box to Julie. "Would you take this up front and leave it on your desk for all to share? I've got to get going."

Pammy followed Julie out of my office, while I slipped on my long black coat and tied the belt. I grabbed my shoulder bag and hurried to the elevator. It was a short ride, four flights to the ground floor lobby. I pulled on my gloves as I walked over to join Crenshaw where he waited for me by the revolving door. I almost laughed when I saw what he was wearing.

In a Victorian-style overcoat, long scarf, and short top hat, Crenshaw looked like a character straight out of Dickens's *A Christmas Carol.* In fact, as an amateur actor, he probably was. Outside his law practice, Crenshaw was active in the local theater circuit.

"Nice outfit," I said. "Where are you performing?"

"I beg your pardon?"

"The caroler getup," I said, gesturing toward his coat. "Aren't you . . . Never mind."

With Crenshaw, it was sometimes hard to know when he was being serious and what he was really thinking. At times, he could be incredibly sweet. More often than not, he was just obnoxious. My best friend, Farrah, called him the "original pompous ass."

We stepped outside into the crisp, breezy air and made our way down the sidewalk toward Main Street. We walked carefully, knowing there could be slick spots in spite of the rock salt sprinkled like breadcrumbs in our path. Snowflakes stuck to every surface, from the cars parked along the curb to the tops of signs and the large red bows decorating every light post. The bows had been up since Thanksgiving, but it was the fresh snowfall that really made the scene look a lot like Christmas. It ought to, I thought, since the holiday was only a week away.

We turned right at the corner and continued down Main Street, walking past downtown shops with cheerfully decked-out storefronts. When we passed Moonstone Treasures, I slowed down to admire the window display: gracefully draped garland and glittery five-pointed stars framed an artful arrangement of red and gold candles. Just then, the door opened and the store owner herself hurried out, raising her hand in greeting.

"I had a feeling I would see you today, Keli," she said. She approached us and gave me a hug, enveloping me in the scent of rosemary, patchouli, and orange blossoms. I smiled in return. I had known Mila Douglas for years, but we had become closer friends last February when I had helped catch the criminal who had been harassing her and breaking into her shop.

Crenshaw regarded Mila with a raised eyebrow. With her white velvet tunic over black leggings and the strands of silvery ribbons crowning her brunette shag, she looked like a cross between a snow queen and rocker Joan Jett. I ignored Crenshaw and complimented Mila on her window display.

"Thank you, dear," she said. "I can hardly believe Yule is only four days away. I still hope you'll join—" She stopped mid-sentence at my warning look. Mila was forever trying to coax me into joining her coven, but I preferred to follow a solitary spiritual practice. Only a small number of people knew I was Wiccan. Crenshaw was not one of them.

"Will you stop by later?" she asked. "I have something important to tell you."

"Um, is tomorrow okay? I'm not sure what time I'll get off today, and Wes is coming by tonight."

Crenshaw crossed his arms and tapped his foot on the snow-covered sidewalk.

"Oh, I'll just tell you now," said Mila. She took my hand and spoke quickly, her breath forming puffs of fog in the cold air. "I had a vision this morning," she said, "and you were in it. So was Mercury, the messenger god." She paused, and squeezed my hand. "There are two things you need to know. One: You will soon have a visitor from your past. Two: Someone in your midst is going to die."

Connect with Us

Visit us online at
KensingtonBooks.com
to read more from your favorite authors, see books
by series, view reading group guides, and more.

Join us on social media

for sneak peeks, chances to win books and prize packs,
and to share your thoughts with other readers.

facebook.com/kensingtonpublishing
twitter.com/kensingtonbooks

Tell us what you think!

To share your thoughts, submit a review,
or sign up for our eNewsletters, please visit:
KensingtonBooks.com/TellUs.